Midnight Movie Creature Feature

Edited by TW Brown

Cover, Interior Art and Design by Shawn Conn

Dedication

For everybody who stayed up late at night to watch the scary movies after their parents went to sleep.

Foreward

Vampires…werewolves…zombies…witches. Those are some of the basics when it comes to horror. Yet, there is so much more. People like Roger Corman opened the door to some great schlock. Over the years, horror has gone through so many changes, and not all of them good.

When I think of horror…really good horror…I want my monsters! I actually wrote a college term paper in one of my writing classes about the decline of actual monsters in today's scary movies. It seems that we, the consumer, are content to sit through one incarnation after another of what I—and many others—call torture porn.

Roddy McDowell had a great line in *Fright Night*, "You kids today, all you want are crazed lunatics running around in ski masks…hacking up young virgins." It seems that there was a bit of prophecy in that 80s classic. Most of the so-called monsters in modern day horror are disgruntled men (or women on those rare occasions) who use various power tools in mildly creative ways to slay the newest batch of coeds.

Welcome to the May December Cinemas! Inside, you will finds various tales of terror that will make you cringe…or even chuckle at the cheeziness. You've paid your admission and can journey to any theater you like. So, grab your popcorn and welcome to the show!

I want to take a moment to thank the folks of Booked Podcast for their incredibly entertaining discussion involving one of the stories in this anthology. I urge our readers to become their listeners.

Let's all go to the lobby…!

TW Brown
June 2011

Contents

A GOLEM IN OZONE PARK

Starring **Jim Sylvestry**

A Golem in Ozone Park
Starring Jim Silvestry

It was definitely a late hour, and the roaring rain outside would turn even the most foolhardy stumblebum into a shut-in this night. But here at Ravi's doorway stood Abby, hugging herself and drenched like a sewer rat, her saucer-sized turquoise eyes wide with fear and despair. She was seventeen, and her stooped posture betrayed adolescent discomfort with her unusually tall and gangly frame, but those knowing eyes of hers could have been beaming from the skull of an ancient, harried shaman.

"We have to go, Ravi," she intoned gravely. Her voice sounded weak from the cold and the rain. Had she somehow walked all the way from Brooklyn Heights to Richmond Hill, Queens?

"Come in, Abby," Ravi replied. His own voice did not sound much better. He had been in a deep whisky-coma, and his throat still burned from the pack of unfiltered cigarettes he inhaled just a few hours ago.

He did not remember hearing the doorbell, or a knock. Maybe he was still half-asleep. Or maybe this was just that thing that Abby did: pulling him toward her; pulling them all towards her. Stumbling far ahead as they try their damndest to keep up with her.

Abby shook her head methodically at his invitation. "It may already be too late," she sighed.

She was shivering through her drenched purple hoodie. There were damp strands of her red hair matted to her cheeks.

"Whatever crisis you've dreamed up now won't get any worse during the time it takes for you to dry up," Ravi said, gently tugging at her sopping arm. Abby wouldn't budge.

Making this physical contact with Abigail summoned Malik, her protector, now standing directly over her left shoulder

1

and shooting down Ravi with a death stare. He had been somewhere near the whole time, of course, standing frozen like an ice
sculpture in some shadow, eyes locked on Abby, hands on hilts,
able to strike down a distant threat to her in the time it takes to
sneeze. It had taken Ravi a long while to get used to Malik. The
youth was pretty in the way that women were, yet stoic and
deadly in the fashion of Ravi's former colleagues in the Mossad
at Tel Aviv. Quietly arrogant and ridiculously graceful, Malik
was a royal pain in the ass during most social situations. But
Ravi knew that Abby was safe when he was near; and Malik was
always near.

Neither Abby nor Malik made a move to enter Ravi's dingy
apartment as the rain continued to hammer down on them.

"You have to get dressed and come with us," Abby said.
"Bring your guns and your gear. Uncle Sean and Wanda are
meeting us."

"You should have called them first, Abby. They could've
driven you."

Abby didn't respond, and still remained outside the door.
Clearly her mind was no longer involved in this present moment,
but had raced into the next.

Ravi had spent so many nights over the past few months
chasing after half-understood hunches from Abby's dreams and
visions, leaping between nightmare scenarios in rapid-fire succession. Prior years of his life were dedicated to assassinations,
bombings, interrogations, countdown crises and last-minute cav-
alries in the Middle East. Ravi knew how to spring into action,
how to click on a dime into crisis mode, how to stumble and race
through confusion with the hope that clarity would catch up with
him soon.

But the endless pain and fear of Abby's eyes never ceased to
unnerve him. And tonight of all nights, he just wanted a good
night's sleep.

But this wasn't in the cards for him. Not tonight.

Ravi stooped in the back of the moving van, clutching his rifle like a wizard's staff, mulling over the fragments of surreal information that had been offered to him. Sean Flynn sat across from Ravi, smiling and chuckling, red-faced and silver-bearded, bulge-bellied and twinkle-eyed like a department store Santa. Flynn never showed fear. Perhaps this had something to do with his former career as a diocesan exorcist. Either he'd seen all the other-worldly horrors that a man could see and had developed an apathy, or the horrors he'd seen were so beyond scope that dwelling on them would drive him mad. Another possibility was that he already was mad.

"What are you so damn excited about?" Ravi asked. Flynn had actually been singing some illegible song under his breath while he polished his Uzi. *Singing*.

Flynn beamed a mischievous smile at him. "It's been awhile since I had me a good golem," he said, his brogue ridiculously thick for a man who spent only a few pre-adolescent years in his native Ireland. "The Rabbis always kept their special affairs to themselves. The bishop wasn't exactly on their speed dial, if you hear me."

Ravi shook his head. "Golem," he muttered. "Of all the crazy things I've done...now here I am, hunting golems in Queens. What would my Bubbe say if she were alive today?"

Flynn laughed raucously. "She'd say, 'Good for you, lad! Now the world's a better place with one less killer mud man to deal with!'"

"But you should know, Ravi, I think the plural of golem is *golem*, not golems. Like sheep, and beer. *Golem*."

"It's golems," Ravi replied. He wanted to share in Flynn's amusement, but his instincts were too busy preparing him for a particularly non-humorous outcome.

Flynn appeared to be pondering this. "Golems. *Golems*. No, it doesn't sound right. What do you think, Miss Wanda?"

Wanda, who was driving the van down Rockaway Boulevard in chiseled silence, did not turn around to face them. "You are a pair of assholes for even having this damn fool conversation," she replied in her signature chilled baritone. "Who gives a

3

fuck? There's only one we're looking for, so we don't gotta say golem or golems or whatever the hell you say. Foolishness."

Abigail startled Ravi with her sudden cough. For a min-ute he had almost forgotten she and Malik were there. Abby was nestled into a fetal ball against Malik's shoulder, her always-wide eyes anything but tired. Even though she had accepted a change into dryer clothes found in Ravi's apartment—an ill-fitting sun dress and non-matching leggings left behind by an ex and a green khaki jacket were all that could be unearthed from his cluttered mess—she still quivered, coughed and sneezed.

Some protector Malik had been, allowing her to trudge in the rain for hours like that without even so much as an umbrella. But then again, Malik was as equally devoted a servant to her as a bodyguard. He never crossed Abigail, and followed her gentle commands fully and literally, not unlike a golem himself. Malik would follow Abby right off the edge of a cliff without so much as a second thought. Ravi still did not completely comprehend how and when those two ever found each other, or what the ex-act purpose of their union was. He wondered if they understood themselves how this all came about. Regardless, they behaved like kindred souls of in vitro origin, traveling and responding to the world around them like two halves of one person. Despite the coldness of the beautiful youth's eyes, Ravi sensed some-thing deep within Malik that led him to suspect something greater than blind loyalty or convenient companionship as moti-vators for his limitless servitude.

After pondering them for a moment, Ravi was about to ask the girl about their chances of a successfully-timed arrival, but as usual she cut him off before he could even get the words out.

"Don't ask me that," she said with a sharpness that she probably did not intend. "I'm not good with time. It doesn't work that way. The pictures and the words find me at random, I can't control them. I can't even understand what they mean half the time. You know that."

Ravi nodded. He'd become all too aware of the mixed blessing of Abby's "gift."

4

"It's all a crap-shoot really, friends," Flynn sighed wistfully. "Dealing with matters such as these always is. We're humans, and this is the stuff of the supernatural. These creatures and their business do not abide by the logic we've cultivated."

Ravi snorted. "A golem isn't too hard for a dumb human like me to understand. They're mindless mercenaries, amoral thugs. Tools of Jewish vengeance. Puppets of small-minded, angry, impulsive despots. Sounds like the stuff of the real world to me."

"Why are you just sitting there?" Herschel was screaming, while jumping up and down like an angry child. "I gave you an order! Destroy those who have shamed me! Move!"

Tovah was used to these outbursts from her husband. He never differentiated between mild irritations and dire events when choosing the need to perform them. Perhaps his raging was called for now, however ineffective it was.

The behemoth continued to sit against the low stone cemetery wall as if in contemplation, or more accurately, deep depression. It was almost anticlimactic after the ceremony of its conception, which involved a long monologue of ancient language which Tovah was ashamed to not fully comprehend. The old words were recited off the computer scan of that insufferable tablet from Yemen by Herschel in his most dour prophetic tones.

Then there was the swirl of red gritty dirt from the opened sack, recovered from the grave which Tovah had unearthed with little help from Herschel; swirls rising up like ribbon-thin cyclones, melding into each other, fusing the stabilizing dirt midair at extreme angles until the giant was fully formed. And then, what a spectacle it was to behold how it stumbled and thrashed as it tried to gain its bearings, felling tombstones and their little withered piles of visitors' rocks like dominoes, despite Herschel's best efforts to quell it with his immediate, shrill commands. Something born at breakneck speed of stuff so flimsy should not now be so hard and so very dangerous.

The golem loomed some thirteen feet high as it rampaged, the black oval pits of its empty eye sockets and the gaping pocket that served as a mouth of sorts betraying no additional emotion. The old letters which carved themselves onto its brow were the only feature on its face that told a story, albeit in one word: *truth*.

Tovah was born with an understanding and appreciation of fearful things, but nothing quite prepared her for the sight of this inhuman creature and its infantile rage of confusion. Never mind the other things that began to pop up out of the graves around them: the roving, creeping corpses who stumbled like drunkards, first towards them, then quickly away, perhaps upon discovering the newly-reformed golem and thinking twice of sticking around. It all made Tovah's blood run quite cold; yet she refused to show her panic. She must be the calm one, as always, the rational one, even in the very midst of irrationality.

But after a few moments of birth throws, the golem froze like the statue it should have been (in a rational world) and plopped backward onto the ground, drawing its mighty knees to its high chest and hugging them. So very much like a child. And this is how it remained.

"I am your creator!" Herschel was now screeching at it. "I brought you back to the living world! You'd still be a bag of old dirt in a pine box if not for me! You must do as I say!"

Tovah could no longer bare this high-pitch fervor, but knew better than to outwardly defy her husband. Imagine if word got back to Crown Heights—on top of everything else that occurred this night, and the bloody nights that would follow—that Herschel's wife was disrespectful and disobedient. No, that would not do, no matter what the end result of all this was. She would have to be tactful.

"Maybe it's frightened," she whispered as she willed her hand to stop quivering while gently resting it on Herschel's shoulder. "Clearly, it's confused. Everything we've read about these creatures professes their lack of intelligence. Perhaps it needs to be told to do things in small measures. Baby steps, Herschel."

At first, Hershel veered with hostility to face her when she began to speak, raising his own hand in a threatening gesture. His violence was one thing Tovah did not fear; rare as the beatings were, they fell upon her weakly and were unmemorable. When she finished with her advice, he actually, after a moment, nodded thoughtfully and once more addressed the creature, this time with a thin layer of restraint.

"Stand up," he said.

And, in another terrifying moment, it did.

Ravi had only been living in the United States, and Queens specifically, for a few years, and had much to learn about the neighborhoods of the city. Ozone Park was a mere twenty minute drive from his own Richmond Hill, but it might as well have been a different country given its isolated properties. First ordained as a vacation resort due to its closeness to the beachside Rockaways, the town soon fell into the blue collar residential trappings that seized the rest of the borough. Over time, John Gotti and the Italian Mafia took control of the neighborhood and laundered their blood money into the local pizza shops and delicatessens, before Rudy Giuliani and the feds swept in and cleaned them out. Now the inconveniently distant, decaying, industrial hamlet was populated largely by West Indians, and generally forgotten by the rest of the city. All of this, Ravi knew well enough.

What he was now learning, quite rapidly, was that at some point, for some reason, a cemetery in Ozone Park became a preferred destination for turn-of-the-century Jews to bury their dead. Yet no significant Jewish population ever resided near the Bayside Cemetery, and quite frankly it showed. There was no evidence that any extended effort had been made in over a hundred and sixty years to maintain the grounds or repair damaged stones, and the entire stretch of earth was tangled in weeds, smashed by fallen trees, tarnished by vandalism and withered by erosion, while the inky sky-bound snake of the elevated A-train rained its sparks all across the corroded mess, night after night, for a century.   In short, the knotted hills above ground perhaps painted a more macabre picture then whatever was rotting beneath it.

But maybe the current situation with the zombies provided the first exception to this.

It was Abby who had led the way from the parked van, as always, much to everyone else's reluctant acceptance. Her pace was spry, but those probing eyes (as always) pulsed with terror for what lay ahead. Malik (again, as always) was her gilded shadow, hiding that annoyingly-gorgeous and multi-ethnic hodgepodge of a mug behind that silver plate mask (eerie in its simplicity) that he wore for "battle." and of course he flashed those damn twin samurai swords of his, long and pale like serpent's teeth. How graceful, like a dancer, he stepped over the unkempt cemetery ruckus. What a profoundly different stock that kid was made of.

Stumbling with a particular lack of grace in the middle went Flynn, drawing his bearded lips into a deliberately pert frown when he'd clearly prefer guffawing at the thrilling absurdity of it all. His holy waters and relics would be of no use here, yet the barrel-bellied fool seemed to have no qualms waving his submachine gun about like an enchanting rod. Ravi checked himself— it was never wise to underestimate Flynn, however hard the former priest tried to paint himself as the carefree comic relief.

Ravi himself took the rear with Wanda. Of all the others, he identified with Wanda the most. Built nearly like an American footballer with serpentine dreadlocks, the no-nonsense ex-cop was disciplined and down-to-earth, the latter an unusually useful quality when dealing with threats so particularly "unearthy." Her preference for sporting gigantic surface-to-air weapons that projected explosives belied her training, yet undoubtedly proved to be her niche. Unlike Ravi—who was summoned into the fold under pretense of a paid mercenary gig—Wanda got mixed up with their lot through a set of odd circumstantial events. She had a chip on her shoulder and much to prove, yet her reasons for staying were her own.

And so they proceeded in file, through the pitch and mesh of the unhinged grounds of Jewish burial, where the feet of all corpses were supposed to be facing toward Israel beneath the surface. Only the quiet rumble of the electric train above, the din of the distant traffic beyond, and the beating of their collective hearts within, were heard at first. Perhaps there was hope that they had made it on time, before that damn fool renegade rabbi unleashed that holy hell from below.

But then came the creaks and the thrashes, inconspicuous to the untrained ear, yet only too telling for those in the know. Next came the stench of fetid rot, and the chattering of ancient, wasted teeth with no gums, lips or throats to buffer them. And there they were, those nightmare silhouettes with their grabby arms and irregular-shaped skulls, trudging towards down them from atop a low hill, pushing the unwilling crew of hunters into a tricky circle between the stones.

"We're too late," Abigail sputtered. At times like this, it was necessary to have someone state the obvious, to remind everyone of what was up and what was down.

Surprisingly, Flynn took the first shot. Several loud rounds of his little machinegun shattered the head of one attacker. It kept coming, but without its head there wasn't much trouble-making for it to partake in.

After satisfying himself with Abby's relative safety—wedged between the edge of hill and a crumbled headstone—Malik was the next to enter the fray, dancing like quicksilver into a close-quartered throng of creepers and smiting them swiftly with his silvery blades. With his moonlit mask, the young man looked like a supernatural force himself, a heavenly opposing energy to the raiders' deathly murk. Ravi hated Malik most of all when he found himself admiring him.

Ravi felt Wanda hesitate before lowering her comically enormous firearm and rushing the creatures with her almighty nightstick, the only police tool not confiscated at her termination. She had a hunger for pyrotechnics, but was smart enough to know that starting fires in a place like this would be unwise. Close melees with zombies were dangerous of course—some variations could spread their plague with their bites, rendering their victim into one of them. Others just liked to eat live flesh, and their teeth certainly hurt as they clamped into your bicep.

Ravi settled for popping a few of their kneecaps with some well-timed rifle rounds. The rotted joints exploded and the torsos crashed to the earth, writhing pathetically and helplessly. He was by no means a pacifist—if killing something that was already dead could be considered homicide—he just didn't see the point in getting his hands dirty against foes that could be so easily neutralized by a wisely-placed bullet.

In truth, Ravi loathed zombies. He loathed them to the very core. Perhaps zombies were most effective in war against men just like Ravi, who had killed and mangled so many hundreds of flesh-and-blood targets over the decades. Targets with faces and names and families, all of which Ravi had to block out of his registry in order to pull the trigger and get the job done. Targets who did not fall away with eloquence or convenience when contact was made, but instead popped, snapped, splattered; hideous realities on every level. But then, to have it all rise up again, pursue you, devour you…it was nearly too much for any soldier to bear.

Flynn tried to explain the differences between zombie strains once, but since science did not even acknowledge their existence, he had little information to support his theories. Flynn divided all zombies, with comic simplicity, into Runners and Stumblers. These tonight, fortunately, were Stumblers, slow on the approach and easy to outmaneuver, only deadly when right up close. The full roster of zombies in any given horde were either all Stumblers or all Runners, no mixture of both and not much predictability as to which they will be when they rise up.

Ravi noticed that these particular Stumblers were behaving strangely, even for zombies. They seemed half as interested in flesh consumption then any horde he'd encountered in the past,

10

and were more inclined to keep moving, as if being pursued. Zombies were not supposed to have the brain power to gauge threats; they always engaged, never fled. And yet there was no doubt about it. These zombies were trying to get the hell out of there.

Most of these were little more then skeletons, having been buried below the ground within little more than a pine box, or no box at all (old Jewish burial traditions praised the closeness of flesh and earth) for a century and a half. It was rare for organ-deprived remains to reanimate, and there seemed little purpose in eating people when the chewed flesh would just tumble out of their ribcage cracks onto the earth below. Perhaps the zombies understood this on some level. They comprehended the cruel pointlessness of their resurrection and just wanted to keep stumbling until they fell apart somewhere down the road. Sadly, though, Ravi doubted this. Something had manifested nearby that was potently awful enough to make the dead dig up their own graves and retreat.

And there was little doubt as to what that might be.

The slaughter was over after a few hazy, confusing minutes. It did seem like a slaughter, not a battle. The undead men and women put up little to no resistance, and were not permitted to flee. As his friends regrouped around him, Ravi felt an iron sickness within.

"What is wrong now?" Malik demanded sharply. "These were unnatural things. They could not be permitted to carry on like that. They would've bitten someone, somewhere, at some point. We are lucky they went down so easy, without biting any of us."

"I hear that," Wanda added with a nod, her tone less cavalier than her words.

Ravi looked up at Malik and contained his burning desire to destroy him.

"Yes, so very lucky," he whispered. "So incredibly easy."

He felt a firm hand clasp his shoulder: Flynn.

"Put it out of your mind, lad," the older man said with un-characteristic gravity. "These weren't Jewish people. They

11

weren't people at all; just cursed things. We only broke them down again, to their natural state. It had to be done."

"We have to put them back in the ground," Ravi heard himself say. "They suffered enough indignity in life."

"We will," Flynn replied, "when we're done here."

Suddenly, Wanda did a double take. "Where the hell is Abigail?" she shouted.

Malik immediately followed suit, and shouted something unintelligible.

Ravi's heart leapt. "Dammit! Malik, where did she go?"

"She was there…right there where I left her," Malik insisted furiously while pointing at the nook, as if saying the words forcibly enough would will her back there.

"She's wandered off," Flynn said, now exhibiting genuine fear. Abigail was his niece, and perhaps the only living person he truly loved.

"Of course she did, she always does," Ravi cursed. "She went to find the golem herself. She's probably stumbling toward it in one of her trances, like these damn zombies."

Malik threw down his swords and screamed again, his voice muffled behind the mouthless silver mask, while beating his own temples with knotted fists.

"Get your shit together!" Wanda yelled at him. "Even you can't watch her every second."

Flynn pointed to the hill where the bulk of the zombies first appeared. "If the zombies came from up there," he said, trying to muster a calmer tone, "then the Hecht grave, and therefore the golem, are that way. Undoubtedly Abby is headed there also."

Nobody had to say another word; they were off.

The smallest voice in Abby's head—the one which was assigned to remind her to do practical things like eat, bathe, dress—was whispering now that she should slow down, wait for her friends, *do not move any closer to this thing alone, you*

dummy. As per usual, the other voices in her head spoke with such force and urgency that this trifling reminder had to be ignored. Had to be, or chosen to be: Abigail was never sure of that. It certainly didn't matter now.

The zombies had frightened her. Not because they were grotesque, or dangerous, but because they were in pain. She had felt their pain splash and gel all over her like poisoned water, and it shook her to the very core.

But that is not why she moved. Abby did not, *could* not, run from the type of suffering that frightened her, because there was no place to run from it. It was all around.

Rather, she moved because the voices told her to do so. Sometimes the voices called from within her, and other times they called from the distance beyond. This time it was the latter, and when these voices beckoned, she had to come. Such was her lot in life.

She heard their calling not with ears, not with her mind. The processing vessel was buried deeper within Abigail. It was her soul that heard the calling.

Many voices had come and gone for as long as she could remember. She liked to think of them as different voices each time, for some reason, although surely this wasn't exactly accurate. One voice called her to have her Uncle Sean meet and enlist Ravi under the guise of paid mercenary work, and another voice drew her to Malik in an open field up north, while many other voices before and since led her to uncover all the things in life that most people did not know existed, or believed to be the stuff of man-made fiction. This particular "voice" which led the way for her now was first heard the moment Rabbi Scholl arrived at the Brooklyn Heights apartment where she lived with her Uncle Sean. It began as a rumbling, throaty whisper as soon as the door was opened for the long-bearded holy man to enter, but as the conversation between the two old friends Sean and Hyman (ironically unintelligible from Abby's vantage at the top of the stairs where she tried to eavesdrop) seemed to grow more dire in tone, the whisper had already swelled to shout. The language was not quite clear, but the words set requisite pictures in her head. These were puzzle pieces that she would have to assemble before it was too late. This had become her mantra: *Before it's too late.*

Uncle Sean's explanation gave some clarity to the jumble of depraved images that had begun their dance in her head. It seemed that a brash, angry young rabbi named Herschel from the synagogue where Rabbi Scholl presided had been the source of some recent trouble for the community. He had revealed himself to be an upstart, a perpetrator of intolerance and quarrels against those he deemed unexemplary of the true faith, as well as those outside the faith. Herschel's brand of hate and calls for vengeance were not commonly found in the peaceful Orthodox sects of Brooklyn, and in due time the controversial, self-proclaimed "prophet" was unofficially frozen out of community affairs.

Sensing the unspoken slight, Herschel announced his mission of revenge against his former community. He and his wife Tovah went missing for several weeks, and some believed them to be mercifully gone for good.

When rumors made there way back that Herschel was actively seeking a golem to use as his ultimate tool of vengeance—a specific golem, first summoned by his own ancestor to fight any possible variant of historical Jewish enemy, no less—most scoffed at the unbridled silliness of the notion. But Scholl, who had seen a great deal more of the world then his brethren, knew better. On top of that, Scholl knew Herschel to be the worst possible person to get his hands on a golem: a spiteful, stubborn, slighted fool. The chaos that could ensue from an improper summoning, let alone a misguided attempt at controlling a golem, could be irreparable. Rabbi Scholl knew that Uncle Sean had experience in dealing with such problems. Scholl's faith led him to Sean Flynn in much the same way that this barely understood voice now led Abby to the next chapter.

Abby shot back into the present with a snap. She had wandered several yards deeper into the unfettered darkness of the graveyard, and had no conscious memory of the journey. But in a fashion that was growing more and more common for her, she had found what she was meant to find.

14

Move, an impulse commanded her, *move, move, move*. This wasn't any sort of foreign, supernatural voice; this was her central nervous system doing its job. And "move" she did, leaping sideways like a ballerina as the ruddy behemoth nearly tore right through her.

It happened so fast. Abby was often slow to process the events that actually occurred around her in the material world, preoccupied with the constant dumping of puzzle pieces into her brain as she was. She usually relied on Malik to pull her out of the way when danger found her. How foolish she was, to leave him behind now, yet how lucky to survive what she just brushed against. She might not be so lucky a second time.

On the ground, entangled in dead weeds and now painfully bruised on her ribcage from the awkward dive, Abby turned up to glance at the passerby. The thing that nearly ran her over was about the size and mass of her uncle's van. One would expect its footfalls to be thunderous, earth-shaking; but it moved with terrifying silence.

The grave of Eli Hecht, Herschel's ancestor, was visible in the distance, relatively remote from the other graves (like his descendant, Hecht was not so beloved in his time), freshly excavated by a single shovel that now rested near the hole. The scene also exhibited other signs of recent disruption: newly-felled trees, recently pulverized headstones, and two new corpses hastily dumped inconspicuously near where Abby fell. She mistook these for fallen zombies at first, a man and a woman, until her eyes locked onto the bulging orbs of the dead man's, now and forever frozen in fear. She was unsurprised that Herschel and his wife met such a fate; there were few alive with the know-how to truly control a golem, and a simple command like "Come this way" could result in a fatal trampling as the golem moved towards the designated direction.

As the creature barreled out of sight, Abby found she could barely take her first, shaky breath before the thing reappeared for another darting pass from a different angle. It appeared to be marching stiffly, purposelessly, in uneven circular patterns. During this new pass, Abby caught a marvelous glimpse of the creature's *face*: giant empty eye sockets, a crudely-hewn fissure of a mouth, and that archaic forehead tattoo. Absolutely no living person, and probably a blessed few among the dead, knew how the spell to animate a golem actually worked, or where and how it originated. Speaking the words of the spell over the pile of enchanted earth of which the golem was first molded merely reconstructed it into its previous manifestation. Perhaps this face, and the other crude streaks of detail that jutted across the creature's frame, were the renderings of the golem's original creator, or perhaps they simply were what they were.

One reason for this lack of understanding regarding the golem's origin is the fact that a golem's animated lifespan generally existed in very short shifts. They were often used as tools of defense against invaders, and only in a final hour, last ditch effort at that, given their dangerous and unpredictable nature. Yet legends were often kind to the golem, describing them as God's gift to man, allowing humankind to create life from earth in the same fashion that God created them. Golems, of course, were understood to be inferior to man as they lacked souls, intelligence and free will. God must have looked down at his golem-harvesters in the same way a nuclear physicist must smile at his child as she played with her harmless chemistry set from the toy store. In some stories, they were long-lived servants of man, tending their fields and serving them their meals. Other tales had them actually passing for human, and it would take the soul of a true prophet to identify them for what they were.

This particular golem was not going to pass for human anytime soon, nor would it be serving any beverages tonight. It's crudely anthropomorphic design perhaps only served to give it a mobility that its original creator could understand. This creature was made to defend, to kill, and nothing more.

And yet…(Abby rolled off the path of its second pass almost a moment too late) there was something there that called out to her. Objects often spoke to her too—if "speaking" was the right word. They told the stories of their creators, and their handlers throughout time. Yet this new voice wasn't quite that.

There was emotion there, muddled and rudimentary as it was. Buried deep in the vacuous pit of its existence, this creature exhibited something that could pass for feeling.

And what were the feelings? Confusion. Despair. Loneliness. Fear.

Abby could relate.

As the golem came for its third, rapid pass, Abigail rose to her feet as quickly as she could, the pain in her side pricking her like hot needles. She stood to face him, head on. She did this not to be foolhardy, or defiant, or privy to sweet surrender. She just needed a moment of clear stillness. She needed to be sure. And, amazingly, as the golem came nearly upon her, merely a few feet from plowing right over her as if she were little more than a plastic lawn ornament, it suddenly stopped dead in its tracks.

The moonlight played strange tricks in the shadows of its black eye pits. The giant was hovering over Abby in complete stillness, and its own great shadow stretched over her like an intangible drawbridge. She was an ant in the wake of a mighty sequoia. Yet still, the golem did move against her. Instead, it just continued to stand, continued to probe her. Yes, it was probing her, contemplating her. That much was certain.

A golem without a master was a thing without purpose. It was expected to do what this golem had been doing up until this point: thrash, rage, endlessly march, crush everything in its path. But something about Abby had stopped it, at the very least distracted it. Did the golem see that she was not about to attack it, or try to control it? Did it sense her compassion, her empathy? Abigail had to be careful; she did not want to project her own emotions onto this thing, which was supposed to be lifeless, as much an object as the jacket she was wearing. Objects told the stories of the people who touched them. They did not tell their own stories.

But in those dark sockets, Abby saw a glimmer of something alive. She was sure of it now. The creature was curious, interested, and, strangely…grateful? Yes, it was grateful.

Grateful to meet a person in this dead place, in this cruel world, that understood it, even remotely.

Everything that was commonly understood about golems was incorrect.

Abby couldn't help herself. She reached her hand out to it. The golem looked down at the gesture and flashed amusement…joy. The moonlight caught the etchings of the symbols carved into its head. The word they spelled was "truth."

Then the golem's head exploded with a flash of fire and a sonic boom, hurtling Abby backwards with its force, dropping her flat on her back, nearly stopping her heart as she landed, her lungs squeezing shut, her body a live wire of pain. Before the specks of color consumed her vision, she watched as the headless statue jerked to the left, then to the right, as if trying to catch a glimpse of its distant attacker with the eyes it once had on the head that was once there on its shoulders.

In a movement like sand passing through the narrow bend of an hour glass, small rivers of red dirt began to crawl from various angles back into the neck hole of the golem. Even as they continued to gather, the dirt rivers solidified, thickened, shaped. The golem was now reconstructing itself, and those kind vibes it once projected were nowhere to be found. As Abby struggled to reclaim her breath, she felt her heart break for the golem, and knew it was time to be afraid again.

"Why did you shoot?" Ravi shouted to Wanda as the two lay low in the bushes. He had been watching the silent movie of Abby and the monster unfold through the crosshairs of his rifle, not yet ready to pull the trigger, seeing what he knew Abby saw and trying to believe it.

Wanda, while obviously shaken, was glaring back at Ravi like he was the world's biggest idiot. "What in the hell did you expect me to do? I had to do something!"

She had fired a rocket from her massive contraband weapon into the creature's head, which was now regenerating itself onto its neck, as exploded golem heads were apparently prone to do. This had not been the plan. In fairness, there wasn't an actual plan to begin with.

"It won't be happy now," Flynn said. "I'm going out there to get Abby."

Before Ravi could stop him, before anyone could even react to this new plan of action, Malik was already racing to meet the golem, swords and mask ablaze in silver deathlight. He had begrudgingly promised to be still, to wait for the right moment, before any engagement was attempted. Perhaps he saw this as the right moment, or perhaps he had just thrown this promise out the window when he found he could no longer watch Abby in danger. At any rate, his split second decision changed the rules entirely, and Ravi loathed him for it. Loathed him, and was grateful to him at the same time, hateful little prick that he was.

The tips of Malik's two samurai swords stabbed into the creature's chest. Only the tips made their way through before the golem swung its arm through Malik. Malik went hurtling like a silver comet into the Hecht tombstone, leveling it. It went crashing down with him into the open grave, likely onto the poor bones of old Eli, who probably now regretted his undead decision to stay and watch the show.

Even as he found himself springing into action, running for the golem with his useless weapons with Wanda and Flynn flanking him in even pace, Ravi found himself watching Abby as she outstretched her arms to where Malik fell, wordlessly pleading, breathlessly sobbing.

There was simply no time to ponder Malik's fate now.

The creature, head fully remade, now spotted his new attackers and took the offense to them in a mighty, swift, silent charge. Not expecting this at all, Ravi caught his heels mid-run and nearly stumbled. Flynn and Wanda fared little better in this tactic change. Then, in a crushing, rapid moment of unfathomable pain and wonder, Ravi was hurtling through the air, the graveyard and the sky spinning in circles around him.

Was he struck? Kicked? Thrown?

It hardly mattered as he came crashing back down to Earth, head still spinning as if he remained airborne. His skull had connected with a headstone on the way down, and he felt the hot blood rushing down his neck, down his shoulder, down his waist and leg. There wasn't much time now.

Shockingly, he was on his feet again, although his body pleaded for a more horizontal position. The night sky was alive with flashfire as Wanda and Flynn unloaded their weapons into the golem's torso. This was not even slowing it down as it rushed them. It was about to make a beeline through them. They and Abby were three points on a straight line that the golem would pass over. What would be left of them would resemble the clumsy heaps of flesh that were once Herschel and his wife.

There was only one way to deactivate a golem according to legend…and according to Flynn. The process was utterly ridiculous in theory, and would be the perfect fool's errand in practice. Flynn, Wanda and Abby were certainly in no position to pull it off now. Neither was Ravi, technically. But that was not about to stop him from trying.

His head felt lighter than air as his clothes began to cake in redness. This would be something if he could actually do it now. This would be one for the record. Feebly, he fumbled against the smashed headstone behind him, in part to secure his balance, and in part to claim the tool he needed. His hand pried loose a hanging chunk of the stone. He knew his grasp was tight around it, his knuckles whiter than it, but he could not feel it in his hand. He couldn't feel any part of his body. It wasn't the fear or the pain which consumed him now, but something more tranquil. He could slip away now and be fine with it.

No, no, I can't. Think of the others. Think of poor Abby. Think of the legacy of my people. Yes, think of those things.

He was walking up to the creature, clutching his jagged stone. It was less like walking, more like dragging his own body forward.

When he was close enough, he leapt. In a movement that felt more graceful then it probably appeared, Ravi was now latched onto the golem's back, arms squeezing its wide neck, which was thicker then a telephone pole. Belying what he had just seen in regards to the loose, reforming dirt of its head, the golem's hide was now the consistency and thickness of a mountainside. It thrashed wildly, trying to unhinge Ravi. The golem was moving with wild desperation, perhaps sensing what Ravi was trying to do. Here was a fool's errand indeed, yet this particular fool was not going to let go so easily.

As the golem jerked to and fro, and Ravi swung limply against its shoulders as if he were a light wool scarf, the sound of stone scraping against stone pierced Ravi's eardrums like nails on a chalkboard. With one arm gripped tightly around the golem's neck in a bloodless vice, he had positioned himself awkwardly over the giant's shoulder so that he could see a little bit of his own handiwork. His carving stone had found the correct character among the letters of the head's imprinted tattoo: the *aleph*, resembling a crooked "x," which came last in the line of lettering across its forehead. It was remarkable that the battered old sliver of tombstone was able to carve into the hide of the golem's head at all; perhaps this one area was designed to be softer, for this very reason. This could have been the golem's Achilles heel, if Achilles were standing on his head.

If the golem had a voice with which to scream, this is what it would be doing now as details of the *aleph* slowly began to wither away against the heavy strokes of the carving stone. But soon, the creature's movements, slowly but surely, grew more lethargic. Its arms lowered, now stiff against its sides. It bowed his head, even as Ravi continued to hack into the front of it. It now seemed resigned to this action.

The Hebrew word for "truth," upon removal of the trailing *aleph*, becomes "death." It was as simple and bizarre as that. Change the name of something, remove a single letter from its spelling, and the thing loses its power. Hebrew was funny that way. Perhaps Ravi would laugh about it one day.

In another sudden instant, sudden as everything that happened before it, Ravi crashed into the grass below. Loose red dirt, the lifeless and immobile remains of the golem, rained down on top of him. The spell had been broken once more.

Ravi lay there on his belly for what seemed like hours but was probably seconds. He was nearly out of consciousness, and knew he shouldn't close his eyes until the bleeding from his shattered skull was plugged.

His eyes met Abby's. Flynn and Wanda stood behind her, both frozen in disbelief at what they had just witnessed, but it was mostly Abby's expression that caught his attention. She was a weird kid, for sure—always was and always will be—but as he saw every possible human emotion project themselves in those giant turquoise globes, he thought he finally, truly understood her. Abigail was the only person alive who could feel everything at once. That must be a hard way to live.

In the moments before the blackness finally consumed him, Ravi thought of his victims in the battlefield, his victims in the bombed vehicles, and his victims in the interrogation room. Then he thought of the bones of the Jewish dead, strewn about him like so much rubbish. And lastly, he pondered the red dirt that covered him, and the silent scream of his last victim.

The A-Train roared above in the distance for one more pass. The passengers would be oblivious to the events that transpired just a few feet beneath them. That oblivion must be the state of true bliss.

Perhaps it would be good to remain in the blackness. Perhaps it would be pleasant, and restful. That would be a nice thing indeed.

A Golem in Ozone Park

The Lure
Starring Chantal Boudreau

Buck pulled the brindle hound puppy out of the passenger seat of his pick-up truck, and held it up for Walter to get a better look at it.

"You said you were okay with the runt of the litter right? I mean—I'm cuttin' you a deal and all. My hounds are the best in Kings County, and this little feller's got some good growin' potential. He may be small now, but just look at them there paws."

Walter grunted, scuffing the dirt with his feet and not even bothering to give the pup the once over.

"I ain't worried about that, Buck. You don't need to sell me on the pup. I told you I wanted it and you'll get yer money fer it. I don't care if it's the runt. I just want me a dog."

After Buck had handed the animal to Walter, he scratched at his greying beard.

"So yer finally gettin' a replacement for Farley? It's been a while since he went missin'. I figured it might still be one of them open wounds with you, after what happened with Billy."

Walter frowned a little and shrugged, still not meeting the other man's gaze. The sullen, sandy-haired man cradled the puppy carefully.

"I'm managin'. It's kinda lonely in that big house by myself—plus I don't like huntin' and fishin' alone. Don't need yer best hound—just somethin' to take the edge off a little and help out a few ways."

Buck, the older of the two, had already been through his own empty nest experience, only under much different circumstances. Buck's son had left to join the army and his daughter had married and moved away. Then his wife had died of cancer. That was when he had focused his efforts on breeding the best hunting hounds in the region.

"Heard from Sheila lately?" he asked Walter.

He figured since he had already breached the topic of the younger man's dead boy, his estranged wife would be no more taboo. Buck had always heard the death of a child often resulted in marital break-up, and Walter and Sheila were living proof. Perhaps if it had not been so sudden, or if there had not been so many questions surrounding the tragic event and finger-pointing regarding blame, things might have ended differently for the couple.

Walter shook his head, still fondling the pup, his eyes downcast. "Haven't heard from her since she sent for her things. She moved in with her sister up in Glendale. They were always pretty close. She ain't comin' back."

The way Walter spoke made Buck suddenly feel very uncomfortable, as if he were treading somewhere he ought not. He waved towards the puppy.

"Well, he's yours now. Treat him right, and I'm sure he'll be a loyal friend. I gotta' get goin'. Good luck settlin' on a name. I always have a hard time with that."

Buck left in a bit of a hurry, anxious to escape the presence of his tense and brooding customer. He could see why Sheila had left, if Walter had been this way before her departure. At the same time, Buck felt bad about abandoning a man who admitted to being lonely, but his discomfort outweighed his guilt. Once in his truck, he peeled away.

Walter watched him go with empty steel-grey eyes, clutching the puppy more tightly.

"I think," he murmured coolly, "I'll call you Bait."

The puppy was small for his age, but was more stubborn than Walter had been expecting. It whined and struggled as the sandy-haired man with a perpetually stern expression knotted the rope around its neck.

"Sorry, little feller, but it's gotta' be this way. That devil fish got Farley and Billy. If I'm gonna' have any chance of takin' my revenge, I gotta' have a good lure. I ain't quittin' 'til that monster is as dead as my boy."

Walter blamed the fish for all of his sorrows. It had started when he and Billy had gone on one of their regular fishing trips to the creek. Billy had been sulky, because of the beating the night before. It wasn't something that Walter had wanted to do, but he had stuck to the same methods of discipline his own daddy had used, and Billy had been starting to act like a little smart-ass. Since Walter's daddy had sworn by it, Walter had been obliged to whip the saucy out of the boy. Still sore from that encounter, Billy had kept his distance from Walter, fishing a fair stretch away.

Farley was a good hound, but as much as he was faithful to Walter, he had been around when Billy was born, and as far as that dog had been concerned, Billy was his boy. On that basis, he had hovered by the boy's side, instead of sticking close to the man.

Walter hadn't cared much if his son liked him, as long as Billy respected him, and he hadn't worried much about the boy as long as Farley was around. Shrugging off his son's scorn, Walter had hunched his shoulders and focussed his attention on the task at hand, lowering his line into the swirling waters of the creek. He had been enjoying the swish of the current and the feel of early morning sunlight on his back when his tranquility had been disturbed by a flurry of barking followed by a loud cry of dismay from Billy.

"Farley!" the boy had yelped. "Something got Farley!"

Walter had scrambled to his feet and jogged over to where Billy had been standing, gaping at the water. The unhappy man had arrived just in time to see a large ripple marking the spot where some sizeable creature had dipped back into the murky waters of the creek. There had been no sign of the dog. Walter had reached over and cuffed the boy upside the head.

"Yer supposed to be watching fer gators, dumb-ass! Farley was just a stupid mutt and didn't know better! Now he's gone and it's all yer fault."

Billy had cringed away reflexively, but his facial expression had contained no guilt, just fear, and not the fear of his father. When he spoke, the child's tone had been defensive.

"That weren't no gator—I know what they look like. It was a fish, a really big, ugly fish with huge horny points and giant wormy bits hanging off its face. It lurched right out of the water and snapped Farley up off of the bank..."

"There ain't no fish in that creek big enough to tangle with the likes of Farley. Quit yer tale-tellin', boy," Walter had interrupted, shoving his son away from the bank's edge. "This fishin' trip's over. There'll be blood in the water, and if there's one gator, there could be more. Now we gotta go home and tell yer mom. She's gonna' be mighty upset over this, and if you don't change yer ridiculous fish story, I'm gonna' give you a lashin' worse than the one I gave you last night."

"But I ain't lying. It was a monster fish," Billy had insisted.

It had taken a back hand that had drawn blood to shut the boy up, and that should have told Walter something right there.

The sullen man sat back and sighed, tugging the rope tight on the puppy. While he wasn't trying to choke the runt of a hound, he wanted it secure enough to make sure the critter could not squirm loose. It gave a series of high-pitched yelps and started to shiver.

Billy hadn't changed his tale when Walter had reported the incident to Sheila, but he had remained silent the entire time, neither confirming nor denying what his father had had to say.

Walter rose to his feet, and started dragging Bait towards the door, but the stubborn pup refused to go. It curled its tail under its rump and Walter found himself sliding the animal across the slippery kitchen tiles in the direction of the back door. When he got to the stoop, the door open, the impatient man took a few steps back and bent down and scooped up the puppy in a single motion.

"Yer not gettin' out of this, Bait, so there's no point in trying."

Walter tucked the tiny dog under one arm and grabbed up his shotgun with the other. Then he started for the creek.

The Lure

A couple of months after Farley's disappearance, one of the locals had managed to capture a giant gator in the creek not far from their regular fishing hole. Walter and Sheila had agreed that it was likely the one responsible for taking their hound, and when there were no other sightings in the next few weeks after that, they had both decided that it was safe to fish the creek again, although Sheila had held out against it longer. Billy had been especially reluctant to go, even braving his father's wrath by suggesting that he might refuse to return to the creek.

The boy's will was not as strong as it might have been after years of beatings whenever he had chosen to disobey or disrespect his father's wishes. A few solid blows and a few strong threats had been enough to convince him to change his mind.

Walter knew that he should have paid attention to the boy's concerns now, but hindsight was 20/20. Billy had been saucy from time to time, and a little thick-headed, but had never been a bad kid. After all, Walter had raised him proper.

When he and Billy had arrived at the creek that day, the boy had purposefully avoided the spot where Farley had been taken. He had edged his way a fair distance downstream from his father instead. Walter had been a little more on his guard that day, not entirely convinced that the danger of gator attacks was a thing of the past. This time, he had been much quicker to leap to his feet when he heard his son cry out.

This time, although surprised, Billy's shout had been a joyful one. "Farley, Dad! I saw him in the water! He's not dead!"

As Walter had headed his way, Billy had scrambled over to the edge of the bank, tossing his fishing rod aside, and had leant in towards the murky water, searching for more signs of his canine friend. Walter had known that it was impossible for Farley to still be alive down there, but the boy had seemed mesmerized, his eyes unfocused and his mouth slightly open.

"Get back from the edge, boy!" Walter had yelled, in his sternest tone.

Billy had been beyond hearing him. The frightened man had rushed forward, but a few seconds before his son had been within arm's reach, the worst thing ever had happened.

Walter shook himself free from his memories, happy to forget that horrible one from the day that he had lost Billy. As hard as he tried, however, that moment returned to him in nightmare after nightmare, and he was reminded of the tragedy every time he slid into his cold double bed at night missing the warm presence of his wife. He had always treated Sheila right, but things had never been the same after he had returned home without Billy. He hadn't exactly been surprised when she had left.

Walter grumbled to himself and put Bait down on the ground. They were at the creek now, and in an effort to release some of his pent up rage, Walter gave the puppy a hard nudge with his toe. It yelped and cringed away from him, moving into place in the process. Walter bound the rope to a protruding tree root at the water's edge and then sat a few feet away, gun in hand, and waited. Bait tugged futilely at the rope and whined pitifully.

Walter was tense, expecting the same gruesome sight at any moment as had met his eyes the day that Billy was taken. The devil fish had leapt straight out of the water, more dolphin-like than fish in that one act. Billy had described it quite well when the monster had snatched Farley, only he hadn't really told his father just how terrible the beast actually was. It did have horny protrusions that jutted out of its face and back like vicious weapons it might use to fight off foes or spear prey, but they were gnarled, and bits of rotting flesh clung to their points. Its scaly skin was a mottled greenish-grey, riddled with pus-white ick and reeking of death and the creature did have wormy strands that hung from its face, dripping with a transparent slime.

Walter had only glimpsed the devil fish's eyes for a brief moment as its needle-toothed gaping maw had closed over Billy, but those plate-like bottomless pits had struck terror in his heart. What he had seen there was demonic, like staring into the depths of Hell itself. He could not keep himself from shuddering at the memory.

Walter sighed, impatient to end this war with the fish, one that had started when it had robbed him of his dog. It would not end until Walter or the fish was dead. He had tried to grab Billy and pull him free from the monster's jaws during the attack, but all he had been left with was the hood of his son's coat.

Returning home to Sheila with that and the tale of something pulling their child into the creek had brought with it doubt and blame. Billy's loss had set off another round of gator hunting, and while Walter had kept the nature of the creature that had taken their boy a secret from his wife, she had held him at fault for taking Billy back to their old fishing hole so soon after Farley had been taken, and for convincing her that it was an acceptable plan.

This resentment, along with the fact that Walter had taken to spending every free moment perched with his fishing line and his shotgun by the creek, waiting for the opportunity to blow the devil fish out of the water, had driven Sheila away. He had come home one day after yet another unsuccessful vigil to find a note and no Sheila. She had told him that they were finished and that she would send for her stuff. Walter had spoken with her briefly on the phone since, but that day had been the last time he had seen her.

Walter was still hunting the devil fish on a daily basis, but his spirit, soured from failure and frustration, had driven him to new extremes. He had decided that since all of this had started with the monster seizing and devouring his dog, then perhaps that was what was required to lure it back again. He had chosen a puppy because it would put up less of a fight, and it would be a tender morsel.

After a few hours of waiting, with no sign of the fish, Walter wondered if he had been mistaken. Maybe Bait wasn't what the monster wanted.

Walter decided it was time to test this theory. He got to his feet, setting the gun aside, and untied the rope from the root. Then he tossed the puppy into the creek.

Walter gathered up his gun again with one hand, holding onto the rope with the other, and waited. The puppy's cries echoed around him, and the little dog thrashed about in the muddy waters in a desperate panic. If that didn't attract the devil fish, then it clearly wasn't interested.

31

Walter eventually pulled the puppy out again. It was not quite dead from exhaustion and from inhaling water during its struggles. He watched, disgruntled, as the animal lay feebly on its side in the dirt of the bank, its flanks heaving. Walter had heard tales of anglers who had trouble reeling in the prize fish in areas commonly used for catch-and-release competitions, not because the fish had learned to avoid the lures, but because they had become accustomed to a certain type of bait with more appeal than what the average fisherman had to offer. They had escalated their tastes.

He was sure that was the case here. The devil fish had started with his dog, and that had been sufficient in the beginning, but its tastes had escalated once it had gotten its teeth into Billy. The monster would not be satisfied with dog flesh now. The fact that it had rejected Bait was proof of that. If Walter wanted to draw the demonic creature to him, he would need a better lure.

"So you like my puppy?"

Walter had gotten Bait a proper collar and leash and had treated him well after that failed attempt, feeding him the best puppy food, and grooming him carefully. Within a few weeks, the animal had plumped up and was now a cuddly ball of brindle fluff. Walter had started taking it on walks, purposefully passing the sorry excuse of a house where Marcie lived along the way.

The girl happily sat at Walter's feet, fondling the round squirmy pup. Marcie was the local wild child; a scrawny thing whose scruffy dark hair was always in tangles, whose clothing was always in rags, and whose skin was always patched with dirt. Her daddy had abandoned his wife and four children years ago. They struggled to survive off of the meagre amount provided them by welfare and her mother was too busy watching her younger siblings or sniffing out handouts to worry about what Marcie was into. The girl had free run of the neighbourhood, unsupervised, and generally did as she pleased.

"What's his name?" Marcie asked, shielding her brown eyes from the sun with her hand as she gazed up at the puppy's owner. Walter could barely make out the freckles on her face through the dirt there.

"His name's Bait," Walter admitted.

Marcie giggled, both at the name and the fact that the little animal was now licking some of the dirt from her face.

"That's a dumb name for a dog."

Walter shrugged and gave her what he hoped looked like a friendly smile.

"It seemed fittin' at the time, with what's been goin' on around here with all the gators and stuff. If you like him, you can come play with him at my place whenever you want. The little guy gets lonely there since there's no kids at the house and, a lot of the time, I'm too busy to pay him the proper attention."

Marcie had known Billy from school, on the rare occasion that she hadn't been playing hooky. She was aware of his disappearance and the departure of Walter's wife that had followed. She pulled the puppy into her lap and cuddled him, but she frowned slightly.

"I dunno...maybe..."

"Well, you might wanna check with yer mom first, anyway. She may not like the idea of you hangin' round my place."

This drew the hostile response that Walter had been hoping for, one that suggested if the girl did show up at his house to visit the dog, no one would be aware of her whereabouts.

"She ain't my keeper!" Marcie spat. "I take care of myself—I been doin' it fer some time now. I go where I want, when I want, an' if I decide to come see yer dog, she don't need to know about it. Ain't none of her business."

"Alrighty then—I leave it up to you. I'm headin' home to whip up some biscuits and stew fer supper. If yer hungry and wantin' to visit Bait, come on by. I'll have lots—too much fer one person."

Walter turned and started towards his house, leaving the double temptation to simmer in the girl's thoughts. Bait might prove to live up to his name after all.

"Whad ur yeuh doin'?" Marcie drawled groggily, drool trailing down her chin, and her head lolling back.

She had not anticipated that the stew would be drugged. As soon as she had passed out at the table, Walter had tied her up, making sure she was bound tightly and was secure enough not to be able to escape her restraints. He could not allow her to get away.

Nobody would miss her at first, even though he had kept her overnight. He knew that she had run off before, and it would likely be 48 hours before anyone would seriously start to look for her. If he let her get away now, he would never get a second chance at catching and killing that devil fish, and he was not about to let that grudge go. It did mean that he had to act fast. He would take her out to the creek at the first light of dawn.

"I'm preppin' my lure," Walter growled, as he checked the ropes that held her. He didn't want any of them coming loose while he was carrying her out there.

"Whaa?" she sighed, still not fully in control of her faculties.

"I ain't plannin' on messin' with you if that's what yer worryin' about. I ain't sick like that. I just need yer help to catch me a fish, and I knew you wouldn't be willin'."

Marcie whimpered a little, but realized that it was pointless to fight. It would just waste what little energy that she had, and that she might need later.

As soon as he was done inspecting the ropes, Walter grasped the captive girl and hoisted her over his shoulder. Then he carried her to the door and grabbed his shotgun which was propped against the outside wall. He did not bring Bait with him. He would not need the animal this time. With a groan in response to his heavy burden, Walter headed for the creek.

"How—how am I supposed to help you catch a fish?" Marcie mumbled, now more alert.

"There ain't much to it. Yer just gonna' have to lie on the creek bank, and maybe wriggle a little," Walter replied breathlessly.

"How's that supposed to work?"

"Don't fret over it. Leave that up to me," Walter grunted, his face growing red with strain.

When he finally reached his destination, he dropped Marcie into the long marsh grass and leaned over to catch his breath. She complained loudly about the rough handling and started to squirm a little, which was just what Walter had been aiming for.

Once he was feeling somewhat rested, he dragged the bound girl over to the spot where Billy had been when he was taken. As he had with Bait, he left her close to the water's edge, and then he retreated a short distance, shotgun in hand.

It was a brisk morning and the biting wind added to Walter's growing irritation, as he waited for the appearance of the devil fish, and the monster did not come. Marcie continued to be quite vocal, protesting her treatment and telling Walter that it wouldn't be long before her mother would have people looking for her and that they would figure it out and come for her. Her ranting Walter could ignore. That much did not bother him, and the more active she was, he thought, the better the bait she would be.

Hours ticked away, and soon it was mid-morning. Walter was growing enraged; it would seem that Marcie was not proving to be any better of a lure than the pup had been. What more did the devil fish want? Finally losing his cool, he set aside his gun and stomped over to her, preparing to use similar tactics as he had with Bait, and dangle her in the water. That, he figured, would do it if anything would.

As he neared her, something caught the corner of Walter's eye. He turned to glance into the water and his heart leapt at what he saw there. It was a face, a familiar face. All reason escaped him, his brain flooded with positive emotions, and in a daze, he was soon leaning over the murky water's surface trying to get a better look at his son.

"Billy?! Billy?!"

The face got closer and closer, and Walter could register nothing but the joy he felt that he would soon have his boy back. By the time he was aware that the smiling face of his son was floating on the end of a wormy growth, it was too late.

Walter barely heard Marcie scream, as the jaws of the devil fish closed over him.

The Lure

A Zinger Must Die
Starring David Perlmutter

The time machine, which bore an uncanny resemblance to a standard glass fish tank, revealed itself in a blazing streak of light that rainy evening in Halifax, Nova Scotia, halfway between the green Common and the imposing mass of the Citadel, at the intersection of Bell and Sackville. The rain was wet on the ground, as it usually was in Halifax at that time of year, and it would cause the streets to be difficult to tread for those of the strangers' persuasion. The year was 2010, the time late fall, just after a particularly decisive period in American politics, in fact, but the occupants of the machine were not of either this time or this place. They had come on a mission from the future, a mission which they had primed themselves to succeed in. Well, one of them anyway, but her enthusiasm for the planned action and her reckless disregarding of what would result from their actions more than made up from the slightly more tepid response that her colleagues had for the whole affair. This enthusiasm and bravado on her part was in spite of the fact that they knew they would face members of the human race at their intellectual peak and prime, and that they themselves could never be considered "human" by any conventional definition of the word.

But, then again, humans had always treated the cartoon race, of which these supposedly noble three were part of, as their bastard offspring; the chief skeleton in their closet of unparalleled achievement. Once conceived in a light-hearted vein by human beings for their entertainment, and, to a lesser degree, their edification, the cartoon race had undergone in the future a long and painful process of attempting to gain their equality with human beings on and off the screens where they had lived. This gain occurred only when the human race finally eliminated itself in catastrophic nuclear warfare. But the shadows of what the human beings had done cast long shadows beyond the period in which they existed and perished, and carried with them a heavy legacy that was only now just beginning to be dealt with in this future time. Even living and working in an area where humans as they had existed for thousands of years were now long gone, this intrepid trio still felt the "curse" of being "different" in some way, form or shape from the rest of the world; a "curse" that had first imprinted itself among the human beings to express their revulsion towards the "differences" cartoon characters had vis-à-vis them, and was retained in the races that now succeeded and competed with the cartoons for land, political favors, money and other benefits of their future world. Cartoon characters had always inspired ridicule, contempt and disgust when they made contact with "real" human beings, wherever they were, whatever time period they chose to navigate in, whatever form they chose to live their lives in. Why should this time, when the humans were still firmly in control, be any different?

The entire sordid imbroglio had been Bess' idea, to begin with. Most of the good ideas were hers, as she would be the first to tell you, her splendidly out of control ego allowing her nothing less. It was she, after all, who had discovered the tragic fate of the first and only African American to serve as President of the United States during the human era, thanks to a close perusal of a dog-eared copy of Howard Zinn III's *A People's History of the United States in the 21st Century* in the school library. It was she who had fallen madly in love with him based solely on the full-color photograph of him on his inauguration day, the day when all of the promise of his election campaign seemed fulfilled, however brief and tragic that period ended up being amongst the American people. It was she, after all, who had managed, after much perseverance and not a few bad words and deeds on her part, to track down one of the few still existing copies of the sweatshirt worn by his supporters back in 2006, the one with his name and the year on it above his now legendary slogan:"YES, WE CAN!" The very sweatshirt she now wore proudly on her extremely icthyian chest. And it was she who feverishly convinced her closest friends, Osler and Malvolio, in spite of the extreme amount of doubt that at least one of the two young men seemed to possess about the enterprise, that this was something that they *had* to do to set the world on its right course. They went along out of friendship (and, in Osler's case, his as yet undeclared love for Bess, which he, as a teenager, as they all were in spirit and mind, found constantly difficult to fully and adequately vocalize to her...or anyone else, for that matter), even if, privately, they might have had second thoughts about what, exactly, it was that they had ended up committing themselves to.

Bess was also the first to make sense of the environment where they were. Halifax in 2010, after all, was a particular time and a particular place that needed to be accessed in a way possible only through incredibly thorough and specific calculations, as Bess herself would be the first to let you know. Checking the machine's digital indicator, which had been precisely set to "HALIFAX 2010" by her own fin, and then checking the coordinates on Google Earth Retro with her FinPod, she let out a shriek of delight when she discovered that her precise calculations were entirely accurate.

"We did it!" she shouted. "We're here!"

Her companions, asleep for what they had assumed would be a long flight, said and did nothing. Displaying one of the rapid-fire mood swings common among cartoon females, she whirled around rapidly, adjusted the orange headband decorating her red hair, and shouted at them: "WAKE UP, DAMN IT!"

Osler was up in an instant, his stringy black Afro almost standing on end. He wrapped his fins nervously around the Glock pistol Bess had assigned him to carry and stood up immediately. Malvolio was in a deeper sleep and not aroused by this shout, so Bess resorted to pulling him up by the pompadour-shaped fin attached to his head like a rooster's coxcomb and slapped him sharply in the face. That was what worked.

"We here already?" Malvolio said when he was revived.

"Of *course* we are!" snapped Bess. "How long did you *think* it was gonna take us to travel through time?"

"Coulda sworn it woulda been *longer*," Malvolio muttered.

"Don't be silly, Malvolio," Bess answered. "With these new precision time travel tanks we can make it here and back in no time—so long as we get back here in time, of course." She punctured this phrase with a feminine giggle that belied the utter seriousness with which she approached this mission—which reasserted itself almost immediately as she turned her gaze to Osler.

"For Pete's sake, Osler!" Bess said. "You're gonna *rust* that Glock with all that sweat of yours you're getting on it!"

"Sorry!" Osler, eager to please Bess and avoid evoking her wrath, quickly shoved the gun in his hair for safe keeping while parting his nose-less face to reveal the braces on his teeth as he said this, all the while continuing to sweat nervously. "But I just wanted to…be prepared!"

"Look, guys," said Bess, "I know that you know how much this means to me…"

"Yes," the boys said with resignation.

"…and how irrevocably things will change once we're done here…"

"Yes," they said again.

"…so I cannot stress this enough. WE CANNOT SCREW THIS UP! We go down the street to the studio, kill the bastards who greased the wheel that created the screwed-up world we live in, and then get back here promptly so we can get back home in one piece. In the meantime, don't *say* anything, and don't *do* anything that will fix things any more wrong than we want it, or things will get very difficult for me- and for YOU! UNDERSTAND?"

"Yes," the boys said with finality.

"And *then* will you be happy, Bess?" Malvolio said. "Really?"

"I will," said Bess.

"And then," added Osler, hopefully, "you might have more time for—"

"Enough talk!" Malvolio interrupted curtly. "We're wastin' time when we could be *icin'* those chumps!" He holstered the

42

harpoon gun Bess had assigned him on his shoulder and walked off down Sackville.

"Wait a minute, Malvolio!" said Bess, as she ran off with her own weapon—a Winchester rifle—in her fins. "That's the *wrong way*! Come *on*, Osler!"

Crestfallen, with yet another attempt to voice his affection for Bess trounced by time, Osler followed along meekly.

They made their way silently and quickly down the road to the CBC television studios (they first went to the radio studios, in a separate building across the street before realizing their mistake). Following this, they headed down the hallways, unnoticed by the security staff, until they found the room they wanted. It wasn't hard to find.

It was the writing room of the comedy series that had unwittingly triggered the chain of events that had led to their mixed-up world with a singular, ill-timed and badly thought out joke; the wrong that the trio from the future hoped to avenge this night.

What could be seen from the room was not much, given that the room was enveloped in copious amounts of smoke, both of legitimately purchased tobacco and more illicit substances that had been clandestinely shipped in to Halifax harbor under alternate labels. In addition, there was, it seemed, a considerable amount of alcohol being consumed as well, as the aliens frequently heard small amounts of whiskey and Jamaican rum poured into small shot glasses and then rapidly drained.

"Do we do it now?" Malvolio whispered as the trio crouched in the hallway behind the room's door.

"Not yet!" Bess hissed. "As soon as they tell the joke..."

In the midst of the smoke in the room and the haze of alcohol, the four human stars of the show—Jones, Critch, Hall and Crawford—were in the midst of debating what would be going into the following evening's broadcast, along with McAuliffe, the story editor, and the head writers, Tingley and Howell. The latter had changed the topic over to the upcoming November midterm elections, and now began to pitch a concept idea to the group, in the "news report" style that was very much the program's *raison d'etre.*

"I got it!" Tingley said as he filled his glass with rum.

"We *know* that!" cracked Howell. "But what's the joke?"

Tingley wrinkled his brow in disgust and read his "joke", hastily scribbled on a brown paper towel from the men's room.

"'President Barack Obama'," Tingley read, "'made it clear today that he will not allow the Republicans nor the Tea Party to prevent him from initiating his agenda in Congress regardless of the results of the midterms. Speaking in the rose garden today, the president made this comment: 'All I can say, in the words of a great poet of my race, is that they picked the wrong nigga ta FUCK with!'"

The room exploded in laughter. But there was nothing of the sort from the hall, as much as Osler and Malvolio would have liked to join in.

"That's the joke!" Bess declared. "Come on!" Furious, she loaded her Winchester loudly as she entered the room, flanked by Osler on her left and Malvolio on her right, which served to gain the ungainly humans' attention.

"All right!" she said angrily. "Hands up!"

"What is DIS?" shouted Critch, his Newfoundland accent more pronounced in proportion to the amount of alcohol he had consumed. "You cain't just come in here and—"

"GET YOUR GODDAMN HANDS *UP!*" roared Bess, as they obeyed her. "We haven't got any time for your BULLSHIT!"

"Speaking of *bullshit,*" countered Crawford, his arrogant manner heightened by his weed consumption, "you mind explaining yourselves?"

"The only explanation *you* deserve," snapped Bess, "is this: we are cartoon characters from the year 2350, and we have come a long way back to correct all the wrong you have caused us since you started here. We say you *caused* it specifically because everything bad that happened to us began exactly because of that shit-heeled Obama joke you just told!"

"And are we to assume that *you* are an Obama supporter?" cracked Hall, also a Newfoundlander and as drunk as Critch. "Even if we have difficulty believing that crock of *shit* you call an excuse for para-military action?"

Malvolio's fins grasped the trigger of the harpoon gun as he aimed it directly at Hall's head.

"Don't be callin' my *best* friend a *liar*, you stuck up BITCH!" he shouted. "Or else I'm gonna go all MOBY DICK on your human ass!"

"It's all right, Malvolio," Bess said calmly as she patted his fin with hers. "She doesn't know the right way to treat us. NONE OF THEM DO!"

"Look," said Jones, yet another *Newfie*, who wandered up to Bess and friends with alcohol-laden breath. "I doan mind them barging in here like that! Gawd! I half expected the Tories to be doing dat to us any day now! But I do think we ought to hear 'em out first!"

"You *crazy*, Jones?" shouted Critch. "Last things we needs in here is somebody given us some goddamn sob story! Specifically since they ain't done nothin' to us…and they won't, if they's smart about it!"

"Still," Jones insisted, "I'll believe them if it sounds good, there! So," she said to Bess, "start talking!"

"With pleasure," Bess said soberly.

She proceeded to explain, in detail, to them about the future where they had come from. How a small group of crazy Tea Party enthusiasts in Buffalo were going to catch the program with the joke in it later that week, and they would take that as permission to travel to Washington and lynch Obama from the nearest tree like the "nigger" they thought he was. How Joseph Biden proved to be incapable of smoothing things over with his predecessor's panache, and how he was driven out of office by another Tea Party mob. This in turn led to the complete control of the United States in the hands of the Republican Party, with every "election" in subsequent years becoming more and more of a farce.

At the same time, Bess, Osler and Malvolio—and the many other members of the cartoon race they represented—had been driven more and more outside of the shadows in which they had existed away from their weekly existences on television. They had been forced into a position where they had to constantly fight for their citizenship, if not their survival, in a new Republic that made merely being a liberal a position akin to treason. And finally, how Obama had been deified by the defenders of the democratic faith *a la* Lincoln, and he was now something to be cherished for his ability to support and deal with people who were not of his background, an ideal that their generation hoped to fully restore by taking action against the Republican elite.

"And it all had to do with the fact that you Canadian ASSHOLES lambasted him when he needed our support the MOST!" Bess shouted.

"'Tit didn't!" objected Critch. "It 'twas them Buffalo lunatics that lynched him. We just made funnumim, is all!"

"Don't contradict me!" ordered Bess. "It's all in the history books. Howard Zinn III is *not* a liar…and neither am *I*! I *love* Obama and what he stands for to us, and we are going to fix things so that he actually gets to do what he *wanted* to when he was in office…"

"Wait a minute!" said Crawford. "Howard Zinn *The Third*?"

"Yeah," said Osler, "a big wheel in our world, historywise."

"Where we come from," Crawford arrogantly stated, "there's only *one* Howard Zinn! And he's enough of an *asshole* as it is!"

With the panache of a veteran Nantucket whaler, Malvolio fired his harpoon gun. The grappling hook buried itself deep in Crawford's chest, poking out in an ugly way from his back. Malvolio reeled the hook back, and Crawford's dead body collapsed on the ground as his entrails and organs fell out.

"Oh," shouted Bess, "you've done it now, Malvolio! Now we've got to kill *all* of them!"

"You sure?" said Osler.

"It's the only way now!" said Bess.

"Fine," Malvolio said, "I wanna kill me some more humans, anyhow! Racist bastards!"

"RACIST?" the other humans exploded.

"We're *Canadians*, asshole!" snapped Critch. "We ain't no…"

But before anything else could be said, Malvolio had fired the grappling hook out at him again, this time scoring a direct hit to Critch's brain. While he continued reeling Critch, Osler and Bess proceeded to fire point blank with their guns. The bullets flew quick and fast, but the immortal 'toons would not be swayed in their determination. By the end, all the humans in the room were dead, either of gunshot wounds or what Malvolio politely called "filleting".

"Well," Bess said, surveying the damage, "it's done. They won't tell that joke—or any other ones."

"I suppose," Osler said, "that we can go home now, right?"

"That's right," said Bess, with a feminine trill.

"And then," Osler continued, trying to build up towards telling Bess his feelings, "I can finally tell you about how much…"

"SHIT!" Malvolio interjected. "The *cops*! They've found out about us!"

"RUN!" shouted Bess.

Breaking through the windowpane of the room, and wondering how in the world they had been discovered so fast, the cartoon trio, alien to this time and place, began running away from the Halifax Police as fast as they could towards their makeshift time machine, entirely unaware of what they were now coming back to.

We have not heard anything from them since.

THE PIT

A FATHER'S VENGEANCE KNOWS NO BOUNDS!

STARRING
TERRY ALEXANDER

The Pit

Starring Terry Alexander

Carl Sunderland held the night-vision binoculars to his eyes. The gas mask he wore for protection against the noxious odors surrounding the small farm house kept the eye pieces from setting properly. He spotted a splash of movement in the tree line a quarter mile from the old house.

"Tipton," he mumbled. "Wait, no there's two of them." He focused the field glasses on the dark brown creature following the gray. "Well they're in for a surprise."

Carl rented the farm house months ago. Its remote location, far from any town with no neighbors for a mile in any direction, suited his purpose. A thick forest bordered the fence line on three sides. A long serpentine trail led from the dirt road to the house. A large strip mine from a bankrupt coal company stretched along the back; over time, rain turned it into a small lake.

Carl scanned the clearing, knowing the beasts would have to cross through the high grass to reach him. He soon found what he was seeking, the heavy growth moved in an unnatural manner mid-way through the empty pasture. He focused on the waving plants vaguely making out the crawling dark shapes.

He checked the loads on the modified .45 automatic. He'd commissioned a gunsmith to fashion the special silver bullets months ago. He's ordered five hundred rounds and only used twelve. Maybe he'd get lucky tonight and burn a few more.

A smile touched Carl's lips as he glanced at the full moon high in the heavens. Yeah they were in for a surprise. Returning the pistol to the holster, he circled the waiting trap to the safe room. He wanted a ringside seat for the action.

Soft pads carried them noiselessly through the thick high grass. The gray male led the way, the brown female close behind. They moved cautiously, hoping the movement of the tall grass wouldn't give them away.

A bizarre mixture of odors drifted on the wind. The male hesitated filling his nostrils. The wolf's senses isolated the scent of rotten meat, blood, and something else; a harsh, searing smell, and underneath it all the scent of the old hunter.

A low growl came from the female; she didn't understand the need for stealth believing only in speed and strength. Her youth and inexperience could jeopardize the hunt. She had no fear of man, thinking of them only as prey, food to fill her hungry belly. This one was different, this human killed their kind, and death held no fear for him.

The pair drew near the old house. The mingled odors confused their sensitive sense of smell. The gray saw the three dead cows scattered around the perimeter of the old wood-frame structure. Every instinct screamed at the male to leave, to run away and wait for another time. Its human desire for revenge cancelled the wolf's natural caution. The beast slowly moved to the porch, easing its massive weight on the thin boards. A board near the door creaked. He froze rooted to the spot.

The old hunter would hear, he would be waiting inside, prepared for their attack. Large nostrils sniffed the air, the man smell was stronger, but so were others. The scent of blood driving him wild; his human mind suppressed the urge to taste the hunter's blood. It eased from the porch to circle the house and search for a safer entrance.

The female grew impatient, she rushed forward, smashing the door to splinters and bounding inside. The gray raced after her, this foolish act could endanger them both. Still he couldn't risk her killing his hated enemy. That pleasure he reserved for himself.

An overhead sheet of plate metal slammed to the floor behind the male, nearly catching his foot. The human was tricky; the gray had never been trapped before. Tears filled his eyes. Harsh scents burned his nostrils, rendering his sense of smell useless. He glanced at the sliced onions and crushed garlic scattered throughout the room. Dead, bloody rabbit carcasses dangled from huge treble hooks attached to the ceiling. Entrails dangled from the ravaged bodies, dripping blood and gore. The male ducked under the fleshy ceiling, only to be overwhelmed by the strong onions at his feet.

The werewolf blinked, fighting back tears. His blurry eyes focused on the female, frozen in the center of the room. Sensory overload rooted her to the spot. She shook her head from side to side looking for the hunter's scent or a way out.

A random drop of blood fell from the dangling carcass overhead. It splashed on the tip of the female's nose, driving her into frenzy. She jumped upright, her mouth gaped open. A loud growl came from her throat. The male leaped forward, keeping below the line of hooks.

Her head and shoulders slammed the dangling hooks. The rabbits began to swing and sway like a row of pendulum's. The female's jaws locked onto a tender morsel. Two sharp barbed hooks hidden inside penetrated the solid roof of her mouth. The third shredded her tongue and hooked into the lower jaw under her teeth.

The lump of cold flesh muffled her high pitched howl of agony, reducing the cry to a pathetic whine. The female fought the metal kiss of the hooks. Her actions drove the barbs deeper in her mouth. Her frenzied movements dislodged several rabbits, the naked treble hooks found the flesh along her arms, shoulders, and neck embracing her limbs with their cruel grip.

The gray tried unsuccessfully to free her, only drive the barbs in deeper. Through blurred eyes he watched the old hunter emerge from the small alcove at the far end of the room. The human lifted his weapon. The male knew instantly he had to flee. To stay would mean certain death.

Crouching below the baited hooks, the monster gathered his strength. The leg muscles bunched in its thick legs. The creature leaped straight up, releasing the pent up energy like a spring. It crashed through the sheetrock ceiling in a rain of white powder and falling debris.

A naked barb lodged in its hand, the sharp hook penetrated the flesh catching on the bones behind the knuckles. The hook and line stopped his momentum short of the roof; it crashed among the wooden rafters. Pain shot through the wolf's bestial arm, racing from fingertip to shoulder.

A loud explosion echoed through the small house, followed immediately by another. Two smoky holes appeared in the ceiling punching through the roof

Large canines sank into the flesh at the wrist, biting at the skin, muscle, and tendons. Crunching through the joint, the wolf spit the hand through the hole. The severed limb circled and twisted at the end of the line.

The monster cradled the wounded arm near its belly. The sharp claws on the remaining hand slashed at the plywood underside of the roof. A small hole appeared, and the creature tore at the opening, enlarging it. Shingle grit filled its nose and mouth.

A third bullet tore through the ceiling near its foot. The wolf tore at the roof with renewed vigor. It jumped at the hole; fur covered shoulders scraping along the edges. It forced itself outside, standing on the pebbly roof. It threw back its head, gazing up at the full moon. A loud mournful howl filled the night, vibrating the air. A fourth bullet punched through the wood and shingles, burning the werewolf's thigh. The monster leaped to the ground, running for the forest.

"Damn it." Carl Sunderland listened to the werewolf's howl, knowing he'd squandered an opportunity to kill Tipton. Things hadn't gone exactly as planned. He'd never be able to trap him again. Tipton was too smart and clever, regardless of what form he possessed.

The female strained against the hooks, a choked snarl issued from her ravaged mouth. Carl approached cautiously, the female reached for his throat, her claws slicing the air. The silver treated cords held her short.

"At least I've got you." He lined the sights on the female's chest. "You won't kill again." He squeezed the trigger. The explosion rang in Carl's ears.

The female's eyes widened, she jerked against the bonds. Her breath came in ragged gasps. Her body convulsed once and slowly went limp, the hooks and cords supported her weight. The body began to sway back and forth, lending a psychedelic effect to the change from beast to human.

Carl gazed at the pretty face, a young woman with sandy hair and a line of freckles across her nose. A pity he had to kill her. "I hate it when they're young and stupid."

The thumb sized, black-edged hole in her chest caught his eye. "This is interesting." He gazed at the claw-tipped hand swinging in space. The fingers flexed and curled, fighting the hook. Carl pulled a silver bladed dagger from his boot top. He poked at the hand with the blade. The fingers immediately closed around the weapon, the sharp edge slicing into the flesh. "Yeah, this is interesting."

Carl drove away from the farm two hours later; he watched the inferno's reflection in his rearview mirror. The old place had gone up like a tinder box, aided by the gasoline he added inside and out. He hoped the flames would prove hot enough to render the girl's body to ash.

Carl sat at the far table of a small café in a Podunk town in Southeastern Oklahoma. He kept his back to the wall, facing the door, watching everyone who entered. He knew Tipton had followed him, he felt his eyes on him, waiting for the full moon to strike. Carl knew the moon cycles well, he couldn't afford to let one sneak up on him.

He sipped at his coffee, the place actually made a good breakfast, nothing fancy but good none the less. Bacon and eggs, scrambled just like his mother used to make, and the biscuits were just to his taste.

The bell jingled above the door signaling the arrival of another customer. A tall, thin man entered; his face drawn and pale, baggy eyes set deep in their sockets. A large bandage covered the stump end of his left arm.

Tipton's ice-blue eyes fastened on the older gray haired man. "Coffee." He said to the waitress on his way to the far table.

"You look like hell, Tipton." Carl's hand closed on the knife hilt in his vest pocket.

"Go to hell, Sunderland." Tipton took the chair across the table.

"Care for some breakfast, my treat." Carl shook a cigarette from the pack on the Formica table top. He pulled a lighter from his pocket and puffed it to life. "You know that hand of yours moved for two days. I threw it in an ice chest; I'm gonna burn it when I have the chance."

"You're a sorry bastard." Tipton turned his eyes to the plump waitress who delivered his coffee.

"So they tell me." Carl flipped a length of ash to the empty plate.

"You're enjoying this." Tipton blew steam away from his coffee.

"Almost as much as I enjoyed killing that bitch that ran with you." Carl's mouth set in a grim line. "I almost had you the other night."

"But you missed. Amber was young and inexperienced, and sometimes sacrifices must be made. But you didn't find your daughter, you didn't find Rachel."

Carl fished his billfold from his hip pocket; he pulled a five and threw it on the table as a tip.

"You think killing me will make everything normal again. That you'll get Rachel back and live happily ever after, well that's the farthest thing from the truth." Tipton sipped at the hot liquid.

"Honey, you want a refill?" The hefty waitress circled the various tables with a fresh pot.

Carl shook his head.

"Top it off, please." Tipton smiled weakly at the waitress, as she filled his cup, holding any comment until she moved away. "There are more of us than you can imagine; we're like weeds in the garden. You can't get rid of us."

"I *can* get rid of you. I'll keep killing your kind until I get my daughter back."

"Sunderland, I despise you more than any human on the earth, and I know you feel the same about me." Tipton shook a cigarette from Carl's pack. "I'll give you a chance to kill me and get your daughter."

"What's the deal?" Carl asked, sliding his lighter across the table.

"You and me on the next full moon, the survivor wins Rachel." Tipton lit the cigarette. He inhaled deeply filling his lungs with smoke.

Carl nodded. "Alright, I'm game."

"You name the place." Tipton smirked. "You're going to need all the advantage you can get."

"Gravel quarry five miles off the Possum Hollow road. I'll see you there in two days." Carl pushed back his chair rising from the table. "Don't worry, I'll get the coffee."

"Remember what I did to your wife?" Tipton smiled. "I'm going to enjoy eating your heart. I hope it tastes as good as hers."

Carl parked his black pick-up a mile from the abandoned Possum Hollow Gravel Company. A small grove of trees shielded it from any prying eyes that might happen to come along the rutted dirt road. The prospect of such an encounter seemed remote. From the look of the overgrown vegetation, no one had been here for months, possibly years.

The early afternoon sun baked the area in its harsh relentless glare. He pulled two duffel bags from the floor board. Carl had to prepare for Tipton's arrival. He knew this area well, having scouted it previously to lay a trap for the lycanthrope. His time was limited so he had to place his many surprises and get some rest before nightfall.

Sweat drenched his shirt before he covered half the distance to the pit. Carl took a moment to rest under the shade of a massive oak, his burdens proved to be heavier than expected. He lit a cigarette and drew the smoke deep into his lungs.

He glanced at his back trail, Tipton could follow it easily, but knowing the man's mentality Carl knew he would ignore it when he turned into the beast. Tipton was an aberration among his kind, retaining much of his human knowledge after the change. That quality made him the most dangerous.

He threw the butt to the ground crushing it under his boot sole. The pit wasn't getting any closer and he had work to do.

Carl Sunderland waited in the darkness, his black clothing blended with the shadows. The night-vision goggles strapped across his eyes gave an excellent view of the pit. During the afternoon, after he planted his traps and cached weapons around the interior of the pit, he found the perfect hiding spot: a deep slash cut into the steep side of the rock wall, it had taken him nearly an hour to scale the vertical incline to reach his shelter.

He longed for a cigarette, but resisted the temptation. Tipton could be out there anywhere, just waiting for him to make a mistake and give his position away. He looked at the entrance, a gentle incline on the south side of the quarry, built to allow access to trucks and tractors. He'd planted a special surprise for Tipton there.

Carl's eyelids grew heavy, he blinked several times fighting sleep. He needed to be at his best to battle Tipton. Carl glanced up at the heavens, the full moon hung high in the western sky. It had to be past two o'clock. *Where is he? Where's Tipton?*

Mosquitoes buzzed around his head, landing on his unprotected ears and neck. Carl ignored the impulse to slap at the pests. A hint of sound reached his ears, the faint ringing of a bell. *What's going on here?* A frown touched Carl's face. He peered out toward the lip of the quarry. A low chorus of bleats mixed with the ringing. *Sheep? What's Tipton up to?*

The sound grew louder, coming directly toward the entrance. An old ewe wearing a bell on her collar jumped onto the road, followed immediately by the entire flock.

"Damn." Carl lifted the .243 Remington to his shoulder. He caught a glimpse of the werewolf running behind the sheep urging them forward. A story told by his grandfather filled his mind. During the Second World War soldiers drove flocks of sheep over suspected mine fields to protect men and equipment. Tipton was updating an old strategy.

The first explosion rocked the quarry, sending dirt, gravel, blood and bones rocketing into the air. Another blast shook the ground, dirt rained down on Carl's makeshift shelter. Tipton stood on the lip of the quarry staring at his gory handiwork.

Carl snuggled the rifle butt to his shoulder, for a brief instant the crosshairs centered on Tipton. The werewolf vanished, before he could find the trigger.

The panicked sheep raced around the bowl shape of the quarry, milling at the lowest point near a stagnant water hole. Carl licked his lips, a nervous tickle settled between his shoulder blades. He lowered the rifle to the ground. *Where's Tipton? Where did he go?*

A rain of pebbles fell from the rock wall above, clattering off the larger stones. Carl twisted his body, searching the vertical sides. The hairy form of Tipton plunged through space toward him.

"Shit." Carl fumbled for his pistol, tearing it from the holster. A set of razor sharp claws dug into his shoulder, plucking him from his perch. The .45 fell from his hands bouncing off the rocks to fall to the ground below.

Carl twisted his body in midair to prevent the massive weight of Tipton from driving him into the unyielding earth. Stars exploded before his eyes, his breath exploded from his lungs upon impact. He lay on his back struggling to breathe. Tears misted his eyes. Tipton's blurry form towered above him.

A talon-tipped foot smashed his chest, cracking two ribs. The werewolf pinned Carl to the hard, rocky surface, grinding its extra weight into Carl's ribcage. Sharp stones tore at his back. Carl pounded his fists on the foot and ankle to little effect. His vision darkened, his desperate blows grew weaker and weaker.

In desperation, his hand stretched for his boot top and the hidden silver dagger. Bending his knee, he managed to scrape the top of his boot; the elusive handle remained out of reach. Tipton threw back his head, his snout pointed toward the round, glowing disk in the heavens. A primitive, guttural roar exploded from his mouth.

"No, dammit, no," Carl said. "I'm not going to die this way." He gritted his teeth, straining to reach the knife hilt. His fingers brushed the bone handle. The index and middle finger squeezed down on both sides, inching it from the scabbard. The dagger moved and inch, then two. Carl, on the verge of unconsciousness, tugged the knife free.

The sharp blade sank into the flesh behind the werewolf's ankle; its deep bite slicing through the Achilles tendon. Tipton fell to his knees, his left leg unable to support any weight. Carl drew several huge breaths, filling his starving lungs.

"Die, you bastard!" Carl lunged at the wounded beast. Tipton twisted his torso at the last instant, the blade buried into the monster's shoulder. A roar of pain burst from the wolf-like mouth. He jerked away from Carl, the old hunter lost his grip on the bloodslick handle, leaving his weapon in the werewolf's heavily muscled flesh.

Carl struggled to get to his feet; his left arm dangled uselessly at his side. He stumbled toward a huge oblong stone in the center of the quarry. He gulped air through his mouth, trying to urge more speed from his weak, tired legs. He knew Tipton would recover quickly.

The boulder seemed so far away, Carl gritted his teeth, forcing his exhausted body toward the weapon hidden there. A loud roar and the crunch of gravel sounded behind him. Even with one good leg and hand the werewolf could rip him apart easily. After an eternity, Carl touched the pitted surface.

He circled to the far side, palming the boulder for support. He saw Tipton closing the distance; even hopping on one leg the werewolf was fast. Carl's hand closed around his weapon, lifting it to a firing position.

"Come on, you know you want to kill me." He turned to face Tipton, the beast quickly closed the distance between them. Carl gripped the sawed-off twelve-gauge double-barreled shotgun with his good arm, pointing it like a large pistol. The weapon jumped in his hand, the noise nearly deafened him as he squeezed both triggers. The silver pellets struck the monster solidly in the chest.

Tipton fell heavily, his arms pawing the air. A gurgle broke from his blood splattered jaws. Carl staggered over to the mortally wounded creature. Slowly the savage features began to change becoming human. Tipton coughed, dark blood frothed his lips.

"You did it," Tipton's voice sounded far away. "You killed me." He blinked several times.

"Where's Rachel? Where's my daughter?" Carl pressed the ejector button on the shotgun; the empty casings sailed over his head. He jammed two live rounds into the barrels. "Where is she?"

"She'll find you." Tipton rattled a final time and lay still.

Carl shook his head, his arm throbbed mercilessly. He exhaled a deep breath; slowly he turned up the inclined road. A small fur covered figure met him at the entrance. Her belly swollen and full, obviously a pregnant female, she growled, showing large incisors.

"Rachel, Rachel, is that you?" Carl pointed the shotgun toward the creature.

The Spine-Tingling Tale of the Crystal Golem

Starring Tom Ribas

Jules rappelled down the lengthy black cord leading from the rooftop to the center floor of the museum. The grappling hook was attached to the side of an opened window, part of a triangular prism of glass that adorned the tip of the building. His strong legs and arms flexed as he slid his weight down the cord, moving quick and silent. Then he reached the end and his black stealth boots quietly touched ground.

Several feet away there arose a tall glass case lighted by twin spotlights and protected by a mobile gridwork of interlacing security beams. The red beams would sound the alarm if any part of Jules's body touched them, moving in complicated patterns up and down and side to side. With the confidence of an expert knowing what to do and the swift reflexes of a cat, the thief lunged, dashed, and bent his way through the complex web of lasers. He reached the end and took a breath. Now he stood directly before the glass pillar showcasing the ultimate prize— *The Lost Purple Diamond of the Mayans*.

Jules was the greatest jewel thief the world had ever known, and had amassed the world's largest black market collection of priceless gems pilfered from all over the globe. He'd never been caught, had mastered his trade down to the minutest detail, and now he was one foot away from the object of what would be his greatest conquest: the rare diamond with a purple sheen caused by an uncommon structural defect.

The Purple Diamond thought to have been lost forever in the mists of time, possibly taken by Spanish conquistadors, or perhaps just disappeared in whatever mysterious disaster the Mayans themselves vanished in. Archaeologists had been frustrated over the years by the many references to the diamond in Mayan hieroglyphics, engravings on walls that seemed to indicate they attached special magical abilities to it, often using it as a centerpiece in rituals and ceremonies. The glyphs would then become less clear, growing confused by an indecipherable story about some kind of invading presence that destroyed and brought senseless destruction, without any guiding principle or reason. Whatever that presence was, it was inexorably linked to the Mayans' inexplicable disappearance from the Earth.

But just six months ago, in a ruined temple on the Yucatan Peninsula, a British archaeologist found a secret passageway that led to a hidden chamber below the lowest known floor of a ziggurat, and there the Purple Diamond was discovered, preserved through the years in all its glory, resting on a hidden altar.

And now that the diamond was almost in his grasp, the master thief prepared for the crowning achievement in his already stellar career. He took a glass cutter from his belt and deftly moved the tip of the rod clockwise against the case. He pulled the other rod away and a circle of glass held by a suction cup detached from the pane; Jules reached into the hole and grasped the diamond in both hands. Reverently, he lifted the jewel off the pedestal and held it under his eyes, staring into the glittering, shimmering contours of its surface.

At last! Now I've truly done it! The Lost Purple Diamond of the Mayans, thought to have been only legend, the most priceless and sought-after jewel in all the world, and now it's all mine!

A faint tinge of energy coursed through the diamond and ran up both his arms with a tingling sensation. Jules continued to stare at the surface of the great jewel in his hands, practically hypnotized. The current of energy came again, stronger this time.

Oh yes, it is yours, all right. It is yours, along with all the burdens which that entails.

"Who said that?" Jules asked involuntarily.

The face of a long-haired man with dark skin aged by wrinkles, wearing a tarnished turquoise headband and a jade earring in one ear, appeared on the top facet of the diamond. He spoke directly to Jules: *This is the voice of Yax Pasaj, the chieftain entrusted with guarding the jewel and ensuring that its dark power never be used again by human hands; to ensure that the great tragedy that befell my people would never happen again.*

The energy coursed harder through the thief's body. It became visible to him as raging blue fire that surged from the heart of the stone. It pulsed harder and harder. Jules could feel his body being taken by an unstoppable, ungovernable force.

"WHAT IS THIS?!" Jules shrieked in fright.

Ha ha ha ha, this is the CURSE..............................of the CRYSTAL GOLEM!

Jet and Ruby lay sprawled atop each other on her queen-sized bed. Music played on the stereo as they read comic books.

Jet looked at his watch and noticed the time. He put down his pulp "Monster Movie" Creature Feature comic and started to get up. "Well, better get going," he said, patting her leg so she'd let him move out from under it. "I need to help Pro-fessor Hornblende with an experiment." Jet studied crystallo-graphy at the local university, sometimes helping his professors in the lab for extra credit.

Ruby leaned up on her elbow. "Jet, don't you think you should consider changing your major to something a little more practical? I mean, there probably isn't much of a job market in crystals these days."

"Honeybunches, we've been over this a thousand times. Crystals are what I do. I've loved them ever since I was a kid."

"I know, Love Muffin, but sometimes I wonder about your future. I don't want you to be disappointed because you can't find work as a crystallographer."

"You know, Margaret Thatcher studied crystallography. Look how she ended up."

Ruby studied him with her wide, blue eyes and said, "Are you saying you want to end up an uptight British lady?"

Jet looked at her for a second and burst out laughing. He ruffled her red, pointy hair and said, "You screwball kook. What am I going to do with you and your raging wit?" Then he walked to the side of the room and took an amethyst he had given her off a dresser, and sat back down on the bed. He held it up so it shone and sparkled in the overhead light.

"You see this? This is perfection. Crystals are more structured and logically planned than anything else on Earth; they reveal to us God's purpose and his mathematical plan for the world. Hundreds of years of heat and pressure have forged this wondrous, geometric work of art: notice the shining mirrored faces, the flawless interior without any traces of inclusions or contamination...a beautiful sense of symmetry and balanced space...the solidity...the density...no air bubbles, chips, or slippage between atomic planes...perfect luster and vivid saturation..."

His voice drifted off as he continued to stare into the bright, reflective surfaces of the crystal. He seemed dumbly mesmerized by it; Ruby leaned up to him and said, "Do I need to leave you two alone?"

Jet broke his gaze away from the crystal and saw that she was mocking him. He burst out laughing again. "Oh, you nut. How I love you!" he said and leant and kissed her passionately.

Ruby appreciated the affection and pulled Jet towards the bed. She knocked the crystal out of his hand and it fell to the floor.

Jet broke away and said, "Gosh! I'm late. I've got to see you later, darling."

"Will you call me later tonight?"

"We'll see. If I have time."

He left the bedroom and Ruby could hear him exiting through her front door and down the small flight of stairs. She got up and picked the crystal off the floor, placed it back on the dresser. There it rested, watching her, waiting silently.

It was not too long afterwards that she received a phone call. She picked up the phone, said, "Hello?"

"Ruby! This is Dr. Hornblende! Something terrible has happened!"

"Dr. Hornblende? What's happened?"

"A horrible monster has attacked the lab! It's destroying everything in town! You must warn Jet!"

"But Jet already left—"

"No! NO! AIIIIIIEEEEEE—" The phone clanged and she heard a weird, oddly musical roar. Then just a dial tone.

She hung up and dialed Jet's cell phone. He didn't pick up. She tried again. And again. But still no answer. She tried the TV; it only showed only test patterns.

Ruby sat in the empty silence of her bedroom, seated on her bed with her legs crossed, back against the wall. She tried to smoke a cigarette. She got up and started to pace in a circle.

She couldn't stop thinking about the "horrible monster" rampaging through Gypsum. Her mind rapidly raced over the countless profiles of monstrosities from the horror movies. There were vampires, werewolves, mummies, ghouls, zombies, frogmen, robots, gelatinous blobs, giant insects, aliens from outer space and so many others. She mentally sketched through the oddest and most atrocious creature combinations she could conceive, Lovecraftian hybrids of gorillas with the head of an octopus, dinosaurs with the wings of a bat. A particularly horrid image came to her mind: a monster with the agile legs of an ostrich and the intelligent head of a dolphin; every one she thought of became successively less anthropomorphic and more terrifying.

How she wished Jet and Dr. Hornblende were safe!

She put out the cigarette and lay back on the bed, unable to calm her frenzied thoughts. She stared at the amethyst across the room.

It began to emit a faint, nearly inaudible tone, resonating with a sonic interference that steadily became nearer. The phonon vibrations of its molecular lattice built as atoms ruffled and shook jumpily about their equilibrium positions; the crystal sensed the power of another of its own. Ruby watched while the tingle hummed louder and a strange source of leant power lit the purple crystal brighter from the inside, glowing with the collective consciousness of the mineral kingdom.

From far below the floor of her room, traveling quickly across rivers of mantle and layers of solid granite, a subterranean meteor was coming fast, heated with the peculiar piezoelectric quality of crystals to change shape as temperature rose, zeroing in on the target its senses had detected; power was coming like a missive from an underground dive bomber, screaming; something old, as old as the four-billion-year-old rocks found on Earth, traveling faster beyond lightspeed at the quantum level, its subatomic particles moving so fast they seem to be in two places at once.

A beam of light pierced from the center of Ruby's bedroom and the Earth opened up to graft a smoldering pit of fire like a portal to Hell. The Crystal Golem arose by orogenesis, to make its dramatic appearance: the lights glistened into an aurora borealis of colors from the fearsome muscles of rock crystal and jewels and gemstones studded in-between. The shoulders were solid spikes of smoky quartz, its tabular pectorals were orange beryl, its abdomen a sheet of blue-green marble. The upper arms and legs were red and brown streaks of realgar, the lower limbs powerful columns of tourmaline. Its hands and feet were blocks of pyrite with smaller cubes for digits; the stony head was gray staurolite veined in gold. In the center of its triangular, orange-red sockets of wulfenite, were flaming red Tiger's Eye locked into a permanent scowl.

It opened its mouth to reveal a tunnel of ringed, sky-blue microcline. A sonic burst issued forth that resonated through the monster's glassy throat and all about the room into a shrill roar of high-pitched music, a crescendo blast of a thousand violins played to an insane squeal.

Ruby was thrown back by the blast, up against the wall, too stunned to scream. The golem charged her, its right arm and massive fist thrust forward. With the full force of its body driving its momentum, it hit the wall mere inches from Ruby's head.

Still slightly weak from its travel, it broke apart into a thousand acicular crystal fragments, spilling a mélange of diamonds, emeralds, and sapphires showering over her head.

As gems rained, Ruby swiftly escaped past the broken golem and ran into the hallway.

The thing's arm reassembled at an alarming rate, the crystals drawn together by a strange force of attraction. The golem ran after Ruby, legs sliding across the floor like Gumby, fluidly breaking through any the walls and furniture to get to her. Everything broke apart like talc against the unstoppable drive of the Crystal Golem, its unrelenting, monomaniacal purpose demolishing everything in its path. Ruby ran out the front door and down the steps to her driveway. The golem boorishly bore a hole through the front entrance and followed Ruby by smashing right over the fence on the front lawn.

A brown Honda screeched into the driveway and Jet leant out the window, yelling, "Get in, get in! Quick!"

Ruby dashed to the passenger side and jumped into the front seat; Jet immediately reversed to get out of the driveway and away from the charging monster. It stomped the ground just where the car had been a few seconds earlier, leaving a gaping hole in the cement. Jet and Ruby skidded off to safety as the golem screamed after them in its frightening, musical wail.

When they were some distance away from the monster, Ruby blurted, "What the hell was that thing?!"

"I don't know, but I heard on the news that whatever it is, it's destroyed half the city. I thought I'd better come back to see if you were safe. It's a good thing I got here in time."

Ruby was struggling to catch her breath. "Dr. Hornblende called and said that it tore up the laboratory."

"*What?* Oh no, we've got to get down there and see if he's okay!"

"What in the world was that thing *made* of? It looked like it was made out of crystals."

"Yeah, well, I did recognize some minerals on its body, and it definitely had traces of pyrite, quartz, and topaz."

There was a long silence, before Ruby said, "You mean crystals can come alive?"

"No. I don't think so. Well, they can grow, I guess."

"Why did it come into my house?"

"I guess it was trying to get you."

"Why me?"

"I guess you must be a threat to it somehow. Maybe to get at me. I don't know. This is weird."

"What was that *noise* it was making?"

"Crystals have very fine acoustic properties. The sound waves of its roar must reverberate through the body before coming out of its mouth."

"Jet, how do you know all this?"

"I'm a crystallographer."

"Did you and Dr. Hornblende have anything to do with this?"

"*What?!* How can you even accuse me of something like that?"

"Well, don't you think it's a bit strange that you know so much about crystals and the first place the monster attacked was the lab and then my house?"

"Ruby, I could never create something like that. I wouldn't even know where to begin. To think that crystals are capable of life—"

"Well, I'm glad you didn't. That thing is hideous."

"Ruby, it isn't *hideous*. It's a fascinating work of nature."

"What?"

"I mean…look at the intricate mosaic of crystals and gems, each type perfectly matching the architecture of its biological systems, the life-like motions and amplification of sound." Jet's voice drifted off and he stared at the road ahead.

Ruby said, "Well, then why don't you two just run off together if you love it so much?"

"God, Ruby! What are you, *jealous* now? Of a freaking monster?"

Ruby lay back in her seat and against the window, brushing her hand on her forehead. "No. No, I'm not...jealous. It's just..." She sighed.

"It's just what?"

Ruby thought back to that day in her childhood, the day that had lingered for so long in memory, now flashing back with crystal-clear clarity. A horrific scene from her past coming to the present, something she could never truly forget. It was the day she attended the International Gem and Mineral Expo as a young girl, in her home town of Opal, Nebraska.

Beneath the wide banner announcing the 1996 Expo, dozens of stands and display cases were set up around the showroom floor, presenting the latest developments in mineralogy. People and their children milled around the wide auditorium, marveling at the individual stands and fabulous demonstrations of rare and unusual geological formations. In the center of the hall there was a very special display, surrounded by a backdrop almost as high as the ceiling. It was colored black and green; on the main wall was spelled out the exciting message: "Dr. Wacky's Magic Goo," and in front of the backdrop was a table, draped in a white cloth, with a silver cauldron that was currently sealed. Next to it were several varieties of rocks and crystals.

Behind the table was a mad scientist. He was wearing a long white lab coat, a red bowtie, and dizzy "swirl" glasses. His hair stuck up in straw-like gray fronds; his pointed nose counterbalanced his wide smile.

Beyond the table and Dr. Wacky were several retractable chairs seating a large audience, a ten-year-old Ruby Watkins among them.

"Ladiiiiiies and germs, wait 'till you see what *I've* got in store for *you!*" Wacky proclaimed in good-natured zeal. "What

I've brought for you here today is nothing less than a gen-u-ine miracle of science, a previously-thought impossibility that has come to fruition through years of continued, tireless contemplation. What I've brought for you here is a magic goo that can make rocks...DISAPPEAR!"

The crowd oohed and ahhed. They begged to have their skepticism proven wrong.

"To show you that this is indeed of science and not just science fiction, I will give you a short demonstration. To my left is a collection of solid rocks and crystals. I'll begin with a common, everyday rock found locally just outside this stadium. You will notice that it is heavy and perfectly solid. Can I have a volunteer come up and test it?"

A little boy from the front row came up, weighed it, and nodded. The rock was indeed solid.

"*Now*, watch as I make this ordinary rock dissolve into pure nothingness, with my magic goo!" Wacky opened the cauldron and revealed a viscous, bubbling white liquid inside that resembled glue. He dropped the rock in, said "Presto!", and pulled the goo upwards with a ladle, scooping it up from the bottom of the pot to show that the rock was no longer there.

The crowd gasped in wonderment and awe. The magic goo was truly not the thing of legend, but of fact.

"Now! If that doesn't knock your socks off and turn you into a believer, let me give you a better, more *scientific* demonstration." He reached over to his collection of minerals and pulled out a piece of glass. "As many of you may already know, the only mineral with a hardness of ten is a diamond, but I don't want to throw away a thousand-dollar wedding ring into the goo, ha ha. So, I'll do the next best thing and use this ordinary piece of glass, which looks similar to a diamond and has a hardness of six point five. Watch as I throw it into the magic goo, and make it...DISAPPEAR!"

The crowd watched with bated breath. Wacky slowly placed the glass over the pot and dropped it in. After a few seconds, he scooped up the goo with the ladle, and showed that the glass was no more. The crowd gave a standing ovation.

Wacky smiled and humbly accepted their praise. He said, "And now here's the best part, ladies and germs: you, for only the low, low price of twenty-five dollars, can take home your very own sample of the magic, rock-ravagaing, crystal-crunching, mineral-mashing goo!"

The children in the crowd immediately bum-rushed the table and started holding their money up to the professor. Two body-guards had to step in to control the surging crowd. Wacky laughed and bid them to be patient; everyone would get their magic goo in time.

Ruby was still sitting in her chair, looking down at the bag of crystals she had bought. She'd used up all her money buying them, and now she didn't have enough for the magic goo. She felt a fool. The crystals were nothing compared to the mir-aculous invention; with it she would have the power to com-pletely destroy rocks, to annihilate matter. She could use it on anything she wished, making any mineral vanish into thin air. What was the point of having a bag of crystals if you couldn't destroy them? Now she'll never have a chance to get the magic goo, because there will never again be another 1996 Gem Expo.

She walked up to the table, watching the professor as he handed out goo to all the excited children. He was using the la-dle to scoop it up and put it into plastic baggettes, handing them to the children in exchange for their money. He had placed a few extra bags of goo to the side of the cauldron, where they were for the moment unnoticed; Dr. Wacky was too busy ladling out the goo to the clamoring children.

She really wanted one of those bags. She wanted it more than anything. It held the god-like power to destroy, to defy the law of conservation of mass. She had to have it. But she had no money.

Wacky was still busy handing out the bags, too busy to take notice of her. She stepped up closer to the table, and to the bags. She was easily within reaching distance. The professor was busy, sweating and furiously ladling goo.

The bags were right there in front of her. All it would take was one little reach. That's it—just reach out and take it.

Wacky wouldn't even notice. He had so much of it; he didn't really need it.

Her hand reached out to take a bag.

She touched it.

Her fingers grasped the plastic.

A hand slapped down on her arm.

She looked up in sheer terror to see the red-on-yellow swirl eyes and hooked nose of the professor glaring down at her. "And just what do you think *you're doing, Miss?*"

Ruby stood frozen with her mouth agape.

A look of deep betrayal passed over the professor's visage as it met with angry realization. "You were trying to...*steal* my invention?" Poor Ruby felt like crying but didn't have the courage to make a sound. "You were trying to...actually *steal* the invention that I've worked so very *hard* on?"

Ruby pulled away her arm and started to back away, cowering in fear.

"Do you have any idea how HARD I've worked on this?! Do you know how HARD I've WORKED my entire LIFE to be able to do things like this?! Do you think that you can just COME in here and TAKE it without *PAYING?* " Wacky's voice cracked on the last word.

Ruby backed into a chair and tripped over onto the ground.

The professor was pointing and screaming hysterically: "Thief! THIEF! THIIIIIIIIEF!!! SECURITY! ARREST her! She was STEEEEEALING! ARREEESSSSSST HER!" The security walked over to the mad scientist and tried to calm him down, but he only got more flustered and screamed even louder. More security guards came over to restrain him. Ruby quietly snuck away and disappeared into the crowd.

And that was the last time she had ever played with crystals or rocks. But she would never forget—the face, the finger, and the accusation.

In the middle of a garbage-littered alley, opening from a busy street, a pile of precious stones lay scattered against a grimy brick wall.

A couple of bums walked into the alley, looking for a place to sleep. One of them noticed the glittering pile. "Oh shit, man! Look at that! Jewels!" said the bum. He ran over and started sifting his hands through the gems. "Diamonds! And rubies, man! We gonna be totally rich!"

The other hobo ran over to the pile and also put his hands through them. "These must be worth a million bucks, man! Look at all these! I wonder who left it?"

"Who cares, man! Just take it before someone else sees it." The two started grabbing handfuls of jewels and stuffing them into the pockets of their Army surplus jackets. Then they heard a strange noise.

"What was that?!"

There was a rumbling from the pile as the gems began to vibrate. The ones that were in the bums' hands flew back into the pile. The trap had been sprung; what had appeared to be the promise of wealth was only a lure to draw unsuspecting prey.

"Oh shit, man! Shit! SHIT!"

The jewels moved of their own accord and the groaning rose louder. They supernaturally assembled themselves into arms, legs, and feet. It grew larger to solidify into a dense mass. A head with two flaming eyes formed.

"Let's get the fuck outta here!"

The bums turned to run, but the creature made of jewels and crystals reached out to grab them by their coats. It lifted a hefty arm and punched one of them straight into the opposite wall, plastering him several inches into the brick and leaving a man-shaped outline like in the Wylie Coyote cartoons. The other one struggled to get free, but the golem held him tight in both hands; it opened to reveal a tunnel of clear, ringed microcline. The mouth grew wider as the golem lifted him closer.

"Aaahhhhhh! Nooooo! DON'T EAT MEEEEEEEE—"

The monster shoved him in headfirst and swallowed. The clear crystals and gems on its body glowed red with the stain of blood. The golem had eaten a man, and gained his knowledge. It now knew how to think like a human.

But the question remained: would it live to regret it?

As Jet and Ruby drove downtown, they witnessed the havoc and wreckage that the golem had already unleashed upon Gypsum. Store windows were smashed and cars were upturned. Buildings were on fire and people were about, frantically trying to put them out. Fire hydrants were broken, leaving geysers of water rushing high into the air. Crazed urbanites ran around willy-nilly looting, screaming, and fighting in the madness that had descended on their town.

Jet slowed. He noticed a couple of guys standing on the sidewalk, looking glum. One was a stocky high school boy with a backwards cap and a letterman jacket. The other was a thin Indian man with his hair parted in the middle and an integrated beard and mustache. Jet rolled down the window to talk to them.

"Hey, what's going on here?" he asked.

"It's the golem, man," said the one in the cap. "It came through here and trashed everything! It even ruined Gypsum High's football field. We were supposed to have a big game this week!"

"And it completely destroyed my jewelry store," the other man said. "That crystalline freak just broke in, smashed everything, and ate my priceless gems! I'm completely ruined!"

It sounded to Jet like these guys had a bone to pick with the monster; he figured they might be useful to have around. "Well, my girlfriend and I have reason to believe that our mutual destiny is intertwined with the sudden and inexplicable appearance of the golem. It seems to be seeking us out to destroy us, so the golem's pretty much guaranteed to show up wherever we are. You guys want to come with us? You might be able to get the revenge you're looking for."

The two immediately accepted the offer and got into the back seat of the Honda. Jet put the car in motion while they introduced themselves.

"My name's Jaidev, but you can call me 'Jade,' " said the Indian man. "In addition to being a store owner I'm also a licensed jewel inspector."

"Name's Jasper," said the high school boy. "I'm the star quarterback for the Gypsum High Giants. GO GI-ANTS!"

"Nice to meet you. I'm Jet and this is my girlfriend Ruby. We're headed to Gypsum University, where I'm currently studying crystallography. My professor and mentor, Dr. Hornblende, was recently attacked and we want to see if he's okay."

The newly-formed quartet listened to a news radio station to see if they could hear any updates on the crisis. They heard a report stating that the National Guard had already been deployed into Gypsum, in order to lead an all-out attack on the golem.

"What are they thinking?" said Jet. "They can't destroy the golem with conventional weapons! The golem is composed of the hardest and densest minerals in the world; no bullet or explosive would ever be able to shatter its skin! This here is just another case of the natural arrogance of man."

"You're getting that look on your face you get when you're being self-righteous," said Ruby.

"No, I'm not!"

"Yes, you are. Look in the mirror."

Jet looked into the rear-view mirror and saw clearly that there was a self-righteous expression on his face. "Aw, shut up."

"Don't you tell me to shut up, Borax Boy."

There was a peal of laughter from the back seat as the passengers voyeuristically enjoyed the quarrel.

"Oh ho ho, looks like someone's sleeping on the couch tonight!" said Jade.

Jasper made the motion of cracking a whip and went, "Kwapish!"

A battalion of armed troops, jeeps, and tanks rolled into downtown Gypsum. They knew where the golem was at all times, using pre-1970's police scanners with crystals built into them that picked up on the golem's musical roar and tracked the signal to wherever the beast was prowling at the moment. The general was riding in the open hatch of the lead tank, the lieutenant-general rolling alongside in a following jeep. They started to hear the unmistakable *clomp-clomp-clomp* of the golem's tread and called for a halt; over the horizon, a bejeweled specter emerged into view, walking in slow, unhurried steps.

The general was a veteran of many wars, and had seen every type of oddity that the enemy could possibly throw at you. He'd dealt with everything from suicide bombers wielding flame-throwers to kamikaze pilots with tomahawks to berserkers with box-cutters in his time. He believed (rightly so, in many cases) that there was no type of problem that could not be solved with the right type of gun.

"Prepare for a full-on attack, Lieutenant," declared the general. "I want to hit this thing with everything we've got."

"Prepare to engage enemy!" yelled the lieutenant.

The battalion stopped and the men prepared for the assault. The general dropped down the hatch and aimed his tank's cannon at the approaching monster. There was a tense moment while everyone had his weapon trained on the golem and only waited for the signal to pull the trigger.

"Ready...aim...FIRE!"

A fireworks calamity of bullets, grenades, and missiles flew into the road ahead of them. The men kept shooting for quite a long time after the lieutenant gave the order to cease fire. The barrage tapered off and they were left with the hazy vision of a giant crater in the center of the street, covered by swirls of dust and smoke. The general came up from the hatch to look.

The smoke cleared and a figure appeared to plodding towards them, in no particular hurry and with a powerful and unceasing drive. *Clomp-clomp-clomp.*

"It's just as I feared," said the general, "we can't destroy it with ordinary weaponry. We have to pull out the big gun. Deploy the Death Ray!"

"Deploy the Death Ray!" parroted the lieutenant.

A covered truck-trailer backed up into the group and the men removed the tarp to uncover a complicated piece of machinery. It looked a bit like a satellite dish with a very long antenna, or an oversized ray-gun toy with a mess of wiring, cables, and bronze tubes attached all over. The truck backed to the vanguard of the procession, and when they activated the Death Ray it hummed and glowed loudly, the lights along the triangular antennae winking on one by one.

The general lit a cigarette and left it dangling from the corner of his mouth. He mounted the steps to the top of the control column that directed the ray- gun and said, "Let's see how you handle ten million gigawatts of pure, unbridled energy, you goddamned sonofabitch!"

The rest of the men started pulling back. The golem kept coming forward and the Death Ray hummed louder. When the target was in range, the general released the safety caps from the firing buttons and depressed them hard. A lance of blue energy shot from the antennae; the ray started making a sound like a car alarm going off underwater. The beam struck the golem directly, and it stopped moving for a moment; the myriad gems and crystals of its body glowed bright blue as they absorbed energy, and the general had to fight to hold onto the shaking controls, his face grimacing and the aviator glasses on his face reflecting bright the blue light of the beam.

The golem glowed brighter and brighter, becoming so intense that all you could see was a blue silhouette standing in the street like a disembodied ghost. The color began to change as light refracted and diffracted by the crystals, the focus of energy becoming channeled and redirected. The blue turned to a ruby-red, turning a fiery red ember that transformed the entire street around them into a giant argon lamp. Colors shifted wavelength to bright pink, then the color of white-hot metal. The laser beam became white as well, and the stream of energy deflecting, focusing, and redirecting away from the golem's body returned backwards to the source it came from. The general was sweating furiously, his hands shaking to try and direct the mounting maelstrom of energy mounting out of his control. The white, burning ghost of the golem slowly stalked forward, against the current, coming in unrelenting steps the long way to the end of the antennae that projected the laser, and gently touched the tip with a single finger.

The tank instantly exploded, and strands of crackling energy rained down from the sky like Silly Snakes.

Clomp-clomp-clomp.

They eventually got to the University and found Dr. Hornblende's laboratory. It was here that the experiments were done with X-rays, neutron diffraction, and molecular beam epitaxy. They were relieved to see that the entire campus hadn't been destroyed, but the lab was in a shambles. They found the professor hiding under a life-sized molybdentite model; his white hair disheveled and glasses askew. He crawled out from under the model and brushed off his lab coat.

"Oh, thank goodness you're safe, Jet!" said Hornblende. "I think the golem came here looking for you!"

"Good to see you, Professor. But I don't understand, what would the golem want with me?"

"Maybe it's because you're the only one who can stop it," said Ruby.

"Well, I have no idea *how* to stop it."

"That's what I've been trying to figure out myself," said Hornblende, as he took out a small red crystal. "Take a look at this. It chipped off when the golem came in here."

Jade took the stone and pulled an eyepiece from his shirt pocket. He studied it and said, "This is genuine rhodochrosite, but it's got some strange discoloration. It's almost as if there's electricity running through it."

"Precisely correct. I believe that the golem runs on pure energy, generated by a mysterious source of power and intensified again and again as it courses through the mirrors of its body, like a laser beam. This suggests that the golem is basically akin to a robot that runs on electricity, and, like a robot, is programmed for a purpose. Most likely, that purpose is total, mindless destruction. But unlike a robot, its crystals have a hardness that allows it to sustain a more powerful electric current than metals like copper and silicon. It truly is a perfect machine, with energy utilized to maximum efficiency, its information processed like the diamond microchips of a supercomputer, and seemingly capable of unlimited strength and stamina. If the golem could be studied, there's no telling what kind of findings it would turn up for research on superconductors."

"But how can a creature made of crystals be *alive?*" asked Ruby.

"It may not be as unusual as you think. Some believe that life might have begun with molecules on crystals, which have a tendency to mutate."

"Hey, Doc, enough with the science mumbo-jumbo," said Jasper. "Just tell us how to kick its ass!"

"Well now, in order to stop the golem we must first discern what its purpose is. And to do that we need more data. So we have to find the golem and study it, to learn more about its behavior and motivation."

"Do you have any idea where it is?" asked Ruby.

"I think it holes up in the industrial part of town where all the abandoned factories are. It's the only place in Gypsum where it would be able to hide and remain unnoticed. I say we start our search there."

The group left the university and set out to find the Crystal Golem.

The golem had cut a swath in the streets, and Jet and his company were easily able to follow it through the Gypsum manufacturing sector to the abandoned chemical plant where it hid. It was standing out in the street doing something unusual. Jet parked his car about a block away and the group snuck into a nearby alley. The golem was covering its face in its hands, a waterfall of diamonds and multicolored zircons streaming down its face onto the pavement.

"What's it doing?" asked Jade.

"I think it's crying," said Jasper.

"I wonder why?" asked Jet.

"Maybe it feels guilty for all the destruction it's caused," said Ruby.

"But that can't be! The golem is programmed to be a killing machine; it wouldn't feel guilt for simply following its nature," said Hornblende.

"I'll tell you what it is," said a voice. "It's existential despair."

They all looked to the other side of the alley where a man was quietly smoking and watching the golem. He had long hair, loose khaki pants, a flowered shirt, multiple rings on his fingers, and a crystal pendant around his neck.

"Who the hell are you?" asked Jet.

The guy looked over at them and said, "I'm Jacinth."

Jasper asked, "Did you say 'Jason?' "

"No, I said Jac*inth*."

"That's a weird name."

Jacinth angrily stubbed the cigarette out under his foot and said, "Dude, you are *seriously* not giving me any positive vibrations right now." Then he calmed a bit and said, "I'm a New Age guru and crystal therapist. I've been studying the golem since this whole hoopla began."

"What's crystal therapy?" asked Ruby.

"Crystal therapy is a type of alternative medicine that uses crystals to remove harmful blockages from the aura, by placing them along the chakras. It's given me all kinds of knowledge about how crystals can be used to heal and focus your spiritual energy, and by extension, how one can heal crystals, to purge them of the dark energy they've absorbed from negative people and their surroundings."

"You want to *heal* the golem?" Hornblende asked incredulously.

"That's right. It's all very simple if you understand crystals. The golem is a living being with feelings just like the rest of us, and like any living being he needs a little love and compassion. It's not easy being a soulless killing machine—at some point you might stop and wonder what the purpose of all the constant mayhem is, as well as why any sane God would choose to create something like you in the first place. You begin to get plagued by heavy existential questions like: 'What do I destroy after everything is destroyed?' It can get to be quite a drag."

"Are you saying that the golem is depressed?" asked Jet.

"Yes. And I'm going to go cheer him up." Jacinth started walking towards the golem.

They tried to stop him, but Jacinth simply waved him off and told them he knew what he was doing. He walked right up to the golem; it ceased its weeping to look at him.

"Hey, man," said Jacinth, "how you holdin' up?"

The golem looked at him with an inscrutable mask made of stone.

"Yeah, I know what you mean. Times are tough, man. I just got out of a really bad relationship recently. I know how it feels to be really bummed out.

"My girlfriend and I would always fight over whether a tomato was a fruit or a vegetable. We're vegetarians, so whenever we had salsa she'd always say that she can't eat it because tomatoes are fruits and not vegetables. I kept telling her that tomatoes *are* a vegetable, and that even if they *were* a fruit it still wouldn't matter because vegetarians can eat fruit. The last argument we had got so heated that she threw a loaded bong at my head. Women, am I right?"

The glowing wulfenite of the golem's eyes continued to stare at the little man.

"So all I'm saying is keep hangin' in there, son. Life can be tough, but you gotta be Zen about these things. Just run with the punches, know what I mean?" He reached out to pat the golem on the shoulder.

The golem's titanic fist shot out and punched Jacinth square in the face, leaving behind a crude "smile" of gemstones like pieces of coal on a snowman. Jacinth remained standing upright for a long moment, before crumpling limply to the ground.

The golem turned to look in the alley. Its gaze flared as it saw them, and it charged.

"Run!" yelled Jet.

They ran across the street, into the chemical plant and bolted the doors with loose boards. The interior was an expansive industrial room with gray, peeling walls, broken windows on the upper story, and the bulky tubes of air circulation pipes hanging from the ceiling. The golem thumped furiously against the door from the outside. Jasper and Jade hurried to a nearby pile of steel pipes and armed themselves for the impending battle. The doors slammed off their hinges and the Crystal Golem stood in the newly-formed opening.

Jade ran at the golem brandishing his steel pipe high in the air. "Die, monster!" he shouted. The golem reached over and backhanded him away like a tennis ball.

Jasper rushed the golem and yelled, "I'm gonna kick your ass!" The golem simply leaned over and swatted him away like a fly.

Then the golem saw Ruby, and its eyes flared brighter; it roared and charged after her, plowing through the ground. Ruby sprinted over to a metal stairwell leading up to a catwalk suspended over huge vats filled with chemicals; the golem followed after her, ascending the struts up to the walkway as King Kong climbed the Empire State building. Jet followed and climbed behind the golem to the walkway, where Ruby was backing up to the edge. Beneath her, below the drop were cauldrons of white chemical. The golem slowly moved towards her at the end. *Clomp-clomp-clomp.*

Ruby looked to the vat below. On it was a faded lettering that said, "DR. WACKY'S MAGIC GOO!" with a picture of Wacky's smiling face by it. This was built at another time, when the Magic Goo was slated for mass production and before Dr. Wacky was disgraced and arrested on charges of selling a highly acidic toxin to children.

Inspiration dawned and she said, "Jet! You've got to push it into the vat! It's the only thing that will destroy it!"

Jet looked at the golem, and its glittering and gleaming perfection dazzled his senses. "But I can't destroy it! It's a thing of greatness! It needs to be studied for the greater good of science!"

"It's either me or the golem, Jet! You can only save one of us!"

Jet looked at the golem, admiring its angular beauty and geometric perfection. It truly was a work of art, one to rival the greatest sculptures in the world. Its perfect utilization of energy powered its fluid movements and incredible strength. It was, aesthetically and mechanically, perfect.

Jet looked at Ruby. She wasn't perfect; she was just a flesh-and-blood creature like himself, with the adherent flaws that come from being human. Her body wasn't as strong as the golem's; much of her energy was simply unused and wasted in the form of released body heat. She was pretty, her ice-blue eyes shone like pure azurite and her red hair suited her namesake, but they lacked the fiery intensity of the golem's eyes that burned like the depths of Vulcan's forge. And her face was attractive, but not quite as geometrically balanced with sym-metrical facets as the golem's.

And yet she was still Ruby, the girl who listened to all his crystallography lectures even when they were boring, the one who made him laugh with her goofy sense of humor, the person who cheered him up when he was feeling down and who cared about him more than anyone else in the world. She might not be as physically perfect as the Crystal Golem, but to him she was far more priceless.

He rushed up behind the golem and gave it a big shove. The golem lost its balance, wobbled forward, and plunged down into a vat of white, syrupy liquid. It roared as it sank downwards, its crystals releasing fumes as they sizzled and dissolved. In time the muck covered up over its head and the monster was no more.

Jet ran to Ruby and gave her a long kiss at the top of the catwalk. Jade, Jasper, and Dr. Hornblende hollered and cheered from below.

Jet and Ruby were once again lying in her bed reading comics. Jet said, "Hey, Ruby, I want to show you a crystal."

Oh no, Ruby thought, *he's going to give me some boring lecture on crystallography. Just nod your head and try to look interested.*

She put down her comic book and sat up. "Okay," she said.

Jet sat up and pulled a small box out of his pocket. He opened it and there was a diamond ring inside.

"Will you marry me?"

Ruby teared up and cried, "Oh yes, yes! Of course, Jet!"

He put the ring on her finger and they embraced. If one were to look closer at the shiny surface of the ring, you would notice the face of a gaunt Mayan chieftain wearing a turquoise crown. Yax Pasaj smiled broadly and said, "I think he paid too much for that ring!" before delving into a howl of diabolical laughter.

The Spine-Tingling Tale of the Crystal Golem

Just the Two of Us
Starring Anthony Bell

Brandon sat in class with his arms folded atop his desk, head tilted, daydreaming as Ms. Dawson taught grammar. Allen Summers sat across the room, but Brandon didn't notice because he was absorbed with the anticipation of seeing his mother after school. His birth mother, that is.

A couple by the name of Beatrice and Marvin were his adoptive parents and had been since he was three. They had always been straight with him. He knew he was adopted, but until recently hadn't known why. They didn't have those answers. Only his mother did.

She had recently reintroduced herself into his life, and he was glad, because his memories of her were few and fading. They were reunited when she'd approached him one day as he walked home from school. It had been weird at first. For two weeks, Brandon had noticed a lady sitting at a bus stop two blocks from the school, and every time he'd walked by she stared at him with interest. She never peered over a pair of glasses, or a newspaper, or let her eyes follow without turning her head.

The first day he noticed the lady staring, he assumed she was fixed on something behind him. The first day he noticed the lady was staring at *him*, he lowered his eyes and walked on, glancing back, although he tried not to.

After the first week, when it was clear the lady wasn't going to cease staring at him as he passed, he switched streets, detouring six blocks to reach his house. It didn't help. She sat posted at another bus stop. He returned to his regular route, saving himself the added distance. He would've told somebody, but something inside advised him against this. She didn't seem menacing, although her blatancy made him uncomfortable. And besides, he wasn't a child.

Then one day she wasn't at the bus stop. Brandon didn't know whether to be relieved or disturbed. After another block, he heard footsteps close in behind him after crossing an intersection. He turned and there she was.

He was too scared to continue moving without looking as if he were a first timer on prosthetic legs, so he faced her, determined to maintain an appearance of composure, maybe even one tinged with a bit of defiance, while feeling like jelly inside.

She was several inches taller than he. Brandon didn't think what assured him of her goodwill was the way she stopped two feet away in a courteous attempt to remain level with him, but really the way her mouth opened in a smile he would think only angels capable of. She pointed at his chest and spoke softly. "Let me see it, Brandon."

He knew what she was referring to, and was not alarmed that she knew of the clover-shaped birthmark just below his collarbone, much less his name. He pulled his shirt down a bit, calmed by her harmless aura.

She smiled. "Just as clear as when you were a baby."

Brandon was tugged from remembrance by persistent noises similar to mumbling. He blinked his eyes and Allen Summers cleared into view from across the room. His lips were moving but Brandon was just beginning to hear what he was saying, as if his voice were being increased with a remote: "...said what are you looking at, four-eyes? Huh, punk?"

Brandon muttered something as the big boy left his seat and approached.

"What was that, dorkface?" Allen said once in front of Brandon's desk, palms planted on top, head dipped forward.

"I-I wasn't staring at you," Brandon said, and looked for Ms. Dawson, who wasn't in class. She must've stepped out; should be back soon, he hoped.

"You was staring at me, all right, because you sure wasn't looking through me." Allen's breath stank, and it took all of Brandon's reserve to restrain a grimace and verbal *yuck*.

His eyes darted around the beefy body, hoping Ms. Dawson would return to the room. "Really, I wasn't. I was daydreaming, that's all. I wasn't looking at you...sorry."

"Sorry doesn't cut it, liar," he said and began to turn.

"I'm not a liar."

"Come again, dipshit?"

The room was silent, as if twenty-seven sixth graders didn't actually fill it. The prospect of seeing his mother again would be badly tarnished if he knew it would occur with a black eye.

Brandon's head was down. "Nothing," he said through clenched teeth. "Sorry."

Allen patted his desk with a hefty hand. "Sorry doesn't cut it."

After school, Brandon went to the corner store and bought a candy bar. While leaving, his hand still pushing the door outward, the first punch connected with his jaw and he began to fall. He felt like a cartoon character, but instead of stars or chirping birds floating around his head in a tight circle, he saw black ovals like leeches sleek across his vision.

The sky suddenly switched places with the ground, so that he saw it while looking straight ahead instead of up. Then his lap commanded his view because he tucked his chin to his chest and covered his head with his arms as best he could.

He curled his legs to his stomach just in time, because he felt the maddening pain of a steel-toed boot connect to his shin right afterward. The beating continued and brought to his attention muscle groups and bones he'd never before noticed. His skull rocked between his arms and the jarring sent the blood in his mouth sloshing around like water in a glass.

After what seemed an hour, he heard the *ding-dong* of the door being opened and heard the cashier, whom he was familiar with, yelling. "Geet off dat boy. Ya hear me; geet offa him, I say."

Hard footsteps clapped away across the pavement while softer ones neared. Brandon was on his side and pushed himself onto one elbow. He opened his mouth and a bowl of blood dribbled out like warm syrup, followed by a single topping that resembled a tiny marshmallow. Brandon ran his tongue along his gums and sighed. He spit a few times to clear his mouth.

"Ye okay der, Brannon?" He was helped to his feet.

He wiped a remaining strand of blood from his chin. "Yeah, Julius. I think I'm fine." Only a bit of blood had gotten on his shirt, but his shins and various other parts of his body were throbbing. "Thanks for scaring him off."

"Wus nutting." He glanced at Brandon and then in the direction the kid had run. "Wus a big kid. Ye chure ya fine?"

"I'm good, Julius, really."

Julius pursed his lips and looked into the distance as Brandon adjusted his backpack and brushed himself off. "Ye be careful, okay, Brannon?"

"I will."

Brandon continued on, saving the candy bar he'd bought instead of eating it as he'd wanted to. He was watchful the entire way. He almost didn't want to see his mother—not Beatrice, but Ivy—because he felt weak and didn't want to appear that way in front of her.

He decided to go anyway, because he relished the secret visits with his mother more than anything and would rather feel weak in her presence than not be with her at all.

He crossed onto the bike path that slithered across most of Ridgeview. As he walked, he rubbed at his chin with his shirt, attempting to wipe off any remaining blood or spit. A few white and red flakes fell like snow. He hand combed his hair and hoped he looked presentable.

A mile later, the bike path intersected with a street which Brandon crossed and followed. Stopping at the corner of Julie's, a cozy diner that served thick and greasy food, he regarded the bike path as he did every day before entering, as if he'd just emerged from a darkened passage in front of a sanctuary.

He smiled and pushed open the entrance door. He smelled frying onions and sizzling hamburger; heard *"...and a side of hash browns, darlin',"*—that would be Rosa, who'd been the head waitress since God alone knew when—and saw a scattered group of people speaking quietly to each other in booths and at tables.

She sat at a table along the front window; where they always sat because there was a big mural painted on the glass. His mother looked lovely as ever, and his smile widened in response to hers.

"Hey, baby!" She rose and squeezed him tight. The pendant on her necklace tickled him as she hugged him.

He brushed his chin against his chest and laughed. He pulled out a chair and tucked his backpack beneath it. His mother situated herself and studied his face in the same unashamed way she'd done at the bus stops. He lowered his eyes.

"What happened?"

"Nothing."

"You don't have to lie to me, honey." She licked her thumb and leaned across the table, then wiped at his cheek. "Now hold still, B; you missed a spot. Open your mouth."

He did. She placed a hand under his chin to tilt his head back and then peered inside. She sat back and sighed; fingered the pendant at the bottom of her necklace. He thought it was a religious symbol. He'd heard that a lot of people in jail became religious.

"Who did this to you?"

"I'm not sure," he said. "Sucker-punched me; didn't get a good look at him."

"Then who do you think did it?"

He shrugged, avoiding her gaze.

"You can't let people push you around, baby, or else they'll make it a habit."

"I know." Then, thinking that wasn't a strong enough response, said, "I would've fought back, but it was so quick that I didn't have a chance."

She spoke softly, as when she'd first approached him, and he was powerless to resist because all he heard was love. "What's his name, B?"

"Allen Summers."

She touched her pendant again, as though absorbing strength because the name of her boy's attacker somehow brought home the pain of the encounter. "Has he done this to you before?" And out of concern as only mothers can, the stream of questions began.

Brandon grabbed her hands. "Mom, mom, mom—slow down, okay? One question at a time. Breathe."

"I'm sorry, baby. I just, well…"

Their usual waitress came to their table. "Hey, sweeties! And how are we today?"

"Alright, now that we've gotten to see you," his mom said. "Looked like that young man was trying to sweep the great Janelle off her feet."

"Not my type,"—she cupped the side of her mouth with her hand—"too cool for his own good."

"Hmm. Well, honey, I'll take the BLT, please, with ice tea."

"And you, sugar?"

Brandon always blushed when she called him that. "I want chicken strips today. Water is fine for me."

"Alright, sweetie. Y'all give me a second and it'll be on the way."

Janelle left and Brandon answered some of his mom's questions. "He's hit me before, but never in my face. It's always been in my stomach or arm. He thought I was staring at him today, and I guess maybe his self-esteem was lower than usual or his pants were too tight, because—" his tongue slid over the gap, "—now I'm a tooth short."

"Have you told anyone, your friends, teachers, Beatrice or Marvin?"

"No."

"So no one else knows?"

"No—well, Julius does, but nothing specific. He scared Allen away today because it happened outside his store, but he doesn't know the kid or anything." The waitress came back with their orders. Once she was gone, he said, "Mom, can we talk about something else?"

"Oh, okay. I'm sorry for putting you on the spot. If you're sure you're fine, I guess we can leave it be for now."

They chatted on around mouthfuls of food. He couldn't believe he'd been scared earlier when deciding whether or not to tell his mom the truth. He knew now that she would never see him as weak and felt silly for adding that he would've fought back when he really wouldn't have, because that would've only gotten him pummeled worse.

He smirked at his previous insecurity and reveled in the glowing presence of his mom. There were good times in life, but this was a *great* time, and he couldn't wait until he could be with his mother forever, as it always should've been.

Sunshine detoured around the painting on the window like water around a boulder and shone in stripes along Brandon's face and exposed forearms. It was warmth that seemed to originate from inside of him and flow outward, and he thought, as he sat across from his mother, that yes, it truly was a great time.

When the time to go did arrive, his mom stood, sighed, and smiled down at her son. They waved bye to Janelle and walked out of Julie's together and loitered in front of the large window for a few minutes.

"Okay, baby," she shaded her eyes with one hand and admired the bright blue sky above, "we go our separate ways for another day…"

"But not for long," Brandon said, completing the sentence that had become their departing ritual.

They hugged and Brandon trotted toward the bike path, determined to keep his eyes forward. Looking back was too much a yearning gesture, one more glance for fear it would be the last, but he had no reason to yearn because he would see her tomorrow, and the next day, and on and on until they could be together for good.

He crossed the street and entered the bike path, which was well lit despite the thick copse of trees it ran through, but still dull and dimmed in his heart compared to the sanctuary he'd just left. Every day that he entered he wanted to turn back, wanted to yell *"Mom!"* and run to her, because every day he feared that he somehow wouldn't find his way again. The pathway between the life he'd always known and the life he was meant for would somehow be hidden, so that he'd search and search without ever again finding it.

But he couldn't run back. His mom wasn't ready yet. Everything wasn't in place. Soon, though.

Soon had never felt so long in coming.

Allen Summers used his key to enter the house, then slammed the door behind him, partly to annoy the housekeeper, and partly because he seemed to have a chronic need to periodically slam stuff.

"Allen, what have I told you about slamming doors?" he heard from the kitchen.

"Not to do it." He walked into the living room to set his backpack on the recliner.

"Then why do you persist?"

"Why do I what?" He shook his head and made an ugly face.

"Why do you persist—why do you keep doing it?"

"I'm forgetful."

"Would being grounded help you remember?"

He took on a whiny imitation of her voice and mumbled so she couldn't hear. *"Would being grounded help you remember?"* He reverted to his own voice: "No."

"Then you should work on that; it's not a hard thing I ask."

A minute ago it was told, now it's ask. "Whatever."

Allen went up the stairs to his room, *slammed* the door, then flopped on his bed. He turned on the stereo, from which, during the next hour, the sound of heavy metal blared.

Allen's hands were locked beneath his head and he faced the ceiling, eyes closed. A smile flirted with his lips as he thought about earlier that day.

A while later, a tasty aroma drifted into his room. Dinner time—one thing the weirdo lady was good for. He flipped off the stereo and dashed down the stairs, hitting the ground floor with a loud thump.

In the kitchen he saw the maid with clamps in her hand and two salad bowls on the counter to her right. He stuck his tongue out.

"Be polite unless you'd enjoy that between these tongs."

"What are you talking about, lady?" *How did she know?*

"Allen," she said, dropping spaghetti onto a plate from a foot up so it made a loud splat. "I have a name, and you'd better start addressing me properly. I could talk to your father about this, if you'd like."

His silence related his sentiment.

She continued: "So what's my name, Allen?"

"Veronica."

"Good! Now sit down, shut up, and eat your food— including the salad." He did, but slowly, because thinking about his father lessened his appetite.

The man was a lawyer and lived at work, and his way to deal with his son would be to send him to a military school; said it would fix him up. Allen tried to avoid looking at Veronica, but it was difficult because she was so interesting, in a creepy I've-got-to-keep-my-eyes-on-you-so-you-don't-try-something-sneaky sort of way.

She takes those books with her everywhere! A thick hardbound volume was open before her as she ate. One of the pages it was opened to was full of writing, like a normal book, but covering the other page was a drawing of something that resembled a gargoyle, around which were little paragraphs of tiny print.

She had tons of them. She'd read through a book every few days. One afternoon she left one sitting on the coach while she cleaned upstairs. Allen flipped through the book, reading a sentence here and there, but mostly glancing at the pictures. It was creepy stuff; like something a witch in a movie would carry around. A few days later Veronica had left the same book on the kitchen counter while out grocery shopping, but this time a note fell out of it after Allen began flipping pages: *Peeking is rude, Allen.*

Since then he avoided her and tried not to even glance at her books when he could help it. Eating dinner, however, he couldn't keep his furtive eyes from her or the book before her. He'd had a few dreams about her, and thinking of them always made him go cold.

Veronica finished long before him and set her dishes in the sink, then told Allen he could wash them tonight. He wanted to say it was her job, but didn't. He finished his own meal, including the salad, and began cleaning up. When he was almost done, he looked into the living room. He could see her from where he stood at the sink. She'd moved his backpack from the recliner and now sat there with her legs tucked under her and the book in her lap. A lock of hair hung over one eye. He wondered if she could tell he was staring, like when he'd stuck his tongue out at her, although that had probably just been a good guess.

She glanced at him.

He jerked and splashed soapy water on himself.

"Do you need something, Allen?"

He turned and shoved his hands back under the water. "No," he said and fumbled with a plate. He heard the dull thud of the book being closed. Foot steps. The rustle of jeans.

"Then why were you staring?" she said from behind him.

Allen didn't believe in werewolves and vampires, or ghouls and ghosts. He believed in what he could see and touch and feel and smell. But as all humans, he had doubts that arose in certain situations which logic failed to explain. Sometimes she knew things she couldn't; and gave off an aura that left him feeling exposed.

He hadn't done well with lying today. "I don't know," he said.

"Really?"

"I guess I spaced out."

"Spaced out. Hmm."

He thought he could feel her breath tickling the hairs on the back of his neck. He wanted to turn and face her, because being unable to see her was...not scary—he didn't get scared—but...uncomfortable. Yes. It was uncomfortable, but he didn't want her to know that's how she was making him feel.

"Well," she said. "Are you almost done with the dishes?"

"Yeah."

"Good." She walked off with the book in her hand.

The next morning Allen slept in until after ten because it was Saturday. He hadn't been woken late last night for a talk, so he figured Veronica hadn't spoken with his dad before leaving.

He lay among the comforter for a few more minutes, deciding what to do for the day. He wanted to be out of the house for sure. Veronica had given him the shivers, and he felt weird in a place where she spent so much time, even though that place was his home. Some fresh air would be nice. Maybe he'd go to Swans Park, or the river.

He rose from his bed and tiptoed across his floor as he gathered clothes to wear. His foot crunched what must have been a potato chip, causing him to scrunch his face and hold his position like a mime. There were no responding sounds.

He wiped off his foot and then dressed. He took to the sides of the stairs while making his way down and held his breath until he reached the front door. Loud snoring echoed in the hall. He took care opening the front door, and even more when closing it.

The air was crisp, but polluted with the smell of cigarette butts that sat in the ashtray on the front porch railing. He grabbed his bike from the side of the house and began to pedal his way to the park.

His T-shirt rippled against him, but he was warm because the sun was out. Birds chirped like women and flew round and round along an intricate racecourse known only to them. He wished he'd brought his paintball gun.

It was as he was passing the taco stand that he saw something. When he turned his head to get a better look at what he'd glanced peripherally, nothing was there. He coasted on his bike and turned around, traveling by the taco stand again. There were several cars parked behind; a stack of cinder blocks; a small bush. Nothing that resembled what he thought had been at the edge of his vision moments ago.

He turned around once more and stood on the pedals of his bike while checking the area. Nothing. The person manning the stand gave him an odd look. He'd probably gotten his eyelashes stuck together, that's all.

After reaching Swans Park, he set his bike in a rack with two others, then took a seat on a nearby bench. There were a few swans floating close to the shore on the large pond. He left his seat to bring back a dozen baseball-sized rocks. He let them clatter out of his shirt and onto the bench, then tossed one up and caught it a few times to assess its weight.

Remembering the cane that the old man had thrown at him the last time he tried to do this, he looked around first. There was no one at the chess tables yet, or anyone else around that he could see. He spent a minute more looking around like a drug dealer about to exchange product for payment, and then, seeing that he was alone, lobbed the rock with a grunt at the closest swan. The bird squawked as the stone splashed feet away; it swam off.

Allen quickly picked up other stones and began lobbing them at the swan. He started to run toward the pond, stopping every few seconds to hurl another rock. The swan continued to squawk, and flapped its wings a bit. When he had only two rocks left, it started to rise from the water, wings pushing down with long strokes.

Allen tossed his second to last rock and let out a whoop once it hit the bird in the back, causing it to fall. He reached the edge of the pond and stood breathing hard with the other stone in hand, waiting for the thing to move, or even twitch. The white bird floated on the surface, and that was all.

He hurled the last rock at the bird. "Chicken shit." He spent the next twenty minutes at the bench, watching the corpse, wondering if it would sink or continue to float.

He wondered where the owners of the other bikes were, then decided he didn't care. One bike was purple and the other had a card in its spokes. He grabbed his pocketknife and slashed a hole in each tire of both bikes. Cold air whistled out. He smiled.

Once finished, he mounted his bike and cruised about the park. He kicked over a garbage can on his way, but was disappointed to see that there wasn't much to spill. He came to the bike path and turned onto it. He knew this section would wind through a moderate-sized forest and lead to a residential neighborhood where he used to steal when he was younger.

The tree branches curved toward each other and created a tunnel. There were shadows everywhere, but none grabbed his attention until one moved with him instead of being passed by. It was moving among the trees to Allen's right. A deer, maybe? The bushes and twigs remained quiet among the thick foliage of the forest. Nothing snapped in an animal's wake.

Allen braked to a stop, one leg resting on the pedal and one propped on the pavement. He blinked his eyes, then rubbed them. Sunlight penetrated the first dozen feet or so, but beyond, the forest became hazy. There was definitely something there, though. He thought he could make it out; had to be a huge dear, with antlers or something. He peered some more, then closed his eyes for several seconds. Opened them again—

And fell backward onto his ankle. Pain sparkled. He scraped his palm and cried out. He scrambled out from under his bike, huffing and glancing at every shadow among the forest across from him.

For some time he couldn't move. A trickle of urine escaped him and he was afraid to look left or right, fearing it would be there.

He wanted to yell for help, but who would hear? After a deep breath, he looked and didn't see anyone down the stretch he'd traveled so far, and much less was visible in the direction that he was going, because the path curved fifty yards ahead. He didn't even know if his voice would work at the moment.

Birds chirped on as though nothing were amiss. He studied the forest for a minute. Two minutes. He had the strongest urge to hop on his bike and speed away, but now felt childish even thinking it. Also, he might be imagining things.

It had only been glimpsed, an image emerging from the dark background, and it had appeared like a hologram. There'd been a huge, scaly arm that floated in the air, and a head above the arm, connected by an invisible neck. The head had been massive, reptilian in appearance, with large jaws that had smiled wide when Allen had opened his eyes. *Could that be right?*

He got up; convinced he must have been seeing things. The picture had been insubstantial enough to have never been, as though some thought or image from his mind had been strong enough to, for a second, imprint itself on his eyes, like an after-image. Or maybe it was a hallucination caused by the weed he'd smoked with Carl a few days before. That could happen, right? He decided 'yes' and rode off.

How wrong he was.

Monday morning boasted exuberant students whom, fresh from their weekends, were asked to be quiet several times by Ms. Dawson before she could take roll.

"My, my, class," she said, a big smile on her face, "What weekends we all had. Okay now, Ashley…"

"Here."

"Aaron…"

"Here."

"Allen…"

"Present."

From his seat, Brandon watched Allen, wondering why he felt the need to say "present" when "here" worked fine. He wasn't a class clown—that was Jose Mantilla's job—or funny; so he thought it stupid that the boy didn't use the response everyone else did. It was as though it made him feel superior.

His eyes bored into the boy's skull as he wondered what made him tick, what was really going on inside of there. Why he acted the way he did. If there was something silly he was scared of that only his mom knew about.

So that Allen wouldn't catch him staring, he returned his attention to Ms. Dawson. He said "here" when his name was called and doodled with his pencil until roll was complete. Then they watched a short documentary on the effects of CFC's on the ozone layer.

Sitting with his chin on his arms, he started to doze, so halfway through the program, he began whispering with Mandy, a girl who was part of his desk group.

He smelled the perfume first, and then felt the hand rest on his shoulder as soft hair brushed his face when she leaned close. "Brandon, I know how exciting this video is, but will you and Mandy wait until it's over to discuss it?"

"Sorry, Ms. Dawson."

"Yeah," Mandy said. "Sorry."

She left as she'd come, like a silent breeze. Brandon watched her go and then waited until after the documentary to discuss how exciting it was with Mandy. When the recess bell rang, he walked out of the classroom to the playground without hurry. Kids streamed past him like banners and conversation mixed with laughter prevailed throughout the halls. Once outside, he sat on the curb that separated the asphalt area from the grass and watched a soccer game.

His eyes became unfocused and the ball changed into a white blur bouncing back and forth between block figures as in foosball. It seemed slower this way, as did all the days since meeting his mother. In the morning she was usually the first thing on his mind; either her or the boner that he invariably woke with. In class, math equations on the board were constantly replaced with his mother's face. As he walked home, ate dinner, took a number two (which was a little embarrassing, but his mind always wandered when he did), and as he laid in bed waiting for sleep.

At times he felt guilty, as if he were somehow betraying his foster parents. They'd cared for him and loved him since forever, and all he could think about was his mother, the one who gave birth to him. He couldn't help it, though, and wanted to leave them a note for what consolation it might be, but knew he couldn't. Maybe someday. He loved them, to be sure, and would miss them from time to time, but he *belonged* with his mother.

There was a tiny tap against his head, and he looked up expecting to see raindrops, but saw nothing but clear sky. The tap came again and this time the pebble bounced into his lap.

Allen was behind him, standing up. Several others kids stopped what they were doing—playing marbles, tetherball, farting with their armpits—to watch.

At times such as this, he wished the boy were dead, or had never been born, wished that some monster would come along from a nightmare and eat him up.

Brandon held his eyes, but said nothing. The two stared each other down for a minute like gunslingers about to draw. Allen ended the contest with a kick of gravel. Brandon raised his arms and blocked his face, then stood up and brushed off his shirt, remembering what his mother had told him about letting people bully him.

"How's your jaw?" Allen said, and winked.

"Better than your face." It was the first thing that came to mind and he realized how weak a comeback it was once it left his lips.

Allen had squared features, giving him the look of a stupid person, but other than his brutish appearance, there was nothing immediately wrong with his mug that would credit the insult, such as a black eye, a fat lip, or a missing tooth, for instance.

"You like being socked, faggot?"

"You like looking stupid?"

Allen moved as though to step forward and beat the hell out of Brandon, then stopped. He stepped back, head shaking. His lip quivered almost imperceptibly, but Brandon saw it. Allen appeared as though he'd seen his own death. Brandon would've laughed if it hadn't been so unexpected.

The next moment, the big boy ran across the courtyard as if a dog were chasing him. A duty followed his progress with a frown. He ran across the street bordering one side of the school, then on and on and out of sight.

Brandon turned around. The jungle gym and two slides were in the gravel pit and a few kids played chicken on the monkey bars. There was nothing that could've sent Allen running. Maybe he was using drugs. He'd heard about some high school kids bringing weed around, but it could be a rumor. Who cared; this made the best story in history: big bad Allen Summers running from school looking as if he were going to piss his pants.

Allen ran the entire way home, his heart thumping like horse hooves and lungs pressing against his ribcage like a growing beast.

He burst inside and closed the front door; collapsed to the floor on his back and panted. The ceiling was a plain white surface and the memory of the creature was suddenly superimposed on it, so he closed his eyes and clasped one hand to his chest, hoping to slow his heart.

God, what was happening? He was gonna beat that little punk's ass, then—*bam!* it was there. That creature, whatever the hell it was. And there'd been more of it this time, too. And clearer, as if to prove it wasn't his imagination; wasn't the weed. No, it was real, all right. In addition to the massive head and arms, he saw the neck and bulky shoulders that connected them, part of the waist and half of the legs that held it up. Its arms hung well past the knees, like those of an ape, and from the fingers extended thick, dark claws.

It had reached for him, dear God—*had reached for him*. He had a vague idea from his gut that it couldn't hurt him, at least not yet, but he didn't think he could handle watching it lunge at him like a dog on a chain for much longer before his bladder let go. So he had to run.

He squeezed his eyes shut even harder, the sweat from his brow sliding down over his temples. The images began to fade. He breathed heavily for a while longer and cracked one of his eyes, then the other, and when he didn't see the creature against the ceiling any longer, opened them.

The soft *slap slap* of slippers approached and Veronica came into view upside down over him.

"You look as if you've run a marathon." Veronica held another book in her hand, with one finger marking her place between the pages. "What are you doing home? Is it a half day?"

"Uh, yeah; half day," Allen said. "Totally forgot until they reminded us this morning. Teacher's conference day, you know."

"So why are you sweating yourself dry?"

"I, um, just wanted to get back early so I could meet a few friends at the park."

"You're a bad liar, Allen. Maybe you were running from the police instead of participating in a marathon. Is that it, have you been bad?"

He grunted as he sat up. "Why do you care, anyway?"

She regarded him for a moment, then: "Because life is short and I am not your enemy. I would enjoy seeing you on the right path, but don't see how your current habits will ensure that."

"Are you gonna tell him about this?"

"Your father doesn't need to know. Besides, you seem to have enough to ponder already." She glanced at her watch. "Well, I need to get some groceries and run a few errands. I'll be back around five to make dinner. Play nice, Allen." She left him sitting there.

Brandon swallowed a bite of his sandwich and continued: "So there I was, ready to fight—I was going to, too—and then he gets spooked, like he saw a ghost or something. He started backing up as if someone was coming toward him, but no one was there. Nothing."

"What do you think scared him?" his mother said.

"I don't know." He leaned forward, causing his mother to do the same. "I think he was doing drugs," he whispered. He sat back. "But I could be wrong. I don't know what else would make him think something was there when it wasn't, especially something that would cause him to run away from school."

"Strange."

"Sure is." A lady passed by leading a small boy by the hand.

"Hey, mom?"

"Hmm?"

"When do you think you'll be ready? To take me with you, I mean."

She covered one of his hands with her own. "Soon, baby. I'm just waiting until this last project is finished so that all my loose ends will be tied up."

"Okay. What should my new name be?"

"That's up to you, honey. What would you like it to be?"

"I don't know..."

"Buster?"

"What?—no."

"Baxter?"

He laughed. "I'm not a dog, mom."

Her hand flew to her mouth. "You're not?" She walked around the table and smothered him with kisses while ruffling his hair. "But you're just *so* cute."

He half-heartedly tried to fend her off. "Mom, that tickles." He giggled and squirmed in his seat, eventually slipping to the floor.

"Gotta live one there, Ivy!" Rosa said from across the diner.

"Sure do," she said over her shoulder. She helped him up, a face of joy. "How about Bucko?"

107

Watching her boy approach Julie's was Ivy's happiest moment each day. She loved how the wind would blow his hair in his face; and he would brush it away, much too concerned with his appearance as boys his age were. She loved him however he looked, and as he approached she always tried to imagine those missing years.

Some days these thoughts angered her, because they would lead back to why he was taken from her, and then she would remember that life wasn't fair, and irony was a sorry son of a bitch. She herself was an orphan growing up and never became established in a foster home. The families weren't her family, and she could never quite escape that fact enough to be comfortable and trusting.

She had no blood family she knew of. After getting pregnant, everything started out fine. Then he lost his job. He drank a little and couldn't find work after six months, so he drank more. A year went by; liquor became the requisite sixty-four ounces of agua. Then he began beating her. She remembered sitting in the bathtub with Brandon held in her lap, the door locked and braced by a chair; wet eyes and a lonely heart. One night he returned home early from the bars. He hit her, and hit her again. Brandon walked into the room, roused from sleep. He sucked on a thumb. He was shoved backward into the wall.

Something in her broke at that moment. She took her son back to bed, soothed his red, teary face, and tucked him in. She kissed his forehead and that was the last time she saw him in a very long time.

The knife rack; his chest; blood; tears and memories; a black eye puffing up. An animal rage filled her; she yelled with each stab, and screamed pain and anger for the three years of keeping quiet.

They took her baby away from her and she went to jail. The adoption was closed, so she was not privy to any information concerning the adoptive parents.

She learned a lot about herself with so much time to think. There were no coincidences. She learned that; and belief was everything.

She found her baby boy, and it didn't take as long as she assumed it would. He was hers, after all. And soon it would be as it always should've been.

Watching him leave Julie's was the saddest part of her day, but she managed to keep her eyes dry. It wasn't much longer and everything would be in place: his birth certificate, history, location, house, job. It was all covered. She'd learned about patience, and although it was frustrating, haste and emotion was a mixed-drink worth declining every time.

Allen didn't show up for school the next day. Rumors were probably flying around about his running away. All the little sissies would jump on the episode like paparazzi. Plus, he needed time to make up a believable lie that would explain his leaving school.

He left the sidewalk for a large field of tall grass bordered on one side by a grove of evergreens. Wind rippled the field, turning it into a wave of greenery which rustled in response. He didn't have any plans; just walked aimlessly.

The ground was firm beneath his feet. A few of his friends and he would come out here in the rainy season and splash in the mud and tear skinny trenches through the soil with their ten speeds because their dads were too cheap to buy them dirt bikes.

There was a dirt trail that had, over the years, been trampled into being from the undergrowth in the grove. It led toward the northeast side of town, and more familiarly, the Pit.

He wasn't going to the Pit. Although he'd done tons of stuff out there—broken windows, blown up frogs with firecrackers, lit a cat on fire—he would never go alone. With friends, yes, but never alone. He wouldn't admit it to his buddies, but the Homeless Warehouse scared him. Every kid knew the stories. He glanced at the trail, anyhow, which started up a low hump of land and disappeared into the trees.

A groan built in his throat, suffocated and died in his mouth; he didn't dare open it for fear that he would scream.

It was there, walking parallel to him by the edge of the trees. It passed the trail and stopped, as he did. It was more substantial than before, gaining reality with every additional appearance. Except for a few splotches of its body that were still transparent, and other spots that were still invisible, Allen could see the entire creature, which now included a thick, spiked tail like an alligator's. It was reptilian, but with the physical structure of a man, at least seven feet tall.

Allen felt cold beneath the sun. He remained still and concentrated on keeping his breathing very shallow and slow, because he held to the wishful notion that it might not have seen him, that if he were quiet and unmoving he'd go unnoticed.

It was still there when he opened them.

He began walking as he had before glancing toward the trail, but kept his eyes directed at the creature as he did so. Slow; he wouldn't run. The creature followed parallel to him, its long arms swinging with heavy momentum, its tail running its own trench into the ground.

Allen stopped.

It stopped.

He watched it the way any prey does a predator. He was cold but sweating, and was developing cotton mouth. This time he kept his eyes open and counted to one hundred, hoping the creature would slowly dematerialize and wisp away on a roll of wind. It didn't.

He began moving again.

It did, too.

Tired of walking around without a destination, he decided that running back home was what he craved most in life at the moment. He dashed to his left over the field, away from the creature. He didn't dare look back. His shaking body didn't seem totally under his control. He was sluggish, as if his motor controls were damaged, and couldn't run fast enough. Several times as he sprinted away he was on the verge of releasing a shriek, sure that the creature was right behind him and that an instant later he'd feel his back opened up in one powerful swipe.

He was nearing the end of the field. The sidewalk was coming closer, seemed to run toward *him*. Past that was the street, and farther on several houses around which, if he managed to travel, was a busy street that guaranteed public. People equaled safety. He got the feeling that now the creature would confront him only if he were alone.

The smell of wild flowers was brought to him by way of the wind and he began to smile, thinking he might make it, because he was close, so close. He had to make it. His arms pumped at his sides and he willed his large body to run as though leaner and faster, to—

A rock jutting out of the ground tripped him. The fall knocked the air from his lungs. He rolled onto his back, fearing the next and last thing he'd ever see in life would be the snarling mouth of the gigantic creature, jaws opened, teeth gleaming...

But he didn't see an inhuman amount of razor-sharp teeth that blocked out the sun. He saw the field of tall grass and the sway of the tree limbs in the distance. He looked left and right, wanting to cry, breath coming in static bursts, snot gathering on his lip. It was gone.

Allen got to his feet. He walked backwards until he'd crossed the street and bumped into the side of a house, jerking at the sudden contact. He rounded the corner with one glance back, then ran.

They met for what would be—or should be, if all unfolded as expected—their last time at Julie's. His mom beamed at him from over their usual table and he couldn't help but show his excitement in full force; his mouth was open the entire time they were inside the diner because his smile wouldn't allow it to close. He even chewed with a smile.

After eating, she took the chair next to him and began adjusting his hair and plucking off little fuzz balls that stuck to his shirt.

He laughed. "Mom, I'm not a monkey."

Her hands flew to her cheeks. "My God! You're not? All this time..." She shook her head. "I thought for sure that after you told me you weren't a dog, that you must be a monkey."

"That would make you a monkey, too."

"A true statement, young man, so I guess you're not."

"What, monkeys aren't cute, mom?"

"Not like puppies," she said and ran her hand through his hair.

Brandon leaned into her as she continued to stroke and scratch his scalp. "It's gonna be great, huh? Just the two of us, like the song."

"Yeah, baby, just the two of us." She gazed out the front window of Julie's, through a break in the painting, and thought how much warmer the sun felt with her boy in her arms, how much lighter her heart felt when with him. *Just the two of us, like the song.*

She raised her wrist and looked around her boy to check the time. "Honey, we're almost there. Just one last part to play." She kissed his head.

Later that night, after eating dinner with his adoptive parents, Brandon rode along the bike path and left it to travel along streets he was unfamiliar with. He was fine, though, because he had directions scrawled on paper. It wasn't yet dusk, but twilight was forcing the sun down as it took shift in the sky. The air was felt fresher than ever before, and neighborhoods were quiet.

Brandon took to the sidewalk and rolled gently right and left in lazy progression. He alternated between whistling and humming. He looked up and the sky was clear of clouds. The faint brilliance of the stars shone through as dusk fell. Brandon took this as a good sign.

Several blocks later, he took a turn on an unknown street for a slight detour from his destination because he didn't want a connection made, however slight the possibility. After a while his vision drifted, so that he watched where he was going and could ride around toys and bumpers of cars that extended from lawns and driveways into the sidewalk but didn't *see*, at least not farther than ten feet in any direction. The world lost its figure and gave way to thoughts of his mother.

Tomorrow!

That's when it would begin, his new life with his real mother. They would run away with new names—well, she already had hers, so only he would have to get his—and to a new place neither had ever been to. She had it all figured out.

It was so close. One night's sleep away, but they already had it planned that he would stay with her for the night, not that he would sleep. Earlier that day at school, he'd asked his buddy Brent if he could spend the night at his house. Brent had called him after school to tell him it was fine, but that his mother wanted to speak to his mom to make sure she was fine with it. Beatrice was, and offered to drive him there because Brent's house was on the other side of town. He'd declined, saying that he wanted to enjoy some fresh air.

"But, Brandon, that's a ways away," Marvin had said.

"I know, but if I take my bike I could be there in, like, thirty minutes."

They had looked at each other for a moment before responding, but Brandon had interrupted before they could get their first words out. "I'll be fine, honest to God. I know it's kinda far, but I'll be fine." They still looked doubtful, so he added, "I'll call you as soon as I make it over there. I'm not a kid anymore, you know."

They'd relented after making him don his helmet, which he'd quit wearing when he was eight.

He rode another block, took two more turns, continued down another block, then ditched his bike so that it rested along the curb, he kicked at the spokes until several bent. He stood over the bike while ripping a part of his shirt. Once he had the cloth free, he dropped the ragged piece; it landed on the bent spokes.

He smiled to himself, feeling criminal in his actions, knowing, as would everyone else the next day, that he'd never reached Brent's house.

Allen cringed as if struck. "Why?"

"Because," Veronica said, "It needs to be dumped."

He kept his eyes on the TV. "So why don't you do it?"

"Because I'm washing dishes and you're an able-bodied young man, that's why. Now get off the couch and do it."

"I don't want to go outside," he said, then clamped a hand over his mouth.

Silence in the kitchen. No dishes met the wash rag under a stream of water; no shoes tapped to an unheard tune. Then: "Why don't you want to go outside, Allen?"

"I don't—I mean, it's really cold out there right now."

"Really?"

"Yeah."

"Seemed warm to me when I got home; looks warm out there still."

"That was hours ago."

"Allen, I don't want to argue with you. I really don't. Would you not make a big deal out of this and just dump the damn trash. It'll be a twenty foot walk through the cold that you're so averse to feeling."

"So what to feeling?"

"Aver—oh, never mind. Take out the trash, dammit!"

He looked out the window; the grey hews of dusk settling. There was no movement. He put on a sweater. Once he'd made two donkey ears of the plastic and tied the top of the trash bag, he pulled it out of the container and dragged it behind him toward the front door. He glanced at Veronica, who'd resumed washing dishes. A shiver ran up his spine and lodged in his brain.

The air was warm outside…as they'd both known. He stood on the top step for a minute. His legs felt like stone, and he didn't want to do it. He didn't necessarily feel comfortable inside the house, being with Veronica, but outside was an unsafe zone. At least with company he was safe from the creature. He felt like dropping the garbage on the side of the house, but didn't want a lecture from his dad.

They, along with the neighbors, dropped their trash in a Dumpster. It was farther away than twenty feet—a few hundred feet at least, across a backyard and thin gravel alley, finally to rest on blacktop by a parking lot for the blue apartments. That was quite a walk. Three hundred feet.

At least.

Allen scanned the neighborhood for several more seconds, his legs feeling heavier and heavier as the time passed. He moaned and planted one foot on the second step, then onto the cement walkway. Six more steps and he was on the driveway. Not bad so far. He was cool. Everything was all right. After crossing the driveway he stepped onto the grass of his neighbor's backyard. He held the garbage bag off the ground and it bumped against his leg as he walked. He didn't like it making sounds, sounds that could muffle something approaching.

He swung around, his heart increasing a few beats. Nothing there. Everything was still cool. Come on, only two hundred feet or so to…

(then he'd have to walk the length again, all the way back)

…the garbage bin. He came to the alley and stopped. He heard a bird chip in the distance. He looked up and down the gravel passage and then walked across it. If he ran, jogged, or even scurried on his way to the Dumpster, he knew he'd lose it. He'd scream bloody murder and rant and rave until he was held down so a doctor could inject him with a sedative.

On the asphalt now. He was on the asphalt and, still, all was good. His eyes darted here and there, never focused in any direction for longer than a second or two. Thirty feet away; he was close. So far so good.

There. He was at the blasted thing! He glanced around once more, lifted the corrugated black lid, which blocked out the sky for a moment, heaved the bag over and let it go *plop* inside, then dropped the lid.

It stood behind the Dumpster, viewable from the waist up. The thing. The it. The creature.

Allen stared up at it, his feet stuck to the spot. He swallowed reflexively, which was hard, as if he were trying to down an egg.

It stepped to the side of the Dumpster; a fully visible, monstrous reality. Allen compensated with three steps backward.

Seeing it from across the field, Allen had guessed it to be about seven feet tall; he was wrong. It must have been at least eight, maybe even nine feet in height. It stood erect as a man does, but was a lizard in every other aspect. Its thick tail rested on the ground like a crescent moon. It was gigantic. Colossal. The large scales that covered its body were dark green and glimmered like freshly polished armor. Its head was …was…goddamn. Its mouth was bared, and its teeth were like dozens and dozens of long daggers jutting from its gums; saliva dripped in globs to pool on the ground. Its eyes were the worst part, though, because they contained intelligence, a purpose.

Allen didn't get it, didn't understand why this creature was after him. He was just a kid, with chores and an allowance and a prick for a dad.

"No," he moaned.

The creature seemed to smile.

Veronica watched through the kitchen window. She closed the tome sitting on the counter before her and reached for the hollow of her neck, where her pendant hung; a piece that could easily be mistaken for a religious symbol.

Just the Two of Us

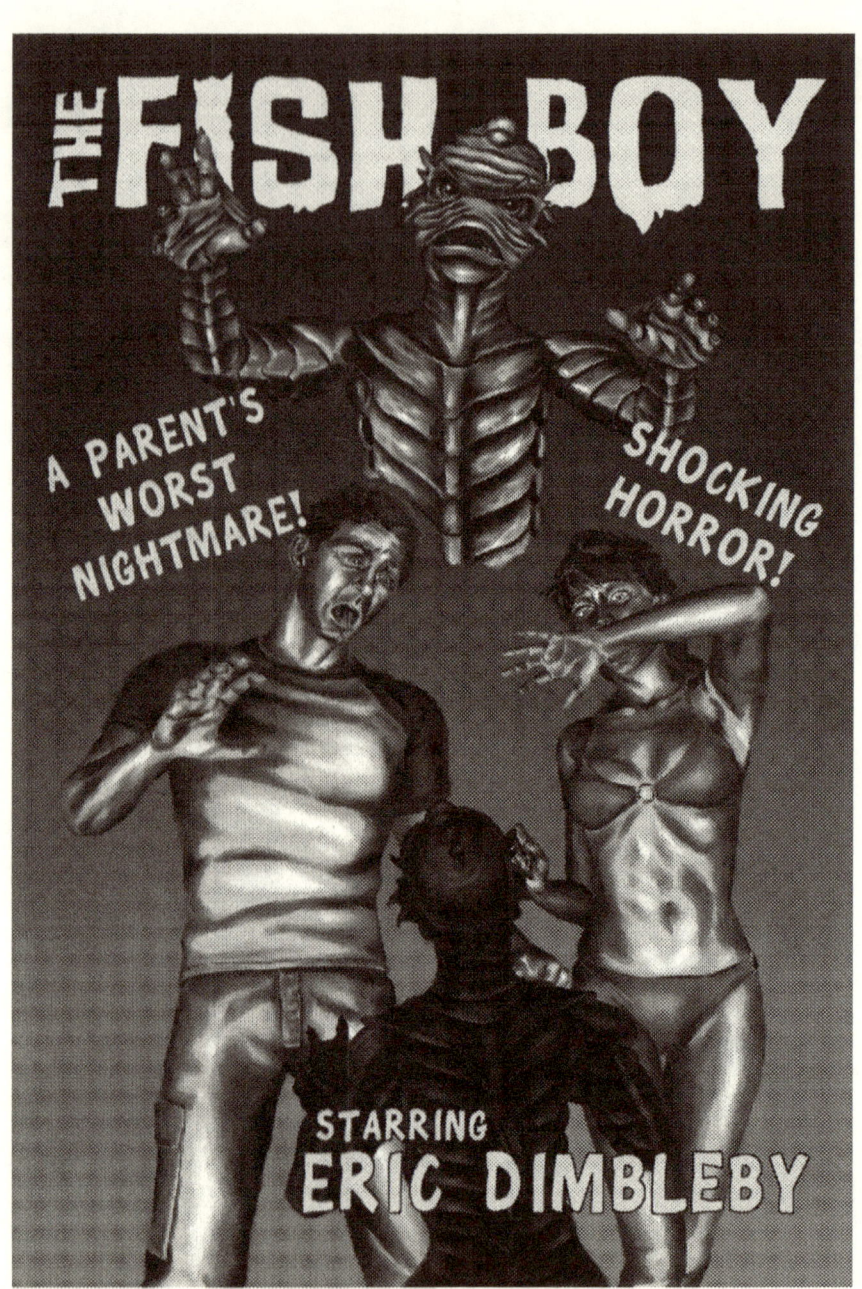

The Fish Boy
Starring Eric Dumbleby

The Fish Boy popped his head through the surface of the meandering dark river to spy upon the unknowing invaders. He had watched them since dusk, casting their fishing lines deep into his home, trying to snag a dinner that rightfully belonged to his people. They had come to frolic and swim and fish in his chilly river, but they may have never expected that one of the fish would cast a line out for *them*.

His protruding floppy eyelids (one of his many genetic permutations that put him a notch above the rest of his river brethren) flicked away droplets of tainted water in an attempt to find aquatic purity once again. He could feel the filth of their ways all over his body, seeping into his mouth and over his gills. Urine was one thing, but feces was another altogether. One of the children had taken a swirling tan defecation in the river right above his underwater nest. Soon after that, they had strung up a dead fish on one of their sand-implanted oars, and a more deplorable act of aggression the Fish Boy could not recall. But that was neither here nor there. Today was not about revenge. Rather, it was about completeness, a sense of self-actualization for the Fish Boy. He was to become whole, once again.

The night was chilly, but comfortable for the humans.

They seemed very much to be enjoying themselves.

The Tall Hairy One was singing to his kinder while his mate looked on, preparing food from shiny bags. The Sweet Smelling One and the Dirty Scowling One watched their father with wondrous gazes, observing his every sound and undulation in his voice. They laughed and engaged in merry, something which troubled the Fish Boy at his core. It had been beasts like them that had caused so many tribulations for the Fish Boy and his people. Without their encroachment upon his world, the Fish

119

Boy's own parents would still be alive, of this he was sure. But still, there was also envy.

The Fish Boy gurgled in the void of darkness, digging his feet into the silt beneath the lazily moving river so that he would not drift too far away from their encampment. He wiggled his webbed toes and crouched low, submerging his head beneath the water to breathe deeply, coming back to the surface revived. He could survive for several hours outside of the water, unlike his ancestors (even from one generation earlier) who could only withstand a few minutes before choking upon the precious smoggy air of mankind, flopping about the ground in their final throes of death. Evolution, for the Fish Boy, had come in leaps and bounds.

He watched invaders upon his shores with regularity, especially in the summer when they took to canoes and kayaks, pleasuring themselves in his backyard to convince their deepest psyches that they had not completely destroyed the natural world just yet. Men in business suits, yapping by water coolers on Friday afternoons about their upcoming weekend adventures into the wild; down a river, up a mountain, along a trail, beneath the ocean, hang gliding through the rainforest, wrestling snakes, eating fire, and spelunking caves. They were tourists in the natural world, witnessing it in their sickest form of self-denial, knowing in their foggy brain matter that the clock was ticking, that the virus that was the human being was ravaging it all one morsel at a time.

When the Fish Boy watched them, he spat disdain from his flapping gills. Human beings were repugnant forms of life, to be wiped out in due time. The Fish Boy, of course, remained the pacifist and never took to that matter on his own. That was the job of their own vices and diseases. They never died of old age as the beasts and fish of the world often did. They died of their own stupidity, one by one, like lemmings from a cliff.

But this group...they were different than the rest. The Tall Hairy One had deep round eyes that reminded the Fish Boy of his own father. And the Tall Hairy One's mate was something special as well, yet less definable. A sense of subtle unspoken delight emanated from her to him, a vibration that the Fish Boy could not put his finger upon. She called to him with words that could only be translated as "home" with tremolos of comfort darting through the chilly June air.

The night masked the Fish Boy from the Barker family. He stood in the ticklish current of the Saco River, entrenched in blackness, while they sat around a warm crackling fire. He was their home invader, chewing popcorn and calculating his next move from an uncurtained window, observing his illuminated prey as they watched the Late Show from within their well constructed comfort zone. Had they been able to see the Fish Boy standing waist-deep in the river, his freakish round eyes and agape mouth painted upon his tapered scaly fish-face, then they may have run away into the night, away from the sandy shores of the Saco River, screaming in terror at the mere sight of the monstrosity.

Jimmy Barker strummed his poorly-strung Alvarez guitar in an attempt to impress upon his children the fact that he "had once been in a pretty successful punk band in the nineties." They weren't buying it, and when they asked their mother of their father's former spit-and-kick rebellious rock glory, she would only say that, "Daddy tells fish stories. He lies because he hates us." At this, Jimmy would shake his head, smiling at Patricia with that classic you-got-me snicker. Patricia was not so good at returning the gesture, instead opting for a bitter sneer.

Patricia poked the metal pronged skewer through a series of rock hard stale marshmallows, convinced that the fire would bring them back to life, like Jesus on a cross dripping with white gelatin. As she laid them across her knee, into the dancing flames, she sipped at her wine cooler and said not a word. Her vacant stare was one that she could easily lose herself in. *Anywhere else but here* seemed a fitting place for her in most family situations. Perhaps she resented them for taking away that career in accounting; or for forcibly removing her from Friday night bar hops with her girlfriends.

"Daddy, can you play that Violent Femmes song again?" Gabe asked of his father, his gritty unwashed face displaying a smile that Jimmy could not easily deny. Ever since Gabe had crossed the threshold of Age Twelve, everything had changed. Gone were the days of his innocence. Now the boy knew how to manipulate his parents and he never turned down the opportunity to do so. He only enjoyed the Violent Femmes song because it had the word "fuck" in it, which his father would never censor... hence making his mother angry, hence initiating a fight between them, during which Gabe could get away with whatever miscreant activity he deemed appropriate use of his time.

"You betcha, kid," Jimmy replied, picking at the first few notes of *Add It Up* by the Violent Femmes, which contained Gabe's favorite lyric of :

Why can't I get/Just one fuck?"

By the tenth note, Patricia had snapped out of her zombie stare and squashed the idea like the party-pooper she was known to be. "You kids need to get in your goddamned tent. We've got a long day of canoeing and fishing tomorrow and you can barely keep your eyes open, anyway." She looked over the flames at her children, who sat across from her with newly formed scowls upon their faces, ready to fight the good fight on the matter.

Jenny, Gabe's younger sister (by only one year, which she never failed to bring up), protested without a thought on the matter, "But we're on vacation, Mom. Don't you know what that means? No friggin' rules!"

She glowed after the inciting statement, smiling her biggest fake smile. It was true, since their father had stated that very same sentiment at the beginning of their journey, that they were engaging in a "weekend with no friggin' rules". In reality, he had been talking about himself and his escape from the swelling hatred of his office—that infested place that was crammed to the hilt with rules and policies and regulations and utter dipshits. He so very much hated the employment aspect of his life, and sought to destroy those harsh feelings with every vacation he could financially afford for his family. Even being at home reminded him of the office, for that was the place that he came each night to lick his sad wounds in the life he had never wanted.

"Well, that's your opinion. Rules are one thing, but exhaustion is another. If you two don't get a good night's sleep, then your father and I will have to do all the rowing tomorrow. Not to mention all the fucking whining we'll be forced to listen to. And we will not be happy with that. *Not at all*. Isn't that right?" Patricia reasoned, looking to Jimmy for backup. He was staring into the fire, quietly moving through the Violent Femmes song in his head, fingering the notes on his guitar, stopping only to rub his itchy beard when he could not remember the proper note. "Isn't that right, *Father*?" she repeated, louder and in the vernacular of black-and-white-sitcom-mother-in-an-apron.

"Oh...yes," Jimmy said, snapping to attention. He took a swig of his beer and plopped it back into the built-in beer cozy on his beach chair. "That's right." He had no clue what she had said, but grinned at his children to let them know that he was supposedly very much on top of things. Patricia sighed, eyeballing her children, wishing they would just disappear for the night.

She badly needed to drink. Hard. Fast. Deep. To smother her thoughts and feelings.

Gabe stood up first, kicking at the sand with a snarky gripe. "Fuck this," he mumbled, walking towards his tent in defeat. He knew better than to continue a squabble with his mother, for it always ended the same.

"You see what *that song* taught him?" Patricia blasted at her husband, never missing the chance to remind him of his parental faults and pour salt on to the very same wounds she had created with her claws.

"He may be a pushover, but you can't get *me* to listen to your reasons. Have some more booze, why don't you?" asked Jenny, crossing her arms at her chest, staring into the fire in an implication that she was not going anywhere, not anytime soon. Her mother glared at her, but she remained a reflected Medusa.

As Gabe unzipped and plodded into his tent, wiping away the gritty sand that had clung to his bare feet all day, Patricia scolded his younger sister, "You march into that tent right now, young lady. Or we'll wake up extra early and get in our canoes without waking you up. We'll leave you to live on this beachhead for the rest of your miserable life. How would you like that? Huh? Would that make you happy?"

There seemed a vein of truth beneath her mother's vicious statement and even Jimmy was taken aback. "Geez, honey. A tad harsh?" he queried, slinking back into his turtle shell upon catching the laser-beam stare of his rebellion-countering wife. Likewise, Jenny's face fell blank, coated with nothing but dread at the nightmare scenario of being left to fend for herself in the trees and sporadic buggy beaches of Saco River. How far had they traveled since last seeing any other sign of human life? Miles....many miles, at that. More than she could guesstimate with her limited metric knowledge.

"You wouldn't," the young girl said in defiance, the blood now fully drained from her face. It seemed entirely possible that her mother would resort to such tactics.

She had once left Jenny behind in the supermarket, pounding on the tiled floors with her fists as a terrorist attack against her mother for denying her a bag of licorice candy from aisle six. Patricia had marched out of the Shop N' Go, into her car, and turned the ignition. She was halfway out of the parking lot before Jenny caught up to her, screaming bloody murder for her mother to open the car door and to not abandon her. That thought had never been vanquished from her mind, and it remained a poignant possibility for Jenny to be forever left to fend for herself in a cold harsh world.

Jenny went to the tent and slept, begrudgingly so.

Her parents quickly broke out a bottle of cheap whiskey and indulged until they could no longer feel their fingers or toes. "Those kids got the devil in them," slurred Jimmy, to which Patricia agreed with a half-asleep nod. Patricia despised chit-chat when she was drinking. It simply annoyed her.

The intention of drinking was to shut down, like a robot being deactivated. It was not the time for fluffy banter or deep discussions. Jimmy continued to talk through the remainder of the evening, and she continued to ignore him.

She burped and Jimmy chuckled. He could not remember her being so very inebriated, not since their earliest days in college when they had first met. She had been prettier then, as would be expected, but she wasn't nearly the raging bitch that she had become in more than the decade and a half since. But still...

"I love you, honey," mumbled Jimmy between belches of foggy whiskey, hoping that the words would help to put him back in her eternally good graces. But Patricia was snoring, propped in her chair by the still roaring campfire, and Jimmy decided to partake in the same. They never made it back to their tent.

The Fish Boy, meanwhile, had grown bold in his deep analysis of the Barker family. During their brief skirmishes and marshmallow consumption, he had taken careful notes of their dynamics. Each had a prototypical behavior, as he found existed in most mixed groups of people (regardless of genealogical relation). These people were different, though. They reminded him again and again of his own family. He, too, had a groveling younger sister, always quick to lash out, but just as quick to offer a rosy hug or kiss on their father's oily scaled cheek. Their mother had a streak of loving compassion through her, much like the Barker woman, that overturned all, causing smiles in her brood, one and all.

Standing over their tent, the Fish Boy breathed in their scents once again, drunk by those titillating moments of cool childish breeze. Less than twenty feet away, he could hear the cacophonous sounds of the elder humans snoring, apparently deeply affected by the liquid they had been consuming.

He closed his buggy burning eyes, his mouth wide open, and he imagined himself as a much smaller Fish Boy, swimming and playing in the river with his pep-pep, mother, and sister. On that fateful day when it had all gone to shit, they had collected a box of discarded human food that had been left on one of the beaches. Inside the box was an odd assortment of salted meats, wrapped in greasy cellophane. It had made his father's stomach churn, but the Fish Boy had chewed on them voraciously, one after another until he likewise felt ill. Drifting in the river, lying on their backs, they found great solace in the fact that they had not been forced into hiding by any humans on that day.

They were normally vigilant about being spotted. If only one human was to spot them, and even worse—record the evidence—then it stood to reason that an entire army of the dumb bastards would be coming right behind, with guns and nets and speedboats and cigars galore. The Fish Boy and his breed were unique, that which humans had never before encountered, and the plan was to keep things that way. Such was the advisement handed down from generation to generation in their family. The humans were to be kept at a considerable distance. It was okay to steal from them, or scavenge their garbage when they were eventually downstream from their underwater fortress of fallen trees and branches. But one was never to make direct contact. Not under any circumstances. The bleeding heads of the Fish People were nothing more than trophies for the people of the land-roaming variety.

On that day, his sister and he had played a game of hide and seek in the murky bottoms of Saco River. During one of the Fish Boy's turns to hide, he had drifted further than their predetermined playing field. He had known that he was out of bounds, but he cared not, for victory was more important than abiding by rules.

When the sharp silver hook had caught him in the mouth, he struggled against it, whipping his body and reaching up with his webbed hands, working away at the painful hook in desperation. His family would be so angry with him! As he tugged at the hook, it only created more of a frenzy, dancing and pulling on him, shooting rivulets of pain through his headspace. Pulled to the surface, a gaggle of frightened men looked upon him.

"What the fuck is that?" one of them shouted.

"That little kid's got a goddamned fish face. Get your gun, Brock!" another called out in response to the sight of the disgustingly bizarre Fish Boy. With a jolt of energy, the Fish Boy banged his fin-hand against the side of the boat, groaning in discomfort.

Brock had come to the edge of the boat, his three companions cheering him on. Training his rifle on the Fish Boy's head, he inhaled and readied himself for the glories of the strangest fishing story ever told. The Fish Boy was the Sasquatch of the fresh water world, and Brock was to be his eternally famed executioner. "Glory, glory, hallelujah," whispered Brock as he pulled the trigger.

By the time the bullet had exited the chamber, the entire boat had been flipped over in a scrambled moment of confusion. The Fish Boy's father had toppled it in an act of unquestioning heroism while his mother worked at the hook in her son's mouth. They gurgled statements of love and fear to each other as the fisherman clambered through the water awkwardly, startled and terrified to be in the same water as their otherworldly prey.

Brock was able to quickly turn the row boat back over and climb in, but his mates struggled to do the same. "Get in this boat, you dipshits! They're getting away," Brock grumbled.

With the hook safely removed from the Fish Boy's torn lip, his parents grabbed each of his two arms and began their descent to the bottom of the river. He was in shock an unable to propel himself, so they thought it best to keep together as one family unit. Though it was only twenty feet deep, it was dark enough at the bottom to stay out of sight of their pursuers, mixed with the cloudy bulges of silt and mud. Once they were safely at the bottom, his mother dabbed at his lip with her fin-hand, fearful of his torrential bleeding. She asked him *what he had done* in their special language of whispering noises and squeals. The Fish Boy was so very regretful that he could not properly express it to his parents, his mind still reeling from the attack. They were disappointed in him, but would forgive all to spare his life.

"They're still down there, fellahs. Gonna bag us some mutant fishies, what you say about that?" Brock insisted to his clan of beasts, all of whom grunted in revelry, although they were collectively dissatisfied with being dumped into the lazy river. They were terrified of the things, Brock included, but their terror was overridden by a desire to live in infamy among the hunters and fishermen of the world.

"Lookee there," said Trent, Brock's brother-in-law, pointing to a swirl of blood that was coming to the surface, intermingled with tiny oxygen bubbles. "We must have got that son of a bitch good with the hook. We tugged pretty hard, musta damn near took its fishy little face off, aye?"

Brock looked to his rifle, waterlogged from their tipping. "Reserves," he mumbled, pulling up the floatation seat at the back of the boat. Inside, wrapped in thick clear plastic, was a spare shotgun. He had brought it along, just in case they had such an incident.

Trent had tried to talk him out of both weapons, but had failed. *We're fishing*, he had insisted to Brock, *not hunting*!

With the shotgun trained on the blood slick, like the bulls-eye on a target, Brock thanked Jesus Christ for the smallest of blessings and pulled the trigger. He pulled a second time, re-loaded. Five shots later, the blood at the surface had increased five fold, and he grinned with satisfaction as two bodies came to the surface. He leaned over, poking the Fish Boy's mother's ex-posed rounded breast with the tip of the gun. "Get that fishy motherfucker out of the drink, Trent. I don't know if I should eat it or fuck it. Or better yet, I'll hang this bitch on my wall. We're gonna be famous, boys."

Beneath them, the Fish Boy wept in a way that only fish boys weep, coming back to his senses just long enough to lose them again, distraught with his loss. Not only had his parents been brutally executed right before his eyes, but he would also have to leave his home. They would know of him now. Once their people viewed the bodies that they were about to bring back to shore, it would be a field day on his life. They would come for him. But maybe that would be for the best, that cruel demise. And what would he tell his sister?

The rules. He had broken the rules and his family was torn asunder.

And now, the Fish Boy stood above a family that reminded him so very much of his own, and he could not help but weep in that same special way. He sniffed the air again, reaching down to unzipper the tent. If he was to insert himself into a new family, then it was only just that he free up some space, first and foremost.

Gabe squirmed in his sleeping bag, half asleep and dreaming of the fat fish he would catch the following morning. Though the boy had always rebelled against their vacations into nature, a primordial part of his childish human fabric craved the pristine dirt and dander of the outdoors. He would never let on to his parents how much he enjoyed their vacations, but they secretly understood, especially his father.

When the Fish Boy wrapped his webby fin-hands around the bottom of the sleeping bag, the boy made not a peep and continued to snore like his sauced pair of guardians. The little girl in the sleeping bag next to her brother, likewise, continued on in her submerged state of REM sleep. *Perhaps*, thought the Fish Boy, *they had all been drinking that hideously debilitating amber liquid.* When his new parents were initiated, there would be no more of that liquid. It seemed almost a poison.

The Fish Boy dragged the sleeping bag, boy inside, away from the tent. The restrictive sand was difficult to maneuver him through, but the Fish Boy managed. It was far too important for him to fail.

The young boy opened his eyes to see the gruesome facade of his repulsive captor, the greasy shining face of a monster- part fish, part human- glistening in the campfire's light. Gabe started to scream but his sounds were plugged by the floppy cold fin of the thing, opening and closing its large mouth, gills pulsing in a slow rhythm as it studied the boy. Gabe's screams, beneath that slippery plug, became less forceful as the air escaped his lungs and his breathing ceased.

The Fish Boy pitied the young boy for what he was forced to do. He had witnessed so many fish in his day, flopping in the sand, kicking and fighting for a breath of oxygenated water to pass through their mouth, to pass over their gills in sweet sustenance. Like them, the young boy squirmed. The Fish Boy tightened his grimy grip, looking across the sand at his new parents, still passed out from exhaustion and that amber drink. They would need their rest, for tomorrow would be their proudest day.

When the sun drenched their slobbering faces, Jimmy and Patricia awoke. They looked to each other, their eyes encrusted and sticky by their previous evening's indiscretions in the category of alcoholic consumption.

"You bitch," Jimmy said as he gagged on his own cottony mouth, for some reason his initial instinct to lash out at his wife for any number of grievous thorns in his existence. "Sorry," he added soon after, ashamed for his gut reaction. Luckily, she had not heard him.

Patricia felt as though she had been run over by a melting ice cream truck that had recently burst into flames. Her face was sticky but hardened, a mixture of thickened saliva and bug bites upon her cheeks and nose.

"Water," she wheezed through crackling lips, falling to her knees and crawling towards the river. Reaching the water's edge, she lunged forward, dunking her head and shoulders into the flow of the river, gratefully smiling beneath the aquatic sanctity.

Jimmy, on the other hand, took right to cleaning up the mess about the extinguished fire—beer bottles and food wrappers for the most part. He folded up the beach chairs and packed away his guitar in its waterproof baggie, lugging each component to his and Gabe's canoe.

"They're still asleep?" he asked of his wife, who was rubbing the invigorating river water into her face, digging away at the disgust in what she had done to herself the night before. "It's well past dawn. They're usually the first ones up," he noted, dipping his sore feet into the river, a chill escaping up his spine as the frigid pulse of it took him over. God, he loved being in nature.

"Go wake them up, dummy. We need to eat breakfast and get our asses back on the river if we're going to finish the next leg by lunch. Time's a'wastin'," she said, a wretched scowl on her face.

Jimmy jumped into action because that was what Jimmy did when she was in that particular brand of funk. Keep the peace. Abide and abide again.

"Yes, ma'am," he said with a hint of hidden irony as he pulled back the tent flaps, poking his head through to witness his two lovely little lumps still fast asleep in their bags. He shook each of their feet in turn, saying softly, "Wake up kids. It's time to get a move on or the old hag will claw our eyes out."

Gabe stirred, as did Jenny, but neither poked their heads out from their bags. Jimmy stayed put, in search of confirmation (via proper eye contact) that they had escaped the clutches of sleep. Were he to walk away without validation of that fact, he would surely be back again in ten minutes repeating the same wake up call. "L-E-T-S, G-O," he insisted, louder this time.

They stirred again. Gabe sat up like an undead vampire rising from the grave, but Jimmy quickly discovered that Gabe was nowhere to be found. Looking into his eyes were the glossy lifeless eyes of a fish. Beneath the head were the thin white shoulders of a child.

The Fish Boy rolled over, rubbing next to Jenny's sleeping bag. He moved to a crouching position. He was glad that his father had awoken him; he needed to resuscitate his oxygen from his lifeblood in the water. He felt woozy for a moment, stumbling as he stood.

His new father took several steps back from him, screaming aloud and falling into the sand. "Patricia, something's happened to Gabe!" he cried out, trembling as he reverse crab-walked his way through the sand. "Holy fuck, that's not Gabe at all!" he cried in reconsideration, sand grating into his eyes in his fearful thrashing.

Patricia turned to see her young Gabe wearing a mask. He looked more pale and skinnier than usual, but she chalked that up to her liquified brain matter. The mask was a nice touch. "What a crock. Nice mask, Gabe." She tried to recall when he would have picked up the blueish-green fish mask, presumably at one of the tourist traps they had happened through during their drive up north. "Get your sister up and get ready for a *very* abbreviated breakfast."

Jimmy turned to his wife with the eyes of a lost child. She had not looked close enough at the thing that had emerged from their children's tent. The blind bitch had not seen the look in the thing's (his son's?) vacant dead eyes, or the pulse of his gills.

As the Fish Boy dove into the river gleefully, his heart went atwitter at how much fun they would have together. His new family was terribly amusing, especially with the strange noises they made. Could they not see how much their new son loved them? In the end, they had no choice to love him, lest they fall under the same wrath as had the Fish Boy's predecessor.

"My dear, your gags are absolutely ridiculous," she called after Gabe, following him into the water up to her knees. The stream felt stronger today than it did the day before, perhaps from the heavy rains that had dumped further north in the preceding days.

The Fish Boy leaped from the river a full five feet, cajoling in the air with a spray of mist. It was at this moment that Patricia came to understand the words of her husband, that the thing with the fish mask was not her son- that it was not a mask at all, that is was an integral part of the fishy beast.

Her piercing scream echoed along the surface of the river like a skipping stone.

Patricia backed away, finding footing in the sand again. The thing that had taken Gabe's place emerged from the water, standing on his lanky ivory legs with river water dripping from his awkward pale body. And for a moment—just one fleeting moment—the monstrous fish-child smiled at her, water dumping from its gills. The mouth opened and closed several times, as if flexing, and the lips curled back just enough to send jolts of terror through her nervous system. "What have you done with my son?"

"Jenny?" Jimmy groaned as he imagined the worst for his daughter, she who had been forced to sleep only inches away from the fish-beast throughout the evening. What if it had eaten her? What, just what if, the mutant had raped her?

He poked his head through the tent flaps again, whispering for his daughter, "Come on, sweetie. Daddy needs to get you out of here."

He shook at Jenny's feet and a second beast sat bolt upright. The Fish Girl reached her scrawny arms out in an attempt to embrace her new pep-pep. With a squeal of joy, she batted her mutated eyelids multiple times. She'd been so anxious throughout the evening, awaiting the moment of her revelation, alongside her brother. Finally, she would meet her new parents. They had possessed (according to the Fish Boy) all the qualities that would, in time, melt her infantile heart.

Jimmy fainted, his face down in the lap of his daughter's piscatorial replacement. The smell of pond scum drifted in and out of his nose, and he dreamed of his children's births, of them emerging from between Patricia's legs, sea kelp and slimy pulsing tentacled squids in place of the pinkish-hued cherubs of reality.

"What have you done with my son?" Patricia asked again, rivers of salty tears descending her face. "WHAT HAVE YOU DONE WITH MY SON?" she blasted angrily, falling backwards on to her buttocks beside her canoe as the Fish Boy inched his way forward, intent on hugging and kissing his beautiful new mother.

Along with her question, her hand reached behind her for one of the oars. She decided very quickly that she would thrash this mutant fishy son of a bitch to death. But instead, her quaking hand fell upon her son's face, cold and rigid. The first fact that came splattering against her frontal lobe was that he was not breathing. Her eyes then confirmed that her boy Gabe (he who had first asked of her if he could one day "pway da gootar like pop") was a deeply bruised purple color, his eyes as lifeless as the walking talking bait who had stepped in for him, who had slept snugly in his sleeping bag while they snoozed away their drunkard habits and sadness.

"What have you done with my son?" she begged, leaning in close to her dead child, caressing his face with her hand, asking the question of both God and the Fish Boy simultaneously.

The Fish Boy leaned in close to his new mother. He would suckle on her breast by nightfall, as would his sister the Fish Girl. He turned as his sludgy arms wrapped around Patricia, looking to his sister with a smile. The Fish Girl had dragged Jimmy from the tent, stripping away his clothes to see his true nature, taking quick notation of his strange genitals, looking next to her brother who possessed no discernible features like those of their new pep-pep.

She emitted a high pitch noise at her brother, who responded with a similarly piercing reverberation. Things were back to normal, on some level. They would never forget their own parents. They would forever wonder where their bodies had been dragged away to—mounted in the den of a sickly human. But life moved on. For every bridge that burns, two more are built.

The Fish Boy squeezed tight to his mother and imagined the delicious fun they would have together.

The Fish Boy

NATURE'S FURY UNLEASHED!

AND THE DARK GROWLS BACK

Starring: AARON DRIES

And The Dark Growls Back

Starring Aaron Dries

One

They shouldn't have run. But at the time, it seemed there was no other option.

Lila and Sam held each other in the back seat of the car. She could feel his breath, warm against her neck. Her hands on his arm tricked Sam into thinking that they would get out of this okay, that he would always be around to *be* touched.

The car bumped along the unpaved road and Sam had to work hard to keep down the fairground hotdogs he'd devoured two hours before. The shock of what he'd done had numbed his body, but his stomach felt alive and violent.

Sam cranked down the window and cold air rushed inside, changing the air pressure. Their friend Paul, who was driving, asked him to close it because it was making his ears thump. "I can turn up the air-con if you're hot," Paul said. There was no reply. "Are you guys hot?"

"We're fine!" Lila snapped, guilt settling in as soon as she'd spoken. She had no right to bite at him. None whatsoever. In fact, she should be reaching over and planting a kiss on his cheek.

Without Paul they would still be at the fair, huddled in the dark.

Lila told herself to stop being so hard on him; to hold herself together. She forced a smile and held her chin high, refusing to wipe the tears from her cheeks. To do so almost felt like giving in. Lila had decided to wear her tears like a scar. A reminder of where they were and what they had yet to overcome.

She tucked a lock of her auburn hair behind an ear with shaking hands. Whatever air of confidence she'd been trying to uphold fell apart.

137

"I'm sorry," Lila said, searching for Paul's eyes in the rear-view mirror. He avoided hers. "This is just so fucked up."

"I know," Paul said.

She could hear the fear in his voice. It made him sound younger. They had been speaking in rushed, half-sentences, their minds scattered and seeking distraction. Fear made children out of them. And try as they might, there was no distraction good enough to keep the reality at bay.

Sam had killed a man.

It was four in the morning and they were driving through Icelandic twilight. Everything was swathed in a blue wash that made the landscape seem clean and crisp. They'd never felt so alien.

It would be dark soon, and they wanted to get to the cottage before sundown. Time was a hawk above their heads, ready to swoop in and feast. And their crime was the rock against which the bird sharpened its beak.

Sam, Lila and Paul were all twenty-two years of age, their birthdays separated by mere months. The two boys had gone to high school together, and their respective *Facebooks* were full of photos of each other. Sam and Paul finished each other's sentences and told their stories in back-and-forth banter that disorientated the listener.

Lila and Sam had been in a relationship for two years and had met in Australia. She was from Auckland and he from Sydney. He bought her a drink in an overcrowded bar and later, they'd kissed on the beach.

She loved him for his humour and for his innate ability to draw the best out in her.

But now Sam had fallen silent, his face lost in shadows. She could feel him shaking. If ever there had been a time for her to be strong…it was now; and unlike many other times, she would have to initiate her courage on her own.

I can do this, Lila told herself. *I can. I can.* It became a mantra in her head, the words running together until they had little shape or meaning. Her defences fell. The truth crept back in.

They were making mistake after mistake.

They shouldn't have fled the fairgrounds and they shouldn't have involved Paul. Lila studied him in the rearview mirror, his puppy-dog eyes breaking her heart. Oxygen vanished from her lungs. She started thumping at the windows, stirring her boyfriend from his nowhere-state.

Sam had once owned a goldfish named Flipper. Flipper had done laps in her bowl for six months, seemingly content with her basic, familiar surroundings, until the Sunday afternoon when Flipper decided she'd had enough. Sam found his fish on the dining room floor, covered in a thin layer of carpet grime, her mouth opening and closing in great, painful gasps. Screaming, the child dropped to his knees, scooped his fish up and dropped her back into its bowl, only to watch it float to the surface. Sam cried the afternoon away, his father's hand on his shoulder, comforting Sam in a way he never did again.

Lila had the same look about her.

Clambering for air...flopping around in her seat.

The same panic overcame him, and in his mind he saw his girlfriend bobbing facedown in a pool, her hair an auburn star floating in the water. His nausea disappeared and he straightened, grabbing Lila by the sleeve of her blouse. "Stop the car!" he yelled.

Paul swerved off the road. The wheels hit the loose dirt, and fountains of dust flanked the vehicle. The car screeched to a halt. Sam opened Lila's door and pushed her out onto the grass. The same hands that had moments before been shaking and cold, were now strong. He supported her neck and held back her hair. Lila vomited into the dust, lifted her head and took a gulp of air.

Paul stepped out of the car and watched the couple collapse against each other, their syncopated breathing slow and rhythmic. He felt a pang of jealousy. He had never felt so out of the loop and so far from his best friend.

They were surrounded by acres of flat land formed from ancient volcanic rock. Everything was covered in foot-thick moss which, when stepped on, felt like the cushioned floor of a jumping castle. Days before, the three of them had bounced up those hills to watch birds riding the wind. They had then continued to the cottage and eaten baked sheep's head, toasting to their trip over shot glasses of Brennivin Schnapps with shark flesh floating in it.

Paul smiled, and for a brief moment forgot that Sam had killed a man. That they had run.

It all came back and he gripped the car door. His knuckles turned milky-white and he felt blood pounding through his veins. "We'd better keep going," he said. There was no confidence in his voice. No authority.

They didn't listen. Lila and Sam sat in the twilight, the stars growing bright above them.

"I'm sorry," Sam whispered. "I'm so sorry."

Two

The cottage sat at the base of a dormant volcano, washed in blue moonlight. Two flags, one Icelandic and the other Australian, flapped in the cold wind at the end of the porch. The three figures marched up the concrete steps, passing a collection of garden gnomes and polished rocks.

It was dark.

The cottage belonged to Paul's second cousin, Bentley, who had immigrated to Iceland fifteen years prior, worked as a commercial fisherman, and married a local Olafsvik girl. They raised a family on the outskirts of the city and built the cottage together in the valley. Back when prices were reasonable; before the economic crisis crippled the country.

Their only neighbours were the hills. Nearby, there was a saltwater river that stretched all the way back to the North Atlantic ocean. It was a quiet, peaceful place. Except for the wind. *The wind howled.*

Bentley had taken them to the cottage earlier in the week. It was he who'd made the baked sheephead—caramelized potatoes on the side. The backpackers had toasted to him. Bentley was back in Olafsvik with his wife and children. Sleeping. They had left the fair hours before the murder, dizzy from the rides, their faces red from all the laughter.

Three

Paul opened the door. It swung wide and slammed against the wall. They stared into the mouth of the cottage, searching the shadows for movement. Sam knew they were alone, but that didn't stop him from feeling like he was being watched, that somewhere inside the cottage there were eyes staring back at him.

And that those eyes did not look upon him with kindness.

Paul swallowed hard and fumbled along the wall until he found the light switch. When he flipped it, the room filled with a blinding yellow glow.

The kitchen was just as they'd left it two days ago: clean, but by no means tidy. Plates had been left to drip-dry near the sink and the beds in the above open loft were still unmade. A hallway led to a wardrobe-sized bedroom and en-suite. The walls were lined with family photographs, books, topographic maps and drawings. A ladder stretched up from the living room floor to the loft, where their travel backpacks were laid open like disemboweled bodies, spilling clothes and dirty socks.

Paul closed the door; it made the cottage feel smaller. Sam and Lila turned to him, their eyes wide and uncomprehending. "*What now?*" Sam asked. He thought coming to the cottage would solve everything. That it would save him. He was wrong.

"We wait," Lila said, massaging her neck.

"Go up into the loft and try to get some sleep," Paul suggested. "There's a shitload of food left over from the other day. I'll make some soup for us."

"I'm not hungry."

"Sam, you will be later. Get some sleep. Trust me." Paul smiled kindly, but he could tell that Sam didn't appreciate being told what to do. He turned to the refrigerator.

Lila switched on the hallway light. "Go up, babe," she told her boyfriend. "I'm going to brush my teeth and then I'll join you. I just got to wash my face or something. I feel nasty."

"You don't think we should call the police?" Sam asked, going to the window. He saw nothing but his own warped reflection.

"I don't know what to do," Paul said, running his fingers through his hair. His stomach was in tight knots and he felt the first stabs of a migraine behind his eyes. As a child, he'd suffered from headaches so severe they had resulted in hospitalization.

He remembered the metal table. How it had slid into the mouth of the CAT scan. The machine hovered above his head like a crown, flashing lights and squawking robot noises. Even in the machine he could hear the doctors whispering.

Tumours...cancer...

Those words hadn't computed in his mind at the time. They just didn't make sense. There were other whispers, too. *His parents*. They appeared calm and collected in his company, but at night he could hear them crying in their bedroom.

All of his results came back negative and the headaches faded with puberty. His parents changed after that. They had hardened, and were less compassionate. *But he was alive*. Even though words like *tumours* and *cancer* didn't make sense to him as a child, the word *alive* did. He knew its value, its delicacy. Paul was thankful.

But every time he felt that first stab of pain, he remembered the sickening thud in his head, the voices of doctors. It made him feel so small.

"So, what? We just sit here and wait this out?" Sam asked, pacing back-and-forth.

Paul leaned against the kitchen counter. He felt himself deflating.

"Shit like this just doesn't up and leave, you know," Sam said. He stood still and pulled at his hair.

Paul winced; it hurt to watch his friend like this.

Sam fell onto the couch, exasperated. When he closed his reddening eyes he saw blood on cement and the spinning lights of the Ferris wheel. The distant jingle of carnival music. He drew his knees up to his chest and for the first time since primary school, Sam turned to prayer.

Four

The small confessional booth smelt of mothballs and fart. Or at least, that's what the kids used to say. Everything was made from polished wood, except for the leather pad used to cushion their knees and the metal grate separating them from Father Mason.

The priest seemed impossibly old to all of the children at James Bridge Catholic School. The students would swear they heard him creak when he walked, as though he himself were fashioned from the same wood as the pews they were forced to sit on.

"Excuse me, Father, for I have sinned," nine-year-old Sam would say. "It's been two months since my last confession." He spoke in whispers, terrified that the other students—who were lined up outside the booth in Indian file—might hear what he was saying.

Confession was compulsory and Sam hated it—they all did. It was a distrusted bi-weekly event. Distrusted because all of the children suspected that the details of their confession were passed on to their teacher, who would then mark grades with their sins in mind.

They also hated confession because it was so frequent. As a consequence, they were often at a loss as to what to say. This happened to Sam a number of times. He would kneel there, "umming" and "ahhhing", never forgetting the pressure of time, because every moment that passed was a dreaded moment closer to Father Mason's retorts. That was always the worst part. Mason's breath would fill the booth with a foul, sour musk.

"Okay, Father. I...ahhh...pushed my brother off of the trampoline. I'm sorry."

Yes. That was always a good one.

"Uh-hh, I felt pretty bad about it."

"Yes, of course you do. What else have you to confess?"

Sam's sweaty fingers were intertwined. Crisscross shadows from the grate divided his face into sectionals. He felt as though the walls of the booth were closing in. A draft stirred the rosary beads dangling from the door handle. The tiny, silver Christ-figure, splayed on his crucifix, tapped against the wood.

A rapping in the sweaty dark.

"Father. I was at a fair in Iceland. Someone made a pass at my girlfriend. I was stupid. I pushed him. He pushed me. I punched him and he fell and he cracked his head open on the gutter. He bled everywhere."

Five

Sam's eyes flicked open. He didn't scream, or bolt upright like people always seemed to do in the horror movies he sometimes watched—and rarely enjoyed. He didn't like the roller coasters Lila had dragged him onto at the fair, either. He hated pig hunting with his friends on their parents' farms back home in James Bridge.

Sam just didn't like being scared, and even worse, he didn't like having to convince others that he *wasn't*. It always left him feeling shamed. Fatigued.

He sat up on the couch, rubbed his neck and looked around the room. Lila was nowhere to be seen. He assumed she was sleeping in the loft. Paul was still in the kitchen, stirring pots. Sam looked at his watch. It was five-thirty in the morning, and he was still a murderer.

Steam hovered around the kitchen ceiling; the bulb gave off a hazed miasma of golden light. The windows were open, and the air sucked out the steam in occasional gasps. Sam smelt the bubbling soup and his stomach clenched. His hunger caught him off guard. He cracked his back and watched his best friend of many years continue to busy himself around the kitchen, unaware of his presence.

Paul was a good guy, and always had been. He held himself in a quiet, reserved way that some people mistook for either stuck-up, or queer. Sam had defended his best mate's character more than once, but he did it without reserve. He would defend Paul physically if he ever needed to.

But anyone could tell that they were polar opposites, from their looks to their attitudes. Many had commented on it- even Lila.

Paul was tall and lanky; Sam short and solid. Sam was quick to anger; often fueled by machismo, or alcohol. What Paul lacked in backbone, he made up for in loyalty and insight. It had proved enough to get him through school, out of James Bridge and then abroad.

Sam wished Lila were next to him. He felt naked and exposed without her. In many ways she'd become the drink he clutched to his chest when he stood alone in a nightclub; not an accessory—but his buffer. She made him look as though he knew what he was doing.

Paul was bent over a pot, licking a wooden spoon. He looked drawn and tired, like a man who'd been up all night. Like a man coerced into into something he didn't deserve.

He looks like that because that's exactly what he is, Sam thought. Guilt settled in. He crossed the room and touched Paul's shoulder. Paul didn't flinch, or react. Sam wondered if his friend had known of his presence all along and avoided it.

"You're awake," Paul muttered.

Sam nodded. He looked down at the pot and saw large, bald sheep bones rolling in the soup.

Paul threw down the spoon and pivoted around, his face contorted by fear. He drew Sam into a hug.

Six

The room was full of dancing people and Lila saw him through the strobe. She was at the club with three older girl-friends. It was her birthday. A party hat was strapped around her neck, the elastic tight across her throat. She had been drinking gin and tonic from a chipped glass, enjoying the bitterness of the lime wedge.

He approached, half-dancing, half-walking.

Lila gave him the once over and then went back for more. She could see the muscles through his fitted shirt. His sleeves were rolled up, revealing tattoos on both forearms; a caged bird on the right, the word "family" on the left.

The music throbbed. It seemed to push them closer. Lila finished her drink and slammed down her glass. Confidence flooded her body; she tingled. For a moment she feared she might be sick.

He could have looked anywhere in the room and yet he'd looked her way. At her.

The confidence evaporated. She tried to grasp for it, but it was like trying to grab at smoke; it floated away, leaving her naked.

The stranger swooped in. His face grew huge before her. In his eyes she saw the sensitivity he was trying so hard to hide. "My name's Sam," he said just loud enough to be heard over the beat. "What's yours?"

She watched him re-arrange her pointed birthday hat so that it sat on the top of her head. "There we go. Mu-uuch better," he said, leaning in close.

Lila told him her name.

Seven

Lila watched from the loft, her sleeping bag wrapped tight around her. The living room light glowed on her face. It highlighted the curves of her cheeks, glimmered in her pupils.

It felt good to see the boys embracing. It had been a long time coming. Tensions had been building between them on their five-month long travels. They had almost come to punches in Vietnam over a crooked taxi-driver with a skipping metre. Paul wanted to let it go, but Sam had refused to be taken advantage of. It had nothing to do with the money loss, just the principle. Lila hated their stubbornness and stormed from the cab.

There, she had faced a river of motorcyclists. Hundreds of people buzzed by and somehow managed *not* to crash. Nobody stopped for pedestrians; it would only eventuate in a massive pile-up. The only way to cross the road was to calmly walk into the traffic. *To assimilate with it.*

The concept had always terrified her, but she had no choice now.

Lila swallowed her anger and stepped onto the road.

A similar conflict had arisen at Heathrow Airport when Sam had discovered that customs had cut the locks off his backpack. Instead of getting angry at someone responsible—or at someone authorized to make a difference—he directed his anger at his friends. Lila hated how passive-aggressive he could be. It made her feel like collateral damage.

Yes, their hug was long overdue, and it had nothing to do with misspent money, or broken locks, or any of the other issues they had bickered over. All that shit didn't seem to matter any more.

One punch at a fairground made it all meaningless.

It wasn't about the past anymore. Just the future. And how that future was slipping away.

Her phone vibrated under her sleeping bag, startling her. She'd forgotten she even had it with her. Lila snatched it up and read the three terrifying words printed across the screen.

ONE MESSAGE RECEIVED.

She didn't know why...but she looked at the windows below her.

Moments before, they had been safe. Alone. Now, a battered-up phone, some decent coverage and those three words reminded her that they hadn't escaped. *Not really.*

147

They had loaded themselves up into Paul's cousin's car and headed for the cottage, tucked away between two dormant volcanoes beside a river that that lead all the way to the ocean.

The windows were dark. *But what was in the dark?*

Lila remembered reading about Nordic mythology in one of her travel guides. One paragraph haunted her now—myths told by parents to keep their children indoors after twilight.

Trolls living in the rocks. Their chattering heard on the wind. They moved quick, leaping from shadow to shadow. Nimble and crafty.

Recalling the mythology now, Lila could almost feel the warm breath of Icelandic grandmothers against her neck as they drew close to whisper their hand-me-down tales.

Lila wondered if the trolls were out there now, running across the landscape. Or perhaps they were nearer than that. They could be outside the window now, looking in and studying her, sharpening tools crafted from dead birds and volcanic stone, salivating—

Keep yourself under control, Lila told herself. She rubbed her arms, kneading away the gooseflesh. It took great effort to draw her attention away from the window and the secrets it held. She focused on her cell and unlocked it with a quick jab, hoping that the message she'd almost forgotten about would frighten away the images in her mind.

The message was from a girl named Pala, a local who'd taken them clubbing in Reykjavik. She had accompanied them on their adventure north.

Pala was the one who had suggested the fair.

And it was there that they'd met the young man who made a pass at Lila.

Lila couldn't remember what he looked like. When she searched her memory for his face she only saw a blur with probing fingers. His touch had been like fire.

Pala had followed them to the car park after the fight, her face streaked with running mascara, blonde hair whipping in the wind. It had been *she* who had ushered them all away from the scene of the crime.

They might not have run were it not for her screams.

Lila read the message.

SPOKE TO MEDIC. MANS NOT DED. POLICE LOOKING 4 YOU. COME BACK. PLZ. IT WIL B OK. XX

She had to read it three times before the words sunk in. She sat up so quick her head swam. The boys turned towards her. Sam's face was expectant yet torn. Paul was rubbing his forehead.

"Guys," she began, gesturing to her cell, "he's okay. *Oh Jesus.*"

"What?" Sam stepped forward. "What is it, babe?"

"He's alive!"

Eight

The volcanoes were flat silhouettes surrounded by stars. Sam could hear the flags flapping behind him. He sat on the lawn at the rear of the property next to the humming generator, his knees buried deep in the grass.

Paul and Lila watched him from the cottage doorway. Their shadows fell long over the land. They hugged each other, laughing and jumping like children. The wind changed direction, blowing cold air into their faces and rattling a set of wind chimes they hadn't even known were there.

Somehow, those chimes reminded them of where they were. Of what they had outrun and what it was they were so happy about.

One punch had changed everything. And a single text message made it better.

They were dancing for their lives, not for the man who lived. Paul and Lila settled, feeling selfish. They stepped back into the cottage, leaving the door open.

The chimes twinkled gentle music.

Sam could feel the weight lifting from his body as though it were a tangible thing. It didn't disappear- but it lessened.

He studied the sky. It was so huge. So *incomprehensible*. It seemed such an infantile realization, but it dawned on him nonetheless.

I'm nothing.

"Thank you," he said to the dark.

And the dark growled back.

Nine

Sam's screams filled the valley, drawing Paul and Lila back out to the porch. Paul's instincts told him to go back into the cottage and lock the door; that it was too late. He grabbed Lila by the wrist.

Their eyes hadn't adjusted to the dark; when they looked at the lawn they saw nothing. But they *sensed* movement. Jerking. Tearing. Ripping.

The screaming stopped.

A moment slipped by. A bird cawed somewhere; it was a lonely sound.

The thump of approaching footsteps. Sam stepped into the long rectangle of light thrown from the kitchen door. His ashen face. His blood-soaked shirt.

Some part of Paul's brain told him it was *his* turn to scream, but the wires were crossed and a single bleat, almost a giggle, escaped his lips. Lila pressed close against him. She felt warm.

Sam's right arm dangled from his shoulder by a thread. Blood gushed from his stump in quick-spurting fountains. He yelled again, spinning on the spot, a red circle painted on the grass.

Paul watched his best friend—the man he'd embraced in the kitchen minutes before—stop and try to catch the pendulum that was his arm. He missed. The thread of meat snapped, recoiling like a rubber band.

Sam saw his tattooed limb hit the grass. He fell to his knees and made as if to reach for it, sending his senses into disarray. He was right-handed, so it was natural for him to bend over and pick it up with that hand. He lost his balance and fell to the ground, collapsing under the phantom sensation. His jutting collarbone perforated the soil as he rolled and hollered.

There was no pain, just confusion. The stars above him burned so bright he had to squint. The sky turned white. The growling descended again; a torrent of sound. He tried to breathe but he felt like he was drowning. There was an intense pressure on his left thigh. White turned to black.

Lila watched her boyfriend being dragged away, slipping into darkness. The fingers of his left hand carved divots in the lawn. And then he was gone.

Ten

Paul was at the hospital with a bucket between his knees. That morning's headache had been the worst. The nurse was patting his back. Her name was Violeta and she spoke in a funny accent that reminded him of James Bond villains.

The blanket his grandmother had crocheted for him fell to the floor. Violeta picked it up and wrapped it around his shoulders. It itched at his skin but he didn't want to be without it. It reminded him of home; that there was always somewhere better to be—and that that somewhere should never be forgotten.

Paul fell back onto his mattress once the nausea passed. The curtains stirred, knocking over the get-well cards on the bedside table. He felt hollowed out; the headache curled up inside him like a crab in its shell. He was ten years old and wanted to die.

"Make it stop," he said. "Please, just make the hurt go away. I hate it."

Violeta stepped in front of the window. The room darkened. "Back in my home, we have an expression. Don't get between the goat and the cabbage," she said, crossing her arms. "Paul, you're between the goat and the cabbage. You're stuck but these doctors here will help you out. They're good peoples." She looked him in the face. Her breath smelt like sour fruit. "You'll be fine, but toughen up."

Eleven

Paul forced Lila back inside. He was shaking all over but held himself steady as he slammed the door shut, flipping the deadlock. His face was flush against the wood. The smells of the boiling soup wrapped around him.

Lila scratched at his shoulders. "Get away," she screamed, pulling at his hair. "Jesus-open-the-door-and-let-him-in!"

"No, Lila!" Violent pain tore through his head.

Paul didn't want to say it, but there was no other choice. If he didn't acknowledge what they both now knew, they would remain behind that door, frozen and unable to do anything. Let alone defend themselves. "He's dead, Lila. Jesus...he's gone."

There. He'd said it. It didn't make it any more real, but it did light a fire in him. The pain in his head burned away and he emerged on the other side in control.

Paul ran to the window. The wind picked up and sucked the air from the cottage, his hair blew wild around his face. He closed the window, slid the copper latch into place and looked through the glass. In the second before pushing away from the sink and flicking off the kitchen light, he saw the shape of the creature on the lawn.

Just a second.

It was as big as a car. He didn't see its head—just blood against white fur. And two black eyes.

The cottage went dark. "Quick," Paul yelled. "Up the ladder to the beds. Now!"

They heard it climb up onto the back porch, overturning chairs and snapping one flagpole. The sound of its roar shook the walls, stabbing their ears.

Lila hefted herself up the ladder.

Paul looked over his shoulder and saw the shadow at the window. A matted snout shattered the glass without hesitation, shards clattering into the sink. Its head breached, followed by one silhouetted arm and the sleek arch of its spine.

Lila disappeared into the alcove and Paul started climbing. "Get your phone," he screamed. His sweaty palm slipped on the final rung and he tumbled to the floor, landing on his feet but jarring his knees.

The creature pulled itself through the window. It seemed impossible that something so huge could get through something so small, and yet Paul had watched cats squeeze under bedroom doors in a similar way. The creature pulled and expanded, stretched, and spilled into the room. It knocked the pot of soup onto the floor, sending a wave of boiling liquid across the floorboards. Paul felt overcooked potatoes slide under his feet as he attempted to climb the ladder a second time. Each heft pinched the nerves in his knees, but he forced himself through the pain. He could hear the creature uttering dumb grunts as it licked soup from the floor.

Lila offered her hand and Paul took it. He thumped onto his sleeping bag. Paul could smell the Issey Miyake cologne he wore. It was a part of the fabric now, and again his mind shot to better places.

His home in Australia. His bed.

Paul rolled onto his back, remembering where he was. The air was hotter in the open alcove but that had nothing to do with the sweat covering his face. Fear had wrung the water from him. He felt dampness between his legs when he swished around to kick the ladder off its feet. He'd pissed himself as well.

The creature stepped into the pale glow from the living room window. Its jaws opened, revealing sharp teeth that glimmered as if with an inner light. It had velvety lips, as black as licorice. Blood dripped from its nose. The room shook when it lumbered and its claws tore up the floor.

Eight feet above those scratches, Lila and Paul scampered back from the edge. They pushed themselves flat against the rear wall, bent double under the peak of the roof. There was a small round porthole that overlooked the front lawn and the car they had arrived in. The window was too small to escape through; its presence a total mockery.

"What is it?" Paul asked, more to himself than to Lila.

The grandmother, her face as lined as the land she had lived on her entire life, bent forward on cracking limbs and whispered in Lila's ear once more. Lila saw the Icelandic landscape and the bulging volcanic rocks in the open flats. Only they weren't rocks. They were alive. They moved. When they stood tall they blotted out the stars. The grandmother retreated back into the dark, leaving behind chills and myths.

What *was* it? Paul's question hung in the air, as tangible as smoke.

Thoughts of grandmothers, of trolls in the fields faded away. Lila blinked, a tear slipped into the crescent of her lip. She could taste the salt. It tasted real.

"Bear," she said.

The word sat between them, leaden and impervious. Lila hadn't understood what it was until she had said it aloud. Not really.

A big fucking polar bear.

It didn't make sense to either of them—although nothing was making sense by that point. *Iceland didn't have any polar bears.* There was little to no snow, and even less in the way of resources for them to live off. The country was a grey rock covered in moss and pavement.

In her travels, Lila had learned that misconception surrounded—and in many ways, defined—each and every country. Australians kept kangaroos as pets; all Canadians lived in the snow; Iceland was full of ice. There was no truth to any of them, but as she stared into the black eyes of the bear, she found herself praying that all of those cliches would *somehow* become true. BANG and it all became fact.

Yes, she had a pet kangaroo. Yes, she had experienced a white summer in downtown Vancouver. Yes. There was ice in Iceland.

If the misconception were true, then the monster was a monster no more. It would be just another animal. Natural. Dangerous. Just another lost and hungry creature.

It might as well be a troll, said a voice in her head. The voice of the grandmother.

Lila and Paul's minds started to roll backwards, drawing hypothetical lines between the hypothetical dots. They both started with the certainty.

Blood. Bear. The window. The lawn. The dark.

The volcanoes? *No.* The fields. *No.* The river?

Yes, the river.

Paul and Lila's thoughts were intertwined. They didn't speak, but their minds worked in unison.

The river lead to the ocean.

Polar bears had been known to migrate significant distances, from continent to continent even. Paul recalled reading an online article about a female polar bear from Greenland being shot on the Iceland's northeastern coastline. He shook his head in disbelief. And yet the evidence that such a story could be—and was—true was screaming him in the face.

It *had* been known to happen. It *was* happening.

Had. Was. Paul shivered. The two words were like the *born* and *death* dates chiseled into the face of a headstone. His headstone. And between those two dates—those facts—was the dash that somehow related to his life; everything that he had experienced...all of his fears and love.

Now that Paul and Lila's minds had pinpointed -and justified- the origins of the bear, their thoughts wound forward, drawing the narrative between the no longer hypothetical dots. And that last dot ended on them.

The polar bear had migrated.

Its great paws ploughed through water, a white blur amid the blue. It lived off small fish and its fat reserves, like a whale. It slept on its back when fatigued, and fought off shark attacks in the mornings and evenings. As it drew closer to land it passed schools of Orca snatching seal cubs from the waves.

The polar bear entered the river system.

It moved fast, the current ushering it along. It passed unseen through towns, terrified by the sounds of ferries and fishing boats. Its hunger grew.

The polar bear came ashore.

It pulled itself from the river, struggling to adjust to its own weight after months of being afloat. After resting, it went in search of food, only to find none on the land. It climbed over rock and averted hot springs, its snout buried in the moss. Hunger drove it on.

The polar bear had smelled their food.

It caught the scent. Meat and fats. Oils and barley. Its stomach constricted, pain tearing through its massive body. The creature was almost crippled by its desire for food, and yet it pushed onwards through the night.

The polar bear found Sam.

Its jaws clamped around his arm and pulled him apart. After dragging him back into the shadows, it clawed through the soft flesh in his side, stretching the skin open until his stomach fell onto the grass. The smell was unlike anything it had ever experienced. It fed, gluttonous and messy. It was not satisfied.

The polar bear broke into the house—

Paul and Lila stifled their cries with the palms of their hands. Sam, the best friend, the boyfriend- was no longer alive. He was on the lawn, he was *in* the belly of the creature. His parents in James Bridge slept unaware that their son was dead.

Devoured.

It all started to become real.

Fear was sending their bodies into fluctuations of extreme sensitivity—to light and touch—and then the opposite. Numbness. Lila had to concentrate hard to avoid another panic attack. Sam was no longer around to hold her, to provide comfort and support.

No.

Sam was dead. He was in pieces.

Dead. Pieces. Pieces. Dead.

The repetition of these facts sobered her.

Lila fished through her jeans for her cell phone, but couldn't find it. She exhaled, heart broken. Lila was realizing how easy it was to invest in the smallest of things when faced with extreme danger. How hope itself could be dangerous. Crippling.

It was Paul who saw the phone. It was half-tucked under a pillow at the edge of the alcove facing the living room. He gestured for Lila to stay put and began a long, delicate crawl towards it.

Pain zapped through his knees as he moved. Every time he shuffled, another floorboard creaked and he would grow still. He prayed to someone he didn't believe in to save them from the creature. He crept further, leaving behind a trail of sweat.

The phone stared back at him.

By the time he was close enough to reach out and grab it, he had full view of the living room and the kitchen. The wind was blowing hard through the shattered window, it stirred the wet locks of his fringe.

The bear took up the majority of the living room. Its hind-quarters had knocked the television to the floor and when it attempted to stand up, Paul heard the pop of its joints...the crunch of broken glass under its paws. The bear's head bumped against the low-hanging bulb, shattering its seventies-style casing. It stood eight feet tall; and even then, Paul got the impression that it wasn't fully erect. Its head was bent low, sleek as an otter. He saw its eyes twinkling. The hair on its belly was twisted and matted into dags, streaked with blood and grease. Even from the alcove, he could smell its stench: sewer water and brine.

Paul snatched up the phone. A minor victory. He backed up, unable to take his eyes off the beast. Lila touched his leg he held back a scream.

He wanted to make the call, but didn't know how to unlock the phone. Lila grabbed it from him, frustrated and crying. The alcove filled with green light. Paul grabbed a blanket and threw it over them. Instant warmth. The glow from the display screen burned brighter.

"What's the number for police here?" Lila asked.

"Shit, I don't know."

"Is it 911?"

"Oh fuck me," Paul moaned. "Just call it."

"No."

"What you mean, 'no'? Just do it."

Lila was already dialling. She held the phone to her ear. Paul poked his head out from under the blanket. There was no relief; the bear was nowhere to be seen but he could hear it thumping around in the kitchen.

"Pala?" Lila whispered into the receiver.

"What are you doing? Call the police!" Paul wanted to strangle her.

"We're in trouble, hon," Lila began. "We need the police... Yes, the police. We don't know the number. Please, hon, call them for us and send them to Paul's cousin's place. It's about an hour and a half out of the city...Paul, what's the address?"

He gave it to her, bit his knuckles. He felt guilty for doubting her.

"Pala, it's a fucking bear. A big fucking polar bear." Lila found herself laughing; stupid and high-pitched. "Oh, hon, I don't know. It's big and...Pala, it killed Sam." Lila laughed the laugh of those who don't know what to do, or how to react. "Hon, it killed Sam."

Paul saw the sorrow in her eyes, despite her rigorous, forced smile. That pain ran deep.

"Just call me back to let me know you got through to them, okay?"

Two ah-hum's later, she hung up, held the phone between her palms and squeezed. "I can't believe this is happening," she whispered.

There was a terrific thud from the living room. They snapped down the blanket, forcing themselves as flat against the rear wall as they could manage. Their heartbeats pounded in their ears.

A huge, blood matted paw sailed through the air and slammed against the alcove floor. Long claws dug into the wood and when it withdrew, it took a sleeping bag with it. Its roar shook the port window behind them. There was tearing. Paul's mind flooded with images of Sam, wreathing under the creatures maw. The tearing was his stomach ripping open, drowning on his own innards.

Lila searched the room for something to defend themselves with. There was nothing, just their travellers backpacks, which now that they were partially empty, had little weight to them. She rolled onto her back and kicked at the port window.

And screamed.

Paul stumbled backwards, gripping his chest. "Oh, fuck me!"

Lila's foot was imbedded in the glass. It had not shattered. It had caved in with her ankle imbedded halfway through.

Paul had once seen a *National Geographic* documentary about morray eels on late night television. The needle-sharp teeth of the fish angled inwards, making escape impossible once it had latched onto your flesh.

The angle of the broken shards were the same. The only way for Lila to break free was to force herself *through* the portal. That wasn't going to happen.

The window ran red. Freezing Icelandic air blew through the small cracks in the glass and whistled. This coincided with the ringing of Lila's cell. The small space filled with green light again. Paul couldn't tell if the phone was on silent or not, her screaming and the howl of the bear drowned out all other noise.

Paul always measured chaos with rationality. He was a man of logic, and had excelled at mathematics and science in his school years. Reason had always been his ally. And the presence of the bear made a mockery of it all. His best friend was dead - had been eaten alive. Paul felt betrayed. By fact, if nothing else.

He was no longer at the top of the food chain.

The bear was rewriting their place in history.

Twelve

There was another crash.

The bear could hear their screams. It had their scent. The rich stench of their skin, of their sweat, of the piss in their jeans. Such sweet odours were far more enticing than the reek of the spoiled food in the refrigerator, the soup on the floor. Fear had tenderized their flesh. It sensed this.

The bear was victim to its hunger and it wouldn't stop until it was full.

Muscles that were accustomed to leaping from icebergs, swelled as the bear prepared to jump. It shivered, shook its head and reached up into the alcove again. The noise of its prey drove it on. Their screams were its music.

Its muscles released and the bear jumped.

Claws scratched and dug at the floorboards. Dust sifted from the rafter beams, raining over Paul who was still trying to dislodge Lila's ankle from the window. It was useless. Lila couldn't help writhing; the pain was too immense. But the more she moved the more the glass carved her to the bone. Paul's hands and arms were lathered in her dark, oily blood. He could taste it on his lips. It was both sweet and bitter at once.

Lila bent her head as far back as she could manage. She watched the bear pull its upper half into the alcove. A surge of strength pounded through her and she dragged herself upright, the muscles in her stomach crying agony. Her fingers dug at the loose flesh around her ankle.

Lila realized that the pain had faded away. It was strange...she felt as though she'd dipped her leg into a pool of cold water. There had been that first, frigid step and yes, it had hurt; *but not really*. In some ways, it was almost pleasurable. Now there was just the echo of pain thumping through her body, interrupted only by the pop and sever of stray nerves. When that happened, her eyes bolted open and the darkness that lurked nearby vanished.

Her jeans were black with blood. The smell of it made her want to vomit, but seeing the dripping mess kept her determined. *I'm not going to black out*, she told herself. *I'm not. I'm not. I'm not.* Lila had heard of mothers overturning crashed cars to get at their trapped children—her will to survive was the same. She tore at the strands of flesh about her exposed bone; whittling herself away.

Paul and Lila froze still as the cottage groaned. The floorboards under their feet pulled away from the walls and nails drove up into Paul's knees. The head of the bear was sideways in the room, snapping at the air, its claws digging divots in the wood as it scratched for grip. The bear didn't know what was happening, but its prey did.

And there was nothing they could do to stop it.

There was a moment of silence before the fall. Paul looked into Lila's eyes and smiled. There was no reason in it. No science. *Just instinct.* It was a lightning bolt of happiness. It burned bright and faded away.

The floor beneath them collapsed under the weight of the bear. Dust and wood splinters exploded around them. The walls shook, crying protest, as the alcove split in two, pinching in at the middle. Paul didn't have time to grab onto Lila—or anything. He scrambled, desperate and afraid, and slid into the funnelled floor, diving into the cloud of dust.

The bear roared.

Lila felt the floor disappear beneath her. She snapped against the wall—a thud to the head—and hung upside down, suspended by one leg from the window, the shards holding tight.

She felt darkness drawing close again. Blood rushed to her head, swelling her face. Dark blots painted her upturned vision, but through the bruises she saw the dissipating cloud, and through it, pinched tight in the middle of the collapsed floor, she saw Paul.

The roof was now sixteen feet above him. The alcove floor had collapsed in a V, with him pinched tight at its apex. He couldn't see his legs. Paul tried to breathe but no air passed through him. There was an intense pressure on his torso, a pressure so overcoming that it blocked out everything else. His shivering fingers touched the unbelievable inversion of his stomach. His fingers sensed the bulging fabric, but the skin beneath registered nothing.

Oh shit, he thought. *I'm stuck.*

He was pinched in half.

Air. I need air.

Nothing.

I'm winded, he thought. *Yeah, that's it. I'm winded. Just give me a minute—*

Blue moonlight slit through the dust, landing on the head of the bear. Its eyes were full of pain. Its hunger had tortured it for so long.

Paul watched it stand before him, its head disappearing into shadow. He sensed its power. It was an almighty thing. Heat radiated from it in waves, soothing the chill that tickled his cheeks. He was so cold. Paul wanted a blanket to wrap himself up in. A blanket like the one his grandmother had crocheted for him; the one he had wrapped around his shoulders when he was sick with the headaches. It had been such a good blanket. It always made him feel better.

He looked for it and died.

Lila had stopped screaming, and in her final moments of consciousness, saw her last true friend grow as still as the dust about him...and longed for him immediately.

She was alone now.

Helpless and numb, she watched the bear descend on Paul's body and wrap its jaws around his head, drinking out his eyes. It yanked hard, its paws digging at the loose floorboards, crossing wires somewhere in the room and filling the space with sparks. Paul's pinched torso burst open and his intestines danced in the strobe light.

Lila grew calm.

In the flashes of light she saw another shape in the room. The silhouette of a man. It grew larger and, like the pain, everything else faded away. Except for him. The stranger. The bear and its feast; the slopping and the chewing as it bit away Paul's jawbone and gagged...all gone. Swallowed up by nothingness.

There was just the man as he walked closer. His swagger radiated confidence. He started to dance.

Lila could taste alcohol in her mouth. She tried to place it. Was it gin? Maybe. Lime? She couldn't put her finger on it- and it didn't really matter anymore. All that mattered was the man. The man and the way the strobe light lit up his hair. His eyes. Somewhere, there was music.

Beat.

Beat.

"My name's Sam," he said into the dark. "What's yours?"

The Visitor
Starring Kelley Kombrinck

OHIO-Small Town Celebrates Mythical Being—(*from the November 3rd edition of the Tusc Valley Times-Reporter*)

It's time once again for the greater Tuscarawas county area to cast a bemused eye south down route 77 towards Griffithstown. It's the weekend after Halloween and their annual, "Autumn Harvest Sasquatch Festival" kicks off this Friday at dusk (or roughly 5:00 pm). Far from a typical, small-town festival, Griffithstown's celebration revolves around the area's notorious reputation as a hot-spot for sightings of the legendary Sasquatch.

For decades, Griffithstown (along with the nearby town of Cornwich and the adjacent Ami Pierce Township) has boasted frequent "sightings" of what eyewitnesses claim is Ohio's version of the infamous ape-man. In the last thirty-five years, nearly seventy of these accounts have been reported to the Tuscarwas County Sheriff's office. Also reported are strange howling sounds attributed to the creature and occasional sets of over-sized footprints, one set of which was photographed in 1979 and published in a book about UFOs and other strange phenomena.

Far from keeping their notoriety hush-hush, the citizens of Griffithstown celebrate their status as Ohio's crypto-zoological epicenter. Each year since 1980, the town puts on their "Autumn Harvest Sasquatch Festival" the first weekend of November. The festival's activities include arts and crafts, games, rides, and a large parade, among other things; all in commemoration of their (alleged) hairy, outdoor neighbor. The festival atmosphere is one of high spirits and good cheer. Many of the festival-goers boast having caught glimpses of the elusive beast themselves—but no one fears for their safety. They regard the creature as a town treasure.

I've seen him four or five times in the last fifteen years or so," says Merton Squibb, 51, of Ami Pierce Twp., "The last time he was out at the back of my south field standin' at the fence. He's got no reason to hurt nobody. We all want to keep him safe."

(Article cont'd on page C-4)

It was Thanksgiving and the snow had come early. By the time everyone was on their second round of dinner rolls, heavy flakes began to swirl and fall from dark clouds that clung to the sky. It started slowly, floating lazily down like tiny sky-dwelling jellyfish. By dark, however, it was clear that the snowfall was not going to let up, and was probably going to get worse. A smooth layer of white powder covered the lawns and fields that had been beaten into submission by the season's earlier freezing rains and frost. The wind started gusting across yards flinging handfuls of the stuff against walls and windows, covering driveways and making sidewalks slick.

At Aunt Mindy's house where Brooke and Cliff spent each Thanksgiving and Christmas, the children of relatives both well known and obscure, watched the snow with squealing delight. The family was spread across three large, round tables in the huge dining room at the back of the house. The walls were a soft, buttery yellow and the tables were draped with simple but elegant red tablecloths. It was comfortably warm and lit by lamps that cast an equally warm glow. Conversation at the kids' table turned quickly to the impending Christmas vacation, Santa Claus and what presents they expected to find under their respective trees.

Cliff sat at his table, nibbling on a buttered roll and looking out the window at the whitewashed scenery with disquiet. He did not share the children's enthusiastic opinion of snow. He hated it. He hated cold and ice and everything else about winter; in fact, secretly (or sometimes not-so-secretly) he even hated

Christmas. Brooke, sitting next to him, was talking to her cousin Libby about something, laughing occasionally. She wouldn't be bothered by the weather at all; she thought the snow was pretty. In his own world, Cliff simply sat staring out into the gloomy afternoon and sighed inwardly.

The babble of voices became a wash that swam in and. Cliff wasn't listening,though he caught bits and pieces of conversation. He was considering getting up to grab another Pepsi when he realized that Libby's husband Mark was looking at him expectantly. Cliff suddenly wondered if Mark had been trying to talk to him. Mark was a small, timid looking man with thinning hair and a growing beer gut. He seldom spoke to anyone (other than Brooke's brother Brad, who was in the living room watching a football game) and Cliff had taken to ignoring him. Now he flushed with embarrassment; it was clear from the look on Mark's face that he had said something to Cliff and was awaiting a response.

"Sorry, man, I was off in Oz. What'd you say?" Cliff asked.

"I said, it's gonna be a rough ride to our place if this snow keeps up."

Shit, Cliff thought, *he's right*. Cliff and Brooke had driven up from Cincinnati that very morning straight to Aunt Mindy's but were staying at Mark and Libby's new house overnight. They had only just moved in the weekend before and had been remarking off and on all day about how far off the beaten path it was.

"We've hardly seen more than a couple of cars go by all week long," Libby had said. She'd meant it to be a boast about the peace and quiet but Cliff was a city boy and something wasn't as charmed by the stillness of the country as his wife's cousin..

"You guys should be careful when you're comin out that way. There ain't no lights or anything." Mark nodded and took a sip from his cup of punch. "It's *real* dark."

"Oooh...and spooky, too!" Libby leaned forward and turned her attention to Cliff. "We live right up the road from the

Warlock's Grave. Has BB ever told you about the Warlock's Grave?"

"No," Cliff cast a sidelong glance at Brooke. *BB?* He smiled crookedly, "BB sure hasn't."

Brooke rolled her eyes at him. "It's just a story the kids around talk about." She turned to Libby. "Jeez, you guys moved all the way out *there*?" She shook her head. "That really is the boonies."

"I know it is, but I love it." Libby nodded, her tall, teased bangs swaying back and forth. "But back to the Warlock's Grave. Cliff, there's a little graveyard off the side of the road, not even a mile up from our new house. It's very old; in fact I think it's a historical site. Anyway in the very back of the cemetery, near where the fence meets the woods, there's a grave back by itself away from the other stones."

"Would this be 'The Warlock's Grave'?" Cliff asked.

"Yeah. The name on the stone is worn away though everybody thinks it says David something. But the birth and death dates you can read."

There was a space of seconds where the room was quiet. Everyone was listening along with Cliff even though they all knew this story well.

Libby surveyed her audience with a grin and continued. "Born October 31st 1781, died October 31st, 1906." She paused for a heartbeat or two to let the information sink in and then went on. "Underneath that it says, 'May He never wake'."

Cliff felt an unexpected chill slip down his neck and along the backs of his arms. He mentally calculated the age that the dates on the supposed gravestone suggested. Then Brooke was standing behind him, her hands resting on his shoulders.

She picked up the thread of the story, speaking in a low, breathy voice. "At some point people started saying it was a Warlock that was buried there and that his ghost haunted the cemetery and the woods. People didn't like driving past there at night and sometimes said they could see a tall, white figure standing at the fence watching them as they passed by."

"Wow." Cliff leaned back in his chair. "Maybe we should've stayed at the Motel 6 instead." He chuckled and the spell was broken. Brooke and Libby burst into giggles and Libby's two little boys Dylan and Garrett followed suit. Aunt Mindy smiled broadly and asked if anyone wanted some pumpkin pie and several of the older aunts and uncles raised their hands to show they did indeed want some pie.

Mark sat quietly, looking out the window into the gathering dark. "Damn. It's startin to snow again," he said it out loud, but no one was listening to him.

Shortly after five o'clock, the clouds had decided to invite some of their own friends and family over for Thanksgiving and the sky had been trapped somewhere above their fat, shadowy bodies. The lovely shower of white that had floated to earth so gracefully earlier had become a swirling haze. The local weathermen all agreed this was going to be a record breaking blizzard; maybe the worst since the big storm of '65. These newscasters advised that people stay off of the roads, especially in the rural areas and to batten down for the night.

Around eight-twenty, though, the sky had managed to push its way back past the clouds, letting the full moon sweep the ground like a searchlight. The snow slowed, but did not stop altogether and it seemed that this might be the time for anyone visiting family to make their way back home. Cliff and Brooke bid everyone who had lingered at Aunt Mindy's a goodnight and a happy Thanksgiving and said they were going to make a run for Libby and Mark's. Libby and Mark, themselves un-fazed by the insolent weather had left a while earlier to visit with Mark's family for a bit.

Cliff and Brooke had driven through the main center of town and, after a few twists and turns, finally wound their way onto the country road that led to Libby and Mark's new house.

They drove for what felt like a long time, and the landscape began to feel desolate, at least by town standards.

As far as other houses, they had only passed two in the last ten minutes and these looked dark and not well kept; maybe even abandoned. The scenery was pretty though and Cliff watched it go by with vague interest. On one side of the road the ground climbed up a gentle rocky slope. Short, stout pine trees grew in sparse little patches near the bottom, giving way to their taller cousins as they marched up and away. On the other side lay winter-barren fields, the husks of their harvest stamped flat by the cruel weather of late November. These fields sprawled from the edge of the road until they gave way to dense woods, now denuded of leaves and pointing to the sky with skeleton-finger branches. A sparkling blanket of snow covered over the fields marred only by the sporadic tracks of animals that had passed by.

"Oh my God I'm so *full*. I'm not sure I can stay awake." Cliff took one last drag on his cigarette. He opened his window enough to shove the butt through. A whistling blast of cold air slipped in and bit at his fingers as the cast off stub flew off into the darkness behind them.

Brooke grinned. "Yeah, I feel like *I'm* the stuffed turkey"

It was very cozy inside the car. The heater blew warm air at them as Nat King Cole sang the song about the chestnuts. Still, Brooke was driving cautiously. The road seemed to have been hastily plowed a couple of hours earlier but it was still slick with moisture and a stiff wind was blowing skirls of snow everywhere. "I kind of wish I'd known they were going to Mark's Mom's house to eat again after Aunt Mindy's; we might've just stayed there."

"Well they don't ever tell anybody anything. They just sort of come and go as they please, don't they?" Cliff definitely wished they had opted to stay at Aunt Mindy's house. They could be playing euchre with Brad right now, or in their room, fooling around quietly. Instead, here they were feeling their way along this slippery byway trying to find a house they'd never been to before to stay with people who he actually found slightly annoying.

Earlier in the day it had seemed like a nice idea; getting some quality time with the out-of-town family, maybe playing games or watching a movie. However, after having stuffed themselves full of a pilgrim's feast at noon, scrounging for scraps and snacks all day and then eating again at dinner-time, both Brooke and Cliff were uncomfortable with their pants buttoned.

"I'm sorry." Brooke sighed.

Cliff reached out a hand and put it on Brooke's leg. "Eh, it's not your fault. They're the ones that—holy shit, what is *that*?" He sat straight up in his seat, putting both of his hands on the dashboard.

"What's what?" Brooke's eyes didn't leave the road ahead of her.

"Slow down, slow down. You don't *see* that?"

"Well I *am* trying to watch the road so that we don't die."

"Seriously, slow down and look over here." Cliff pointed out of his corner of the windshield and rolled his window down all the way letting in a sheet of cold air that crawled down the collar of his shirt making him shiver. "Jesus *Christ!*"

Brooke slowed them to a crawl and looked out the windshield between the swishing wipers where Cliff was pointing. A good distance down the road, silhouetted against the blank-paper white of the snowfall was a large (*very large*) someone or *something* standing at the side of the road. It was maybe two miles further down but clearly visible. It was motionless at the moment.

"That is one really tall guy." Cliff had his head out the window. They were barely moving now as Brooke pulled off the gas and eased on the brake. He could feel the softly frozen crust of snow crunching under the tires as they crawled along the road. He squinted his eyes and cupped his hand over his brow to keep errant flakes out of his face. "What's he doing out there?" He shook his head. "Damn, that guy's gotta be as tall as our living room ceiling."

"Clifford, I think it's just an optical illusion. Nobody's that tall." Brooke smiled, even as she continued to study the impossible figure that hulked well beyond the current reach of their headlights. The idea that a person of that size would be out here walking the deserted backwaters in a blizzard on Thanksgiving at this time of night was funny (though somewhat creepy, she had to admit). *A man as tall as that would be one of those, what do you call them, medical marvels. That or he'd be working in a cheap carnival sideshow.* "I mean, he probably is very tall, *normal* tall, and then the distance plus the weird lighting with the snow makes him look like a giant."

Brooke was still smiling but it suddenly felt wrong on her face. Something about the word, *giant*, soured as it came out of her mouth. It occurred to her that she was trying to convince herself as much as Cliff that the man's size was just a trick of the light. All at once the idea of a man that tall *(Nine feet tall? Ten? In that ballpark for sure.)* standing silent and still in the ankle-deep snow at the roadside was no longer funny in a creepy way. It was creepy in an upsetting way. In fact, when she repeated the thought in her head (*the idea that a person of that size would be out here walking the deserted backwaters in a blizzard on Thanksgiving at this time of night...*) a crop of goosebumps dappled her flesh and the hair on her arms stood up.

"Yeah, I don't know, sweetie." Cliff did not turn to look at her but was still peering out the window and up the road, his eyes slitted against the snow.

It was starting to come down again with confidence. White dots came spilling in through Cliff's window on currents of icy air. On the radio, Nat King Cole had given way to Elvis. When Elvis was done trilling through "Blue Christmas" a commercial for Wooley's Carpet Depot (*Where the discount train always makes a stop!*) took over and Cliff reached forward and clicked it off.

"It looks pretty goddamn big to me. And I think it's moving." He couldn't be sure because visibility had been greatly reduced by the revived storm but it looked like the very tall (*man?*) shape ahead of them had turned slightly towards them.

As if maybe it was turning to face them; to look at them the way they were looking at (*it*) him.

Something about the way Brooke had called the dark figure a giant had unsettled Cliff. It was a silly word really, a fairy-tale word. *Giant*. Might as well say *troll* or *ogre*. It made him nervous though; in fact, it had made his heart sink as if some dire pronouncement had just been passed down upon them. It seemed to be a very dramatic reaction to have over a tall man taking a walk, maybe hitch-hiking. He chided himself for being so childish. *That stupid Warlock story*, he thought. *Can't believe that worked on you. Idiot.*

The car was now inching along at barely ten miles an hour as Brooke lightly tapped the gas every few seconds to keep them moving. She and Cliff had become so transfixed by the thing in the snow that it never occurred to them that their diminished speed might cause a serious collision with someone moving fast coming up behind them. Of course, they hadn't seen another car in either direction since they'd pulled onto this road so the idea would not have carried much weight even if they'd thought of it.

Despite their slow progress they were getting ever closer to the thing in the snow. They were now close enough to it to tell that it appeared to be wearing a fur coat. It was wrapped in a churning chrysalis of snow, and still unlit by their headlights, but both of them (and without speaking the fact out loud) had the impression of a shaggy, wind-blown outline.

"Are there bears out here?" Brooke asked suddenly.

"Well," Cliff paused and licked his lips, contemplating, "I mean, I don't know really. I didn't think so. I guess it *could* be a bear. I don't know how long they can stand up on two legs like that, though."

"But it could be a bear you think?"

"That would be one huge-ass bear, but yeah, maybe." There was a long pause. "I really don't think it's a guy anymore, do you?" Cliff pulled his head back in the window and glanced at Brooke.

"I mean some kind of animal. It's some kind of---*Whoa, what* is *that?* Brooke's nose wrinkled as a foul smell climbed its way into the car through Cliff's open window. It was a smell that reminded her of rotting garbage. It was a hot, wild smell. "Ew God, that's awful." Her voice sounded as if she'd suddenly come down with a bad cold.

Cliff's face tried to collapse in on itself as he recoiled from the smell. It crept up his nostrils and down his throat and it was burning his eyes a little making it hard to focus. He wondered if it was that thing out there that smelled like that. *It smells like a duffel bag full of dead cats dipped in a dirty grease-trap and dragged through a pool of piss*. He didn't know how a thing could carry that odor and still live with itself. *It must not have a nose*.

All of a sudden, Cliff did not want to drive past the rotten smelling (*giant*) whatever-it-was. He didn't want to see it up close. He was getting a very bad vibe and no longer cared what it was or wasn't. There was something very *un-right* about that stinking, hulking form that pushed Cliff well beyond the creeps, and he didn't care if that was silly or irrational.

He realized that his heart was pounding in his chest and that he was getting scared. He decided to ask Brooke to do an immediate u-turn in the middle of the road. He wanted her to drive as fast as she could away from whatever that was slouching huge and hunched (and as they got closer there was no longer any doubt that it *was* as tall as they had initially thought) at the edge of the field.

That's when their headlights finally washed over it and reflected back at them from its enormous silver eyes. It turned its shaggy head and shoulders to look right at Cliff.

It was definitely *not* a bear.

Suddenly it seemed as if time was speeding up and slowing down simultaneously. When it turned its face into the light, they saw it very clearly despite the screen of falling snow. Beneath those outrageous shining eyes were a flat, leathery nose and a jutting lower jaw.

Cliff's eyes weren't sharp enough to pick it up, but Brooke, who had perfect vision, thought she could see long teeth or tusks thrusting out from that jaw over the thing's—what—upper lip?

Moonlight glinted off of them. They looked sharp. Brooke was able to confirm that it was covered in long, thick, dark hair and that it had slumped shoulders and huge arms ending in hands that hung down almost below its knees. Not paws. *Hands*. Hands that were tipped with very dangerous-looking, thorny nails (or claws, Brooke wasn't sure what the proper term would be). They looked like they were made for opening up the bellies of elk or moose (*or people*) and spilling out blood and steaming ropes of guts upon the cold ground below.

"Cliff what *is* it?" Brooke's hands were clenched around the steering wheel, the skin pulled tight around her knuckles, threatening to split. Her voice didn't sound panicked yet, but the concern in it was heading in that direction.

Cliff didn't know what it was. So far it was still just standing there, watching them but he could not credit what he was seeing. He knew it wasn't a bear and he knew it wasn't a man. After those possibilities he ran out of ideas. It really wasn't like anything. He *did* know he didn't want to get even one inch closer to whatever it was.

"I think we should turn around." Cliff began pushing himself back against his seat. That smell was even stronger. It felt like they were being smothered in a jacket made of stink. "Brooke. Turn the fuck around."

Brooke nodded curtly, not needing to be told again. She pressed the gas and yanked the wheel to the left. She had no idea that her eyes were squeezed tightly shut as she tried to turn them around. She didn't want to see the (*monster*) mystery creature any more. She had jumped ahead from growing fear to blossoming terror.

As she tried to turn, the front left tire of the car hit a slick spot on the road and Brooke's evasive move became a shimmying fishtail. "Shit!" She screamed. "Shit! Shit! Shit!"

The car was threatening to toss itself off of the road. The front end swung to and fro, the wheel was steering Brooke instead of the other way around. She fought for control, trying to turn against the fishtail but she only succeeded in making it more hectic.

For a moment, Cliff forgot about his fear of the thing outside and thought only of hitting one of the trees lining the roadside. He slid over towards Brooke till he was pressed up against her side. He reached out and grabbed the wheel. "Hit the brakes!"

As Cliff grabbed the wheel, Brooke let her hands fly away from it and shoved her foot down onto the brake as hard as she could. The front end jerked and Cliff pulled the wheel hard to the right as Brooke pressed the brake pedal. The back end swung sharply to the left, tires screeching, snow flying up from beneath the back wheels and the car came to a rough, stuttering halt.

After taking a few ragged breaths Cliff realized that they'd stopped and scooted back to his seat. He leaned his head against the head-rest and draped his hand across his eyes. "Oh my God that was something. I mean..." And then he remembered the creature. In a frenzy of flailing arms and legs, Cliff spun around in his seat to look out the back windshield.

The car had finished at a point past where the open field ended and small plots of trees and brush made their way up to the gravelly shoulder. The trees were tall and thin and reached their branches out and over the road. Sticker-bushes and brambles, naked of foliage, crouched amongst the trunks like the bones of small animals.

From this spot, however, the long white field, glowing with moonlight, was still visible in its entirety and Cliff saw that the gigantic, dark shape had shambled out into the road and was heading towards them. It pulled itself along in a disconcerting, loose-boned shuffle, its knees bent, its arms reaching out for them. Its eyes gleamed like stainless steel, and Cliff watched, hypnotized, for several seconds as it dragged itself after them. Then its lower jaw dropped open like a trap-door full of upward thrusting teeth and it screamed.

The sound filled the cold autumn air and made it even colder. It crawled under every tiny pebble and burrowed into every knot-hole in every tree. Even the falling snow seemed to pause as if it were chilled by such a sound. It pounded icicles through

Cliff's ears and somehow down into the roots of his teeth. He grimaced, tears forming at the corners of his eyes and spilling down over his cheeks. He had never heard anything like it.

With a jerk of his head Cliff shook off his paralysis. He turned to Brooke. She was also staring out the back window; mouth hung open, eyes wide. Her expression was that of a little girl who had just caught Santa Claus stealing presents rather than leaving them.

"Brooke." Cliff turned, grabbed her arm and tugged on it. "Hey. Hey, come on, babe, we've gotta go." He didn't know he was shouting.

Brooke closed her mouth, turned back in her seat hurriedly and hit the gas. As the car leapt forward into the shadows beneath the overhanging trees, Cliff, against his better judgment, looked out the back window again. A small hiss of air escaped his pursed lips. The thing on the road had reached the spot where the car had just been and was still shambling after them.

It was only a few yards behind them and Cliff got a really good look at it. Its fur was thick and matted, long in some spots and much shorter and courser in others. Heavy, powerful-looking muscles flexed under the dark hair as it moved. Cliff knew that those arms could rip a man to shreds with very little effort. But it was those other-worldly eyes that Cliff kept coming back to; huge ovals with no visible pupils or irises. Just protuberant, reflective silver orbs; motionless and expressionless. Nothing had eyes like that and he couldn't look away.

"Hey, turn around!" Brooke tapped Cliff's hip. "You've got to help me look for Libby's house." Her voice was shaky.

"Jesus, Brooke, it's following us." Cliff still knelt on his seat facing the back of the car. "*Chasing* us."

"Okay, Cliff, but we need to get to Libby's. They'll wonder where we are."

Cliff finally tore his gaze from the back windshield and looked at his wife. "Are you crazy? We're not stopping." He turned back to look at it again, but they'd pulled too far ahead for him to see it clearly anymore. He finally turned around and sat in his seat. He pulled a cigarette out of the pack sitting on

177

the center console, stuck it between his lips and pushed the cars lighter into its slot.

Tall trees lined both sides of the road now, forming a dark archway. Underneath this canopy the snow wasn't able to fall as thickly. There hadn't been a streetlight or a house for miles. "Call them and tell them they should take the boys back to Aunt Mindy's. Tell them..." The lighter popped out, fully charged and Cliff lit up. He took a long drag, opened his window a crack, and exhaled getting ready to finish his thought.

"Tell them what Cliff?" Brooke barked a harsh little laugh. "What should I tell them?"

She realized that she was rocketing along at what was becoming an unsafe speed. She eased on the brake a little (*don't want to slow down* too *much*) as a leaning, yellow sign came up on the right warning of a bend ahead. "Should I tell them we just saw a monster and that it's chasing us?" As if hearing itself being mentioned, the creature let out another blood-freezing scream from somewhere in the darkness behind them. Both Cliff and Brooke winced as if they'd been struck.

They rounded the bend in the road and the headlights picked out what seemed to be some kind of garbage dump on the left hand side of the road. Before they flew past, Brooke noted a rusted out car, broken chairs, a lot of crumbled cement and other debris littering the lot, partially hidden by the shadows. It was the closest thing to a house they'd seen for a long time.

"Yeah, I think maybe you should. It might follow us straight to them."

"Mmm-hmm. Okay." Brooke felt a little hysterical. She took one hand off the steering wheel and mimed holding a telephone receiver to her ear. "Hey, Libby, it's Brooke. Yeah, um, just wanted to let you know that me and Cliff just saw Bigfoot and he's on his way to your house to eat us all up. Yeah. Oh, you *invited* him for *Thanksgiving*? Oh well that's fine then. Bye." She put her hand back on the wheel. "Like that?"

"No, not like that, smartass." Cliff giggled shrilly. He was feeling a bit hysterical himself. "They wouldn't have invited him, dummy. There wouldn't be enough turkey."

Brooke smiled despite her fear. In a moment they were both cracking up and a moment after that they were laughing uncontrollably. She stopped the car in the middle of the road to let the delirious wave of terror-fueled hilarity wash over them and pass. Once they were stopped and sitting motionless there in the dark, the mood sobered quickly. Their laughter trickled to a series of hiccups and sighs until there was nothing left. Brooke's eyes searched the rearview mirror for signs of anything coming up the road behind them. Cliff finished his cigarette and dropped it out the window.

"So you're right." Cliff rubbed his hand across his mouth as he considered their situation. "We can't tell them out and out like that." He shook his head and looked at Brooke with one eyebrow raised. "Have I ever told you that I fucking *hate* your hometown?"

"This is *barely* my hometown. A couple more miles and we're in Griffithstown. I can't imagine why they would move all the way out here."

"Probably because monsters and ghost-warlocks really bring down the property value." Cliff said it to be amusing but the statement fell flat. It felt too close to true to be funny.

"Get my phone out of my purse." Brooke checked the mirror again. She was starting to get a little nervous. She knew they'd put some distance between themselves and that thing and they'd only been sitting for a minute; but it felt like a long time to her. She expected the creature to come crashing out of the woods at the road-side at any moment.

Cliff reached down between his feet to where Brooke stowed her purse and reached his hand into it. He fished around for a moment, feeling past eyeliner pencils, tampons and scraps of paper till his fingers discovered her phone. "What do you want to tell them?" He pulled it out and flipped it open. With his thumb he began pushing buttons, searching her contacts list.

"Well," Brooke said, coming up with an idea on the spot, "Let's say that there was some crazy guy with a gun who ran out on the road and started shooting at us. We'll say he started chasing us down the road and that he might be headed their way. How's that?"

"Yeah, that'll work." Cliff studied the screen of Brooke's phone with squinted eyes, his face glowing blue in the light it cast. "Jeez, where is she in here?"

"She's under LB. Here, hand it to me." As Brooke started to reach for the phone the yowling scream of their pursuer suddenly filled the night again. It didn't sound very far off. Brooke gasped, her face twisting into a mask of terror. Her arms pebbled into gooseflesh and she felt cold all over. "Cliff?"

"Shit!" Cliff shot a look out the back window and then turned back to the front. "You just drive, I'll call them."

Brooke turned the key in the ignition, secretly believing that it would cough, wheeze and refuse to start but it turned over immediately and a second later they were on their way. As they sped off down the tree-shadowed blacktop another shriek pierced the dark. It sounded further away now, but not far enough for Brooke to feel safe.

Cliff found Libby's number in Brooke's contact list and pressed the "send" button. He held the phone up to his ear and frowned. "Hey, Libby, it's Cliff. Me and Brooke were on our way to your house when we ran into...well, into some trouble. We think you guys should take the kids and head back to Aunt Mindy's. We'll explain when we meet up there. It's pretty urgent so give us a call back when you get this." He pressed "end" and rested the phone against his thigh. "Voice mail."

"Maybe they're still at Mark's Mom's house."

As they sped past, the trees on the right-hand side of the road dropped back, letting the moonlight fall through once again, brightening the snow-frosted scenery. Lying, grey and ominous in this illuminated gap, was a cemetery. It looked like a very old cemetery. They caught a momentary glimpse of flat, weathered stones jutting from the ground like crooked, rotting teeth. The monuments were penned in by a waist-high, wrought-iron fence.

"Libby said their house was the next thing after the cemetery. Brooke started slowing the car even though she wanted nothing more than to keep going till they found a way off of this road and out of town. "On the right. Help me look for it."

"Hey, maybe we'll score a two-fer and the Warlock'll come out and chase us too. That would be awesome." Cliff was trying the phone again. When he got Libby's voicemail once more he snapped the phone shut with irritation. "They better be home and just ignoring our calls." He shook his head. "Otherwise, even if it hadn't been for all of this going on," he flapped his hand in the air to indicate their situation, "we still would've gotten all the way out here and just been sitting on our asses." Cliff slid open Brooke's phone one more time and hit "send" again.

After they had passed the cemetery (*no white figures at the fence; thank God for small favors*) the trees had come creeping back up to the road bringing a shroud of darkness with them. Despite there being no leaves on them the trees were very stingy with the amount of light they let through. Because of this veil of gloom Brooke almost drove past Libby and Mark's house. It was set a good fifty yards back off the road and was walled in by trees and grasping shrubbery. An uneven, gravel driveway led up and around to the back of the house. Brooke turned onto this and followed it, the car crunching and rocking over the stones.

From what Cliff and Brooke could see, the house was as dark inside as the yard was outside. It was a one-story brick box with a tired-looking roof. Jutting out from the front door was a crooked walk, slick with freshly fallen snow. There were two large windows at the front of the house on either side of the tin storm door. These probably looked in on the living room. Both had screens that were riddled with rips and tears. The leaf-clogged gutter sagged halfway across its length. The entire house looked like an old woman sadly remembering what it was like to be pretty. Only the small, evergreen bushes that sprouted along the front of the house seemed healthy; aside from these the whole place felt defeated.

Brooke pulled the car up to where the front walk curved around to meet the driveway and stopped. There was no way to see through the windows because the curtains were drawn but no light seemed to glow behind them. Brooke and Cliff sat silently for a few moments, considering what to do next.

Cliff sighed. "Alright. Now what?"

Brooke bit her lower lip pensively. "Well, should we go up and knock? See if they're in there?"

"I'd really rather not get out of the car if possible." Cliff's tone was matter-of-fact but his eyes looked haunted.

Brooke looked back up at the house, and it seemed to look right back at her with mute curiosity. It was dark, but it didn't feel *empty*. She had never had felt this way about a house before. The entire situation had just come upon them so quickly that she hadn't even had time to stop and reflect on the weirdness of it all.

Brooke had a feeling that once they were back in the welcoming warmth of Aunt Mindy's house, surrounded by reassuring light and behind locked doors, she might not even believe this story herself. That was a thought for later, though. Right now she needed to figure out if they were going to step out of their vehicle and approach the house. They would be much more vulnerable outside. The idea filled her with fluttering moth's-wings of anxiety.

"Hold on," Brooke suddenly had an idea, "Let's call Aunt Mindy. Maybe she knows where they're at."

Cliff nodded his head. "That's a great idea." He enthusiastically supported this as a substitute for getting out of the car and going up to the door. He held the phone out to Brooke. "You do it."

Brooke took the phone from him, scrolling through her recent calls till she found Aunt Mindy's number. She sent the call and held the phone up to her ear, pulling her long hair back behind her neck with her other hand. A moment later she looked to Cliff, smiled and made a thumbs-up sign. Aunt Mindy had answered.

"Hey, Aunt Mindy. No. No, not yet, hey listen, do you know if Libby and Mark are still at his Mom's house?" She listened, her smile fading. "Uh-huh. Well because we're at their house and they're not here." Suddenly, something occurred to

Brooke that made her feel instantly better. "Wait, their truck's not here. They must be out. Libby just wasn't…what? They do?" Cliff watched her expression fall again. "They did?" She heaved a heavy sigh. "Okay, well we'll check. Yeah, you try to call her too, okay? Alright. Bye." She set the phone on the dashboard. She looked up at the house.

Cliff waited for her to say something. He let ten seconds of silence go by before he spoke. "So? What? What'd Aunt Mindy say? I hadn't even thought of their car not being here. Does she know where they're at?"

"They park up around the back of the house. They go in through the kitchen door."

"Right. Okay."

"They called her ten minutes after we left to let her know they were home and to see if we were still there. They'd just put the kids to bed. They were worried we might not be able to find the place."

"Huh." Cliff pondered this trying to make sense of it. He was feeling very tired and didn't think his brain was firing on all cylinders. He picked up Brooke's phone off the dashboard and looked at the clock. Eight forty-two. It hadn't even been fifteen minutes since their drive had slipped into twilight-zone territory. It felt like it had been at least an hour. "So did they *all* decide to go to bed or something? Why aren't the lights on?"

"Cliff I'm scared." She was still staring out the window, her hands resting loosely on the steering wheel, her fingers tapping at it nervously. "I think we need to go around back and see if their car's there."

"Right. What if it's not?"

"We leave them a note on the back door telling them to come straight to Aunt Mindy's."

"Why don't you just text her?"

"I'll do that too ,but she's not answering her phone. Maybe its dead or she has the ringer off. We need to leave a note just in case."

"Alright. And what if the truck *is* there?"

183

Brooke looked at him, her eyes wide and shining. "I don't know. Then we knock I guess."

Cliff looked at the naked fear on his wife's face and felt a surge of love and protectiveness sweep over him. He knew that Brooke's concern was now not just for her own safety but for that of her family. Being chased by that horrible thing (which he still wasn't ready to deal with yet) had shaken them both into a daze of deep paranoia. He knew she was imagining all kinds of terrible things that could have befallen Libby, Mark and the boys. Cliff, however, wasn't quite to that level of worry yet. He still believed that they probably just weren't home, but of course they weren't his blood relatives. He hadn't grown up with them. It wasn't the same thing for him. .

"Alright, Brooke. Here." He picked Brooke's purse up from the floor and handed it to her. "Find a pen and something to write on."

Brooke turned the interior light on and opened her purse. She pulled out an old grocery receipt and set it on the dashboard. "What are we doing?" She asked as she pulled a pen out.

"Write your note. Just, 'come back to Aunt Mindy's immediately!' and sign it. I'm going to take it and go around back. If the car isn't there I'm gonna put the note somewhere near the door where they'll see it."

He looked out the passenger window into the dark outside. Anything could be out there watching; anything at all. And now he'd always wonder what kinds of anythings *were* out there, slouching and slithering through the shadows where people rarely go. He turned back to Brooke. "And if their truck does happen to be there then I'll go up and pound on the door a couple of times. If no lights come on then we're booking it the hell out of here back to Aunt Mindy's and we can all talk about where to go from there."

"But it's windy out. What if the note won't stay or blows away?"

"Well, Brooke...I mean, it's the best we can do. You know?" Cliff knew that she was right; that the note probably wouldn't stay but he needed to feel like they'd at least tried and he knew for a certainty she needed to know it, too. "What else can we really do? I don't wanna stick around out here. That thing could be anywhere. It could still be chasing us."

Brooke looked out into the night, her eyes roving wildly from left to right and back again. "Okay. Do it fast then." She leaned forward, holding the receipt against the center of the steering wheel and wrote the note. "Here," she handed the note to Cliff, "I love you." She wished bitterly that the blizzard had kept them from leaving Aunt Mindy's.

Cliff took the note from her, leaned forward and planted a quick kiss on the corner of her mouth. "Love you too. I'll be right back."

Cliff opened the passenger door and stepped out onto the drive. The sound of gravel beneath his feet seemed very loud to his ears. It was grave-quiet out here. He realized they hadn't been passed by a single car since they turned onto this god-forsaken road. The only sound was the wind sighing through the trees making the branches clatter together like chattery teeth. *God, I fucking* hate *the country*, he thought as he walked up the drive towards the house. *Libby and Mark must be the only idiots dumb enough to live out here.* He knew that was an un-generous thought to have and he instantly felt bad about it. Still, it was unnerving, even without the added complication of monsters, how alone they seemed to be.

Cliff walked up to the front corner of the house and passed around to the side. His chest tightened and his breathing hastened. He didn't feel alone up close to the dirty bricks under the shadow of the overhanging eaves. The urge to turn around and see if something was behind him crept up his neck to the base of his skull but Cliff resisted it. He wasn't quite ready to give in to paranoia just yet. If something *was* stalking along behind him he knew Brooke would lay on the horn and scream. Neverthe-less it was an uncomfortable feeling. Cliff was anxious to be done with this and hurried on around back.

Cliff turned the corner and frowned. *Well, shit. This is bad,* he thought. Libby and Mark's old Jeep Cherokee sat in the driveway as silent and dark as everything else around the place.

Worse; he could see the back door of the house laying discarded in the snow next to the truck. It had been violently torn off its hinges. Splintered wood from the door frame hung crazily in the empty space where the door had been. Pieces of lath lay on and around the short back steps that led up to the kitchen. *Oh fuck me, this is* really *bad.* He took a timid step towards the yawning doorway and then another

Cliff knew he should run in and see if anyone needed help. He knew he should see if anyone was (*still alive*) hurt, but his instincts were urging him not to. Each step he took towards the house was more difficult than the last. It felt like he was trying to wade through a river of caramel. Sweat had crept up beneath his hair line in spite of cold breeze that gnawed at him. He was grimacing as if he were in great pain. It felt as if the house was pushing against him, willing him away.

Finally, Cliff reached the steps up to the back door. The damage to the frame was immense. Ugly splinters of bright wood stuck out at crazy angles and he could see the way the metal hinges had twisted and buckled where the door had been yanked free. He knew what had been here. He *knew* it. *How long ago, though? Was it before he and Brooke had seen it standing at the side of the road? Was it after? Had it run ahead of them and then waited here? Was it still waiting within?*

"Oh Jesus." Cliff leaned against the outer wall for a moment. He felt like he might throw up. He breathed deeply a few times, and when he was sure he wasn't going to be sick, Cliff stood up and crept into the silent kitchen.

A strip of moonlight fell through the doorway behind him and lit up a sliver of the kitchen but it was very dark ahead. Snow blew in and clung gently to Cliff's back and shoulders. It had piled up a couple of inches on the floor. The door had been off for awhile it seemed. Cliff wondered if he should call out. He didn't want to. He felt like an intruder. He moved along very slowly and very deliberately, his shoes crunching in the snow on the floor. His body was tensed like a spring. His arms were held out to the sides and his knees were bent. With great reticence Cliff stepped out of the triangle of light that the moon had provided and crept into the shadows. His eyes began to adjust immediately to the gloom and he was able to discern the shapes of furniture out in the living room beyond.

"H-Hey," Cliff whispered hoarsely. "Hey. Is anybody here?" It took an amazing effort for Cliff to open his mouth and speak, even at such a low volume. He knew it should be done though. What good would it be to come into the kitchen, say nothing, turn around and leave?

He moved another few inches into the deepening shadows. "Libby? Mark?" He began to take another step when a sound, loud and strident shattered the stillness. Cliff cried out in surprise and threw his hands up in front of his face. The sound continued for another couple of seconds and then stopped. Cliff's heart was pounding in his chest and his breath was coming hard and fast but he realized it was an electronic sound. In fact, it was a sound he recognized. He'd heard it several times earlier in the day. It was the opening theme from "Sex and the City". It was Libby's text sound. It had come from somewhere very close to him. Cliff's heart kept beating hard as he moved through the kitchen trying to pinpoint where it had come from.

Cliff came around to the side near the sink and was feeling his way along the counter when he stumbled over something lying on the floor in front of him. He nearly fell to the ground, but grabbed on to the edge of the counter (loudly knocking over what sounded like a box of cereal) and managed to keep his feet. He turned, leaned down, and peered at what it was he'd tripped over.

It was Libby's ankle. She was laying facedown on the floor. Cliff's mouth dropped open as he took in the shape of her. In the gloom it was tough to make out details but he thought that her right arm was missing. As his eyes continued to adjust to the low light, he could tell that whatever she was wearing had been mercilessly shredded and torn. He felt his Thanksgiving dinner begin to rise as he realized that her body had been, too. He turned away from her and vomited loudly. The sound of it splashing against the floor caused him to do it again.

When Cliff finished retching, he stood up and looked around wildly. His breath was coming fast again, tearing his lungs and he felt panic bulging behind his eyes. That's when he heard a sound from somewhere out in the unlit hallway. Every system in his body froze at that moment. His breath caught in his chest and his heart stopped pumping. A deep silence overtook him and he strained with every ounce of his being to listen for anything that disturbed that silence. At first there was nothing, but as his ears adjusted to the quiet the way his eyes had to the dark he thought he could just make out the sound of breathing. Yes, it was a deep, hollow breathing, very slow and deliberate; a heavy, rasping sound. Like someone (*thing*) out there in the dark was trying to be just as quiet as Cliff was.

Cliff took a step back, being careful not to step on Libby. His eyes never left the room ahead of him. Without bothering to whisper he called out. "Mark?"

There was a shuffling sound and then the painful squeal of a floorboard that went on for what seemed like forever as if someone very heavy had just stood up very slowly. Cliff decided that enough was enough. He turned on legs that felt like stiff broomsticks and bolted for the door, praying silently not to fall down.

When Cliff came running around the house and down the drive, Brooke's heart started to pound. Without thinking about it she turned the key in the ignition and started the car. He threw a look back over his shoulder towards the house and then slid along the side of the car to his door. He yanked it open, fell into his seat and slammed it shut again.

"Go!"

"Cliff, what happened? Was the truck...?"

"Go!" he shouted. "Just go."

Brooke threw the car into reverse and backed down the driveway, watching through the rearview mirror. She could hear Cliff next to her breathing hard and wondered what had sent him flying. Now she was more scared than ever. She reached the end of the driveway and backed out onto the road.

"Cliff, I texted Libby. I haven't gotten an answer back yet though."

"And you're not going to." Cliff shut his eyes and rubbed them with his fists. "Come on, we gotta go."

"What do you mean by that?" Brooke turned her head and looked at Cliff. "What happened back there? Is she okay?"

Cliff looked back over his shoulder out the back windshield. "Never mind. We've gotta get out of here. *Now*."

"Not '*never mind*'. You tell me what you saw." Tears formed at the corners of her eyes. *"What happened to Libby?"*

"Drive faster." Cliff said as they pulled away from Mark and Libby's house. He grabbed Brooke's cell phone from the dashboard and opened it up. "We'll talk about it later."

Brooke stepped on the gas and they shot forward. With tears streaming down her cheeks she began to sob. "Fuck you, Cliff. We'll talk about it now." Her eyes flicked from the road to Cliff. "Who're you calling?"

"911."

Brooke grimaced and squeezed her eyes shut, her foot still pressing on the gas. "Oh *Jesus!*" She snuffled back snot and tears and looked at Cliff again. "You tell me what happened!"

Cliff looked up from the phone in his hand to respond but anything he might have said was swept away in a bolt of terror. "Brooke! Look out!" was all he had time to say.

What happened next only took eight seconds.

Brooke looked out the windshield. They were approaching the decrepit old graveyard, bouncing along and still accelerating. If they'd been going just a little faster both she and Cliff would have probably died when the giant black shadow came running out from between the crooked stones. It stepped over the fence and darted out into the road in front of the car. It turned its massive bulk to face them, its silver eyes implacable and flat and it let out one more unspeakable scream that went on and on for an eternity.

Then, the collision.

Dual air-bags deployed. Shattering glass. Screeching tires. Crunching metal. The force of impact like hitting a walking oak tree. A blur of dark hair. Huge arms flailing against the hood. Claws shrieking against steel. The unending scream.

If Brooke would have had time to hit the brakes, either she or Cliff (or maybe both of them) would have been thrown through the windshield. Neither of them had on their seatbelts. As it was, they both slid forward, their heads slamming into the rough nylon of the airbags, and were then bounced back into their seats. Neither of them heard it happen, but both front tires had been blown out.

Then it was over.

A minute went by. Two minutes. Brooke and Cliff didn't move. The car was making a hissing sound, but neither of them noticed. Brooke, in fact, had been knocked unconscious, her head lolling on her neck against her window.

Cliff, meanwhile, began to stir. He moaned and sat up. There was a sharp ache in his right arm. He tried to flex it and cried out as a spasm of pain shot up his arm all the way to the shoulder.

"Oh god*dammi*t!"

Using his left arm, Cliff reached out and grabbed onto Brooke's headrest and pulled himself upright. He squirmed, turning himself in his seat so that he could reach the door-handle with his left hand. His hurt arm got squeezed between his body and his seat and he gritted his teeth against the hot agony in his wrist. He reached out pulled the handle, pushing the door open with his foot. He leaned forward, putting his feet on the ground and gingerly stood up. His whole body was one massive ache. He shuffled around to the front of the car, his previous fear muted by shock.

The damage to the front end of the car was amazing. The hood, grille and bumper were dented inward where they'd hit the creature. It looked like they'd hit a telephone pole. The hood ornament was gone and a plume of steam rose into the air from the crushed radiator. Long, ugly scratches reached from the windshield to the headlights. Cliff saw that the tires had exploded; tread hanging off the rims in rubbery strips. The windshield had a spiderweb of cracks radiating out from the lower right corner where the hood had pushed back into it. Incredibly, the lights were still shining but something was obscuring the one on the driver's side.

Cliff limped around and knelt down. A patch of coarse, dark, hair was matted against the light in a wet, red smear. He reached out to touch it and then thought better of it. There was more hair and more blood on the grille. There was also blood spattered all over the ground turning the white snow almost black. This reminded Cliff of what it was they'd hit. He stood up hastily and spun around. He looked out into the road where the creature should have been laying, dying or (*hopefully*) dead.

The road was empty.

Cliff was confused. The car had slammed into that thing at nearly forty miles an hour. Even if it had only been injured, there was no way it could have managed to drag itself off into the woods that quickly. He took a few uncertain steps forward, searching the road for more blood and hair. He walked as far ahead as the headlights illuminated and found no trace of anything. It appeared that they'd hit an invisible force field. He stood out in the road a moment longer, looking right and then left off into the dark trees. He scanned the old cemetery from which the thing had come running. It was filled with black shadows. It revealed nothing. Cliff wasn't sure how he felt about this turn of events. It was all so far beyond the scope of his understanding that he just shook his head and decided to focus on getting someone out here to help them.

He dragged himself back to the car and gently settled into his seat. He scanned the dashboard for Brooke's phone but it wasn't there. He leaned carefully over, trying not to move his right arm too much. He reached down between his legs and started feeling around the floor at his feet, groaning at the pain in his hurt arm. After a few moments of scrabbling around on the floor mat, his fingers closed over the phone. *Thank God.* Next to him, Brooke was starting to regain consciousness. She was moving her head back and forth and groaning. Cliff thought she was probably going to be okay. He reached out and tenderly stroked her face with the back of his hand. He really loved her.

Cliff held the phone down in front of him and dialed with his thumb. He held it up to his ear and waited for the response.

"911, what is your emergency?"

"Hi. My name is Cliff Morgan and you're not going to believe this."

(*From the December 5th edition of "The Cincinnati Enquirer"*)

Local residents disappear in bizarre missing-persons case- A Cincinnati couple was reported missing last weekend in the city of New Philadelphia, Ohio, two hours southwest of Cleveland. Cliff and Brooke Morgan of Mt. Healthy had been visiting family over Thanksgiving when their black Volkswagen Jetta was discovered wrecked and empty of passengers on Gimlin Avenue, a back country road.

At approximately 9:07 pm, 911 received, what the dispatcher called, "a very strange call for help," from Mr. Morgan. He reported that he and his wife had hit some sort of large, unidentified animal with their car and that they needed assistance. He also reported that there was some problem involving family members that they had been visiting and that an ambulance should be sent as well. When law enforcement and Emergency Services arrived on the scene, they found the battered car but no sign of Mr. or Mrs. Morgan.

Upon investigating the home of Mark and Elizabeth Welker, the family members Mr. Morgan had requested help for, it was discovered that they too were missing along with their two sons: Dylan, age 6 and Garrett, age 4. There were signs of forced entry into the Welker residence as well as signs of a struggle within including blood and torn clothing.

A large-scale search has been mounted by the Tuscarawas County PD and has been widened to include the area surrounding the nearby towns of Eastchurch, Dover and Griffithstown. So far no traces of the missing have turned up. This is not the first time that someone has disappeared on this particular stretch of road.

(*Continued on Page A-11*)

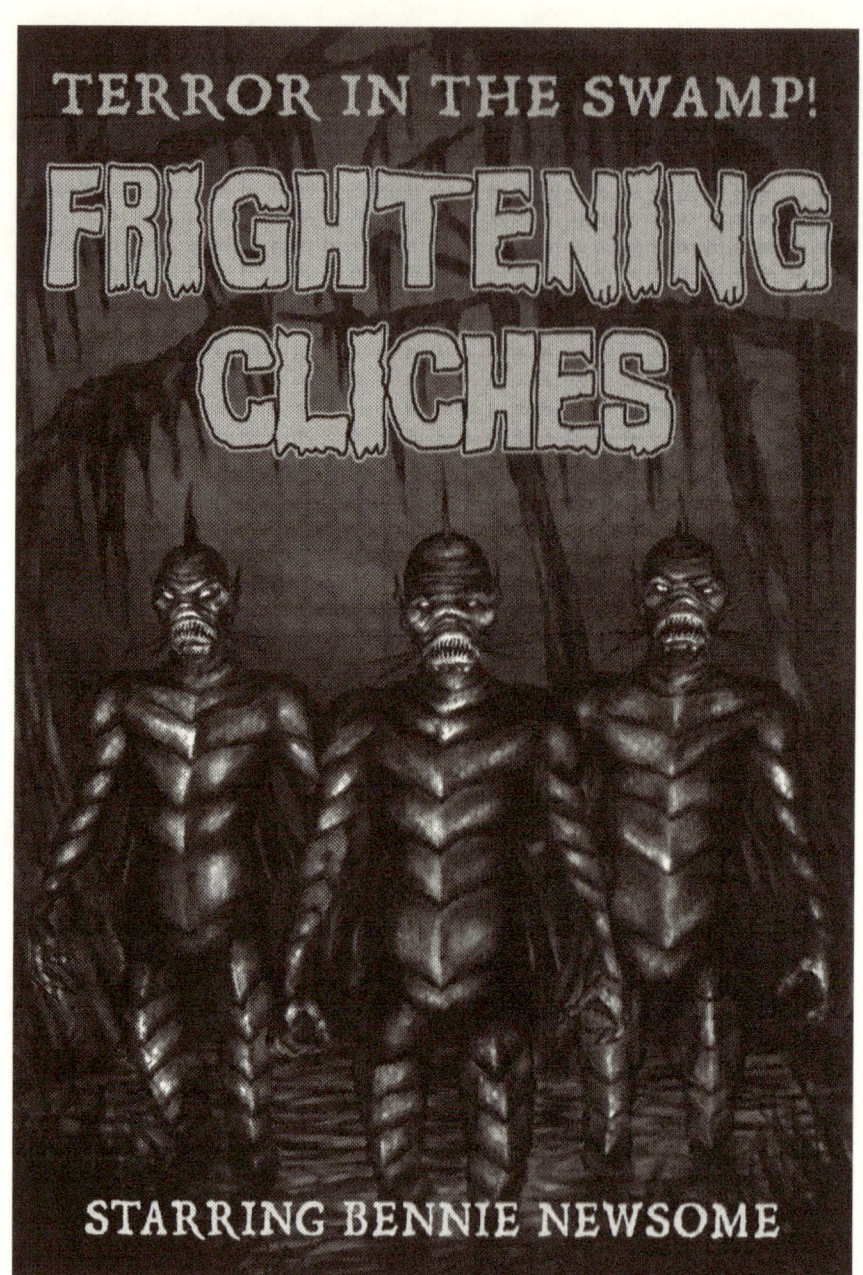

Frightening Cliches
Starring Bennie Newsome

-1-

An unusual noise caused Tonya Devur to sit upright in bed. Beads of sweat caused by the sweltering summer heat began to roll down her face because of her new vertical position. Not only was her face covered in perspiration, but the salty bodily fluid had soaked through her thin night shirt.

At that moment, however, Tonya was not concerned with the uncomfortable dampness. She was more troubled with the sound that had disturbed her restless slumber. The woman's body was rigid. She held her breath to better hear the noises around her.

There was a low whispering sound coming from the whirling, plastic blades of the box fan situated in the open window. Tonya heard the customary, incessant noise that made crickets infamous. And accompanying the insects was the maddening croaking of the native frogs.

None of that is the noise I heard, the woman told herself.

The hoot of an owl sounded somewhere in the distance.

That's not it either.

After a long moment of sitting and listening, Tonya decided that it had to have been her imagination. She was in the process of laying back down when she heard the eerie sound again. It was a slight thump coming from downstairs.

I know I heard it that time! the woman exclaimed as she sat back up. Tonya turned to her right and began shaking her husband from his seemingly hot and uncomfortable sleep.

"Ugh!" Malcolm groaned from both the intense heat and being awakened. "What is it?"

"I heard a noise downstairs!" his wife whispered harshly.

"You didn't hear anything. Go back to bed." Malcolm decided to lead by example by rolling over and closing his eyes.

Tonya shook her husband again before his snores could resume. "I heard a noise from—"

Thump, thump!

The woman gasped then exclaimed, "I heard it again!"

Malcolm sat up and gave his wife an angry, half sleepy-eyed stare. "Well, what do you want me to do? If you did hear something, I don't wanna go and find out what it is! That's how people lose their life! Always trying to investigate!"

"What if it's a burglar?"

Her husband's brown eyes widened as if to say, *what did you think I was talking about?*—then he shrugged his shoulders to emphasize his nonverbal statement. "All the more reason to stay up here! We have a lock on our bedroom door, and if you let the thief take all that he wants, he will most assuredly leave."

Disgusted by her husband's cowardice, Tonya angrily swung her legs over to the side of the bed and located her bedroom slippers. Malcolm ran a hand across his balding head and sighed at his wife's obvious passive-aggressive tactic. "Where are you going?" he asked, knowing full well that she did not plan on going anywhere.

"I'm finna go and see what's making that noise downstairs."

"You ain't going downstairs."

Without saying another word, Tonya rose to her feet and shuffled over to the door. The sound of her slippers sliding on the wooden floor cut through the relative silence. Malcolm let out another defeated sigh before throwing the cover aside and looking for his slippers.

"Get back in bed," the man said. "I'll go and check."

Tonya smiled triumphantly and hurried back to bed. "Thank you, baby!"

Shut the hell up, was what Malcolm happened to be thinking, but he replied, "Yeah, yeah, yeah." The two phrases basically meant the same thing.

Malcolm shuffled over to the door with its peeling paint and undid the lock. By the time he had the door open, he was regretting his decision to buy that house in Louisiana. It seemed like such an excellent choice in the beginning.

-2-

Malcolm Devur was a renowned author who had written several novels and over a hundred short stories. In the beginning, his mind was like a vast well, full of imagination. Combine that with an unmistakable talent for the written word, and you have yourself the recipe for a successful career. At least, that was Malcolm's thought, but he went to the well one day, dropped his bucket in, and came up without a story. The man's source of supposedly endless imagination had dried up.

"What's a creative writer without imagination?" Malcolm asked himself as he slowly strolled down the long, echoing hallway with its creaking floorboards. Lights were steadily being turned on as he walked by light switches—the horror writer was not a fan of the dark.

Malcolm had done all he could to overcome writer's block, but his problem was that everything had been done to death: werewolves, talking dolls, zombies, vampires, ghosts, goblins, demons, and the most notable monster of all...humans. Their story had been told from every angle, which inevitably made them a cliché. The monsters had been written as both villains and heroes, done in every setting imaginable, placed in every situation conceivable, and killed in every way possible. Oh, and outer space! Do not get Malcolm started on the dullness of outer space—the place where undead monsters and their reputations went to die.

Malcolm chuckled to himself and shook his head while descending a set of rickety stairs. To him, a monster going into outer space was like a well-known movie star reduced to doing commercials for a living. Their career was practically over.

Thump, thump, thump!

Malcolm froze in the middle of the staircase when the racket brought him from his contemplations. The unnerving clamor was coming from the kitchen.

He held his breath and struggled to listen over his loud, thudding heart. The sound originating from the kitchen was consistent and forceful, as if someone was beating on the backdoor's window. A panicky soul trying to gain the homeowner's attention perhaps?

But who knocks without pause? the man asked himself. *And if they really wanted me to answer the door, then why not come around to the front and try the doorbell?*

The questions only confused Malcolm more, while causing his already rapidly beating heart to pick up pace. A nervousness overcame him, and his palms began to sweat. For the second time in less than three minutes, Malcolm was wishing that he and his wife were still in their cozy home, back in Alabama.

But noooooo, he thought sarcastically as he continued down the stairs with more caution than before. *You were convinced that you needed a change in scenery to jumpstart your dead imagination. You just had to purchase an old, isolated colonial home near a Louisiana bayou.*

Ironically, Malcolm wrote stories that made people sleep with the light on, but he was an easily frightened man himself. He was afraid of the dark, he couldn't sleep with the closet door open, and he kept the space beneath his bed filled with clutter so no monsters could hide under there. What scared him even more than imaginary creatures that went bump in the night were ridiculously large houses stationed in the middle of nowhere.

When his realtor first mentioned the huge estate, Malcolm thought that the place was just what he needed to get his horrific, creative juices flowing. But after listening to the creepy groans the house made and enduring the sensation of being watched by unseen eyes, Malcolm was ready to abandon his newfound inspiration. It was only his first night in the house and he was ready to pack up his bags and head for the state line.

And now there's someone rapping at my door with a lot of hostility! he fretted. *I don't know how much more my nerves can take!*

SMASH! As if on cue, the sound of shattered glass filled the house.

Malcolm stumbled down the rest of the stairs and purposely fell onto his belly. Someone was actually breaking into his house! "WHO'S THERE?" the man asked in his loudest and burliest voice, hoping to discourage the criminal. "I'M 'BOUT TO WHOOP SOME ASS!"

The only reply he got was the sound of his backdoor lock being disarmed.

Resolute in his decision to scare the intruders away, Malcolm low-crawled across the living room floor, receiving several carpet burns in the process. Like a military soldier, he snaked his way through the living room. His left leg came up, his right elbow went forward and he crawled. Now with his right leg up, and left elbow forward, he crawled.

Despite his apparent bravado, thirty-six-year-old Malcolm was terrified. The man was filled with a strong desire to dash back upstairs and dive under the covers, but contrary to what he told his wife, he believed that the burglar would come seeking the owners of the house. If the intruder was brave enough to break in with people at home, he probably did not have a problem with killing.

Eventually, a frightened Malcolm came to the doorway that connected the kitchen and living room. Still on his belly, the man pressed his body against the wall and peeked around the doorjamb. Moonlight streamed in through the kitchen's sheer curtains and illuminated the outdated room. Malcolm looked past the sink and beyond the table that seated four. The noisy refrigerator was put into his peripheral, allowing his focus to go straight to the open back door. Malcolm was able to clearly see a humanoid form. He heard glass crunch beneath the trespasser's feet as the guy entered his kitchen.

Malcolm quickly removed his head from the doorway. Scared stiff and not knowing what else to do, the man began to make deafening sounds that resembled a great cat. He roared, he screeched, he wailed, and he hissed. *Maybe the burglar will leave if he thinks I have a panther in here,* Malcolm thought frantically. *If he doesn't think I have a panther, then maybe he'll leave if he realizes I'm crazy.*

Instead of hearing the footsteps flee out the backdoor, the individual continued to slowly head toward the living room.

SMASH! More shattering glass, this time from the living room window, caused Malcolm to let out a high-pitched lioness shriek. He turned toward the latest assault and saw three more figures struggling to climb across the broken shards of glass that still remained in the wooden frame.

Malcolm was able to see the new arrivals a lot better than the first, and what he saw nearly caused him to die from fright. At first Malcolm thought his eyes must have been playing tricks on him, but after rubbing his eyeballs and squinting for a moment longer, the man decided that what he saw was real.

-4-

"What's the matter?" Tonya asked when her hysterical husband rushed into the bedroom and slammed the door shut behind him. "I thought I heard a tiger downstairs!" The woman suddenly cowered into the bedcovers and asked, "Did a tiger somehow get into our house?"

"Put some clothes on!" Malcolm shouted as he turned the light on, then hurried over to their shared dresser. His hands trembled with fear as he pulled on the knob of the drawer. Seeing that his Parkinson's disease-like symptoms were slowing him down, Malcolm took a moment to take a deep breath and try to calm his nerves. The man counted backwards from ten, took another cleansing breath, and looked at his hands. They still shook uncontrollably.

Without moving from the bed, Tonya asked, "Why do I need to put clothes on? What's wrong?"

Malcolm turned and looked at his wife as if he had forgotten she was there.

"Baby, what's the matter?"

"Swamp monsters just broke into our house," he said while returning to his raid of the dresser drawer. Malcolm could not believe what he had just told his wife. He, the master of horror fiction, was actually admitting to being under attack by swamp monsters.

I was just talking about how all monsters had basically become clichés, now I'm running from the worst cliché of all. Swamp monsters! They're creatures mentioned in children's tales for goodness sake.

"A swamp monster?" Tonya asked to make sure she was hearing her husband correctly. "Did you say swamp monsters broke into our house?"

"That's exactly what I said!" Malcolm screamed. He was angry at the fact that he had to repeat his farfetched claim. The man snatched a shirt out of his drawer and slammed it shut. "There are at least four swamp monsters downstairs in our living room! Swamp monsters! Green humanoid blobs that drip swamp muck and algae! Swamp monsters!

"I knew I shouldn't have come to Louisiana of all places," Malcolm muttered to himself. "I mean come on! Swamp monsters! Really?"

Instead of showing fear as Malcolm had expected, his wife began to laugh. Tonya was all too familiar with her husband's reputation as a storyteller, but he was really stretching the truth that time. "There's no such thing as a swamp monster," Tonya stated.

Once he had his shirt on, Malcolm went to another drawer to remove a pair of pants. After he had a pair of jeans in his hands, the man came to a halt and asked Tonya to be quiet for a second. He silently indicated that she listen, and his wife reluctantly obeyed.

Thump, squish…thump, squish…thump, squish.

"Do you hear that?" Malcolm asked.

Tonya nodded her head.

"That's the sound of swamp monsters coming for us," he said in a matter of fact tone.

Tonya, who had every right to be skeptical, sat on the bed watching her husband move madly about the room. She had to know if Malcolm was pulling her leg, or not; therefore, the woman resorted to her secret weapon. "Put it on something," she demanded.

Malcolm spun toward his wife and exclaimed, "I'm a best-selling author! Why would I come to you and make up a stupid ass story about swamp men breaking into the house? Don't you think I could come up with something a little more creative than that?"

Tonya stared at her husband with a hurt expression on her face, a pained look that Malcolm was all too familiar with. He knew from experience that her damaged ego would transform her mood into angry defiance at any moment, and an argument was the last thing either of them needed.

"I'm sorry," Malcolm said quickly and with a much calmer demeanor. The man took a deep breath and fought to reign in his out-of-control emotions. "I'm more than a little frightened right now, and you're not helping matters by questioning me. If it makes you feel better, I put it on everything. With my right hand on my heart and left hand toward Heaven, I swear to you that there are swamp things in our house."

Tonya had never seen Malcolm conduct himself so oddly before, and his actions caused her to believe that there was some truth to what he was telling her. Spurred to action, Tonya slid out of bed and dropped to her knees.

"What are you doing?" Malcolm asked.

"Praying," she replied as she took the usual position.

Malcolm let out a frustrated growl and hurried over to his wife. Tonya's solution for everything was to pray. Malcolm was not as religious as his wife, but he entertained her whenever she felt like they were under demonic attack, or being blustered by some evil spirit. But that particular moment was not the time for praying and he told his wife so.

"Now is not the time for praying," Malcolm said as he put a hand under her arm and lifted her up from the floor. Tonya looked at him with another expression that he was also accustomed to seeing. One that said, "blasphemer!"

"Why isn't this the time to pray?" she wanted to know.

"I'll tell you why this isn't the time for prayer," Malcolm said as he threw his wife some clothes to put on. "The Bible says we, meaning it, wrestles not against flesh and blood, but against principalities and powers." He pointed in the direction of the living room and said, "That's flesh and blood downstairs—in a manner of speaking. We're on our own."

Malcolm was not a religious man, but he learned a long time ago that the easiest way to control a Christian woman is to know the Bible. Tonya would tell him he was wrong all day long, but she wouldn't dare refute words recited from her holy book.

True to her nature, Tonya admitted that the Bible—not her husband—had a point. The woman took the clothes given to her and began dressing. As she pulled her shirt down over her head, Tonya asked, "Well, what are we going to do?"

What are *we going to do?* the man asked himself. That was a good question.

They could not remain in the house. The swamp monsters had already infiltrated their home, and he did not know his adversaries well enough to know if he and his wife could hold out in their room. Were the swamp men strong enough to knock down the door, would the lock withstand their barrage? Could the monsters liquefy themselves and slide through the gap beneath the door? Did they have to be back in the swamp before daybreak? These were questions he had no answers to. Malcolm had been ten years old the last time he came across a book that mentioned swamp monsters. There was not enough literature on the subject.

Since staying inside was not possible, he and Tonya would have to escape into the great outdoors. That choice also came with its own problems. It did not take a horror writer to know that going outside during the midnight hours was a bad idea, but he had no other alternative.

After carefully weighing each option, Malcolm announced, "We're going to make a run for it."

-6-

As soon as he had made his proclamation, Malcolm looked over at his wife. Although he always claimed to have never noticed whenever she brought up the subject, the woman had gained substantial weight over the years. Tonya was a little over two hundred pounds and had the stamina of a rock.

Malcolm glanced down at his belly which was protruding over his fastened jeans. The man readily admitted that he was not in the best shape of his life either, but he was a lot better off than his wife. And if they found themselves having to do a lot of running, which was most likely, Tonya was going to be in a lot of trouble.

I never thought of it before, but people in both horror books and movies are always physically fit. Malcolm grabbed his sneakers from the side of the bed. *I guess we're about to find out if an out-of-shape couple can escape the clutches of swamp men.*

"The swamp monsters have already made it to the living room," Malcolm said as he hastily made his way over to the closet. He opened the door and reached up onto the top shelf to remove a shoebox which had been hidden behind a stack of miscellaneous items.

"Right now they should be on the front set of steps, if they're not already in the second floor hallway. As soon as we leave this room, we're gonna make a run for the back stairwell. Assuming that the coast is clear, we'll dash through the dining room, through the hall, and into the basement. We can reach the outdoors by going through the basement, then we make a run for the car."

Malcolm removed a handgun from the shoebox. He had originally purchased the weapon to battle alligators if the animals happened to crawl out of the swamp lands. Now his gun would be used to fight another denizen of the bayou.

Malcolm checked the magazine to make sure it was full of bullets, then he clicked the piece into place. He grabbed an extra box of ammunition and placed it in his pocket. "Are you ready?" Malcolm asked Tonya once his gun was locked and loaded.

"Yeah, I'm ready."

Malcolm turned to face his wife, then came to a sudden halt. "You taking your purse?"

Tonya looked down at the designer bag hanging off her shoulder, before giving her husband a blank stare. "I always take my purse with me."

"Yeah, but we're...you know what, never mind."

The scared couple walked over and unlocked the door. "Alright," Malcolm whispered. He held the gun with its barrel facing the ceiling and dangerously close to his face. "On the count of three we're gonna rush out the door and sprint down the hallway to our left. Understood?"

Tonya nodded her head nervously.

"One, two—"

"Malcolm, wait!"

"What's the matter?" the man asked as he watched Ton-ya walk away from the door and proceed to their dresser.

"I forgot to grab my cellphone."

Tonya had her back turned to her husband, so she did not see the dumb look Malcolm gave her. "Are you serious?" the man asked. "This is a life or death situation and you're worried about your cellphone?"

"We may need it," Tonya said as she unplugged the device from its charger.

"But there's no wireless reception out here."

"Well, we may need it when we get to where we're going."

Malcolm let out an irritated sigh. Tonya, not daunted by her husband's mood, waltzed back over to the door. "I'm ready," she said.

"We can die at any moment!" the man fussed. "But we mustn't forget the cellphone!"

"I said that I'm ready!"

"On the count of three!" Malcolm whispered harshly. "One, two—aw, crap!"

Tonya asked, "What's wrong?"

"I gotta pee."

Tonya gave her husband an unbelieving stare that rivaled the one he had given her only a moment ago. "You complaining about me going back for my cellphone, but you can't hold your urine until we get someplace safe!"

"I won't perform to the best of my ability if I know I gotta go to the bathroom," Malcolm insisted. He smiled then added, "And that goes for running from swamp men, too."

Tonya was not in the mood for one of his dirty jokes. "Well, hurry up!" she yelled.

-7-

Three minutes later, Malcolm rejoined his agitated wife at the bedroom door. "Alright, let's do this! You ready?"

Tonya glared at Malcolm. "Are you ready? You've been in there forever!"

"I've been holding it for a while. Anyway, on the count of three. One, two, three!"

Malcolm yanked the door open and Tonya was the first to run out into the well lit hallway. The first thing she saw were slimy, green creatures approaching from her right side. To be honest, Tonya had not completely believed her husband. Not until the woman caught a quick glimpse of their hollow, black eyes and their facial features that happened to be permanent grimaces. The lead swamp monster reached out for her, putrid green muck dripped from its hand.

"AAAAAAAAAHHHHHHHHH!" Tonya screamed as she darted from the creature's reach. She bolted down the hallway just as Malcolm emerged from the bedroom.

POW! A shrieking Malcolm fired his gun, knocking the first swamp man back a step. As Malcolm followed closely behind his wife, he shot three more times. Only one bullet found its mark, but it did very little to stall the undead monsters.

"I can't believe you were right!" Tonya screamed as they ran to the end of the hallway. Their hurried steps echoed loudly on the loose floorboards. "There really are swamp monsters in our house!"

For some reason, Malcolm did not feel like saying I told you so.

Husband and wife fled down a set of stairs that was just as rickety as everything else in the house. They came to the bottom of the dark steps at a breakneck pace, then made a sudden right turn. Malcolm blindly felt along the wall until he found the light switch.

"AAAAAAAAAHHHHHHHHH!" Tonya screamed when the light was turned on. There was another swamp man standing in the dining room.

"How many of these things are there?" Malcolm asked rhetorically as he came to stand in front of his wife protectively. He held his gun up and fired.

The bullet collided with the swamp monster's head, causing it to jerk backwards. Dark green gunk was chipped away, revealing a small portion of an algae-stained skull. Not seeming to be phased in the least bit, the riled creature returned its attention to the pair in front of it. The swamp monster's already evil glare appeared to hold more menace.

"Run!" Malcolm screamed.

Without the slightest hesitation, Tonya raced for the hallway that would lead to the basement. Malcolm prepared to fire another shot, but something unexpected happened. The swamp monster held one of its hands up and its slimy arm darted forward, easily extending over the twelve feet of distance that separated the man and monster.

Malcolm squealed as the swamp monster's tendril like fingers grasped his weapon and snatched it out of his grasp. The beast's arm snapped back to its regular length and the gun was quickly turned on Malcolm.

"Oh shit!" the man yelled as he ducked and ran for the hallway. Plaster from the wall showered the frightened man as the swamp monster began to fire round after round. One of the bullets grazed Malcolm's shoulder just before he could make it to the safety of the hallway.

Malcolm's hand went up to his shoulder to check his flesh wound. *Ain't no fun when the rabbit got the gun,* he thought as he hurried to catch up with Tonya.

-8-

"Oh, dear God! You've been shot!" Tonya exclaimed when her husband finally showed up at the door that led to the basement.

While panting heavily, Malcolm dismissed his wife's worry with a wave of his bloodstained hand. "It's just a scratch."

"Well, what happened?"

"What do you mean, 'what happened'? The damn thing stole my gun and shot me with it!" Malcolm opened the basement door and felt around for the switch that would turn on the light. There was none. "Just great!" he muttered. "We're going to have to go in there blind."

Tonya stared fearfully into the dark abyss. "What if there are more swamp monsters down there?"

"We don't have any other choice," Malcolm said as he took Tonya's hand and led her into the dark underground room. With him leading the way, Malcolm bumped into and stepped on a lot of painful items, causing him to curse loudly. Every time he made racket, the two of them would freeze to see if any unwanted attention had been attracted. When they did not hear wet, sucking footsteps coming for them, Malcolm and Tonya continued onward.

Eventually, the couple came to a stop at the wooden door that led out into the section of yard located on the side of the house. Malcolm felt along the splintering barrier until he found the chain-link lock. He quickly undid the lock, then moved down to the doorknob to disarm that lock as well.

"Alright, we're gonna have to run around to the front of the house in order to make it to the car. There are probably a lot more of the swamp men outside. At least one of 'em is armed, and I'm assuming all of 'em are extremely dangerous. Are you ready?"

"Yeah," Tonya whispered in a tone that really meant no.

"We're gonna run again on the count of three. One, two, three!" Just like before, Malcolm snatched the door open. Tonya bolted out into the hot, stifling night air and her husband quickly followed.

"There's two of 'em!" Tonya screamed when she spotted a couple of swamp men on the side of the house beating on the window.

The monsters halted at the sound of her shrill voice, then turned to stagger toward the startled man and woman.

"I'm gonna distract them!" Malcolm screamed. "I want you to run around them and go for the car! Their arms can stretch so make sure you give them a wide berth!"

Malcolm quickly picked up a red brick from the side of the house, while Tonya went to circumvent the creatures. He threw the improvised projectile at the monster nearest to his wife. There was a thwacking sound as it connected with the beast's skull, allowing Malcolm to gain the monster's attention just like he thought he wanted.

Both swamp things let out a ghastly howl before lurching after the terrified man.

Malcolm bent down to retrieve another brick, then started to run the route his wife had went. "You wanna piece of me?" Malcolm yelled as he started bypassing the monster. "Well, take this!"

He hurled the brick at the swamp monster and sped off. Malcolm heard the soft plopping sound when the weapon hit the beast in its chest, but he did not see the brick get sucked into the creature. Therefore, he was caught unawares when the brick shot from the swamp monster's body with incredible force.

SMACK!

Malcolm cried out from intense pain as he fell to the ground. The back of his thigh ached terribly and his hand reflexively went down to check the rising lump in his leg.

Almost immediately after throwing the brick, the swamp monster who cast the stone held up a hand and let its arm shoot forward. It only had to travel ten feet to take hold of Malcolm's ankle. The battered man frantically struggled to free his leg as the other swamp monster shuffled toward him with its arms outstretched.

Overwhelming fear caused Malcolm to pick up the now sludge-covered brick from where it lay in the grass and began beating on the disgusting hand that held his leg. After three whacks, the monster's hand tore at the wrist causing the beast to let out an earsplitting howl of pain. At first, Malcolm wore a smug smile, but his expression soon turned to one of absolute horror. He lay there and watched as the arm retracted and its missing hand rejuvenated.

Is there no stopping these things? he wondered.

Just as the other swamp monster bore down on him, Malcolm cocked his arm back and threw the huge rock at the monster's head. THWACK! The impact caused the horrifying beast to hesitate just long enough for Malcolm to get up and limp away.

-9-

"Hurry up!" Tonya screamed at her husband as he hobbled around the corner of the house and over to the car.

Malcolm glanced at the front porch and saw what her hurry was. Five more swamp monsters were making their way off the porch and across the lawn. Their grunts and groans filled the air, sending chills down the fleeing couple's spines.

A sore Malcolm lumbered over to the driver's door only to discover that he did not have his keys. Frantically, he felt in his pants pockets. No keys! Malcolm looked to his wife who stood impatiently at the passenger door. "Do you have the keys?"

"Crap!" Tonya exclaimed at her forgetfulness. "Yeah, I have them. They're in my purse."

"In your…what are they doing in your purse? They should be in your hands!"

"Shut up talking to me!" Tonya screamed as she began rifling through the many useless items in her bag. "I just forgot they were in there, but I always put them in my purse," she said. "I'm glad I didn't leave it like you told me to."

"Less talking, more finding of the keys," Malcolm said as he watched the staggering swamp creatures make their way over to them. There was still a bit of distance between him and the pursuing monsters, but he did not know how far their arms could stretch and Malcolm did not want to find out. "Hurry up and find the keys!"

"Just a minute," Tony said as she continued to rummage around in her purse.

Malcolm watched the swamp men come closer with every precious second that was wasted. Howls and groans pierced the night air. The scared man began to move around from impatience, as if he had to use the restroom. While he watched the terrifying creatures to his left, Malcolm heard a groan come from his right causing him to turn then curse loudly. Another set of swamp monsters were coming from the wooded area that surrounded the house.

"I know they're in here somewhere," Tonya muttered to herself. With her eyes directed at her purse, the woman was oblivious to the way things were dangerously unfolding around her.

"Sweetheart, I don't mean to—"

"Here they are!" Tonya shouted with joy as she held up the jingling set of keys. "I told you they were in there!"

"Good! Now throw them over here!"

Tonya swiftly threw the keys across the hood of the car. The cast was way off and Malcolm missed the catch. "Shit!" he yelled before looking around the ankle high grass to find them, which proved to be no easy task in the dark.

Meanwhile, the moaning swamp men continued to close in on them. Majority of them were within arm shooting range.

"Got 'em!" Malcolm exclaimed once he had the car keys in hand. He hurried back over to unlock the driver door, then hopped inside and slammed his door shut. Malcolm reached over to unlock Tonya's door, then he stuck the key in the ignition.

"Let's go!" Tonya yelled once she was safely in her seat.

Please start up! the man found himself pleading as he turned the key. In all of the books he had written, or read, the car never started in dire situations. Malcolm was aware that his situation was very much real, but he also knew that God—the one in charge of reality—was an even more demented writer.

On the first try, the car's engine rumbled to life. "Yes!" Malcolm exclaimed. "God is good!"

"Let's go!" Tonya screamed again, just as one of the soaking wet monsters reached the car and dropped both of its heavy fists on the hood of the vehicle.

Malcolm shrieked, then put the car in reverse. With wide, fearful eyes, he looked into his rearview mirror and saw more swamp things behind the car. "Vehicular monster slaughter!" the man yelled as he backed over the creatures.

There was a loud, jarring thud as he knocked the monsters over, then the car went up as he drove atop the things. It was like going over a speed bump. After running over the swamp monsters with his rear tires, Malcolm was about to drive over them with the front, but the car stalled…then died completely.

The man turned and looked at the dashboard. The check engine light was on. "No!" Malcolm screamed. "No! This can't be happening right now!"

"Maybe you shouldn't have run over those swamp thingies," Tonya whined.

Malcolm gave his wife an incredulous look and said, "Duh! I know that now! Next time I'm in this situation, I'll know beforehand not to run over the monsters!"

"Don't yell at me!"

"I'm sorry," Malcolm said. "I'm dealing with a lot of stress right now. We're just gonna have to run to town. Do you think you're up for that?"

Tonya nodded her head, although she had no desire to go running through the woods along a narrow dirt path with swamp monsters all around.

"Let's go!" Malcolm screamed.

-10-

Malcolm and Tonya hopped out of the car at the same time. Malcolm slammed his door and positioned himself like a relay runner waiting on the stick to be passed. His legs were posed to run, his right hand was held out for Tonya as he nervously looked around at the swamp creatures that were approaching them from all direction.

"Come on!" he yelled.

When Tonya made it around the car and took hold of his hand, something else grabbed hold of Malcolm's ankle. As soon as he tried to run, the man tripped and fell to the ground.

"Malcolm!" his wife screamed.

The man quickly flipped over onto his back to find one of the swamp monsters he had drove over, reaching out from under the car with a super long arm. Malcolm thought he saw death when he looked into the beast's hollow black eyes—his death.

With incredible strength, the creature started to pull Malcolm underneath the vehicle. The man screamed for dear life as he scratched and clawed at the grass to no avail. After he saw that his technique was getting him nowhere, Malcolm lifted his free leg and dropped it with all the power he could muster. He hit the swamp monster's tendril fingers with the heel of his shoe, causing the creature to let go while sending acute pain into his ankle.

Tonya helped her husband scramble to his feet, then the two of them sprinted across the yard. Although Malcolm was limping because of damage done to both legs, he wound up dragging his wife behind him.

"You're running too fast!" Tonya cried out as her husband jerked her along. "You're gonna rip my arm out of the socket!"

"There's no such thing as running too fast when you have undead swamp monsters after you!"

"Hold up!" Tonya yelled. When Malcolm refused to adhere to his wife's request, she repeated, "Malcolm, hold on a minute!"

Still he kept running.

Tonya yanked her hand out of his and came to a sudden stop. "I said hold up a minute dammit!"

Bewildered, Malcolm stopped and turned to face his wife. "What's the matter?"

"My breasts are falling out of my bra," Tonya muttered as she adjusted her top. "I just can't seem to find anything to hold these puppies in."

Malcolm looked to the sky and roared. "Are you serious!"

"Alright, I'm good now."

With a frustrated sigh, Malcolm took his wife's hand again and continued their run across the yard, eventually making it to the dirt road. Instead of leaving the slow moving monsters behind, the pair found themselves running into more swamp creatures. The monsters were rapidly materializing from the treeline that stood alongside the path. The swamp things groaned in that eerie voice of theirs and reached for Malcolm and Tonya as the pair ran by.

Less than one minute later, Tonya was pleading for another stop. "What is it now?" her husband asked around his heavy breathing.

"I'm tired!" she replied.

"You wanna be tired or dead?"

"I can't run anymore! I just can't"

Malcolm let his wife's hand go. He looked at her, then he looked at the approaching monsters. The swamp creatures were everywhere, and there was no way that they could outwalk the things. What could he do?

His first thought was to carry her, but he remembered that his wife weighed over two hundred pounds. Malcolm could barely tote her across the threshold of their new home, let lone run three miles with her on his back. The only solution was to keep running, and Tonya had already made it clear that she could not keep going at the pace he wanted.

I can't die like this! the man told himself. *I'm young and successful, which means I have a lot of living to do. I already took a bullet for her and a brick to the back of the leg! How much more do I have to endure? I've done all I can do!*

"I'm 'ma go ahead and get some help," Malcolm said, more to ease his guilty conscience than to assure his wife.

"You can't leave me out here by myself!" Tonya cried. The swamp monsters were getting closer and she knew that she would not survive out there without her husband.

Malcolm had come to the same conclusion as his wife, but he did not see any other way. He had to survive by any means necessary. He was going to have to leave his wife behind.

"It doesn't make sense that we both die out here!" Malcolm whined, trying to plead his case. "I love you, baby, but I gotta go! One of us has to survive to tell the story...and you can't write. Please don't think bad of me!"

Without waiting for a response, Malcolm turned around and dashed down the road with his both his bum legs. It pained him to hear his wife's screams chase after him. "Don't you leave me, Malcolm!"

"I'll send help for you," he whispered to himself as tears flowed down his face. "I promise I'll send help."

-11-

About half an hour later, Malcolm was sitting in the local police station. The man smelled of sweat, musk, and outdoors while being caked with mud, grass stains, and a bit of blood.

Malcolm leaned closer to the table that separated him and the sheriff. "I came out here to get some inspiration you know? To get away from the clichés and get some new stories, but you wanna know something funny?"

"What's that?" Sheriff Taylor asked in a bored tone.

"After running from those swamp monsters, I realized that although they were clichés, they were frightening! I mean you should've seen 'em! Those things had me wanting to crap my pants! I've never been so scared in my life...and my poor wife,

God bless her soul. I did all that I could to save her, but in the end my efforts were not enough."

Malcolm went quiet as if he was giving Tonya a moment of silence.

The sheriff just looked across the table at Malcolm and gave him a doubting look. He had been listening attentively to the guy until the nonsense about the swamp monsters came up. Now Sheriff Taylor was beginning to believe that the man had killed his wife and was trying to cover it up with some cockamamie story.

Malcolm shook his head as if to bring himself out of his stupor and said, "There's one thing that I got out of this whole episode. I thought that everything had been done to death and it may have, but I haven't done it to death. Like the story of swamp monsters—they've been told before; however, I haven't told my version and no one can tell it like I can."

The man looked up at the sheriff and smiled. "I found my imagination again."

Just when the officer was about to lock Malcolm up, the small silver bell above the station's door jingled. "Sheriff, you wouldn't believe what I found when I responded to the call," Deputy Boyd said as he walked in with a disheveled woman in tow. Twigs and grass stuck out of her mussed hair. Wet soil covered her clothing.

"I found this woman scrambling through the woods near the old Heckman place. Said she was running from some...uh, swamp men."

"Tonya!" Malcolm exclaimed when he saw the woman he never expected to see alive again. He had already began to plan out his life as a new bachelor. "Oh, thank the good Lord that you made it!"

Instead of showing the same excitement as her husband, Tonya glared at Malcolm and growled, "You son of a bitch! You left me out there to die! Luckily, I had my cellphone with me!"

Malcolm slowly turned away from his wife. He leaned in closer to Sheriff Taylor and muttered, "You know what else?"

Frightening Cliches

"No, what?" Sheriff Taylor asked while giving Malcolm a look that said, "You sorry ass excuse for a man."

"You know what else is a frightening cliché? The fact that chivalry is dead, and hell hath no fury—"

Malcolm was unable to finish that statement, because Tonya ran up on him and wrapped her tiny hands around his throat.

Dead Planet
Starring Ryan Hillis

Falling from the star-streaked lanes of hyperspace, the salvage ship, Buzzard, groaned and rattled under the strain of reversion to nonnal space. Captain John Derrick leaned back in his command chair releasing a sigh of relief. Listening to his ship settle, Derrick wasn't sure how many more jumps the Buzzard had left before exploding in a ball of fire.

Recently, Captain Derrick had been forced to resort to cutting corners; replacing or jerry-rigging parts and systems with less reliable equipment because there weren't enough credits for more expensive and proper repairs. The years of countless hyper jumps and numerous dings and scorch marks left from the laser cannons of rival competitors had begun taking their toll on his ship.

Twenty-three years. It seemed almost a lifetime ago since a twenty-seven-year-old Derrick won this bucket from its previous owner in a game of Ardelian Cross. Only four years out of the A-Poe Shipyards, the Buzzard was a glistening, top of the line, sharp-edged beauty. He quickly fell in love with it. Over the years he'd added his own special modifications...if not sometimes illegal ones.

Increasing shield output was one of his first upgrades. Then, after his first encounter with a rival contender, Derrick installed military-grade weapons and engine modifications that, to this day, made it the fastest ship in the galaxy. Now, though, it took everything he had to keep her together. And if this last gamble didn't pay off, he could very well lose his ship and its crew.

Its crew.

They'd been together for so long, he'd come to consider them family. Having survived rough patches in the past, sometimes going weeks without any salvage contracts coming their way, this had been the longest drought of work they'd experienced. So, when Carmona, his communications and linguistics officer, intercepted a distress call coming from a region of unexplored space, Derrick decided to respond. He hoped that this would be the solution to his problems, and that was worth risking it all out here in uncharted territory.

He watched as Carmona's hands deftly glided across the comm panel. Four years younger than him, Carmona was Derrick's kid sister. Growing up, the two shared a special bond with each other. When she was only three, she contracted a rare virus that attacked the kidneys. Needing a transplant, Derrick offered to give her one of his. When their parents died during a hyper reversion while she was only sixteen, he took it upon himself to look after her.

"Scan the planet," he instructed, turning back towards the forward viewport while the last of the creaking and rumbling of deck plates and bulkheads settled. "Are there any life signs?

"No, sir," Tyler reported.

"Have you located the source of the distress call, Joe?" Joe was short for Josephine. Derrick had caught her stowing away after a salvage job fifteen years ago. Hungry and an orphan, Derrick took her in. Over the years, Joe displayed a knack for fixing anything broken, eventually she becoming his ship's mechanic.

"It's coming from a ship somewhere in the southern hemisphere," Joe answered.

"Carmona, begin hailing them on all frequencies," Derrick instructed his little sister. She soon reported no response to their hails. He leaned forward in his command chair, staring at the mysterious planet floating in the viewport in front of him.

Captain Derrick gave Tyler the order to take the ship in, "Land as close to that ship as possible."

Derrick had full confidence in Tyler's piloting skill. Kicked out of the Imperial Fight Academy for insubordination and one too many flight infractions, he'd been the Buzzard's pilot for as long as Derrick had been its captain. Derrick approached Tyler with the piloting job, after watching him pilot a starship successfully through the Rigelian Asteroid Belt with the grace of an Iskarian Sky dancer.

Descending into the atmosphere, the Buzzard shuddered from the turbulence of entry. Gripping the armrests of his chair, he urged his ship to stay together. It violently pitched to starboard. A loud explosion from the rear of the ship tossed the crew from their stations. Derrick struggled to pull himself up off the deck and back into his char. The ship hurtled through the atmosphere. Bulkheads screeched as the pressure of their entry expanded from the heat. Alarms roared and bellowed through the bridge.

"We have a hull breach in the cargo bay!" Tyler reported as he retook the conn. "We're venting atmosphere.

"Pushing the ship's intercom, Captain Derrick called to the cargo bay, "Lewis, Jack, report." The speakers remained silent.

Lewis and Jack were the best two salvage jocks in the galaxy. At least until an unexpected and tragic accident occurred while they were salvaging a derelict freighter from the gravitational grip of a gas giant took the lives of the entire salvage crew. Although exonerated of any wrongdoing, no salvage crew would hire them. Jobless and sporting ruined reputations, Derrick offered the two jocks berths as salvage operators onboard the Buzzard.

Pop!

Pop pop pop!

Rivets from the hull plating exploded from their sockets. Derrick desperately clung to his chair, helpless as his ship began to tear apart. Another explosion propelled the ship faster towards the surface. Tyler launched over his station, landing with a grunt onto the deck. Thrown from his command chair, Captain Derrick slammed against the navigational conn forcing air from his lungs. Pushing off from the conn, he climbed back into his chair. He looked around the bridge at his other crew members. Joe somehow managed to stay at her station. Blood poured from Carmona's nose as she stumbled back to hers.

"Report!" he ordered over the screams of alarm bells, screeching metal, and exploding bulkheads.

"Main engines are off-line. Hull breaches on decks two, three, and the cargo bay," Tyler yelled, climbing back to his own station with blood covering most of his face from a gash above his left eye. "We're in a free fall!"

"Do we still have main thrusters?"

"Yes, sir!"

"Use the reverse thrusters to slow our descent."

"Firing thrusters...now!"

The crew braced themselves as the thrusters engaged. "Come on, hold together," whispered Derrick while the Buzzard convulsed.

"We're slowing down, sir. But it's not going to be enough," Tyler reported.

Sparks flew from exploding stations and lights flickered as the ship struggled to maintain power. The smell of burning electrical wires filled the bridge, no doubt coming from one of Derrick's less legal modifications.

"We're going in!" Tyler announced. "Everyone hang on!"

Firing the thrusters, he managed to level the ships trajectory. Like a pebble skipping across a pond, the Buzzard skimmed the ground. The impact almost jostled Derrick and the crew from their chairs. For a moment, there was a feeling of weightlessness as the ship glided through the air just meters above the planet's surface. Tyler continued to fire the thrusters, attempting to coax a little more drag. The ship struck the ground again, and a loud thud reverberated along the deck plates. Through the forward viewport, Derrick noticed a wall of large trees at the edge of the clearing standing like sentries ...approaching fast.

The ship continued to grind across the surface, and then the rear of the ship slammed into solid ground, sending it into an arching nosedive. Derrick watched as the Buzzard's nose began to dig into the surface.

"Reverse thrusters, NOW!" he ordered.

Tyler pushed full power to the reverse thrusters, tipping the ship back. Realizing his mistake, he quickly tried to compensate.

It was too late.

The Buzzard's rear rammed into the ground. The force of the impact bounced the ship back into the air. Suddenly, it crashed back to the earth, shoving deck plating upwards. Crunching metal and explosions could be heard throughout the ship. The forward viewpoint shattered, shards of perma-glass flew across the bridge. The Buzzard plowed the surface, spearing its way across the clearing, racing towards the towering thicket of trees.

Derrick's grip tightened on the command chair, knuckles turning white. Helpless. Listening. Watching. Closing his eyes, he lowered his shoulders as if it would help soften the coming impact.

BOOM!

The Buzzard smashed into the trees. The collision ripped Derrick's command chair from the deck and propelled him forward into the conn station. Carmona was launched from her station at communications, hurling her into Josephine, both crashing to the deck. At his conn station, the force of the impact catapulted Tyler over his console.

Coming to rest, plasma coolant hissed from ruptured conduits. The crackle and snap of sparks could be heard at several stations. Hull plating groaned as they settled and cooled. Sunlight streamed through the shattered viewport, illuminating the havoc and wreckage of the bridge.

Captain Derrick crawled out from under his command chair, wincing. Blood trickled down into his eye from a cut. After ensuring that his bridge crew survived, he tried calling the cargo bay using the ship's intercom; the system was offline. From the looks of things, that might be the least of his worries.

Turning to Carmona, he said, "Go down to the cargo hold and see if Lewis and Jack are alright. Joe, I need you to go to the engine room. See if you can get main engines on-line." Derrick looked around at what was left of his bridge. "And get us some power back.

Three hours later, the crew of the salvage vessel the Buzzard sat on the ruined command bridge. Jack and Lewis some-how managed to survive the hull breach and crash landing unscathed. Joe returned from the engine room reporting that main engines were gone. Literally. Restoring power would be impossible. She also reported several hull breaches along the ship including the one in the cargo bay. Bottom line, the Buzzard was dead.

Gathered together on the bridge among the wreckage, Captain Derrick wished he'd never answered the distress call. His crew was why he'd come here in the first place and now he'd let them all down. His friends. His family.

"Sir?" Tyler said, pulling Derrick from his reverie. "What about the other ship?"

"What about it?" Derrick asked.

"It could be our ticket out of this mess. It could still be operational. If it's sending out the signal, then there's a chance it may still have power, which means it maybe able to fly."

"If it was, then why send out the distress signal?" Josephine pointed out. "And where are the survivors? They must've seen us crash."

"We don't know the condition of the ship or the status of its crew, Joe," Derrick said, standing from the base of where his command chair once stood. "But Ty's got a point. If that ship can get us off this rock, then we're going to find out...survivors or no survivors."

Little more than an hour after they set out, the crew came upon a narrow stream cutting through a small clearing. With the temperatures already reaching one hundred degrees, Derrick allowed a short break. As they lounged in the clearing, a faint yet unpleasant sound echoed through the surrounding forest sending chills through the group. Uncertain what type of wildlife resided on this world, Derrick didn't want to stick around to find out. Hoping to make it to the ship before nightfall, he ordered them to gather their packs and get moving.

By midday, the blazing sun settled high overhead. The extreme heat began affecting the crew. It seemed to be affecting Joe more than the others. Shortly after leaving the clearing, she began to fall behind. Fatigued and perspiring heavily, she complained of headaches and cramps. Their path led them to the opening of a narrow canyon giving much needed relief from the blistering heat.

"Joe, you okay?" Derrick asked, walking over to where she stood hunched over and leaning against a boulder for support.

Struggling to breathe, she looked up and answered, "Yeah, cap'n. It's this damn heat that's all."

Shocked by her appearance, he resisted taking a step back. Joe's skin had become pale and blotchy. Dark black circles gave way to sunken eyes. The whites of them were bloodshot.

He turned and left Joe to rest. Walking over to Tyler he asked, "How much longer before we reach the ship?"

"An hour. Maybe two in this heat," Tyler said, wiping sweat from his brow."

"All right, we'll rest here. Give everyone—" A loud, throaty growl echoed across the barren canyon walls, interrupting Derrick.

"Um, Captain," Lewis said, drawing Derrick's attention deeper into the canyon. Through the shadows, a lone figure approached the crew. The shadows blanketed it in darkness making it difficult for Derrick to see who it was.

"Hello," Derrick called out. No answer. He noticed that, whoever this person was, he walked funny. "Are you hurt?" he asked. "Do you need help?"

A low growl reverberated through the canyon, amplifying the sound. A gut-churning smell blasted Derrick's nostrils. Gut from the shadows walked a creature that sent them all stumbling back. Carmona shrieked, the thing stepped out into the sunlight revealing a gruesome sight; the flesh that remained, a jaundiced yellow, hung from the skeleton of its wearer. Exposed bundles of reddish fibres and sinew flexed with its every move. Intestines dangled from the gaping cavity of its abdomen, like wet Dojarian noodles. The eyes were a milky white color, the pupils barely visible behind curtain of redness. Its upper and lower lips, gone…exposing bloodstained teeth. Derrick understood why this…thing walked funny; its right foot was missing, causing the creature to shuffle, dragging the bloody stump of its tibia.

"We've got to do something," Jack said, stepping forward, reaching out to it. "Dude, it's okay. We're here to help…"

"Jack, wait!" Before Derrick could pull Jack back behind him, this monster reached out and latched on to Jack. With surprising strength, it pulled him towards it and clamped those bloodstained teeth into his upper arm.

Jack screamed, trying to pull himself away. Jerking its head back, the creature tore a chunk of Jack's flesh from his arm; blood gushed. As the thing went for another homp, Derrick kicked it, knocking it to the ground. Behind him, Joe yelled. Three other creatures were emerging from the forest, all in various states similar to the one that came from the canyon.

"Captain, look out!" Lewis warned as the creature Derrick had knocked to the ground reached for him. Drawing his weapon, Lewis sent a laser blast into its chest. The bolt seared through, leaving a gaping, smoking hole.

In shocked disbelief, Captain Derrick watched as the creature continued to come towards him intent on snaring its prey. Derrick drew his own weapon and quickly fired another bolt, burning a hole through the top of its head, melting brain matter into chunky stew.

"Captain, help!"

Turning around, another creature had backed Joe into a small crevice. Missing one of its arms, it was reaching through the crack Joe had stuffed herself in. Derrick raised his weapon and fired, striking it in the back with no effect. It continued clawing at Joe. Next to him, Derrick heard the hissing of laser-bolts firing as Tyler worked to dispatch his own monsters.

Derrick returned his attention to the creature attacking Joe. This time the laser bolt struck the shoulder spinning it around to face him. Lifeless eyes looked back at him, and it now came stumbling his way. He took aim and sent a hot laser-bolt into the lettered of the monster. The heat from the blast boiled the right eye causing it to burst. Liquefied goo seeped from the socket. The creature dropped to the ground. Dead.

Turning, he watched as Tyler and Lewis finished taking care of the other two creatures that joined the party without injury. Joe rushed from her hiding place and over to Jack who leaned against a rock cradling his blood soaked arm. Pulling out the med kit, she attempted to stop the bleeding.

"How is it?" Derrick asked, kneeling beside them.

"Pretty severe, sir," she answered.

"Burns like hell, Captain," Jack growled through clenched teeth.

"Don't worry, kid" Derrick assured him. "We'll take care of it when we get to the ship."

Standing, he joined Lewis and Carmona where they were examining what was left of the creatures. "What are they?" he asked.

"Don't know, sir" Tyler answered. "But from the looks of them, I'd say they were dead *before* we…um…killed 'em."

"No way," Carmona said. "Those things were *not* dead. You saw them; they came right at us. The dead don't do that."

As if in direct challenge, loud grunting and growls echoed from the forest.

"Well…who…or *what* ever they are, we need to move before more of them show up," Derrick said.

Forty-five minutes later, the crew of the Buzzard stepped out from the comfort of the gorge and into the sweltering heat. The group stood in a clearing surrounded by sparse forest. At the north end, a small but refreshing waterfall fell into a shallow pool. In the middle—standing in contrast—stood a large vessel; the likely source of the distress signal.

"I know this class of starship," Tyler said. "It's a Hovian research vessel."

"Looks as if somebody left the front door open for us," Lewis said, pointing to the open hatch.

"Alright, let's proceed with caution, people," Derrick instructed. "Joe…" he began, but his voice trailed off in concern. Since entering the canyon, Josephione's condition had worsened. She had trouble standing on her own. Leaning against Tyler for support, her breathing was labored and her skin had developed blackish-gray contusions.

Additionally, Jack didn't look to be faring well. Lewis was having to support his weight. Bathed in sweat, Jack's eyes were bloodshot and he had the same peculiar bruising that Joe displayed. Also, the ound on his arm was continuing to ooze blood.

To the right, from a stand of trees, four demonic creatures stepped into the clearing. Their familiar but eerie cries rolled across the wide open space. Even from this distance, Derrick knew that they were like the last beings they'd come across.

"Get to the ship!" Derrick ordered as he ushered his crew forward.

With Tyler and Lewis supporting Joe and Jack, the crew quickly made for the derelict vessel. Following behind them, Derrick drew his weapon; firing a shot, he caught one in the chest. The colt sizzled through its back, disappearing into the forest beyond. He watched in astonishment as the creature stumbled, fell…and climbed right back to its feet.

"Captain!" Tyler shouted.

Derrick turned to see a trio of the cursed creatures between them and the ship. They let out a blood-curdling howl and advanced. All three looked to be wearing uniforms.

From his hip, Lewis drew his blaster and sent a volley towards the oncoming horrors. One bolt found its target, the others missed wide. Carmona took Tyler's weapon from his holster, aiming on the run. The laser bolt burned through the head of the creature, causing it to explode with an audible 'POP'. Blood, brain matter, and skull fragments sprayed across the clearing.

Meanwhile, several more creatures joined the pursuit as Derrick managed to drop the last remaining monsters in front of them. They reached the hatch and Derrick hit the lift button to close it. Captain Derrick, Lewis, and Carmona continued to fire desperately at the growing cluster of creatures as the ramp closed with terminal slowness.

"Who are they?" Carmona hollered, frantic desperation in her voice as she continued to squeeze the trigger again and again.

One of the creatures was able to grip the ramp with its fleshless hand as it rose, trying to pull itself up. Derrick and the others watched as the hatch severed the fingers upon closing.

Outside, the creatures began a ceaseless pounding the echoed through the hull.

The captain turned to his beleaguered crew. "Carmona, take Jack down to the med bay. This is a research vessel so there must be labs and records telling us why its here and what those *things* are," he instructed. "Lewis, see if you can't help find those labs. Report as soon as you find anything. Me an Ty will head to the bridge."

"What about Joe?" Tyler asked.

"We're taking her with us. If the engines are damaged in any way, we're going to need her." As the crew split up, Derrick stood in the cooridor listening to the rhythmic pounding from the horrors outside. Coming here was a mistake. What he'd thought was an answer to his problems had turned into a nightmare.

Stepping onto the dark bridge, Derrick felt a chill creep up his spine. The bridge was steeped in death and gore; bulkheads and operation stations drenched in dried blood. An overpowering stench of decay sent Joe vomiting in the corner. Derrick and Tyler covered their mouths and nostrils in an attempt to smother the stench. Sunlight struggled to penetrate the blood-smeared viewport, bathing the bridge in a crimson hue.

Movement from the command chair drew his attention. "I'm captain of the salvage ship, Buzzard," he announced, taking a step forward. "We're here to help." He stepped up beside the command chair and gasped as he looked upon a cannibalistic nightmare.

Distracted from its meal, the creature turned and reached for Derrick. He stumbled back while attempting to draw his blaster and managed to fire, sending hot photon radiation into the skull of the cannibal. The commotion drew another out from the darkened recesses of the bridge. Grunting in anticipation, the thing stumbled towards Tyler, sending them both to the deck. It latched on with a vice-like grip, sinking its teeth deep into his shoulder and tearing away a chunk of flesh. Derrick fired his weapon, melting through the creature's temple. Grey liquid poured from the hole.

Sure that there weren't any more creatures, Derrick crouched next to Tyler and examined his wound. "You need to go to med bay, have Carmona take care of that."

Grunting, Tyler pushed himself off the deck. "No, I'll be okay. Let's get those engines on line and get the hell off this planet. This place is starting to freak me out."

Derrick turned to see Joe collapsed on the deck. He rushed over to her.

"Sir, I'm burning up," she said between uneven breaths.

"Hang in there," he told her, "we'll get you to medical." Lights flickered to life around him, joined by the welcome rhythmic hum of power.

Lewis arrived at the research labs. The hatchway gaped like a skull's empty eye socket. Red, smeared footprints led to and from the hatch. From the shadows he saw something move. Groans drifted from the darkness. He hesitated a step from the opening. The air held the thick reek of rotting meat. Holding his breath, he stepped through the hatch. With the halo-lamp he'd taken from the emergency kit outside the labs, he shined the beam of light around the room. In the center of the lab stood a cage with a magnetic lock securing the door shut.

Curious, he stepped closer, sweeping the light through the bars. A grotesque hand suddenly reached out, clawing at him. He stumbled back and fell to the deck. Lewis illuminated the horrible being straining to reach him. Grunting. Pawing. Lewis realized that this was one of those creatures that had chased them outside the ship.

"What are you?" he asked.

Careful to stay away from its grasp, he got to his feet and walked around the cage, examining the thing confined within. The creature's black eyes laced with red followed his every step. In the center of its face where its nose should be, there was only a jagged two-inch hole. A gooey mass of black, rotting flesh

230

sloughed from its skeletal remains. Lewis also noticed what could only be the remnants of a uniform.

Could this be one of the crewmembers? He wondered. It was hard to believe that the creature before him had ever been a human being.

Bright whiteness exploded in the lab around him as power was restored revealing several workstaions. Lewis accessed a computer terminal and began scanning the numerous files. After several minutes, one particular file caught his attention subtitled: REANIMATION.

Lewis opened it and began to read. His discovery filled him with dread. He looked up ast the thing in the cage. Dead, hungry, black-rimmed eyes stared back sending chills through Lewis' body.

"You poor bastard," he whispered.

He noticed an annotation attached to the file and accessed it.

Rushing to the ship's intercom he attempted to call Carmona in medical. "Carmona, respond...this is Lewis."

Nothing.

He called Captain Derrick up on the bridge, "Captain, you need to get to the med bay now. Carmona isn't responding to my calls and I think that she might be in trouble...and take Joe with you."

"What's wrong, Lewis?" Derrick asked.

"How much longer before Tyler gets the engines on line?" Lewis asked, ignoring Derrick's question.

"Ninety minutes," Tyler called from his station.

"Lewis, what's going on?" Derrick demanded.

"We are all in trouble. It might be too late."

"Too late for *what*?" Derrick asked. The comm speaker crakled and was silent. An uneasy quiet settled on the bridge. From the command chair, he gave Tyler his instructions, "Get those engines on line...now."

He walked over and helped Joe up. As he turned towards the bridge doors, ther image on the monitors rom the external cameras caused Derrick to pause. Dozens of those creatures had gathered around the ship. Pounding…thumping…battering the hull. Several more were exiting the forest to join the siege.

"Get us off this planet, Tyler."

Boots resonated through the cooridors as Captain Derrick and Josephine rushed to the medical bay, desperate to reach Carmona. Joe stumbled, pulling them both to the deck. Ahead of them, three creatures stepped around the corner and headed straight towards them. Pulling his weapon, Derrick fired three shots. One of the hot plasma bolts ricocheted off the bulkhead, striking one of the monsters with no visible effects. The trio continued towards them undeterred. Aiming at the closest creature's head, he fired again. It crumpled to the deck, boiling brain matter sizzling on the deck plates.

Switching his sights to the remaining creatures, he caught one in the shoulder, causing it to spin and crash against the bulkhead. He swept his blaster towards the third creature as it reached for him.

SMACK!

It fell to the deck with a steel rod planted inits skull. Lewis stood above it. He drew his blaster and fired point-blank at the remaining creature's face.

"Lewis!" Derrick exclaimed. "What the hell is going on? What are these things?"

"I'll explain later," Lewis said, yanking the rod from the skull of the dead creature. "Right now we need to get to Carmona." As he turned, he noticed Joe sitting on the deck, leaning against the bulkhead. He raised his weapon towards her.

"Hey! What are you doing?" Derrick demanded as he jumped to his feet and came between the two.

"She's diseased. Just like the rest of them," Lewis explained.

"Like the rest of *who*?" Derrick asked.

Loud, guttural growls echoed through the cooridors. Drawn by all the commotion, more of the creatures were headed their way.

"More dead coming," Lewis said. "We need to go."

Derrick gathered Joe and followed Lewis deeper into the ship. "Dead?" What do you mean...*dead*?" Lewis didn't answer.

They entered an L-lift and took it several decks down. The doors wooshed open, revealing an empty cooridor. Exiting the lift and approaching the medical bay, they cautiously entered and stopped cold. Across the room, several of the creatures were huddled over a gurney. The smell of decomposed flesh hung in the air like a physical presence. The sound of flesh ripping caused Derrick's stomach to knot as he watched helpless while Jack was torn open and feasted upon.

Derrick quietly motioned for them to back out of the room. As Lewis exited, Joe whimpered. From their flesh-eating frenzy, the dead looked up. Five sets of black-rimmed eyes stared at the intruders. Clambering to their feet, they began to advance.

The captain fired, his bolts burning through one body to the next, but doing nothing to stop their advance. Lewis began firing at the ones coming down the corridor.

As Derrick stepped back into the corridor, a familiar voice called out, "Derrick!" Carmona emerged from an alcove of the lad brandishing a gore-splattered medical saw.

"This way!" Lewis shouted, swinging the steel rod with one hand while continuing to fire the blaster with the other.

Racing towards the research labs, they followed Lewis through the ship. Behind them, the sounds of the monsters faded. A few minutes later they arrived at their destination. Derrick helped Joesephine up onto one of the tables. Brushing a strand of hair from her face, he looked down at her, fighting the feeling of despair that was washing over him.

"She's dying, captain," Lewis said.

"What are you talking about? What is going on here, Lewis?" The deep, desperate groan of hunger drew Derrick's attention to the cage and the creature inside it. "What is *that*?"

"This vessel was here researching the flora and fauna of the planet," Lewis began. "Apparently an indigenous parasite that infects the brain is to blame for *that*." He pointed at the caged creature."

"Are you saying that is one of the crew from this ship?" Derrick asked.

"Yes, sir," Lewis answered. "Shortly after arriving, members of the crew began to fall ill. Within twenty-four hours, anybody showing signs of the infection were dead." Lewis let that piece of information sink in before continuing. "Shortly thereafter they would reanimate with a craving for living human flesh."

Lewis pushed several keys at the computer terminal. "Eventually, the parasite was discovered. Research began on the infected revealing that they demonstrated full necrotic symptoms."

"Necrotic?" Carmona asked.

"The flesh began to rot," Lewis answered flatly. "Once the infected dies, they reawaken to *that*." He pointed to the thing in the cage.

"Why not remove the parasite?" Carmona asked.

"They tried, but it uses the brain as a nest; layinghundreds of thousands of eggs. It was impossible to extract."

"Why stay on the planet then?" Derrick asked. "Why didn't the captain get them out of here?"

"By the time that the crew figured out what was happenening, it was too late. Every member of the crew was at least exhibiting stage one of the infection," Lewis explained.

"Wait!" Carmona held up her hands. "What about the distress signal that we picked up? If they knew that they were infected and without a cure…why risk bringing others to it?"

"They didn't," Derrick answered realizing what had happened. "The ship automatically activated the beacon when it no longer registered any life signs.

"Right," Lewis agreed. "According to the ship's logs, the captain ordered the engines shutdown. She realized the potential danger if this infection got out into the galaxy."

"Is there anyway of knowing if we're infected?" Derrick asked.

"I'm a salvage operator, not a doctor, Captain. But I think Joe's been infected, "he said. "She's going to die. When she does, she's going to wake up as one them."

From somewhere in the ship a rumble vibrated through the deck plates and bulkheads. Derrick knew that soon, the ship would be at full power and Tyler would be sending them and this ship of "infected" into the galaxy. Just as his counterpart had known, he also knew he couldn't allow this ship to reach space. With a heavy heart he pushed the button on the comm panel attempting to call Tyler on the bridge. There was no response.

"We need to get to the bridge before the engines reach full power," he told the others.

"Sir, there's one other thing about the infection. After the dead wake up, I told you they have an overwhelming desire to feed on human flesh. These bites carry the parasites infecting those bitten," Lewis explained. "The incubation period is much shorter; allowing the bitten to transform into one of them in a few hours.

"Jack—" Carmona began to say.

"Ty's been bitten." Derrick told them, interrupting Carmona.

"Then it may be already too late for him, sir." Lewis said.

"Okay," Derrick began, interrupting the stillness that had settled in the room, "we get to the bridge, shut the engines down, and get off this ship."

Gathering their weapons, they headed out of the room. As Derrick reached the opening, he sensed movement from behind him. He turned. Joe lurched at him causing him to reel back, tripping over the hatch and falling to the deck. Joe leapt onto him, her teeth gnashing at his flesh. He struggled to keep her from locking her jaws onto him. A foul stench of decay spilled from her mouth.

"Joe," Derrick pleaded, "it's me."

Snarling. Growling. Snapping. This thing—this creature of the dead—was no longer Josephine. The young orphan girl who stowed away on his ship was lost. Now she hungered for flesh. His flesh. Unable to reach his sidearm, he fought to keep her deadly teeth from biting him. Her weight shifted. His grip slipped. Joe's teeth dug into Derrick's chest ripping a chunk of raw flesh from his body. His vision blurred and pain rushed throughout his body. His head exploded with sudden heat.

"Derrick!"

Through the fire raging in his head he heard someone calling out to him. His sister. He managed to draw his weapon. He placed the muzzle to Joe's temple and pulled the trigger. Her eyes boiled, popping from the intense heat of plasma as the laser bolt exited her skull. Derrick pushed her body off and unsteadily climbed to his feet.

Carmona rushed over to him. "Derrick..." her words trailed off.

From down the corridor, several undead crew members were advancing towards them. "You two get to the bridge. Hold them off." Derrick told them.

"Not without you," Carmona demanded, tears streaming down her cheeks. "We go together."

"I can't, Car. It's too late for me," he said with remorse. "You and Lewis get to the bridge. Shut those engines down and get off this ship. Don't look back."

"Derrick—"

"Go! Now!" he ordered. Pushing her away, he fired into the oncoming undead.

Lewis grabbed Carmona by the arm and pulled her down the corridor. "Let's go. There's nothing we can do."

As they reached the end of the corridor, Carmona looked back. She watched, horrified, as Captain Derrick—the big brother who took care of her, looked her, who sacrificed so much for her and his crew—was overtaken by the horde of undead.

"No!" she screamed in terror.

"Come on," Lewis said, urging her to run. The ship rumbled to life around them as they sprinted towards the bridge. From an open hatch an undead creature stepped out, colliding with Lewis. The creature latched onto him as the two tumbled to the deck, burying its teeth into his cheek.

"Rum, Carmona!" he yelled.

Paralyzed with fright, she watched as the creature tore at Lewis' neck. Another undead crew member walked out of the open hatch reaching for her. She hit the power button on the medical saw. The blade spun to life and she brought it up. The motor bogged when the blade struck its temple. Screaming, she put all her strength behind the saw and shoved the blade through its skull.

She turned to the one feasting on Lewis. Carmona drove the spinning blade into its head. She heard more of them coming for her, attracted by the commotion. She rushed to the L-lift and got in, pushing the button that would take her to the bridge.

Several decks later the lift stopped, and the doors whooshed quietly open revealing an empty corridor. She cautiously stepped out. The ship shuddered and lurched. Carmona crashed into the bulkhead. She sprinted down the corridor towards the bridge.

The engines strained as they began to lift the ship into the atmosphere at twenty meters a second. Bulkheads expanded, creaking as the hull plates began to heat from the friction of exiting several layers of atmospheres.

She ran with all her heart. Her lungs burned. Her heart pounded. Carmona pressed on. The ship pitched forward as it broke through the sound barrier. She was thrown to the deck, knocking the air from her lungs, but managed to struggle back to her feet.

Closer.

Her legs were heavy…exhausted. She fought to force oxygen into her lungs. She crashed to the deck, landing on her back. The steel beneath her was wet…sticky. The smell of copper assaulted her nostrils. She brought her hands up to her face. Dark crimson blood covered her palms. She gasped in horror. Climbing to her feet, Carmona tried to ignore the putrid stench.

At last she'd reached the bridge. The doors glided open and Carmona rushed in, looking around. It was empty. Through the blood-smeared viewport, flames danced across the hull as the ship ascended through the atmospheric layers.

She went to the navigational station, frantically searching the controls that would turn the ship around. She paused, staring at the board frozen in realization. She was the only living, breathing person on board.

She slumped into the command chair, watching while the ship pulled free from the grip of the planet's gravity. Behind her the bridge doors opened. The familiar sound of the walking dead entered. The smell of decomposing, rotting flesh invaded the the entire compartment. The low guttural growls of hunger approached. Her heart raced, pounding to escape. She looked up as the creature stood next to her. Her eyes widened in fear as she looked into the undead eyes of her brother. The distant stars twinkled against the backdrop of darkness as the ship carried its crew of undead into the deep dark reaches of space.

Dead Planet

HAYRIDE

A SHOCKING RIDE INTO HELL!

Starring
JOSEPH A. POLEGA

Hayride
Starring Joseph A Polega

Rachel did not know how to answer her son's question. There had been a lot about it on the news lately and the tales had no doubt reached the schoolyard. Even the kindergarten. She had hoped to avoid the subject, so therefore was unprepared when Evan asked her if there were any such thing as monsters.

Children view things with very literal sensibilities; they accept the world as it is presented to them. Rachel understood this and was very careful in explaining to Evan that such things did not exist.

The boy was not convinced, not that his mother could blame him.

The Ripper had already killed ten. Not just killed, but eviscerated. Torn to pieces. The remains of the last victim were graphically displayed on the front page of the Detroit News leading the public to believe that the attacker was more animal than man.

A state of emergency had been declared across the entire Metro area for the first time since the Detroit Riots of 1967.

There was a night time curfew, rotating patrols of State Police and National Guard, and an onslaught of media convincing the entire country that there was indeed a monster loose in Southeastern Lower Michigan.

People also talked of canceling Halloween, even though it was only early October, until the Ripper was brought to justice. It seemed logical. No one was really in the mood for trick-or-treating.

In spite of everything, Rachel still loved this time of year.

She loved the way the wind was tinged with the aroma of smoke and pumpkin spice. She loved walking along the rows of Red Delicious apple trees at Blake's Orchard in search of the perfect red round treasure. She loved her reaction to the faint air of malevolence always present just below the surface.

Her parents moved a lot when she was young and Rachel's lack of any close friends was an unfortunate side effect.

But Halloween night was always special. It was a chance for her to feel part of a community, like all the other kids, if only for a little while.

The sugar rush didn't hurt either.

Rachel wanted her son to have the same experiences. She wanted him to love this season as much as she did. She didn't want him afraid to be a kid.

She wanted him to know that there were no real monsters; regardless of the claims of newspapers and frightened housewives.

That's when the idea struck.

Sundown Riding Stables was located along the northern edge of Romeo, Michigan; nestled snugly amidst the U-Pick orchards and well-kept row houses of upper Macomb County. They offered riding lessons for any skill level or just rented out horses by the hour if you wanted to take a leisurely stroll through town.

And before the massacre, they were the official home of Slaughtered at Sundown, a double-feature haunted house and hayride that Fear Finder magazine once described as "a delectable feast for aficionados of fear."

It was one of the many haunted hayrides that sprung up across the northern farm communities of Romeo, Armada, and Richmond at the beginning of October.

Rachel and Evan waited in line as the tractor approached them from across the riding paddock. Dusk was fading rapidly but the cold had arrived before the darkness. The bonfire was already lit beside the parking lot drawing a few stragglers nursing cups of cold apple cider.

The crowd was sparse; especially considering that it was opening weekend. Normally, the Romeo Police had to be called in to help direct traffic and control the crowds but their services wouldn't be required tonight.

They only had two hours before the curfew shut them down.

Besides Rachel and Evan, the only other people waiting for the hayride were a mid-twenties couple who bore all the signs of being on a first date and two high-school boys smuggling Miller Lites underneath their Stevenson Titan football jerseys. There were a few nervous-looking patrons in line for the haunted house which wouldn't open until it was fully dark.

Other than that, the only soul brave enough to venture out to Slaughtered at Sundown was the nighttime jock from WRIF who was passing out bumper stickers to mildly interested teenagers between station breaks.

They waited alongside a red-rimmed barn that reeked of the horse manure permanently sun baked into the cladding. Evan looked away from the plastic werewolves and straw-filled ghouls that stared down at him from suspension hooks in the rafters. Creepy music drifted in from speakers mounted on the opposite side of the barn and bonfire smoke hung low blanketing the yard in an eerie fake fog.

First Date Girl scooted closer to First Date Guy, who was all too willing to slip a comforting arm around her waist. The two high school football players stole quick sips from their beers until a Romeo Police cruiser pulled into the parking lot.

The officer shone his spotlight in their direction. One of the footballers tossed him a friendly wave which was duly ignored. He eyed the group with caution as the tractor pulled up behind them. The driver shielded his eyes after he became the focus of the police spotlight.

After a few moments, the officer broke his suspicious gaze and turned the cruiser towards the radio van.

"Well, now that we're not under arrest, let me welcome you to Slaughtered at Sundown," The driver had a friendly face, a large mop of brown hair, and a Romeo High School jacket with *Kent* embroidered across the chest. "Please climb aboard, we have a bunch of friends out in the woods just *dying* to meet you. But please keep arms and legs inside the trailer at all times. We wouldn't want you to lose any limbs...yet."

Kent tried his best diabolical laugh which came out more corny than menacing.

The two high-schoolers jumped up first; selecting spots at the rear and hanging their legs off the back in complete disregard of the driver's instructions. The first date couple sat on hay bales specifically piled in the center of the trailer for patrons who wanted to remain out of reach.

Rachel boosted up Evan who resisted slightly before sitting down cross-legged in front of one of the bales.

Kent hesitated upon seeing the boy. He fixed Rachel with a look of concern but relented when she gave him a stern one of her own.

Rachel sat down next to her son who stared up at her with big doe eyes.

"Do we have to, mommy? I'm scared."

His first tears began to form.

"Don't worry, Angel. You'll see. There's nothing to be afraid of here."

She ruffled his hair and looked up just in time to catch one of the driver's worried glances.

He shrugged in resolve, popped the clutch, and slowly guided the tractor across the riding field towards the darkness of the woods beyond.

By the time they reached the forest, the trailer was enveloped in darkness. The only light was provided by the low beam tractor headlights and a line of jack-o-lanterns strategically placed along to guide the way.

Evan clung tight to his mother, certain that the branches would suddenly spring to life with murderous intent.

Hayride

Mud flew up from the back end of the trailer covering the legs of the two football players in filth. They didn't notice though; their attention was focused on emptying the bottles before reaching the tree line.

Firelight was visible through the foliage, and Rachel was certain she could see workers rushing through last minute changes to the attractions. Scary music and fake screams were piped in from speakers hidden high up in the trees.

Evan cringed at the sound, but Rachel gave him a reassuring pat on the back telling him again that there was nothing to fear. It was at that moment that the Headless Horseman burst through the trees. He rode a large black horse with a silver bridle that snorted and frothed and stomped heavily against the earth. The Horseman effortlessly guided it along with one hand. In the other hand was a shiny steel scythe that he swung over the heads of the unsuspecting patrons.

First Date Girl screamed as the Horseman's steed reared back on its hindquarters. It let out a loud bellow and pawed at the air with its front legs. Evan was sure that the beast would breathe fire from its mouth at any moment.

The Horseman swung wide around the rear of the trailer, past the footballers who threw an empty bottle at him, and raced up the left side towards Evan who sat buried in his mother's lap. He pointed the weapon down at the boy while letting out a bloodcurdling laugh.

Evan's terror paused momentarily as he wondered what kind of magic would allow the Horseman to laugh without a mouth. And almost as soon as he appeared, the Horseman disappeared back into his hiding place between two tall pine trees allowing the hayride to continue towards the entrance of the haunted forest unabated.

The entrance itself was marked by a large hand-painted sign suspended over the dirt path declaring "Welcome to Slaughtered at Sundown, enter at your own risk" in large red letters.

A mannequin with an axe buried in its forehead guarded the right side of the path and ultraviolet lamps illuminated the brush in a deep shade of purple.

Evan shot only cursory glances up at the attractions before burying his face back in the safety of his mother's side. Rachel only smiled; content in the knowledge that her son would learn the truth soon enough.

Two werewolves emerged from the trees on both sides of the tractor. One scratched the wood planking at Evan's feet while the other circled around to terrorize the first date couple. The girl laughed nervously as the werewolf snarled at her from under the cheap plastic of his mask, bought on sale from the local Halloween USA.

Evan wedged himself between Rachel and one of the hay bales until the wolves had enough. They jumped off the trailer as the hayride lumbered along down the path.

The boy returned to Rachel's lap, wiping tears from his eyes. "Is it over, mommy?"

"Not yet, dear. Just relax and it'll be fine."

Again, he was not convinced.

The hayride continued down the narrow path past a make-shift guillotine which decapitated a helpless maiden before their eyes. The football players roared with laughter as a mannequin head rolled towards them covered in red corn syrup that passed for blood.

Evan was so awestruck by the decapitation that he missed the zombies stumbling towards him from the trees. He screamed in horror at the sight of them, but Rachel only noticed the poor quality of their make-up job.

They walked so slowly that Kent had to stop the tractor momentarily so they could catch up.

The zombies had their eyes on First Date Girl who clung tightly to her appreciative beau. Evan shivered as they took mock bites out of her flesh. His tears returned just as Kent put the tractor back in gear, leaving the zombies safely behind.

They continued down a particularly dark and narrow section of the path where branches hung so low that they scraped at Rachel's head. The scent of wood smoke filled the air leading her to believe that some of the would-be ghouls had made a fire to ward off the nighttime chill.

The first date couple whispered sweet nothings to each other as the high-schoolers launched crude remarks at skeletons staked down to long-dead tree stumps.

Evan was slowly becoming inconsolable. Viscous thoughts filled the kindergartener's mind as a demon came streaking down at them from a high wire concealed in the trees. His sporadic tears had dissolved into a full-blown sob.

Rachel did her best to calm him, but the consolation was cut short by the sound of a chainsaw being fired up in the brush.

A giant figure with a pig's face and a red afro wig ran towards the trailer with the chainsaw roaring high above his head. The actual chain was removed for safety but the effect was real enough as the pig-man ran the blade across the wood planking.

Evan screamed out loud and jumped into Rachel's arms causing the first date couple to become truly concerned for his well-being. The girl silently questioned Rachel's decision to bring such a young child to this type of attraction.

Even the football players paused in their verbal assault of the workers to assure Evan that everything would be alright. Kent looked back from the driver's seat but kept the tractor in gear as he rounded a narrow corner flanked by ash trees.

After a few moments, new music drifted in from the speakers. Rachel recognized it as the theme to John Carpenter's Halloween, to this day one of her all-time favorite horror movies.

Michael Myers, or more accurately a high school senior in a Michael Myers mask, was standing in the trees just inches from Evan's side of the trailer. The boy screamed again as Michael raised the fake kitchen knife in his direction. Rachel's shirt was soaked with fresh tears and Evan began shivering uncontrollably.

"Hey, Kent, shut it down for a minute, bro!" Michael Myers had to yell over the sound of the engine.

Kent killed the motor, filling the air with the haunting movie soundtrack and more unconvincing fake screams.

Michael removed his mask revealing an acne-scarred complexion underneath. His blue eyes were hidden under glasses fogged up from the warm breath. He dropped the knife to the forest floor and walked over to Evan with a gentile smile on his face.

"It's okay, buddy." Michael pointed to his face. "See, I'm just a normal person underneath. We're all just pretending."

Evan looked at him inquisitively; the tears were already beginning to dry. Rachel let him up from her lap. She smiled as he walked over and touched Michael's face, poking it as if it were made out of modeling clay.

"He isn't a monster, mommy. He has a regular face."

"I told you so." Rachel's smile spread wider. "There's nothing to fear."

"So he's not like us?"

Rachel shook her head. "None of them are."

"Then can I, mom, please?" Evan asked with an air of anticipation.

Rachel looked around cautiously; scanning the confused faces of her fellow riders. "Okay, go ahead."

Michael shrugged his shoulders in confusion as he looked up at Kent for some clarification. He didn't feel a thing when the boy ripped his throat out.

First Date Girl, had she lived, could have provided the best account of the events that transpired. She could have described how the boy changed. Not gradually like in a horror movie, but instantaneously as if someone had flipped an internal switch. One second he was a normal-looking child but the next he was something else.

Something terrifying.

His face had turned bright red, like one of the cherry tomatoes grown at the neighboring farm. He had narrow feline slits for eyes and long claws in place of fingers. But it was his teeth that she found most disturbing. Evan's mouth had elongated, appearing much too large for his tiny face. The extra space was filled with giant incisors. They were each four inches long, razor sharp, and dripping with saliva.

First Date Girl watched him sink those teeth into Michael's throat and snap back violently; ripping out a large chunk of flesh and bathing the trailer in a river of crimson.She ran off after the boy disemboweled both football players. Their intestines hung down the back of the trailer as if they were festooned curtains. She fled screaming back down the trail, past the pig-man with his chainsaw who was surprised that someone had found their hayride that scary. After rounding the narrow corner, First Date Girl froze in her tracks.

The boy's mother was drifting down from the trees. She floated a few feet off the ground before landing effortlessly as if guided by invisible strings. Her face had changed as well, but the difference was not as pronounced as with her son. It was the eyes; they were a captivating shade of green that was unlike anything First Date Girl had ever seen. She was lost in their beauty as the mother charged.

Rachel made a mental note to stop by the lake on the way back. The boy needed to be rinsed. He was literally covered in gore as if he had bathed in tomato soup.

They rode back on the trailer which Rachel had pointed towards the barn. Kent's headless torso was still in the driver's seat. His hands were tied to the steering wheel to keep the tractor headed in the right direction.

Evan's spirit had risen considerably and Rachel felt satisfied that he now understood.

The police had nicknamed him The Ripper. The newspapers called him a monster. But she was glad that her son now knew the truth: there was no such thing as monsters.

That was not the way Evan saw himself. He considered himself a child, nothing more. That was the way he viewed the world. And Rachel wanted to make sure that nothing would convince him otherwise.

She knew they would have to leave Michigan now. The hunt for the Ripper would increase tenfold after this latest massacre. They would be discovered.

Rachel was thinking Southern California. Or maybe Mexico. Somewhere warm for the winter. She didn't mind moving around. It was a necessity, just like it was when she was Evan's age and her unique nature revealed itself for the first time.

She would teach him to control it just like her father had taught her. Teach him the discipline to restrain the fury. Show him how to disguise his kills to avoid unwanted attention. But that would come in time. For now, just like with all other five-year-olds, Evan's excitement over his newfound talents completely overwhelmed the patience required to master them.

Eventually he would control his power, and when he did, the Ripper would fade into the murky obscurity that marked the home of all great unsolved mysteries. But that would be a lesson for another time. Her son had learned enough for one day.

She looked down at him, his smile a mirror image of her own, and they took to flight leaving only the headless driver of the hayride to greet the next set of passengers.

They traveled east, pausing for a plunge in Lake St. Clair before banking south towards the warm winds of Mexico. And the droplets that fell in their wake were like tendrils spreading a dark legend across the fertile landscape of Michigan to live forevermore.

Hayride

FISH OUT OF WATER

TENTACLED TERROR FROM THE DEPTHS!

Starring CARL BARKER

Fish Out of Water
Starring Carl Barker

Part One – Starters

Tonga Trench
South Pacific Ocean
36,205 ft below sea-level

"Do you mind if I ask you another question, Captain?"

At the sound of Mr Jove's voice, Exelby felt his left hand involuntarily increase the frequency with which it tapped his pencil against the helm of the cramped submersible. Distracted from the detailed charts laid out before him once again, he ground his teeth together in annoyance. Refusing to look round a third time, he ignored the American in the hope that he might fall silent again.

When his illustrious benefactor had suggested that a member of the world press be allowed to accompany the team on their momentous descent into the trench, Exelby had begrudgingly accommodated the old man's wishes. Acquiring funding for expeditions such as this was becoming increasingly difficult in the current economic climate, and he knew well enough to ensure that once you found a money-well as deep and seemingly inexhaustible as the reclusive billionaire Maximillion Schenk, you made damn sure that it didn't dry up on you. Having now spent four extremely long and tedious hours kooked up inside this submarine with the American, though, Exelby was beginning to wish that he'd jettisoned the bespectacled horror less than halfway through their journey down from the surface. The journalist's confrontational nature did not sit well with anyone onboard, and he seemed so hopelessly out of place down here, that Exelby could feel his flesh begin to crawl every time the noxious little twerp opened his mouth.

Thankfully the two of them weren't the craft's only occupants, or he might have strangled Jove with a regulator hose by now. Piccard II was a distinct improvement upon its prototype predecessor and the DSV was able to accommodate a team of four men plus a substantial amount of equipment within its main cabin. Exelby's two hulking Swedish colleagues, twin brothers Lars and Erik Gunnarson, were not renowned for their conversational skills, and so he alone had been forced to engage in the frankly barbaric pastime of polite conversation with the journalist during their slow descent into the depths.

After quickly running out of small talk before passing below 4,000 ft, Exelby had attempted to break the stifling tension with a brief joke by asking one of the twins to pass him a bathymetric chart from the cabinet located 'by Jove'. Being the only Englishman on board however, he quickly discovered that the craft's remaining occupants did not understand his less than subtle punchline and so, cursing vernacular diversity, he had lapsed into embarrassed silence for the remainder of the descent.

As his two-man crew often communicated with each other by means of a simple glance (seemingly possessing a telepathic link which had always baffled Exelby) the only other sound within the sub, other than the low intermittent hum of instrumentation, was the American's irritating voice as he had proceeded to ask a series of increasingly banal questions. Exelby had done his best to humour the man—painstakingly explaining the intricate workings of the LOX Stirling engines in as layman terms as possible, pointing out where the compressed oxygen fed into the AIP system, and going to great lengths to detail the submarine's intended search pattern once they descended into the Horizon Deep. Now though, having come close to gnawing off his own hands at the wrist in frustration, Exelby found himself wondering exactly how far he would need to ram the sharpened tip of his pencil into the journalist's left eye before the man finally ceased babbling.

"Mr Exelby? Did you hear what I said?" asked Jove, leaning forward over Exelby's shoulder and encroaching further into his personal space.

The American's body odour was sharply unpleasant and indicative of the spicy meal he had evidently consumed the night before. Being a scientist, Exelby was used to working alongside people of an inquisitive disposition, but there was something in the way that the American translated his detailed scientific explanations into a handful of hurried squiggles in his notebook that just got under Exelby's skin. Having completely lost his train of thought now, Exelby wearily slipped the pencil behind one ear and turned to face his interrogator.

"What is it that you want to know this time?" he enquired impatiently, noting the smirks being exchanged by the twins on the opposite side of the compartment.

Jove was hunched forward upon the edge of a nearby storage rack, his fashionably tinted spectacles slid down to the very edge of his nose; a ferret in reading glasses. Cradling his notebook in both hands like a newborn, he seemed oblivious to the fact that he was perched precariously atop several expensive pieces of equipment, each of which cost easily more than he could earn in a decade.

"Correct me if I'm wrong, but we are currently at a depth of some 35,000 feet below the surface, are we not?" he enquired pointedly.

"36,200 feet give or take" Exelby replied in a tired voice, wearily beginning to rub at his temples.

Jove slid open his notebook, briefly consulting the contents before looking up again.

"My mistake, I apologise" he continued with a sneer of superiority which did nothing to improve Exelby's mood. "Now, this previously unreported surface depression which you have discovered and, might I add, rather hastily elected to descend into, this...what did you call it?"

"Sinkhole," Exelby answered curtly, hoping to save himself the ordeal of watching the odious little man flick through his notes again.

"Yes, yes of course," Jove grinned unpleasantly, flicking the dirty nail of one finger between his front teeth. "This sinkhole which, by your own admission, shouldn't even exist at this depth, and for which you currently have no scientific explanation..."

"Is there going to be a point to this any time soon?" Exelby growled, baring his teeth.

"Well I just wanted to ask, I mean what I wanted to know is..." Jove began to stutter, clearly flustered by the show of force.

Exelby rolled his eyes and thought about reaching for the pencil again.

"... it's just that you said that the environments in these sinkholes are usually entirely depleted of oxygen and only able to support a variety of bacteria?"

On hearing this, Exelby leant back against the drive console and ran both hands through thinning grey hair before answering. The journalist leaned further forward, as if waiting to catch the words as they fell from the captain's mouth.

"Yes that's right, Mr Jove. In a primarily anoxic environment such as this where water circulation is extremely poor, it is unlikely that any substantial marine life would be able to exist. That coupled with our extreme depth and lack of light means that the chances of us encountering anything bigger than microscopic anthropods down here are remote at best."

Jove opened his mouth hungrily, his curiosity evidently piqued.

"Well if the only thing outside is bacteria, Captain Exelby, then perhaps you wouldn't mind telling me what it is that's making that scraping noise?"

At this, all four men inside the submersible immediately stopped what they were doing and listened. Exelby hadn't noticed it before with his incessant tapping, but now he could clearly make out a muffled scratching noise coming from the rear of the craft. Although the rational part of his brain told him that it was impossible, it certainly did sound like something was repeatedly pushing up against the outer door of the hatch with the unrelenting tenacity of an aquatic door-to-door salesman.

The inclusion of a double-chambered airlock in the craft's design had been one of Exelby's own inventions. Though no direct exploration of the exterior was possible at this depth (the immense pressures being sufficient to squash a man like a bug), it had been his intention to utilise this system to sample the eco-system outside and analyse it for signs of radioactive decay from their primary mission objective.

Moving to stand beside the interior chamber of the airlock Lars, the more experienced of the two brothers, cocked his blonde head of hair flat against the door and listened intently.

"Would somebody care to offer any explanation as to what the hell that is?" Exelby said quietly, staring warily at the air-lock.

The twins exchanged stoic glances with each other but said nothing. Exelby hesitated for a moment or two longer, trying to decide upon the best course of action.

"Perhaps it's a sea monster?" Jove quipped with a scornful expression. The others ignored him for the moment, focused on their visitor.

The faint sounds on the hull continued unabated, each dull impact being followed by a faint scratching sound not unlike that of wet fingernails digging into the surface of a blackboard. Exel-by bit his lip thoughtfully. Despite his many years of experience, this event was not something he had expected or planned for, the unexpected forcing an uncomfortable puncture into the wheel of his mission and leaving him a little disorientated.

"Okay, here's what going to happen" he said, having made up his mind. "Lars, get your gear together and make ready to enter chamber one. Erik, you get suited up and stand by as his back-up, okay?"

Both crewmen acknowledged their respective instructions with a curt nod and immediately busied themselves with prepar-ing their gear. As the cramped cabin quickly became a hive of activity, Jove glanced round at Exelby with a look of bemused incredulity.

"You're not actually thinking of letting whatever that thing is out there come inside, are you?" he asked nervously.

"Mr. Jove, we are quite safe," Exelby assured the younger man, briefly finding the time to affect a satisfying air of condescension. "I intend to open the outer door only for a moment, so as to allow whatever is immediately outside that hatch to be pulled inside, and then once I have closed it and re-pressurised the outer section, Lars here will seal himself into the inner chamber and open the partition wall in order to study whatever we've brought aboard."

"And what if whatever you bring inside doesn't take kindly to being examined like the proverbial lab fish and decides to eat Lars instead?" Jove whined, his voice rising.

"I can give you three reasons why that's not going to happen" Exelby snorted dismissively. "First, the outer hatchway is only two feet square, and in the unlikely event that our visitor is any larger than that, it won't be able to get in. Second, these diving suits are made of a reinforced polymer hybrid which is sufficiently thick enough to protect Lars against both the intense cold of the water and whatever he finds on the other side of that partition."

Jove still did not look convinced and continued to glance sideways at the Swede, who was pulling on the aforementioned hybrid gear over his neoprene wetsuit.

"Third," Exelby continued, "the sudden change in pressure in the outer chamber will, in all likelihood, kill whatever organism becomes trapped in there and so we won't have anything to worry about."

He moved towards the airlock, pausing only to glance back over his shoulder at Jove, whom he noted had begun to tremble slightly.

"And besides," he grinned, "Lars is a big boy. He can take care of himself."

The barrel-chested Swede let out a deep chuckle at this and winked at Jove, who appeared to be slowly turning green.

It was another fifteen minutes before Lars had donned his helmet and checked all of his equipment. He would only require a limited air supply, and so the tank slung across his shoulders was small enough to allow him to squeeze into the interior of the first chamber. Once he was installed, Exelby waited for Lars to give an 'OK' rap on the inner door before beginning to transfer water into the chamber from an onboard storage tank. The hull let out several ominous clangs as the chamber pressure steadily climbed and Exelby had to admit to taking a perverse pleasure in watching the journalist twitch anxiously each time it did.

A green LED blinking beside the pressure gauge signalled that the interior chamber was full and, holding his breath excitedly for a moment, Exelby firmly pumped the lever connected to the outer hatch. A slight swooshing noise indicated the swift influx of water into the smaller chamber and a few seconds later, he pulled back on the lever to close the hatch again before initiating the pressure reversal.

Silence hung oppressively inside the sub, permeated only by the gentle chug of pumps. Without the advantage of a view panel or any cameras built into the cramped airlock space, the three remaining occupants of the cabin were forced to wait impatiently as the seconds ticked agonisingly by.

After almost five minutes, a dull scrabbling sound was heard against the partition wall, and this time it wasn't only Jove who tensed at the knowledge that whatever had been outside was now successfully contained. Exelby felt a bead of sweat begin to traverse his brow and quickly wiped it away, already feeling Jove's sickly gaze pour over him. Another light lit up on the panel as a low motorised whine was heard somewhere overhead, indicating that Lars had manually triggered the airlock partition motor and was slowly coming face to face with their visitor.

Exelby glanced at Erik and saw to his surprise that the still seated Swede's face was unusually tense. Normally unfazed by the often hazardous nature of deep-sea exploration, Erik's face had become a bulged mosaic of raised veins and arteries. His eyes were straining slightly, as if they might suddenly burst from their sockets and a concerned Exelby was about to reach out and lay a hand upon his crewman's rigid shoulder when a loud bang shook the inner hatch of the airlock and made them all jump. The sound reverberated throughout the frame of the tiny submersible like a bell toll and the American swallowed loudly. Unmistakably, something large had just thrown itself up against the other side of the door, and an eerie silence followed before someone whispered quietly in an almost inaudible voice.

"Open the door."

It took Exelby a moment to realise that it was Erik who spoke, so unaccustomed was he to hearing the Swede's voice. Both he and Jove turned to stare at the young diver who sluggishly rose to his feet and lumbered over towards the airlock door, reaching for the release valve as if in a dream. Erik's eyes were glazed over as though sleepwalking, and he bore the vacant listless expression of someone not fully in control of their faculties. Not understanding this behaviour, Exelby instinctively grabbed him by the arm and made as if to pull him back.

"Don't piss about, lad," he growled disapprovingly, but Erik shrugged him away and grabbed hold of the circular door valve firmly in both hands, staring straight ahead like some kind of zombie.

"We have to open the door," Erik said again in a strange far away voice that Exelby was beginning to find more than a little disturbing.

"Erik, what the hell are you doing?" he grunted. "You can't open the interior hatch without flooding the compartment. Don't be an idiot, man."

The Swede's lower arm muscles began to ripple as he struggled to force the valve, the pressure differential having caused it to seize up. Exelby turned to look at Jove who was staring at Erik in open-mouthed horror. Despite his inexperience the journalist had clearly realised that something very bad was about to happen.

"Help me," Exelby cried in desperation as he threw an arm around Erik's thick neck and attempted to yank him away from the door. "I can't hold him by myself."

The Swede responded to this by bending slightly and delivering a sharp blow to Exelby's midriff with one elbow, causing the older man to let out a loud 'oof' as he collapsed onto the deck and began gasping for breath. Jove uttered a gibbering shriek of terror as the door valve began to slowly inch anticlockwise and shrank back across the compartment, attempting to put as much distance between him and the airlock as possible.

"Stop him," Exelby managed to choke, "he'll kill us all!"

He grabbed hold of Erik's legs with the determination of a persistent terrier, but succeeded only in earning himself a rough kick to the face. Jove watched helplessly as Exelby rolled over onto his back, stunned, and it suddenly dawned on him that he was all alone at the bottom of the sea with this crazed Herculean madman. Operating on a mixture of survival instinct and sheer unadulterated terror he grabbed the nearest sizable object to hand, which fortunately turned out to be another aqualung tank and, holding it above his head, Jove hurled the cylinder as hard as he could at the Swede's back.

The tank hit Erik in the base of his neck with a clunk, snapping his forehead forward hard against the airlock door. Jove let out a sigh of relief as he watched the mammoth Swede first slump down onto his knees and then keel over, blood creeping from a nasty gash across his brow.

Beside him on the gantry, Exelby uttered a pained moan as he stirred slowly from unconsciousness, grabbing hold of a nearby strut and hauling himself unsteadily to his feet.

"What happened?" he asked woozily, glancing down at his comatose crewmate in confusion.

"I...erm, well, I think I hit him," Jove mumbled incoherently, seemingly as unconvinced of his heroics as Exelby appeared to be. "What do we do now, Captain?"

Exelby put a hand behind his ear, feeling warm blood trickling between his fingers, and stared down in disbelief at Erik's crumpled form. Six years the three of them had worked together, and he had never once seen either of the twins so much as raise their voices in anger, let alone their fists.

"Now, we tie this crazy bastard up before he decides to do anything else stupid," he said sluggishly.

Staggering back to the helm, he proceeded to oversee the journalist's binding of Erik's hands and feet securely behind his back with several lengths of hose.

"Make sure those knots are good and tight," he observed. "He's one strong son of a bitch."

The young journalist was about to indignantly point out that he had been a boy scout in his youth, when something rapped three times on the airlock door. Jove's words died in his throat as he turned to stare in uncertainty at the hatch.

"Do you think Lars is okay?" he asked in a hushed whisper, not taking his gaze from the door.

Behind him, Exelby made no reply, as he swallowed uncomfortably.

"Don't worry," he said slowly, "there's no release valve on the other side so it can't get in here." His voice was uncharacteristically shaky, as though the captain felt out of his depth for the first time in his life.

"What the hell do you mean 'it'?" Jove asked. "You're not seriously suggesting that it's anything other than Lars knocking on that hatch are you? You said that the pressure differential would kill anything we brought aboard."

Exelby glanced down at the American, his mind swimming with a confusion not entirely resulting from his con-cussion.

"I don't know what I'm suggesting!" he snapped, clearly afraid of unknown possibilities. "But I'm not risking letting whatever's on the other side of that door come in here."

"Captain, sea monsters do not generally ask for permission before invading vessels," Jove began argumentatively, before a muffled whisper at his feet interrupted.

"Let me in."

Jove fell backwards onto the deck and backpedaled away from Erik's body as though he'd disturbed a cobra.

"I thought he was unconscious?" Exelby asked in amazement as Jove peered nervously at Erik's still motionless form. The Swede lay face-down on the deck with his eyes closed, blood pooling beneath his head wound like a leaky sponge.

"I think he still is."

The odd knocking sound came again—three evenly spaced raps against the inner hatch—and then the unconscious twin spoke again, with somewhat more urgency.

"Please, you have to let me in. I need to come inside."

"Okay, move away from him," Exelby instructed, but Jove had already leant forward and placed two fingers aside Erik's neck.

"His pulse is thready and he's hardly even breathing," he said, mystified. "I'm telling you, he's definitely unconscious."

Exelby opened his mouth to argue, but the same eerie whisper passed through Erik's lips and cut him off.

"So cold...so very cold out here. Let me come in. Let me come in where it is warm."

Exelby looked like a man whose sanity was about to slip its moorings and he abruptly spun round in his seat and began to stab frantically at various buttons on the console.

"What the hell are you doing?" Jove yelled, feeling the decking begin to vibrate beneath his feet, the engines stirring hesitantly back to life.

Exelby flashed him a madman's glanre before returning his attention to the controls. "What the hell does it look like I'm doing?" he grunted. "I'm taking us back up."

Jove stared at the submersible's captain in horror."Are you out of your mind?" he yelled. "We have to do something to help Lars. Whatever's in there with him could be sucking his brains out through his nose for all we know."

Exelby spun round in his chair, his face a contortion of frightened insanity. "BON FUCKING APPETIT!" he screamed in reply, half-rising to his feet as if to strike the journalist.

As the submersible began to rapidly rise back up through the impenetrable blackness of the trench, Jove clung to an overhead pipe for support and stared down at Erik's body, which had begun to violently spasm as soon as they began their ascent. The Swede's eyelids had flipped open, his eyes rolled back so that only the whites were visible, and a strange milky substance was oozing from them, slowly bleeding into the cherry-red coating on the deck like cream over strawberries. Hunched tightly over the controls, Exelby risked a glance back at the slowly disintegrating body, remembering the unspoken simpatico between the brothers and triying not to think what might be happening on the other side of that bulkhead.

"Damn Schenk," he muttered to himself as they fled from the murky depths. "Damn Schenk and every last penny of his stinking money!"

Part 2 – The Main Course

Schenk Family Mansion
Beverly Hills
269 ft above sea-level

Mikhel Yuranov stared out through the windscreen in clammy horror, his mouth ineffectually opening and closing like a guppy struggling to draw breath. Before him in the gargantuan driveway, the source of his all-consuming terror stood silhouetted in the headlights of the dilapidated Jeep: a heady throng of well-to-do party-goers gradually making their way in through the impressively ornate hallway of the mansion, casually quaffing from expensive champagne flutes as they walked. The low mutter of mildly inebriated conversation emanated steadily from the crowd. Senators mingled with minor royalty, oil magnates schmoozed effortlessly with cartel leaders and tin-pot dictators boasted loudly to impressionable young women about the considerable size of their arsenals. It was a sight of such unbridled capitalist excess that it near turned Mikhel's stomach; and he already had half a mind to turn around and head back out through the main gate before they were noticed.

As if reading his thoughts, Ivana laid a hand gently across his forearm and looked at him disapprovingly with her intense green eyes.

"No going back now, my husband," she said objectively. "You might as well come inside now that we're here."

Mikhel let out a defeated sigh and threw the Jeep into neutral. "I still do not see why we have to go through with this ordeal," he groaned unhappily. "Surely there must be easier ways to get the money than this?"

Ivana squeezed his arm affectionately, her lips parting into a smile that did more to brighten her elfin face than the chiffon evening dress clinging attractively to her slender figure would ever do. "You know as well as I do that if we do not secure funding for our project by November then the banks will fore-close on our loans and we will be back to square one again."

"There must be other sources we have not explored yet though," Mikhel replied. "I mean, it's not like this town is short of millionaires."

Ivana graced him with a subtle look of withering impatience and tightened her grip on his arm. "Yes, dear, but none of them are as rich or as eminently charitable with their bankroll as Mr Schenk. He's our best chance for success, Mikhel. Why are you being so difficult about this?"

"It's not about convincing him to give us the money," Mikhel grumbled. "It's what it will cost us to get it that worries me."

To say that he was uncomfortable in such decadent sur-roundings would be an understatement of epic proportions. Having been raised on the shores of Zolotoy Rog Bay by parents with barely a ruble to their name; and having spent the majority of his adult life working either in or on the Pacific Ocean, Mik-hel had occupied the last twenty years honing his considerable skills as a diver and marine huntsman. A highly regarded expert in his field, it was fair to say that there were very few sea-dwelling creatures which he hadn't called quarry at one time or another, either for sport, food or, as during the last five years, for scientific research purposes. Still though, the inhabitants of this dinner party represented to him a breed of predator with which he had insufficient experience, and Mikhel hadn't quite made up his mind yet as to whether he was ready to swim with this par-ticular breed of shark.

"What on earth do you mean by what it will cost us?" Ivana asked quizzically, watching him scowl in the direction of the mansion.

Mikhel turned to regard her impeccably raised eyebrow, still amazed that his wife possessed so much bare-boned naivety as to the realities of this world.

"I've heard stories about Maximillion Schenk, that's all," he replied, trying to sound less pessimistic than he was. "They say that after donating money to the projects he is involved in, he has a tendency to meddle in matters that ought not to concern a project's benefactor. That he likes to take control."

Ivana regarded him suspiciously and he could tell she wasn't convinced. "I'm sure he's just interested in finding out exactly how his money gets used, that is all," she countered. "I mean, if you sank millions of dollars into something, would you not want to know how it was spent?"

Mikhel felt his shoulders begin to tense in readiness of the coming argument. "No it's more than that, Ivana," he said firmly. "I talked to several guys who have worked on research funded by Schenk's trust. They said that once his money jammed a foot in the door, he brought in a team of his own people to kick it down, throw them all out on the street, and then change the locks on them."

Leaning in towards her, he laid his forehead against hers so that she could see the concern in his eyes up close. Her skin felt delicately cool to the touch and somehow it seemed to sooth his nerves as he took her hands in his.

"They say signing a contract with Maximillion Schenk is like making a deal with the Devil, Ivana," he whispered.

It was no good, though; his younger wife by some six years was the definite brains of their partnership, and as she leant back against the door and defiantly crossed her arms, Mikhel sighed, letting both his head and his heart fall.

"Fine," he conceded sulkily. "Let's get this over with then. After all, it wouldn't do to keep the Devil waiting."

The sharp slam of the passenger side door told him it was definitely going to be a rough night, and Mikhel sidled reluctantly out of the cab, tossing his keys to the waiting valet.

"This, I do not know how to do," he muttered to himself under his breath, jogging after Ivana, who was already stomping towards the mansion in an obvious huff.

Stepping into the immaculate reception hall wasn't so much like snorkeling with sharks as spring-boarding into a piranha pool wearing only your birthday suit for protection. Within seconds Mikhel found himself surrounded on all sides by a dazzling array of white teeth and insincere smiles. The air prickled with a variety of barbed conversations, and Mikhel suddenly felt more naked than he had ever thought possible. Ivana's fingers slipped reassuringly around his forearm again, their disagreement evidently dismissed for the moment, and glancing at her, he saw that she seemed as equally apprehensive as he was. He returned the caress, slipping his arm around her slim waist for emotional support and together they swam for the safety of the buffet table.

The entire selection on offer for the evening was themed around exotic seafood, presumably in order to reflect their host's recent interest in the world of marine biology. Several tables lay strewn with an assortment of elegant platters containing such varied delicacies as sautéed tiger shrimp, steamed red snapper, mantis prawns, smoked snoek and grilled barracuda. In addition to this, against the walls of the room, a number of large tanks had been erected which housed several live marine predators. Banded Sea Snakes, Blue-Ringed Octopi, Moray Eels and other such notoriously deadly creatures looked on as the rich and famous gorged themselves on their closest kin. It was hard not to view Schenk's unique interpretation of feng shui as some form of aquatic sadism for the benefit of his pets.

For years the great Maximillion Schenk had been renowned for his interest in one particular field; that of man's exploration of space. A direct descendant of the Stauffenburg family line (and apparently related in some way to the same colonel who had attempted to assassinate Hitler), Schenk had elected to invest the majority of his immense fortune into companies such as Grumman and RKK Energiya as soon as he had come of age. The move had turned out to be a wise one as Schenk's companies had made several large fortunes for him by securing lucrative construction contracts with both the Soviets and the Americans to build the majority of their launch modules during the late sixties.

His thirst for knowledge of the greater universe had not stopped there, though. For years, Max Schenk had been renowned as a collector of souvenirs from man's many missions to the stars, pursuing the acquirement of new pieces with an almost fanatical zeal. Anything that had escaped Earth's orbit in order to traverse the heavens and then returned was of feverish interest to him, whether built by his own companies or not, and during the early nineties there were even rumours of him having funded his own space program.

Then, about four years ago, all that had changed. Suddenly and without explanation, Schenk had begun to reinvest vast sums of capital into oceanographic research. At first, he had concerned himself only with emerging technologies such as deep sea mapping techniques and tidal analysis modelling, but his veil of influence quickly expanded to include more hands-on research such as marine anthropology and prototype submersibles. Like some parasitic pot-plant, Schenk's insidious business tendrils had soon wormed their way into every facet of oceanography, ensnaring whatever experts he could find and dragging them helplessly back to the centre of his world so that he might then devour whatever knowledge they could offer him.

This was where Mikhel and Ivana's small but relatively successful bio-research company came in. Despite having published several highly regarded papers on subjects such as squid evolutionary trends and carcaridan mating rituals, they had rapidly discovered that the pursuit of research for its own sake during a prolonged period of economic recession was an extremely costly business. It seemed that the once plentiful pockets of the West were no longer as bulging as they had been led to believe and, upon relocating to America, the pair had soon found themselves in danger of going under.

Having tried and failed to secure further funding from the relevant research bodies, Ivana had suggested that they begin to look for a direct financial backer. Mikhel had been dubious of the idea (and still was for that matter), but having been forced to digest the bare bones of their meagre company accounts by his wife, he had not so much warmed to the idea of putting their baby up for sale as having merely acclimatised himself to it. Still, he had no intention of them becoming lunch for Schenk's Little Corp of Horrors if he could help it.

The bulbous gaze of the mackerel heads floating in the soup bowl did nothing to quench the disquieting sensation of being watched for Mikhel as he stood in a queue of diners, eyeing the crab canapés dubiously. Just as he was about to finally claw his way towards a rather succulent looking lobster platter, the owner of an inebriated voice to his right poked him on the shoulder.

"Hey, don't I know you from somewhere fellow?"

Mikhel turned to find himself facing a fifty-something man clad in a poorly fitting white tuxedo whose receding grey hairline made it look as if he had just received an unexpected shock. The drunkard's finger felt like a hypodermic needle as he jabbed it sharply into Mikhel's shoulder again.

"Now look here, old boy," he slurred unsteadily, "I'm telling you I've seen your face somewhere before."

"You're English aren't you?" Mikhel asked; the accent unmistakable, even drowned under so much gin.

"You're damn right there," announced Mikhel's new best friend as he lazily threw one arm around his shoulder. "Best damn country in the world, she is that."

Despite wanting to rid himself of this human limpet as soon as possible, Mikhel couldn't help but notice that the Englishmen's hands were shaking rather badly as he held on to his glass for support. He silently wondered if perhaps the man's heavy consumption was more of a preventative tonic than a spirit-raiser.

"Have you been back there recently to visit?" he asked, making a ham-fisted attempt at small talk.

"No, no," the Englishmen replied, shaking his head emphatically. "I've been working on a top secret project for Mr. Schenk."

Mikhel stared at him bemusedly, not sure whether to believe him or not. His companion waggled one finger comically in front of his lips as if to emphasise the point.

"High priority clearance don't you know…very hush hush."

Then something changed in his face, and for a moment, a look of inconsolable sadness washed over him.

"Not that it makes any difference of course," he said dejectedly, his voice lowering. "What we brought up from that abyss for him to paw over with his bloody microscopes and boffins. None of that's ever going to bring them back now."

"Bring who back?" Mikhel asked as a pale, bony hand fell across the Englishman's shoulder like a hammer onto an anvil, cutting him off.

"Mr Exelby, my dear fellow, I do hope you're not making a nuisance of yourself to my guests?" oozed a silky voice that somehow unsettled Mikhel.

Maximillion Schenk was taller than he had expected. The recluse's true age was not known, but he was rumoured to be in the vicinity of seventy and Mikhel had expected some doddering grandfather type with a cane, shuffling his way ponderously round the shallows of the room as he watched people gorge themselves on his exquisite banquet. Instead, before Mikhel stood a six-foot-two silver-haired powerhouse of a man who strode amongst his guests like Moses parting the Red Sea. The cane clenched tightly in his fist was for show rather than support, and the brass head at its tip was fashioned in the shape of an octopus wrapping itself around a hapless diver. Schenk stretched out a neatly manicured tentacle and Mikhel took it, surprised by the unrelenting tightness of the old man's grip.

"Mr Yuranov, so glad that you could come along this evening. I've been looking forward to meeting you," Schenk said beaming.

Ignoring the look of recognition which now dawned across the Englishman's face at having finally put a name to a face, Mikhel returned his host's steely gaze without blinking, knowing full well that letting his fear scent the water between them would only embolden the predator further.

"You know of me, Mr Schenk?" he enquired politely through a tight smile.

"Oh, I make it my business to know everything about all my guests before I meet them, Mr Yuranov. Or do you mind if I call you Mikhel?"

"Mr Yuranov is fine," Mikhel replied rigidly, forcing the smile not to dissipate.

"And where is your lovely wife this evening I wonder?" Schenk asked pointedly. "Perhaps chatting up some wealthy industrialist types?"

Mikhel watched Schenk's eyes roam the room in search of Ivana, noting the way his eyes fell upon each group of guests — as if the contents of the wall tanks weren't the only creatures to be regarded as specimens.

"Oh she's around here somewhere, I guess," he replied, not taking the bait. "She's more the socialite than I am."

Beside them, Exelby opened his mouth wide as if to say something, but Schenk turned to him before he could utter a word.

"Why don't you run along, Mr Exelby," the billionaire suggested firmly, making it clear that this wasn't a choice. "I'm sure if you ask at the bar, they'll be happy to refill that glass for you."

Exelby stared at Schenk for a moment with a dull hatred in his eyes that quickly burned itself out before lowering his gaze and obediently trudging away in the direction of the bar. Mikhel watched him go and knew at once that the Englishman was permanently one of Schenk's pets, whether he liked it or not.

Ivana watched her husband enter into discourse with their host from the corner of the room, sipping thoughtfully from her champagne glass. Beside her, the excitable young man with whom she had recently struck up a conversation ogled her over his plate of salad. Vaguely awkward in his mannerisms, the kid had a strangely anxious look in his eyes and continuly hopped from one foot to the other as though dancing on invisible coals.

"I'm sorry, what were you saying, Alex?" Ivana asked, returning her attention to him.

She used the informality of a first name address at the journalist's insistence, but comfortable was not a word to be used in any description of how she felt right now. The reporter (this more derogatory term seemed to suit his loathsome character better) was standing far too close in her opinion; and were it not for the pillar at her back, Ivana would have begun to edge slowly away.

"I said it's definitely in the public interest for the mission findings to be made available as soon as possible. I'd run with the story myself, if it weren't for the fact that Schenk has me watched night and day since we got back."

Her companion's voice held a undercurrent of resentment, directed no doubt in the direction of their host and she wondered what sort of hold Schenk had secured over him.

"And this would be your recent mission into the Tonga Trench?" she asked, struggling to keep up with the reporter's frantic expositions.

"Yes, of course," he replied in earnest, head bobbing up and down like an agitated meerkat. "You see, it's not just the fact that they got killed down there by that thing, no not at all. I mean, people get killed all the time don't they; crossing the street, plane crashes, choking on pretzels for God's sake?"

Ivana was completely lost, but continued to smile politely. The peculiar little man was clearly trying to get something off his chest.

"We're told so often that the core of any story is not the where or the when, but the why. But in this case it's the how that's the important thing. You see, Miss Yuranov, he did it because it told him to."

"I'm sorry Mr Jove, did what?" Ivana said, struggling to follow.

"Took his helmet off of course!" Jove babbled. "Lars was completely protected in that suit. It didn't have room to manoeuvre around in there, to get the upper hand on him you see. But he took off his helmet because it told him to, and now he's dead."

"Are you saying that this Lars person, whoever he is, that he drowned?" Ivana asked, concentrating hard on what Alex was saying.

"I'm saying that's how it started, Miss Yuranov," Jove said gravely, "but then it started to feed, and that's when all hell broke loose."

Ivana was prevented from pressing him further on the subject as their host moved to address his guests from a small dais at the rear of the room. Behind him, thick red curtains obscured what was presumably an as yet unseen tank and it was clear from the look of unbridled pride upon his face that Schenk had something special to reveal to his guests.

"Ladies and gentlemen," he began with the obtuse air of a circus ringmaster. "As many of you are aware, I have recently developed a rapt fascination with that portion of our great planet which resides beneath the sea—an undiscovered country of wonder which as yet has seen fit to keep many of her secrets."

Schenk moved to the centre of the curtains and raised his hands into the air, showman-like.

"However, following a recent biological exploration into the depths of the Pacific Ocean, happily funded by my Marine Trust, it is my great pleasure this evening to be able to introduce to you, a form of life previously unknown to mankind, which I have christened the Sea Unicorn."

"Fascination my ass," whispered a familiar voice in Iva-na's ear. "I heard he was looking for the RTG from Apollo 13 down there."

Ivana turned to find her husband grinning sheepishly at her, his dilated pupils and the vodka clasped in his left hand quickly informing her that he had decided to get through the remainder of the party the best way he knew how. Giving him a scowl of severe disapproval, she returned her attention to Schenk, who appeared lost in his own grandeur. Gesturing majestically to aides at the side of the stage, their host turned about-face as the curtain slowly rose to reveal a large glass tank. An ensemble gasp from the audience told Schenk that his exhibitionism had been justly rewarded and a smug smile quickly tightened across his face.

Ivana stared agape at the strange creature housed inside the tank; despite her plentiful experience, it was unlike anything she had ever seen before. Perhaps three feet in length and half as wide, the thing was covered in a rigid carapace and with a multitude of spindly legs trailing below, it resembled a floating cockroach from hell. At first glance, she suspected it to be some form of isopod grown far beyond the normal size of its genus due to deep-sea gigantism, but upon spotting the bulbous filament protruding from the centre of its head, which appeared to be glowing slightly, she realised that this was something new.

"Is it some form of prehistoric hybridisation do you think?" she whispered, wondering if the creature was a result of some form of interspecies breeding, but Mikhel seemed not to hear as he set about industriously refilling his glass from the vodka bottle he had managed to procure from the bar, swaying slightly as he did so.

Ignoring her husband's current lack of scientific curiosity, Ivana stepped slowly forward towards the tank, fully enraptured by the sight of this unusual specimen. The closer she drew to the tank, the more fascinating the creature seemed to become; so lost was she in her admiration for its sleek lines that she paid no heed to the rounded knot of cartilage at the end of its solitary antenna, steadily beginning to glow more brightly in a series of rhythmic pulses. Several other members of the audience were also shuffling unsteadily forward towards the tank and as more and more guests began to draw nearer, the creature's filament grew brighter still. Even Schenk himself, who until a moment ago had been thoroughly in love with the sound of his own voice, now stood dumbly upon the stage, gazing in through the thick Plexiglas at his prized specimen.

Having finally emptied his bottle, Mikhel glanced up, watching the first few guests beginning to climb up onto the stage with a confused look on his face. Not entirely convinced of his dwindling sobriety, Mikhel watched Ivana painstakingly pulling herself up onto the platform, her expensive dress ripping in two places. An overweight party-goer in a three-piece suit collided with Mikhel as he shouldered past in the direction of the stage, and Mikhel noted the odd glazed expression on the man's face. Glancing round, he saw to his amazement that, with the exception of a few inebriated individuals, the whole party was slowly making its way towards the central tank.

Up on the platform, Schenk now had his face pressed tightly up against the glass, gazing lovingly in at his pet as drool slowly oozed from his slackened jaw. Placing both of his hands firmly onto the edge of the tank, he purposefully hauled himself up so that he hung precariously over the open lid. As if in anticipation to this movement, Schenk's Sea Unicorn hungrily shuf-fled forward, and the zombified billionaire just about managed to dribble the word "beautiful" before pitching himself forward into the tank.

Mikhel's bottle hit the floor—just as Schenk's body hit the water—shattering into myriad tiny pieces. No sooner had Schenk entered the water did the Sea Unicorn scuttle to him and proceed to wrap its many limbs around his flailing body. Despite their frail appearance, the creature's legs were evidently more powerful than they appeared, as it tightened its grip, a red mist began to quickly bleed into the water.

Hardly believing what he was seeing, Mikhel stared in abject horror as, from beneath the creature's shell, several stubby tentacles unfurled themselves and snaked out towards its captive prey. Entering through every orifice, these tubules tore open Schenk's face like a wet paper bag and surged deeper into his head in search of food. The billionaire's lips hung open in a silent scream as the Sea Unicorn feasted upon his soft tissues, half-hidden within the thick ink of his death.

As the creature began its first meal, the remaining drones changed course and begin to amble in the direction of the other tanks in the dining hall. Evidently having not yet quenched its appetite for consumption, the creature's antennae pulsed feverishly, and the nearby guests began to clamber up into Schenk's homemade aquariums. A pair of emaciated supermodels began shrieking in agony from the confines of the piranha tank; the horde of tiny killers rapidly ensuring that they would stay thin forever. A naval officer sat anchored at the bottom of the tank by several weighty medals on Mikhel's right, a blue-ringed octopus slowly forcing its way down his throat.

Fearing for his wife's safety, Mikhel's eyes roamed the room and glimpsed her lying on a metal gantry above the tanks, stretching out her hands towards a writhing mass of sea snakes just below. Many of the guests had already entered the tank, and were now floating below the surface with several of the serpents attached to their exposed flesh.

With adrenaline quickly beginning to counter the alcohol in his bloodstream, Mikhel stared down at the glass in his hand and then up at the creature gorging itself at the centre of this carnage. Realising that he had very little time before he sobered up and became dessert, he staggered towards the buffet table. Thoughts of social faux-pas vanished as he laid his hands upon a pair of gleaming meat cleavers and spun round unsteadily to face the Sea Unicorn's tank.

"This. This I know how to do," he slurred as he lunged forward into the familiarity of the hunt, brandishing both cleavers high above his head.

Somewhere, a gong crashed noisily onto the floor, the sound hopelessly drowned amongst the screams and desperate splashes of fevered feasting. Dinner was most definitely served.

Fish Out of Water

From Rebirth to Reburial
Starring M.W. Williamson

A warm, hard rain fell from the evening sky; which was trading its blush for dark mascara as streetlights lit up in the township below Monterrey Cemetery. Needle-like drops soaked into the porous stones; filling their cracks and eroding them, as if it intended to assist gravity with their eventual destruction. The location of the boneyard did it little service as the area was placed near protected swamplands; the near constant rains of the spring season flooded the gulleys that lay between its rolling hills and well tended grounds.

A middle-aged man named Torrey made a solitary walk between the rows of jutting fingers, his heavy steps packing the soggy ground beneath him. A bouquet of red roses was carried in his hands as he approached the west end of the lot. He had been told that a young girl would be there. A lost soul that frequented this sad collection of those once and still loved.

The pillars of creeping shadow spread over the burgeoning pools of water that choked the grass, engulfing the ground with an increasing pitch of darkness. The blanket pulled over the sky birthed a steady wind that added a chill to Torrey's soaked jean jacket. It seeped past the expensive linen and mixed with the sweat and oil of his skin. No amount of wiping at himself or wringing of his clothes could remove the dampness that made him feel as if he were drowning where he stood.

On the opposite side of flesh, his muscles burned with the exertion of the climb. He wasn't in the best of shape after all. Not anymore at least. Spending his youth in juvenile halls and learning the social skills necessary to survive and prosper in the criminal underworld at the very institutions that sought to redeem him; he had emerged reborn yet not reformed, and spent his life gaining no small amount of notoriety from his manipulation of others to carry out his deeds. He had grown fat and complacent in his mid-life years, dining on the fears and dreams of those who crossed his path.

And now he was the one being used. Given a simple yet ludicrous task by a pig detective, who had a knack of his own for bending people to his will. A peculiar man that Torrey suspected was secretly mocked by his peers, yet spoken of in jealous and possibly fearful whispers between coworkers when his cases were closed.

He spat on the ground, frustrated and bloated in dampness. He was losing interest in his task with his rekindled anger toward Detective Roush. He would turn back. Prepared to face Roush and accept his punishment for not finding the girl and delivering the flowers to her as instructed when he heard it: a soft, hopeless weep that only paused between trembling breaths.

The top-heavy man circled in place. The sound was low and difficult to pinpoint between the falling rain that pounded in his ears; his vision obscured by drops collected upon his eyelashes.

Then he found her.

Zigzagging around the stones, he nearly kicked her crouched body in the ribs. He slipped backward during his attempt to reverse his stampede and landed on the muddied ground. The back of his head must have glanced off a headstone, for when he rose, further muddied and deeply embarrassed, her visage before him seemed to waver and shift in focus.

She crawled toward him, wearing little more than a purple, tattered dress with white frills that were stained and torn. Torrey knew it was certainly not a modern gown. One that had been passed down by her family perhaps—at best—or more likely a remake that was sold to young kids immersed in the Goth culture.

Although he couldn't entirely discern her facial features, Torrey could see that she was in youth's prime. Not much more than nineteen to twenty-three. Her wet, black hair clung to her exposed shoulders, dipping into her ample cleavage. His transfixation with her was only broken for a second as a shift in the light tuned his gaze to fall with surprise on a headstone that bore a surname he had grown uncomfortably familiar with. But he had little time to think about it.

Reaching him, she clawed her way up his body into a standing position. Her petite form seemed to bear no weight against him as she rose.

Her knees wavered, and Torrey grabbed her at the underarms to stop her imminent collapse. Closer now, he could see that her turquoise eyes were red rimmed from her deep sorrow. While petite, amply curved and endowed; judging from the wet dress that coated her like a second skin, her body lacked warmth and substance. With his fingers in her armpits, steadying her weightlessness, he felt like he was holding a life-size doll as opposed to a sensuous, nubile vixen.

Her pale lips offset her olive skin as she mouthed words that he could not hear. He pulled her closer, enjoying the cushion of her breasts and the stiffened nipples that indented his shirt.

The wrapping of the roses in his hand crinkled as they shifted their embrace. Her attention turned to the bouquet still clutched in his hand, and Torrey ignored his growing erection, remembering the task at hand.

"This is an offering to you. From a man named Arnold Roush."

She took the roses from him and buried her nose deeply into the flowers. Once sated by their scent, she plucked a small enveloped card attached to the wrapping. This she put to her nose and deeply inhaled.

A strange smile crossed her lips as her eyes snapped to gaze into the distance. She stiffened, with nose quivering as though she were a blood hound tracking a scent.

"So, look…" Torrey was growing uncomfortable with her strange behavior. At first she had seemed like nothing more than a grieving waif, and now her movements, while implying intense sexuality, were becoming more and more animalistic. Almost predatory.

"…I'm done here baby. But if you're looking for work I could use a few young girls like you in my stable. Y'know. It pays good."

As he turned to exit, the girl threw her arms around him, pulling him down to her height and pressing her lips against his. He thought he heard a delighted hissing as her tongue licked at his teeth.

He tasted a mix of salt and cinnamon as she boldly secreted her saliva into his mouth, as she tickled the insides of his cheeks. Intoxicated by her taste and smell, he succumbed and swallowed the nectar she offered.

Euphoria soon turned to surprise, then fear, as her grip on the back of his head tightened and her tongue pushed past normal human limits; beyond his throat and into his esophagus. Her once frail and weak body grew tense and strong, holding him in place as the kiss intensified.

Torrey panicked, trying to push her away at first, then resorting to punches at her ribcage as the white stars of suffocation swam before his eyes. The world spun as she pulled him down to the earth. His throat was engorged by her endless tongue, which elongated unnaturally and thickened with every inch until at last his insides were gorged with her organ.

A sharp pinch within his torso signaled a lung collapse; and soon after, an intense rubber band-like snap reverberated as she pierced his stomach wall and probed into his intestines.

Breathless, blacking out, Torrey began to seizure as the small strumpet writhed atop him. Her body entangled his, holding him in deadlock until his death throes ceased. Her small mouth made rude sucking sounds as she drank the saliva and bubbling blood alike that erupted from his throat.

Her forked tongue retraced the path through his body, returning to her mouth. Leaning forward to lick his eyelids closed, the girl retrieved the flowers and card lying crumpled next to Torrey's limp body.

With bouquet in hand she stood stoic, savoring the salty sweat that rubbed off onto her fingertips and lips, while gazing into the distance…

…looking right into Roush's eyes as he studied the encounter through binoculars from the edge of the cemetery gates. Spitting away the cigarette that was coming dangerously close to burning his lips, he lowered the binoculars, shaking his head in disappointment. Torrey was meant to leave the flowers close by and speak to her from afar. Not to trip over her and be lulled into death.

Annoyed, he followed the perimeter of the gate back to his car. This area was out of his jurisdiction. He would have to leave the body for the locals to recover. Still, the demon that hunted here had received his message, and accepted his gift.

The layer of crushed rock that lined the roads through the cemetery caught underfoot as he approached his car. Roush cursed as he scuffed the errant stones out of his shoe treads. His agitation increased when he found a man dressed in silver and white sitting in his passenger seat. Scanning the area, Roush found no other vehicle nearby. His own had arrived alone in the lot, and he had remained close enough to the cemetery entrance to hear any other that might have approached.

"How did it go?" the man asked, removing himself from the vehicle while leaving the door open, allowing the rain to spill into the cars interior.

"Those are expensive seats," Roush growled.

"My apologies," the old man lamented. "Material things mean little to me; sometimes I forget that they are important to others."

"Internal affairs? I already see the department shrink as instructed. And sadly have not shot anyone in a while." Roush studied the man before him, taking in the vest coat and pressed dress pants. The old man's clothing was accentuated with silver chains; the impression of several medallions worn against the mans chest were betrayed by his pressed silken shirt. Several of the amulets were recognized, as the detective bore several of similar origin himself.

"I must ask," the old man pressed, unshaken by the hostility Roush displayed, "are you trying to catch that Lamia in the graveyard or court it? You're smart enough to keep your distance. But how many pawns do you have left to sacrifice in this pursuit? Granted one less pimp on the streets can't be considered a crime."

"It's unwise to harass an officer. Tell me what you want and move on," Roush pressed while slamming his car door shut.

The old man bowed as he pulled out a silver identification badge. "I am Drew Huxley. When you run my credentials as you undoubtedly will, you'll note that I and the organization that I serve have credentials with the church and government."

"Get in the backseat crackpot," he snarled; incredulous, producing a pair of plastic handcuffs. He had been the butt of many pranks played by his fellow officers before. His studies of the occult were well documented by his superiors, and the chain of mockery eventually spread down the line to his co-workers. Rather than play the part of the overweight child who mocked himself in order to gain acceptance, Roush had instead introverted. He had never considered himself a social butterfly, and his talents grew stronger regardless of the acceptance of others. Turning inward in such a way had actually increased his abilities as a detective. While the other officers may not have understood his theories or methods, it was his success rate of solved cases that fueled their attempts to embarrass him.

"How exactly do you intend to book me?" Drew asked with a curious tilt of his head. "Will you tell your department that you sent a man as bait? Allowing him to be slain by a demon to further your vendetta?"

Drew turned and placed his hands together behind his back. "Cuff me if you wish, detective."

Roush scanned the grounds around them. There was little room to place another vehicle out of sight. And the rainfall, which grew heavier as they conversed, would affect and microphones placed on Drew.

"I assure you, we are quite alone," Drew spoke, holding his submissive position. "You are my only ride back into the city. I planned it this way so that we may talk more."

The silver haired man seemed almost feeble as Roush bound him, placing a hand atop his head while escorting him into the backseat.

"This is a nice ride," Drew admitted as they began the two hour drive back to Miami. "Cadillac or Lexus? I didn't bother to check. I was more interested in the modifications you've made to it. Bought it with your lottery winnings, didn't you? The hacked police computer seems a bit out of place, but no more than the symbols hidden in the interior here or the holy water mixed with your washer fluid."

The more the old man spoke, the more Roush came to realize that his appearance wasn't a department joke. Drew spoke carefully in a cryptic fashion that one would read about in stories, and yet he had pinpointed many aspects of the detective's recent activities. Looks were deceiving; and this prick dressed to the tee, speaking in a calm, refined fashion, was slowly proving to be quite formidable. In fact his presence in the backseat was stifling from a physical and mental standpoint.

"I possess psychic abilities as well, Arnold," Drew smiled warmly in the rearview mirror as he passed the broken band of the handcuffs into the passenger seat. "My apologies, they were uncomfortable."

Roush fished in his coat pockets for a cigarette. He didn't crave the nicotine so much as he enjoyed the flick of the lighter. Hearing the hiss of the flame and the crackle as it ignited the dried leaves. His smoking grew out of an attempt to appear *normal,* rather than an actual addiction. It was one of many useless facades he had postured throughout the years, yet this one had stuck with him.

Drew settled into the backseat comfortably as he pulled a small metal box from a pocket recessed within his vest coat. The scent of freshly trimmed mint leaves filled the air as he delicately chewed them one by one, savoring the flavor of their delicate green flesh.

"You've been assigned to me indefinitely. The paperwork will be resting on your desk Monday morning. But I was restless and anxious to meet you even sooner. I'm very pleased that my anticipation led me to you this soon, for it appears that you are about to have an interesting adventure with a killing spirit. You are very unique and misunderstood among the general cattle; yet naive and foolhardy at times when displaying your abilities."

"So I'm a CIA initiate? Where's my laser wristwatch?" Roush scoffed through drags of the cancer stick.

"We're more powerful than the CIA. Yet we appear as nothing more than humble servants of the church.

"I've heard of you," Roush rebuffed, trying to gain some sense of control in the conversation. "You're with the Purity. A high and mighty Christian agency with ties into local governments and the Pope as well. Funded by nothing more than hopeful belief and paranoia. A collection of psychics, saints, and psychopaths who claim to do God's work."

"Heard of us in your occult circles have you?" Drew smugly grinned, knowing he had already won the argument. "You clearly know that there is a world beyond this existence. I can help you. I can work with you to hone your scattered and jaded mind to open up all the possibilities you can comprehend."

I'm telling you this, as you already may have guessed, Arnold, because I have you by the balls in every sense but the literal."

"*...to open up all the possibilities you can comprehend.*" Roush's mother had once mouthed the exact same words. She had been a delightful and free flowing spirit. A source of light and hope in a world that was constantly gnawed at by darker forces. It was she who had nurtured his body and mind as a mother should. And beyond that, it was she who tried to teach him to see beyond the veil, into the true reality that held the universe together. His time, along with her teachings, were cut short abruptly as he reached seventeen. Her death left him with no teacher to guide, and no solace to be found in caring embrace.

He sought new teachers. Hungry for knowledge and peace of mind, he poured through the books he rescued from her personal library long before father, a bible thumping zealot, had burned the house to the ground.

"Will it comfort you to know she is well accepted into Heaven? Despite being a pagan and a sorceress?" Drew interrupted.

"Get out of my head old man!" The sedan crossed the yellow lined road as Roush turned to face the backseat. The vehicle regained driving position without Roush at the wheel. His mind guiding its path as the vehicle continued at sixty miles per hour, he poked a finger accusingly at Drew. "You know nothing!"

"I know that you use your gift for little more than slight of hand, and occasionally cheating the state lottery out of the money it draws from the hopeful and desperate." Drew replied in the same calm demeanor. "I can teach you to guard your mind. Further, I can teach you to project it beyond the uneducated limits you currently possess."

Despite Drew prodding him, Roush kept the Lexus at speed and proper course along the road. He was often impressed with himself in the fact that he could steer it better with his will than his own hands, which were growing more shaken with each nightly drink.

"I lament your loss, Arnold." Drew plucked the last mint leaf from its tin and suckled it in the roof of his mouth. "I mean to imply that since we will be together for some time, I can assist you in refining your admittedly exemplar, if not reckless abilities."

"I am not reckless," Roush said with simmering anger. He absolutely hated being questioned, whether by subordinates or self-superiors. "I do as I intend and within the limits of my control!"

"I can broaden those limits, if you allow me the chance. But I must say; before we get to that, what do you intend to do with the Lamia you attracted today? It is migrating, I feel it. It follows you and you alone now. So do we intend to capture or destroy it? And where will such action take place?"

"There is no we or us, sir." Roush returned to the wheel in time to approach the city toll booth.

"Ah," Drew smiled saccharinley, "you intend to confront it in your own apartment. Bold. And I would consider it foolish were you not so amply prepared to take it on in your own turf."

"Get out of my head, old man. Last warning."

"Get me out yourself, Arnold. Push me away like a newspaper page. When you can do this, then perhaps we will get along much better."

His senses should have been dulled by the long drive home, further so because of the alternating awkwardness of silence, punctuated only by Drew's probing questions and anecdotes. Both of which were offered with the subtlety of a sucker punch to the face. Drew had the distinct advantage of philosophy and raw knowledge, which were aptly used to dissect his new "partner," while the latter man could only stew in a tornado of imprisoned anger and force himself to drive more carefully than usual as Drew hit his marks with growing accuracy.

Roush was quite pleased to drop his uninvited passenger off at a late night diner located several blocks away from his apartment complex.

"Wouldn't you like to have someone in your life who understands you, Arnold? Someone who can guide your mind to clearer heights, and your knowledge to deeper depths?"

"No."

"Well, assist me with my case and I will leave you be. Resist and I inform the Purity that you are indeed a warlock and murderer, and a trial will be scheduled."

These were Drew's parting words as he exited to the sidewalk, under neon signs strung stories above their heads. He blended into the crowd easily, seeming to fade right in front of the detective's vision despite the false light and eloquent attire that garbed him, exiting before Roush could answer or form a suitable retort to snub him.

Roush lived well, and could exceed the means of the average detective had he wished it. Yet he chose his apartment carefully, balancing his quarters in a slightly above average building on the outskirts of the city center. His "lucky guesses" at lottery numbers and scratch tickets funded his bank account, which in turn funded his obsession with the occult and occasionally bought him needed information on his day job.

He took a deep breath, standing within the spilling light from the glass lobby doors. The warm breeze that caressed the damp streets brought with it a comforting, if not identifiable scent; a collage of prepared food, vehicle exhaust, human and animal sweat, all mashed together into what could be called a summer fragrance. He imagined every city must have a similar version of this perfume drifting in its air as the masses rubbed together, scouring for every inch of available space in a shrinking world, whilst yet holding onto the hope that they were true individuals and not foolish creatures that willingly caged themselves for the sake of so called convenience.

The lobby doors were left unlocked as he had instructed his nervous accomplice who worked within, leaving out key details of course, about his intended endeavor. The nostril searing stink of the chemical ozone greeted him at entry; unpleasant but bearable to Roush, who had been inhaling pesticide for nearly the last month. A small part in preparation for his expected encounter with the Lamia. It was a simple plan really; bribe the doorman with a few hundred bucks and a promise to help any future traffic violations for him or his family disappear, and *Viola!*...instant accomplice.

In turn, it was said doorman—named Barry—who aided Roush in tainting the well-kept floors of the building with cockroaches. Fumigations were not unheard of at this time of year, and a well accepted choice of action for the owners who lived a time zone away and had the assurances of a policeman that he would personally oversee the evacuation of the tenants and remain to guard the building during the interim.

Summoned by his thoughts, a curly tuft of reddish hair rose from under the desk of the doorman's watch station. Underneath the ginger fire, a chubby, breathless face smiled sheepishly at him.

"Why are you here, Barry? I was specific when I mentioned that no one should remain here tonight."

Barry's chins shook with each word as he spoke his reply. Roush wondered if it was his weight that choked his words or an ingrained nervousness derived from a lifetime of rejection and mockery. Still, Roush reminded himself that this man was risking his job and his life unknowingly by being the needed assistant.

"I j-just stayed to make sh-sure you made it and were the only one in. The building may be empty, but it's my job to guard it," the portly man said with a slip of pride in his voice.

"Understood." The smile Roush offered was slight yet genuine. His presence was at times commanding, perhaps crushing to some who were tamed and grew timid from life's harsh lessons. Barry was such a man. And yet when given a task, or perhaps a purpose, a man like Barry became strong and reliable. Roush wondered if he had to even offer the bribe for Barry to fall in line with him. A little interest and conversation with him may just as easily of spurned his cooperation.

"The tenants won't start returning until Monday as you ordered, detective."

"Well done," Roush sighed, clapping Barry on the shoulder. It was a purposefully exaggerated sigh that he found had often endeared him to others. A show, but nonetheless a displayed weakness which often put people on common ground. It worked. Almost too well for comfort as he only wanted to retire to his apartment and recheck his weapons.

"So what is going down here tonight, detective? I'm ready for anything. Just tell me what to do."

"You should head home, Barry. I'll lock up behind you."

"It's a sting or a setup tonight right? You might need help, someone to watch your back," Barry huffed as he crouched behind the counter and rose again displaying a plastic semi-automatic.

"That's a paint gun, Barry."

"Yeah, I don't have a permit for anything else, but this one bites like a bitch, detective."

Roush teared up as he kept his laughter contained. "It looks pretty mean, Barry. What color are the paint balls?"

"Red!" Barry grinned like the Cheshire cat. "It psyches 'em out. Makes 'em think it's blood."

Anxious and entertaining as he was, Barry was in real danger here. Roush knew he needed to be firm and think quickly to dissuade his accomplice from becoming a complication. He wanted Barry out of here and safely home, but lingering too long to convince him to do that was costing time and lowering the doorman's chances at surviving at all.

"Barry. I need the lobby well lit, especially if you're intent on staying, which I do not recommend. Also I need the hallway lights dimmed. And most importantly, the emergency exits must not be alarmed...and left dark as well. I do expect someone to come looking for me tonight. But they won't risk the light."

"The light?" Barry was puzzled, and almost seemed able to grasp Roush's true meaning. But the detective continued before the doorman could explore the thought.

"Yeah, criminals and underworld types avoid light and cameras. They have this thing about being identified and all. Fix the lights and doors and go home immediately. Or this whole thing could get blown. I'll call you first if I need backup."

This seemed to satiate his accomplice, and Barry immediately seated himself, pounding at his terminals' keyboard, accessing the building control panel. With his gaze intent on the flickering screen, Barry paid no attention as Roush withdrew a small packet from inside his jacket; spreading a thin line of salt and ashes across the doorway and counter-top. "Don't dust anything tonight," was his parting order.

Roush mulled Drew's words as he crossed the lobby to the elevators. Each of the careers he had chosen made friends and loved ones a distinct liability. He learned at a very young age that either could be taken away, or equally as painful; turned upon you given the right circumstances.

At fifteen years, Roush witnessed his assumed father brutally murder his mother. The burly man, much larger and
intimidating at the time, strung her up with a makeshift noose
from the rafters of their Oregon home. He accused her of infidel-
ity and witchcraft as logs were laid below her forming a pyre.

Her killer was partially correct.

Mother had confided to Arnold that she had been visited and
seduced by a dark spirit soon before her marriage. As she traded
vows with her husband to be, a new life was already churning
inside her. The spirit, she claimed, was responsible and Roush's
true father.

The attack had moved her to search for answers beyond the
realm of science and accepted reason. She soon learned much
from her heretic studies, while forming ties with voodoo practi-
tioners and paranormal investigators alike, eventually becoming
deeply accepted into many circles as a priestess; a white witch.

She encouraged her son to learn as well, to explore the middle ground between the science that humanity believed it
understood, and the will and mercy of plausible beings that
dwelt beyond.

He soon came to understand and believe her claims, more so
in his preteen years, as his mind began playing dreams while he
sat conscious in school. Dreams that were proved true to him no
more that several hours or days later. It was then that he fully
accepted his mother's obsession as his own. And sadly, in the
space of a few years afterward, she was gone; destroyed without
trial by a madman mentally conditioned—or perhaps de-
formed—by a lifetime of strict religious indoctrinations.

A soft squish underfoot returned him from thought. A single
red rose lay just inside the elevator door. The edges of his vision
faded to black while his mind grasped the implications of its
presence. The rose magnified in his tunnel vision, bent at its

stem and sat up. The smashed petals fluttered; waving, beckoning him to enter the steel box car.

She was already here.

Wiping at his eyes, he was stepping out; backing into the lobby while keeping a focused eye on the flower that now leered at him. Faceless as it was, it craned itself in his direction, using hidden eyes to watch him as he made his intended departure.

He was crossing the elevator threshold when the doors slammed closed; his body caught off guard, was twisted sideways from the force and pinned between them. He felt tissue bruise as his ribcage compressed a gasping breath from him. The doors continued to press against him, straining to crush him into halves. His veins bulged as blood and heat rushed to his head. The pressure in his cranium felt equal to the crushing force against him, held only at bay by his unrelenting bone structure.

Roush was a large man. Six feet one and holding an impressive physique, especially for a forty year old man who refused to work out or subject himself to a diet plan, he appeared to be in better shape than any fitness crazed high school athlete could hope for.

Bracing his palm and knee against the outside of the door, he pushed away. At last he spilled to the floor, tangling himself as he gulped air and found his defensive stance quickly.

Not surprisingly to him, the doors whisked closed with only the faint rumble of wheels running along unseen tracks; just as any regular conveyance should. The attempt made on his life would have certainly killed an average man, if not by the velocity at which they were closed, then certainly the inhuman strength that continued to press them shut after impact.

He decided to take the stairs; a wiser choice given the circumstances. It was in his favor that the spirit chose to assault him so soon, for if it had been more patient or intentional, it could have waited until he entered the elevator then proceeded to bounce him like a pinball between the basement and the tenth floor, until his remains resembled no more than a sloppy-Joe sandwich in a fine suit.

But instead, the demon chose to toy with him, again as he ascended the plain, monotonous staircases toward the third floor. His steps echoed with small clacking sounds, yet these were soon drowned in the cacophony that erupted as every door exiting the stairwell was pulled open and closed with the speed of a major league baseball pitch. They pounded relentlessly as he grasped the guardrail and quickened his pace. He was not fearful of the Lamia, but here he was vulnerable. The distinction between hunter and prey would be decided within his sanctuary. Apartment 3-03 to be concise.

At his exit to the third floor, his above average attributes were rested further. He rushed in as the door eased open for him, and aptly dodged the hinged projectile as it returned sooner than anticipated. The knob loosened and the surface of the door dented in its final swing. The sheet-rock and frame buckled under the shock of the final closure; leaving jagged cracks and divots of chipped paint to surround the portal.

A single rose lay motionless at his doorstep. Stomping down and rotating his heel, Roush ground it into the carpet that lined the hallways of the upper stories; leaving it behind him in a colorful smear as he entered his apartment.

The interior structure of Roush's home mirrored the others exactly in the building, but it was his choice of color and decoration that gave the two bedroom, one bath unit the atmosphere of a magician's lair. At best it might be compared to an occult specialty bookstore, and worst; it resembled the cluttered interior of the gypsy wagons that held ancient fortune tellers stereotyped in motion pictures.

His walls were bathed in Tuscon Red—with prayers, symbols, and protection wards written across the entirety of each surface, spreading to every room like a magazine foldout. The scripts themselves were written in white, black, and gold, the paint consecrated with holy water; with brush strokes and attention to the finest detail of the written characters that only a true, and expensive, calligrapher could bring to life.

With footsteps unshaken by the adrenaline pounding at his temples, he rechecked the barriers of each room. The lines of salt and ash remained undisturbed. His personal library, as always, remained locked in fireproof boxes, blessed and hidden from curious eyes in a makeshift alcove of his own construction.

The kitchen drawers had been emptied as well of silverware and cooking pans. It was best to avoid sharp and blunt things alike, when inviting a demon into your home.

Roush already carried the weapons he required: a curved silver blade, a pocket-sized notepad filled with his own binding, destruction, and exorcism spells jotted onto its recycled pages, and finally, five yards of high density silver wire, which, it should be noted, was far more expensive than the calligrapher.

He had hoped to find time for a piss and a warm shot of brandy before the show began. In fact he had not truly expected the visitation until much later in the evening, tomorrow evening being his anticipated guess. But this Lamia had reason to be overzealous after all. Among other things, Roush knew how young it was, and for lack of a better word earlier used by Drew; *naive* to its nascent existence as a cursed and light-deprived soul. Nonetheless he was undeterred, if not moved ahead of schedule, by "her" promptness.

He had already seen the tattered shadow of the girl as she floated outside; peering into his windows successively until he was found in the bathroom. With one hand on his trouser snake and the other firmly tipping the brandy in liberal sips; he returned her gaze, which burned into him within the reflection of the bathroom mirror. Her eyes were black pits surrounded with a lizard-like green hue, and remained unblinking as the window glass in front of her began to crack and chip; crumbling as her presence lingered.

"It's more polite to knock first," Roush spoke to her as he placed his glass on the sink and zipped up.

Teeth were bared from her smoky apparition; a circular maw of pointed bone, lacking in top or bottom, beginning or end. The eyes were unchanged. Unable to display anything other than hatred and a murderous will.

Her appearance had changed since the graveyard visitation. Into a less tangible, yet even deadlier form. With a frustrated roar that shattered the window, blowing glass and the sill of it inward, she fled. No doubt to search for a weakness in his household defenses.

Moments later a resounding thud against the wall of the adjacent apartment erupted. It repeated as the Lamia in the next room slammed a medicine cabinet into the sheetrock walls.

Boom! Boom! ...and *knock, knock*. It made Roush smile as he returned to the living room to refill his brandy for one last shot.

It was with a gasp of breath, nearly causing him to drop his glass, that he noticed the photographs of his loved ones staring back at him from their place on the coffee table. The pictures had changed; once smiling faces now replaced with gouged eyes, limbs adorned with tattoos defiling God, and once serene backgrounds that now burned with an inextinguishable fire.

It was a mind trick he knew. Taught in the abyss to the fallen; designed to drive mortals mad, to weaken their will until they were malleable as clay and prone for possession.

"Your parlor tricks will not scare me, child!" Roush grabbed the bottle instead and approached the front door. Outside in the hallway every other apartment doors were torn from their hinges and thrown against the wall, starting from one end to the next, taken down in order as dominoes would fall.

He chugged the bottle until the liquid burned in his stomach and reddened his unusually pale complexion. Grasping the handle of the silver blade attached to his belt he spoke aloud the words that would begin the true fight, wiping away the line of salt resting below his the door, stepping back to avoid its possible swing.

"With respect to the four corners of the North, East, South, and West; with respect to the Holy Trinity, heeding the warnings of Vodun priestesses; by and with my own and free will, given to me by the Almighty; I Arnold Roush invite you into my home for conference. I invite you; the demon once named Alissa, to show yourself now!"

He sensed an unnatural stillness after the words were finished. He knew she was playful and impatient, yet not stupid. In the back of his mind he felt as though the world outside had stalled; frozen in state until this confrontation was decided.

Fueled by liqueur and a wish to end this game, Roush flung the door open with dagger drawn over his head, expecting the demon to rush in and eager to deliver the killing stroke.

There was nothing there. Save for the hallway littered with wooden fragments of the shattered doors, spilled onto the carpet like rice at a fancy wedding.

The ding of the elevator arriving focused his attention. He retreated into his home and held a steady gaze to the outside of the open door. Footsteps approached, neither timid nor heavy. The figure filled his doorway, pausing at the threshold, yet noticeably unafraid. From the light in the hallway Roush could see that it was rotund, with a crop of red hair.

"Barry?" Roush asked, rising from his crouch, lowering the knife.

Barry replied. But his voice was filled with controlled rage. "You were trusted by many, loved by few. And a failure to them all!"

Roush understood, as Barry armed himself with the shoulder strapped paint gun and opened fire. The man was possessed. The hallway exploded into red mist as the gun unleashed its wet barrage. The plaster walls dented and wood splintered from his door frame as Barry ran forward; screaming obscenities while pulling the trigger.

Roush ducked and rolled into the living room. He wasn't eager to test his resilience against any projectile, be it bullet or pellet. That shit still hurt.

Barry laughed maniacally as the paint canister expended itself. It was discarded to the floor as the controlled body neared Roush's cover position.

"Mother died because she couldn't understand your bullshit! You spent your days with her brooding and lamenting worlds beyond! Parallel dimensions? The aspect of Heaven and Hell being defined and compared to the turn of a radio dial? You never appreciated this world, yet you dared to speak of others.

You and you alone were weak. Pathetic. And you slowly dragged her into suicide."

"I…didn't ever expect her to do that. And I didn't want her to." Roush found himself rising, his tears blocked out the twisted face Barry wore; the man's features corrupted by the angry spirit inside him.

Barry lept the couch, pushing Roush to the ground as he mounted him. "I found your books, Father. And I made a deal. Mother would be released from hell, her suicide forgiven, as long as I serve for a hundred years."

"We…the police," Roush stammered, "…never found all of your body. Where is it?"

"Gone," Barry spat, "consumed by the dark, as part of the terms of my agreement."

"I can't believe you did this, Alissa. I should have taught you more. Taught you better."

"I learned well enough!" Barry screamed in his face.

"Then you would know that any bargain with evil is full of loopholes." He lay under Barry's weight, biding his time, waiting for Alissa to waver in her control over the doorman.

"One soul is not considered equal tradeoff for another. Your mother and my wife still burn."

Demons were parasites using mortal vessels for two primary reasons; as a subterfuge vessel to blend in, and also to gather their own strength while residing within a shield of flesh. Seeking to consume and destroy anything that disgusted or defied them. He reminded himself that this creature that spoke through Barry was no longer Alissa. The darkness that she implored her soul to had infused itself into her spirit; corrupting and erasing any traces of the woman she was in life. The resulting thing that claimed her name had also inherited her memories, sorrow, doubt, and rage. Those aspects; it kept and amplified; making itself stronger in the process. It was unlikely that there was enough, if anything left of her inside to assist his escape.

Physically, Barry's body could not match Roush on his worst given day. However, the demon inside did not feel or comprehend the pain a mortal coil held. And therefore, was able to exert it beyond its normal limits of endurance.

Barry laughed as his eyes rolled into his head, leaving the natural boundaries of tissue that held them in place. "There was one other thing I asked. It was for you. You to be shown the pain and suffering you caused us both!" Barry leaned in, a thick trail of drool escaping his lips and running down Roush's neck. "You've been marked, Daddy. You will know the feeling of absolute heartbreak and loneliness. There is another coming. Stronger than I. And your soul will break long before your disembowelment."

This was his moment to turn the tide in his favor. Roush chose his words carefully, he expected they would unseat Barry for a moment at least; giving him time to bind the body with a spell and wind it up in ten yards of silver thread. The Ivory tusk handle of the dagger lay just a few inches away from his grasp. He had planned to pierce the demon through the heart with it, anticipating it to arrive solo, wearing a hellish form. Instead, it craftily engaged him through the doorman. The dagger could be reached and the strike delivered at this point, but not without sacrificing Barry as well. He already had enough blood on his hands and conscience alike. So for now, talking was the primary weapon of choice.

"I've already met my intended assassin. Sadly, it was no match for me. I'd recite its name, but I'm afraid a human tongue has difficulty pronouncing so many consonants."

"Futile bluff," Barry cackled with a glint of superiority in his face, the eyes returned to the proper position.

It was working. With one last push, Roush knew he would be free. "How else would I know that you haunted our family plot at Monterrey? To use it as a hunting ground while awaiting orders from below. Look over my doorway, fallen thing, and see the trophy I collected from your hitman."

Barry did turn to look, shifting his weight while craning to see the lock of red and blonde hair tied together with a silver cross, adorned with sage, hanging over the portal to the hallway. The demon howled in a mixture of shock and anger. But before it could turn back to Roush, the prey took his advantage and planted his feet on the floor, pushing up with his abdomen; he threw Barry off of him.

With thread in hand, Roush hurled toward its resting place below the mounted television.

Barry had no time to get to his feet but he did recover enough balance to blockade his would be captor. Roush was lifted off of his feet and felt the distinct tiling of the kitchen counter top as he was carried from the living room into the cupboards under the sink.

The thread in his hands was turned against him, and Roush felt impending blackout as the demon bound his throat.

A stern voice spoke from behind and above the struggling couple. "You will relinquish the doorman and face us on equal terms demon."

Drew grabbed Barry by the crop of his hair, pulling the head of the possessed body backward. Speaking words in old Latin, some which Roush could not decipher, Drew wrestled Barry away. The two rebounded off of the walls like pinballs in an arcade machine; locked together in a death struggle. The old man was stronger than his frail demeanor and soft spoken monotone gave him credit for. A torrent of ancient Latin exuded with fierce declaration from his lips; a mixture of prayers and commands, some of which Roush could not translate.

Try as it might, Alissa could not subdue nor silence Drew. His mobile exorcism was complete.

Barry began to gag and shudder. Drew thrust his fist into the heaving mouth and pulled the emerging spirit from Barry's throat. The shadow twisted, attempting to break his iron grip.

Letting Barry drop to the floor unceremoniously, the old man continued to hold firmly, unrelenting, as the expelled shadow thrashed and hissed in his grasp. Drew had bound it, with words rather than the stock of tools Roush carried. In his thin fingers the demon was powerless; a black wisp, unable to assume a physical form for retaliation.

"Her fate?" Drew asked a disoriented Arnold.

"It used to be my daughter. And always will be."

Drew pulled out a golden cross and pressed it into the swirls of the shadow. The black tendrils scattered and reformed, feeling pain as the object was introduced.

"You've made quite a mess, Mr. Roush," Drew said matter-of-factly. "One that I can fix. One that you could avoid in the future should you allow me to tutor you."

Drew held the spirit aloft in his bare hands and spoke to the sky, ignoring the thrashing and curses of the tainted soul held in his hands.

"Our Lord in Heaven, please grant passage to this being, once and always your servant, but lost in confusion and anger. Show mercy to this misguided energy, and forgive as you have promised. May the holy light consume the darkness binding this child, allowing ascension. Amen."

The shadow burst into sparks of light, rising upward, disintegrating in flight as they burnt from earthly existence and into the Heaven beyond. Drew's grip, now with nothing to hold, folded into a prayer symbol as he knelt beside an unconscious Barry. He licked his fingers and anointed the unconscious mans head with the symbol of the cross.

"A clear case of designing your own enemy. How unfortunate to have to relinquish the same family member...twice."

Unwrapping the silver thread from his neck, Roush discovered curiosity rather than gratefulness guided his questions. "Why are you here?"

"I stopped by to deliver you the case file for the investigation we will be heading this Monday. It's been a dead end for the common authorities, and the Purity has a keen interest in it. So now it's ours. In the meanwhile, we had best move our friend out of here. The pesticides are still hanging in the air."

"Who are you?" Roush demanded.

"Your new partner," Drew replied without emotion. "I believe we can do great things together. And I look forward to getting started right away. Assuming you have no further family related issues to absolve."

"Old man...your real name," Roush demanded.

Drew smiled, lowering his head as a servant while he spoke; a faint smile of what may be considered regret crossed his lips.

"Michael. There's little more to say until we become better acquainted."

With Barry easily heaved over his shoulder, Drew exited into the red polka-dotted hallway, closing the door behind him.

From Rebirth to Reburial

North
Starring MJ Wesolowski

I've never known pain like it; a relentless gnawing that started in the ends of my fingers and toes, pulling the skin around my nails taught. It's getting worse with every minute that limps by; every shadow that elongates and every degree that drops sends a sheen of agony from my extremities into what feels like the deepest depth of my soul. I cannot move from where I lie, coiled into the corner of this steel prison; I know the metal of the walls, floor and ceiling will take my skin on touch; it is only my weaning body heat and the protection of my clothes that has kept the claws of the scorching cold from me. But as the minutes slump to hours, the idea that I may live through this has begun to fade.

Some time ago, my eyes began to water; I can still feel the tears that have frozen on my cheeks and I dare not change my expression for fear the skin will tear and I will begin to bleed. I am trying not to imagine what my feet must look like, but a relentless image of coiled, frost-blackened toes plagues me mercilessly, gradually snuffing out the dull lamp of hope, which still burns faintly in my heart.

I have a choice either to die of cold, my body shutting down as hypothermia sets in, coiled like a hermit crab in an oversized shell…or to die screaming in the throes of madness, standing before death in the permafrost of the fathomless tundra. Before I make this choice, I need to look back, just once…

i.

After six hours from Pulkovo, Saint Petersburg, we touched down in Yakutsk; the shock of the cold drawing our breath as we followed the small crowd of fur-clad passengers across the desolate strip to the relative warmth of the airport itself. With the

Siberian winter in full force, all that could be seen through the freezing fog was the eerie blinking lights that framed the airport's runways and the hulking shadows of the disused aircraft that stood in regimented lines, like giant, snow clad fossils. Several hours passed as our papers, cameras and sound equipment were unloaded and checked by brusque, suited officials. With the skies darkening and the weather deteriorating, our movements had to be precise, militaristic. We sat, quiet and cold, drinking bitter black coffee as we waited, listening to the mournful howl of the wind.

Thinking back, I only wish I had taken some interest in what we were doing; opened my eyes to the gulf in culture as we left what we knew behind in the warmth and embraced the wild mystery of the frozen north. In truth, I resented it; the cold was already eating into my bones and my head felt fuzzy, as if I'd had too little sleep, or too much. I had no energy and little motivation to undertake this journey. If the circumstances had been different, maybe things might have changed; I will never know.

Half way through series one, I had decided to end my participation on the show. The concept and values that we had started with were original and interesting; this was reflected in our viewing figures and the slightly less snooty reviews in TV listings. However, the more people watched, the more the TV channel pressured our producers for 'evidence', for something 'juicy' that our viewers could 'see'. The response to our show's first series had been somewhat of a surprise amongst the plethora of cheaply produced pseudo-science that filled latenight television. The presenters were ignorant, disrespectful, stamping through the jungles and deserts of faraway places with their size-thirteens; retching gleefully into the camera at Witchetty grubs that a tribe had gone hungry to provide for them. Of course they never found anything; their attitudes to native beliefs made sure they were sold fish scales and gorilla scalps when searching for the half-horse, half-fish, *Mamlambo* in Africa. Entrepreneurial Zulu gangsters paid children to tell stories of the *Tokoloshe* in exchange for aummunition and tobacco from the pockets of the production crew. By night they combed the barren scrubland with ultraviolet cameras, catching nothing but shadows.

We liked to think our show was different, more subtle; instead of trying to catch a monster on camera, we engaged with the people who'd claimed to have seen it. We would eat with them, help them, work for them and recorded endless interview footage. Of course, there were budget constraints, but we managed to overcome them by simply recording the audio of our interviews and presenting it in the final edit of the shows with lingering, long-shots shots of the areas from a single camera.

There was no panicky, infra-red scrabbling after something rustled in the night; we presented the folklore and background that gave birth to the legends we heard and we did it with taste. As a presenter, I liked to step back, let the people speak; let the stories breathe. It gave our show an upmarket, almost intellectual feel, something which was relatively rare in the annals of cryptozoological documentary.

This approach, however, had taken its toll, not only on our representatives at the television channel who had to continuously ward off hints from executives at the channel, that perhaps we could 'sex-up' our show with some light CGI, but on myself and the rest of the team on the ground. For the final episode of series one, we had spent five months in Papua New Guinea, trying to discover why so many 'dinosaur' sightings had been reported in the jungles since missionaries first began spreading their message amongst the tribes; the production company hinting in so many words that we had to actually find something this time and make sure it was caught on camera.

After two of us, myself and Jones, the sound man, contacted malaria, we were eventually allowed to return. The producers weren't happy; I watched the final show from my soaking pillow in a hospital bed, rattling with near delirium and cringing at the cheap stock footage that had eventually been used to pad out a disappointing end to a decent series.

That's why we were here, in an echoing departure lounge in northern Siberia; our destination, the frozen wastes of the Taiga; 100,000 square kilometres of inhospitable, dense woodland, virtually untouched by man. The money that we'd been offered for this 'special', was un-refusable; with a substantial bonus for any sort of evidence of the paranormal we could capture on film. Despite the remoteness of the location and its relative anonymity in popular culture, it sprouted a myriad of idiosyncratic phenomena. The *Chuchuna* was a creature that cropped up in much of the preliminary research into the area; Siberia's black-haired, carnivorous wild man, last confirmed sighting in the nineteen fifties, but who is a staple story of the Tiaga's nomadic Evenki tribes. There were tales of a mummified corpse whose exhumation caused a series of earthquakes throughout the region until it was returned. Not to mention the plethora of flaming, aerial spheres and flame-infused tornados that whirled unrelentingly throughout the lore of the place.

Just do this, I had thought, *get set up for life, then quit.*

Eventually, one of the satellite phones began to trill and Marcin, our interpreter, set down his tepid dregs of coffee and began talking in rapid Russian, pacing back and forth and nodding. He turned to the rest of us.

"We stay in Yakutsk today," he said, his English fluent, but heavily accented, "eat, sleep and tomorrow we take another plane, then we meet our guide into the Taiga."

Maybe it was something in Marcin's voice, maybe it was my tiredness, the cold, the creeping suspicion that I had returned to work too soon from the malaria. Whatever it was, at that moment, a shadow passed briefly over my heart and made the hairs on the back of my neck stand taut.

'*Into the Taiga*'

I felt like we were standing at the edge of something, feet at the brink of some ghoulish, mouth-like drop.

I could not supress a shiver and my whole body vibrated slightly for a single second. Outside the snow fell in an eternal, silent squall.

ii.

It was -46°c when our second plane touched down on the voluminous plateau of pure white snow that stretched for miles around until it hit a hard line of ice-bound forest. The sheer expanse of the place filled me with a strange agoraphobia I had never experienced before. On ground level, the forests of the horizon and even the blunt spines of the mountains we had seen from the plane were obscured by a permanent, icy mist that hung heavy in the air and thus we had the impression of being simply nowhere. We were the only passengers of the plane and after we had collected our own luggage, we stood in a shivering line, scarves over our mouths, passing the cumbersome cameras, tents and assorted safety equipment between us to collect in a large pile on what we hoped was the edge of the runway. A few minutes later, the plane noisily departed, rattling away across the compacted snow and vanishing into the fog. With the wail of the wind, we never even heard it it take off.

This was the furthest you could get to the Taiga by air; we were now to wait for our escort across the last actual road of our journey; the frozen expanse of water that was the Kolyma highway, also known as 'The road of bones'. We huddled closer together, our hands tucked beneath our arms, only our eyes visible beneath our thick, thermal hoods.

Nobody spoke.

iii.

Edik, our guide, drove a tank; it was a huge, ex-soviet machine that growled and rattled across the snow. It was vaguely diamond shaped, with a simple, circular entrance and exit where there had once been a gun turret. The tank rocked sickeningly up and down as it tore a trench through the flattened, ice-stiffened foliage that lined the empty wilderness of the Taiga, belching a cloud of foul-smelling black smog in its wake. The rattling caterpillar tracks effortlessly negotiated every ridge as the tank plunged down every dip and roared through any blockage like a blunt, metal rhino.

The crew and I were compacted between the recording equipment in the hull, packed so tightly in our thermals, knees tucked beneath our chins; we felt every lurch of the machine, but thankfully not hurled back and forth against its metal walls. The tank's inside was bitterly cold and lit only by the dull, grey daylight that seeped in from the two windows at its front. As darkness fell, the only light inside the tank was the glowing panels of controls in the front and a flickering electric light directly above my head.

After what must have been several hours, weary of the clanking violence of the tank's movement, we came to an abrupt halt. Edik turned from his position in the driving seat to regard us; a smile plastered across his face; we grinned back weakly. I had paid little attention to how we had acquired our guide, all I knew about Edik was his name and that he was an Evenk, part of a nomadic tribe that herded reindeer in the Taiga. He spoke in rapid Ewenki to our interpreter, Marcin, before gesturing to somewhere outside and placing a raised index finger to his lips, his head turning his gaze from the tank's window. I opened my mouth to speak and Marcin shook his head frantically, his eyes wide. A few moments passed and we looked to each other and at Marcin, who still shook his head faintly as he followed Edik's pointed finger through the front windows of the tank and into the frozen darkness.

Outside, there was only blackness, interspersed with a whirling grey blizzard. Cramp burned in my legs, and my stomach groaned with hunger. The silence inside the tank was torturous and I could hear the chattering of the crews' teeth. Marcin stayed focused on the view out of the front window and I could hear Edik muttering to Marcin in Ewenki, his other hand now placed over his eyes.

The wind moaned and we moved instinctively closer together as a ghastly flurry of sleet began to rattle malevolently against the metal shell of the tank. More minutes passed and the crew beside me began to get restless, muttering and whispering;

Edik seemed not to notice them, he was still crouched, facing away from the yawning darkness, his body unmoving. He did not seem to care as the crew began to unpack their meagre supplies and bottles of water.

I raised myself slightly from my coiled position and shuffled gently forward, closer to where Edik and Marcin were sitting at the front of the tank. I followed their gaze and it was difficult to make out anything in the blackness, with the reflection of the inner lights against the Plexiglas. As if reading my mind, Edik reached down and pressed a button beside him; the lights inside the tank went out. For what I imagined was several hundred square miles, the only light in the lonely Taiga was the dim, red glow of the tank's controls.

There was no break in the night and still Edik sat, silently, his head in his hands. Never being one to question our guide, I simply sat there, too, staring out of the windows. The minutes began to drag and my hunger, mixed with the crawling jet lag begin to take their toll as I felt my eyelids droop and my vision begin to blur. That's why I could not be certain that, accompanied by some involuntary sleep-twitch, I saw what I thought I saw.

Some movement of the crew in the back was reflected, casting that terrible shadow that passed high over the tank and blocking, for a few seconds, the ever falling snow. My tired eyes must have blurred my vision, projecting the twin red lights from the deck of controls as the stare of twin red, lamp-like eyes that seemingly glanced toward us for a few seconds before disappearing into the night. Edik's sharp inhalation of breath and Marcin's gasp were nothing but simple relief that the sleet had begun to end and we could continue. I shuffled back to the back of the tank, a heavy horror sinking to the bottom of my stomach as Edik turned around, restarted the engine and we began to move. Marcin did not look round and for that, I was glad.

iv.

We began our work the very next morning—I had little idea of how far we had travelled, or for how long; the tiredness getting the better of me and a fitful sleep descending mere minutes after our unscheduled stop in the sleet storm. I put my strange sightings down to weariness, the morning's half-light chasing any shadowy doubts from my mind as we stumbled from the tank into the white-hung tree lines of the Taiga.

Edik had stopped the tank in a small copse and behind us, on the half-path where the tank had flattened the undergrowth, through the fresh fall of snow; branches were already unbending and bushes rising from where they had been flattened. It was as if the Taiga was erasing every trace of our passage. It was difficult to come to grips with the blue, dusky light of the morning; knowing we only had a few hours before darkness would fall again. An odd sadness began inside me, which I quelled rapidly; we were to be here for a while, I could not let the weather get to me on the very first day. At least the sleet and snow had let up, but basic movement in the freezing temperatures was hard.

We were situated a mile south from where Edik's people, the Evenki, had made their camp. We were told that the racket of the tank would have disrupted the huge herd of reindeer that the Evenki were steering through the Taiga, but what we had paid Edik to guide us here would be of great use to their passage and they would be willing to help us make our television show.

After a small breakfast from our provisions, we'd pitched a few of our tents for sleeping and the large white storage tent for the equipment around the back of where the tank sat and we we were ready to go. The plan for the few daylight hours was the camera team were to begin capturing establishing shots if the light was good enough. With the help of Edik and Marcin, to interpret, some of the Evenki would be willing to talk to us on camera about the *Chuchuna*. Edik had told us that there were less and less folk that believed in the old tale, that it was used mainly as a campfire story to dissuade the young Evenki children to go wandering off into the Taiga. However, there was a few of the old people who still talked of the legend or had claimed to have seen one.

After all radios were tested and communication established, three of the camera crew disappeared into the trees to begin filming around the area; a mile or two west, was a break in the dense forest at the banks of one of the Tunguska rivers which the Evenki were following on their herd. Marcin and I set up a rudimentary interview area beside the tank. It was around -30°C and both of us were in thick layers of thermals, only our eyes peeking out from our synthetic, fur-lined hoods. We moved quickly, using eyebrow raises and grunts to communicate. The radios crackled occasionally as the camera crew confirmed their positions.

It was important to keep contact in areas like this; we had found the same in the jungles of Papua New Guinea, city people, unused to such a vast expanse of wilderness could get easily disconcerted, no matter how close they were to camp. People are used to paths, to maps, to knowing that if you walk in a certain direction for long enough you will come to a road or meet another person; that there'll be a coffee shop and a visitor centre at the end. In the yawning wilderness, though, the trees do not end, the landscape will outlast human footfall with ease. The disconcertion that this idea causes, can lead to panic and panic in the wilderness is a thousand times more dangerous than any equatorial dinosaur or Siberian Bigfoot.

One of the digital cameras was set up on a tripod that stood knee-deep in the snow beside the tank; we had laid some reindeer skins that Edik had given us over some sturdy logs to make a long bench and behind was the swift darkness of the forest. The silence of the Taiga was eerie, no birds sang and no creatures rustled in the trees; if Marcin and I had spoken, it would have been in whispers as the grim weight of the cold hung in the air, it's cruel beak pecking spitefully at our fingers and toes.

We were taking a break inside the metal capsule of the tank, drinking day-old coffee from one of the flasks and watching the progress of the camera team on one of the laptops. The GPS map of the Taiga was simply brown circles with the curve of the

Tunguska River in blue. Our camera team's signal was a little blue circle that jerked a few centimetres forward ever five minutes or so. Marcin and I watched in silence before we heard the creak of boots through the snow and the sound of approaching voices.

We stood next to the interview area, watching as Edik led two of the Evenki into the clearing; a man and a woman; they looked ancient, leathery, wrinkled skin which was a deep olive brown, heavy-lidded eyes and black gaps where there was once teeth. They were dressed in their traditional dress, which we supposed was for our benefit, great cloaks of reindeer hide and thick hoods of fur. The horizontal stripes of black, white and red on their fronts reminded me of Native American dress; and this was reinforced further as they approached closer and we saw the threaded beads and feathers that hung around their shoulders and across their foreheads. For the first time during this project, a small flame of excitement began to flicker inside me; it was always the elders of any peoples that had the most valuable stories and memories.

Edik sat them down and spoke to Marcin in Ewenki, who beckoned me over and explained that these people had been herding in the Taiga since they were children and that they had seen a great deal of interesting things. Trying to ignore the pain of the cold in my feet, I spoke quickly into the radio to the camera team, telling them to hold their position and not move as we were to begin filming. I was answered by a crackled confirmation. I noticed from the corner of my eye as I spoke into the radio, that the Evenki elders were muttering to each other and motioning west, the direction the camera crew had gone.

The elders rose and shook my hand, the woman presenting me with an exquisite pair of reindeer-skin gloves that were patterned with tiny beads woven into the wrists. I felt dreadful for accepting them, but knew they would be offended if I had not. I nodded to Marcin who explained them about the camera and the sorts of things I wanted to talk to them about. Their voices did not seem so out of place in the frozen silence of the Taiga, their

314

clucking language rose softly with the faint winds that were beginning to build and whistle between the trees.

As the morning light paled into the beginnings of the afternoon and the faint sun gathered limp light, the Evenki elders told
us of a great darkness that had once fallen over the Taiga centuries ago; a whirlwind that had ripped a hole in the ground and
from that hole same a tall tower emerged, that rose high into the
sky and glowed in the sun.

Marcin and I looked at each other, trying not to appear surprised; this was unlike any tribal story we had heard and
according to the elders, this tower became known to all tribes in
the Taiga as it was visible from all over the land. I looked up at
the horizon, its vast darkness of trees, and imagined the sheer
size that this tower had to have been.

The elders continued, their eyes calm and heads nodding
with what I could only construe as a sadness, or fear.

The tower stood for a time before it began to sink back into
the ground. As the tower sank, it gave off huge booming and
cracking noises that sent the reindeer herds crazy and so the
people kept far from the sinking tower until it was gone from
sight. In its place was a deep chasm that gave out a strange light
and belched a foul smoke.

"The light was a sun..." Marcin said, looking back to the elders and confirming the word in Ewenki.

"The sun?" I looked at them and pointed into the sky and
the faint light that was already beginning to wane.

Both the elders shook their heads, speaking to Marcin and
pointing down to the ground. I followed their gaze and Marcin
spoke.

"They say it was a sun, but not *our* sun, a sun for the land
beneath the earth."

I felt my eyes widen with surprise and leaned forward, my
notes on the *Chuchuna* forgotten as Marcin recited back this
strange story.

"They say that no one went near the hole in the earth and
those who did, did not return..."

The stillness of the Taiga around us was suddenly very lonely. The wind had stepped up its whistling into a moan and the cold began to intensify. I could hear the camera whirring angrily behind my shoulder and knew that the equipment could not last much longer out in the cold. The elders who sat before us seemed uninhibited by the drop in temperature and looked to me, the black wrinkles still in their calm faces.

"What do you mean, '*land beneath the earth*'?" I ventured.

Marcin relayed this to the elders who looked at each other and conferred quietly, their heads shaking. The man made a strange gesture to me with his hands and leaned forward conspiratorially. The woman was pulling her hood tight around her face. The man spoke, his voice a whisper and Marcin strained to hear.

"He says they are like people, the people below the earth. Some see them in the Taiga and name them *Chuchuna*; they are the wild people who eat the flesh of their own and bow to their demons."

The radio gave a sudden explosion of static, making us all jump; I turned around to look at it, my hands shaking now, with what must have been a chill as the temperature felt as if it has begun to descend again.

"Er...tank camp...come in..." The voice on the radio was breathless, panicky.

I cursed and got to my feet, the wind chose that moment to gust violently into the clearing, nearly knocking me to my feet in an icy wave. The feel of it was excruciating against the exposed skin around my eyes and mouth. I grasped the radio and spoke through my teeth; the wind howled around me and the first icy beads of snow began to rattle against my face.

"Tank camp, what is it, over?"

Another burst of static.

"I'm sorry, I know you're interviewing but..." The static came again as if the wind was breathing directly into the mouthpiece. I glanced around and saw the Evenki elders stood up now, cloaks wrapped around them; they were talking rapidly to Marcin who was nodding, his face serious.

316

"We found some..." static again "...it's weird, just ...weird and..." the static roared "...we've been followed...but we ...on film...coming back back now...over."

The radio went dead; its red light fading to a plastic grey. I half heartedly tried making it work, but it felt dead in my hand, like an empty shell. Stuffing it back into my pocket, I turned back to the Evenki elders who were being led back into the trees by Edik as the snow began to come down now proper, a relentless sheet of frowning grey. I raised my hand to the elders and I think I saw the man raise his back, in farewell.

Marcin was wrestling with the interview camera trying to heave it and the tripod into the tank before we were engulfed by the snow. I gathered my notes and the clipboard that he had been holding, which now lay discarded in the snow. We had captured the interview on camera, but for some reason, Marcin had written down a sentence and underlined it twice:

In that cursed place below the ground, they raised the demon of the white silence that walks the winter winds..."

As the wind screamed around us, we retreated into the tank, turning on our lone heat lamp for warmth and checked the laptop for the GPS signal of the crew. They were moving quickly, their pace suggesting a full on sprint back to camp.

v.

"There, just there." Swann pointed to the laptop screen, his finger visibly shaking.

We paused the feed and stared at the image on the screen. The frozen river wound into the middle distance, its banks lined with stubbly outbreaks of trees. It was a desolate, still place and the roaring of the wind outside the tank lent a haunted, ancient quality to the footage the camera crew had taken this morning.

Swann, the head of the camera team, was motioning to a faint grey blob that had appeared on the far end of the frozen water.

"Now play it again."

The shadow seemed to unfurl, morphing gently from a blob into a vaguely human form. It had long, spindly legs and walked upright, its gait was ape-like as it disappeared out of focus.

"We saw a few of them." Swann was looking around the inside of the tank at the rest of us, his eyes wide in the dim light.

"They stayed a distance away, but we heard them in the trees and kept seeing them duck out of sight."

A silence reigned in the tank; save for the shriek of the wind that buffeted its metal sides. This was our moment; we had captured some real evidence, deep in the Taiga on our very first day. However, no one was smiling or even seemed to be considering this sentiment; the camera crew were shaken, and there was no sign of the camaraderie that usually accompanied our expeditions into the wildernesses of the world.

"Now..." Swann spoke again and this time his voice grew harsh, "we found some other stuff, too."

Marcin and I looked at each other briefly. Swann and the camera crew had come haring into the tank some minutes ago, with no explanation of what had gone on whilst we interviewed the elders. Swann had plugged the hard drive off the camera to the laptop, waving away our queries. Edik had gone back to the Evenki camp so was unavailable to speculate on what the fuzzy figure may have been.

Swann's fingers whizzed over the laptop and he opened some more footage from the day; a white blur before the camera focussed onto what was clearly a man-made structure. It was a sort of watch-tower that rose between two trees. About a hundred meters into the air, it stood on four metal legs that were black with age. Foliage grew all over it and the wooden, shed-like structure at its tip was rotted through. The camera panned from the structure, downward to a ruined fence that stood six feet from the ground; topped with limp barbed wire and several inches of snow.

"What is it?" I was flabbergasted to see something so civilized in this empty place.

"It's a Gulag," Bridges, the newest member of the camera crew, spoke up shakily from where he was hunched, in the corner of the tank.

"I studied them during my degree. They're basically labour camps used by the Red Army when they invaded Poland."

"But why *here*? How did they even get prisoners here?" Marcin asked; a stern horror on his face.

"They used the river, I assume," Bridges answered, his voice low and scared, barely a whisper. "The prisoners would have been loggers or miners. Also, where better for somewhere like this? They wouldn't need guards; no one was getting away from here. You could drown in the river or freeze to death in the forest. Only five hundred, from the twelve thousand who were sent here in the forties, actually survived."

"Jesus..." I breathed.

I remembered visiting Auschwitz when I was a teenager and being engulfed by the quiet sadness of the place; its bleak walls and rows of sunken stone sheds that stood in perpetual silent misery. On the screen, this watchtower and this wall, only just visible through the tangled, snow covered trees carried with it the same strange solemnity.

"Did you go inside?"

Swann nodded, he grasped the laptop again and began opening more files.

There was some sort of entrance yard, drenched in snow and only discernable as a yard from the white walls and fences that surrounded it. The camera followed the wall until it came to a huge steel gate that stood squarely at the yard's entrance. The gate was wrought iron and obviously had been there since the camp had been built. It too, was covered with snow, but looking closer, there seemed to be something else, something misshaped about it.

The camera zoomed in and Marcin and I gasped; the gate was hung with bones. Rib-cages in their delicate curls and hands with the fingers dripped through the gaps in the gate's bars Assorted reindeer antlers gave the gate's top, a twisted, spiny crown.

"My God..." my hands covered my mouth now as I stared at the gradually unfolding images on the screen. The camera was panning back from that gate, across the still yard to a raised platform at its other end.

The wooden platform was topped by six wooden poles, around eight feet high; the poles were approximately a foot distance from each other and were decorated with tattered feathers coiled in swathes of a black fabric. What made Marcin and I gasp again out loud were the skeletons that were affixed to the poles.

The camera zoomed in further and we could see where the bodies had been shackled by their feet and their hands, high above their heads. They were each around six to seven feet tall; some still had tatters of flesh around their wrists and ankles, with long, filthy hair that hung in matted clumps. The camera looked them up and down, before focussing hard onto the skulls, which looked vaguely human, but for a sharp protrusion where the nose was. Their arms and legs were long and the shoulders broad. Runes were carved onto the skulls with what looked like charcoal. The camera simply panned up and down this monstrous scene as if unable to believe what it was filming; the breathing of the cameraman on the film was suddenly loud in the tank.

The wind howled outside and we all jumped when the camera view on the laptop abruptly jerked and the man operating it gave a frightened shout. We looked to the crew; Bridges was crying; his head curled into the lap of one of the others and his shoulders shaking.

"That's when we saw more of them," Swann said, grimly, closing the lid of the laptop. "They moved through the forest behind us. Like gorillas, but skinny, long-haired; these great noses on them like snouts."

I could not answer; everyone else was silent, looking to me with expectant faces.

"But, why didn't you...?" A sudden concern began to brim at the edges of my consciousness; if these things had followed the camera crew from the Gulag camp, they would know...

"We told you!" Swann cut me short, his voice just about steady. "Didn't we?" He looked quickly at the others who nodded vigorously. "We told you on the radio that we were followed. If you'd have gone and left us—"

"Where's the phone?" I blurted, whipping around suddenly in the confines of the tank. The others shrank back and Marcin took my arm, his grip firm.

"It's in the tent. Are you going?" I stared hard into his terrified eyes and at that moment, as if to confirm what our fear had gradually been telling us, there was a sound from somewhere in the darkness outside; a sharp scrambling and the scrape of claws on metal. We yelled as one and Bridges began to scream.

"I want to go home! Get me *home!*"

In the small light that flickered in the tank, people began to panic; there were shouts and crashes as we thrashed like netted fish.

"Get me home! I want my mum...please! I want my mum!"

"Shut up, Bridges!" I screamed and there was the sound of a muffled thump, Bridges made an *'oof' sound and was silenced.*

"Stay still!" I shouted, and soon, the others stopped their moving. A full on gale was now screeching against the tank and the sound of pattering feet and fingers came occasionally from the walls.

"They can't get in," I said, my voice only just holding together through the gasping of my panic. "We can lock that hatch from inside."

"What are they?" Swann whispered; his voice hard and desperate.

"They are from below the earth," Marcin's voice was stilted with horror, "and they appease their demon with sacrifice that they may stay alive in the cruel wind of the Tundra."

We all turned to Marcin and he stared around us with his wide, unblinking eyes.

"What did the Evenki tell you, Marcin, when the radio went off? Why did they leave so soon?"

Marcin's usually calm face was pale and his voice came in gasping bursts. "They said to see the demon that walks on the wind, is to be consumed by him."

I thought of those red lamps that had stared down from some dizzy height above us as the tank passed through the Taiga not one night ago.

To see the demon that walks on the wind is to be consumed by him.

The wind roared again from somewhere outside, but this time it carried the deep, predatory growl of whatever it was that walked there.

vi.

The others are dead, or close to it. As the temperature has gradually dropped over the last few hours, days, weeks, they steadily got quieter; curling into themselves beneath their thermals. I hear no breathing, bar my own, alongside the howl of the wind and the thing that walks it. I have tried to speak a few times, but they have given me no answer. Last time I tried to speak, my lips were frozen closed and now they sting with red pain. The water bottles have frozen; I watched their sides burst as the time has passed and the walker on the wind waits, a white shadow with those unblinking eyes.

I have a choice before me and the walker of the wind knows it, too. If he wanted to, his corpse-white claws could tear through the sides of the tank like a clumsy child heaves bright wrapping from a box. He could pour me into the snow and devour me in his jaws while his hideous followers watch on, bowing their shaggy, ape-like bodies to their silent god.

Or he could wait, for the cold to take me or my sanity to fail me.

Time passes slowly in the white silence of the frozen north.

North

Revenge of the Zombie Pussy Eaters

Staring Craig Wallwork

It's a little after 2am at a gay bar in the village called Al's Jizzera, and I'm watching my friend Corbier remove the head from a lesbian zombie by repeatedly stabbing her neck with the leg of a barstool.

The air blisters with the stench of smoke, cancer, sanitary towels and all other things bloody and decaying. Lying face down in a toilet stall, arteries pumping out a strawberry glaze across the tiled floor, is a woman I only know as Pela. Her skirt is hitched up over two perfect arse cheeks, the rabbit's tail of her white knickers on full view. Peeking from the gusset is the white cotton string from her tampon. Zombies are like bears; they can smell blood from several miles away. This is not fact, but my own conclusion.

As Corbier strikes at the yawning wound in the zombie's nape, twisting the barstool leg left and right until I can hear sinew and flesh squelching, I hear him say, "She was willing! Willing!" Corbier is horny. He'd fuck a barber's floor if he had the chance. Pela was the only girl in nearly three years willing to even talk to him, let alone seem remotely interested. Three years without sex. To Corbier's cock and eyesight, that might as well have been dog years. An hour ago they were in a doorway behind this club and he tried to finger her. A little of her menstrual blood made it on the tips. That was all it took. Corbier now has only three digits on his left hand, and will no doubt turn into one of these walking dead within the next few hours. It came as no consolation when I suggested it might not have been his fingers covered in blood.

I clamber onto the washbasin counter and look out through a small gap in the toilet's window. The darkened cobbled streets

325

of the gay village crawl with lesbian zombies all staggering around searching for pussy. A poster for Gay Pride hangs from the wall, a bloodied handprint smeared across the word "Pride." The trills of the women's screams are matched only by that of the trannies and ambulance sirens. Car headlamps frantically throw light against the walls and murky recesses as they manoeuvre out of narrow streets, and every now and then I see a flash of a woman with her legs akimbo, between them another head bobs up and down, chomping. Even men are not safe. Like Corbier, the scent of a woman on your skin can make you just as vulnerable.

I hear one woman scream, "One of my tits has gone!" and I watch her crawl along the floor like she's searching for a lost contact lens, her halter-neck top stained red.

I tell Corbier "It's the end of the world!" but he's too busy wrenching the skull away from the zombie's spine. Like Perseus holding aloft the head of Medusa, he lifts her face toward me. I stare for a moment at the zombie head in his hand. If Liza Minnelli had died of a wasting disorder, this is what her corpse would look like. Her jaw chews on words locked in the vocal chords sprayed across the floor.

I turn back to the window and hear Corbier ask, "I thought these fuckers were supposed to die when you removed their head?"

I point out to Corbier that he may have mixed zombies up with Henry VIII's wives. "You need to destroy the brain," I say, and I notice outside a police car and a female officer getting torn apart by five bloodthirsty dykes.

"What are we doing here?" I ask as Corbier whacks the Minnelli head against the sink in an attempt to crack the skull.

"It was our cocks that brought us here, remember?" he says, a little out of breath. Ah yes, I remember now.

10pm and our friend Gordon is lining up small shot glasses filled with Aftershock; its blue liquid reminding me of mouthwash.

"To our cocks!" he said, and then knocked his back in one. Corbier was next, then Boden, and finally me.

The ink on Gordon's divorce papers was still wet and already he was living the bachelor lifestyle. The air around me was filled with a deep bass drum that shook my inner organs lose, and every darkened cavity of the room was assaulted repeatedly by annoying multi-coloured lights.

The bar, as I remember it, was called Profusion; which was ironic because the place was bereft of anything save for a Chinese barman called Harold, and us four. I was having a shit night. I hate the city. I hate the lights and the noise of the streets and all the fucking weirdos and drunken hordes of young people vomiting in the gutter. It's a cesspit of all that's wrong in the world. But Gordon was happy, happy for the first time in fifteen years now that his marriage was over to Susie.

To be honest, we were all relieved Susie was gone. She had some temper on her. And paranoid? I never met a woman so fucked up in the head. Susie once accused him of having an affair because his breath smelt of fish. The fact that he had been to a sushi restaurant for lunch didn't distract her from throwing all his clothes into the street.

So there we were, Boden, Corbier, me and Gordon with his printed t-shirt that said, "I just lost 200 pounds of ugly fat on the divorce diet!" To last the night, all I needed to do was put up with Boden complaining about his job and the fact he still lived with his mother, listen to Corbier making smutty remarks about every girl he passed, and listen to Gordon tell me how much of a bitch Susie was. I figured in five hours, I'd be home again.

After Profusion we hit a few other bars, one of which we had to leave because Corbier had been slapped in the face by a woman because he asked to smell her vagina. That was one of his favourite lines to a woman. To him it was a win-win scenario. Either they let him smell their vagina, or if they didn't. He offended them by replying, "Well, it must be your feet then."

When we finally arrived at The Missionary, a bar devoid of all moral and pious responsibility, it was apparent there was a significant scarcity of women. Save for the girl who had slapped Corbier—and a few random girls you could throw in a river and skim off ugly all week—nearly every place we went in was full of guys. Boden said the reason was probably due to Corbier being out. Corbier believed it was because Boden was so fucking boring they'd all committed suicide.

It was only Gordon who had the most reasonable explanation. "They're all at the gay village," he said knocking back another shot of something luminous.

Gordon worked with a couple of gay guys and said they were always complaining about all the straight women who drank in the gay village. Straight girls were more carefree, less concerned about the advances of drunken men. In a gay bar, a woman is free to enjoy herself with friends. I suggested it's probably best we don't spoil their fun. To Corbier, that was like Willy Wonka telling Augustus Gloop not to drink from the chocolate river. Ten minutes later, we were in a bar called the Slit Pit.

There was an act, a transvestite called Tranny Wynette. He/she was dressed in gold lamé and singing old country songs that had a gay twist, or supplied a little innuendo like, *If I Were a Little Girl*, *Joy of Being a Woman*, *Will the Circle Be Broken*, *Woman to Woman*, and *Good Girls Gonna Go Bad*. It was all too camp for me, but Gordon got really into it all and even requested Tranny Wynette sing *D.I.V.O.R.C.E.*, which he/she did much to his enjoyment.

Corbier had approached five pretty women in the first ten minutes of arriving and concluded by their disinterest they must have been Vagatarian. He had a point, save for those Corbier had approached, all of the women in the place either appeared masculine in visage, or Cagney and Lacy doppelgangers. Boden said it was like being stranded out at sea, but you can't drink a drop of the water. We decided to move to another bar to see if things improved.

The gay village was a complex little maze of streets and alleys that traversed an old shipping canal. Every street led to another identical street lined with cobblesrone roads, all of which were punctuated with neon lights for clubs and bars with strange and exotic names like, The Velvet Trap, Hussy Galore, Bollix Boutique, and Le Madame. The doors were brimming with men with shaved heads and tight-fitted t-shirts and women with shaved heads and tight-fitted tops. It was like a group of Hare Krishnas had been consumed by Calvin Klein and then spat back out into the street. The music was a constant heartbeat, throbbing against the chest of each dimly lit bar.

As we navigated ourselves around the village, Corbier announced that he wanted to stop and piss. We suggested he wait and use the toilet at the next place, but Corbier was concerned it might get a little too like the Shawshank Redemption. We all ducked down an alley and lined up against its wall like prisoners about to be shot, all except for Boden who never takes a piss outside, and has this really strange habit of always using a cubicle when we're out.

As piss steam rose up from between our legs and united with our breath, I felt Boden's hand tap me on my arm. "Look," he said.

I followed his gaze to see two attractive women against the wall a little further down from us. The one with her back to us was kissing the neck of the other. I whispered to Corbier and Gordon.

"Fuck me," said Corbier, "she's really going for it on her neck."

I felt we'd seen enough and suggested we all leave. Boden agreed, but Corbier, the only person still with his dick out, said he'd catch up.

Before we could move an inch Gordon said, "Look, she's going down on her."

Sure enough, the woman who had her back to us now had her head between the legs of the other woman. Having only seen such a thing on TV, and though morally wrong to observe, we were all transfixed by the blatant act of lesbian sex only a few feet away.

Corbier inched forward for a better view, his hand rubbing his crotch. We whispered to not get too close, but he kept waving us away with his spare hand. It was so dark; it was inevitable Corbier was going to stumble over something. The noise distracted the lesbians and the one eating muff turned to face us. Corbier let out a noise of disgust and ran back to us, forcing his cock in his trousers.

"That dyke is on her bike," he said.

We assumed he meant her monthly cycle. We looked over and the woman staring back at us had blood all over her mouth. Gordon dry-heaved and I held my hand against my mouth, half-expecting something to come churning out. The woman let out a godawful cry, and from dense shadows three other willowy figures in tight jeans appeared, all walking as though a rock was in their shoe. Boden grabbed my arm and pulled me back onto the street.

12:30am. A woman, who looked a lot like a fat version of K.D. Lang, began running toward us. Stopping at Gordon, and with panic in her voice, she said, "There're women in that bar eating each other!"

Gordon replied, "I thought you'd be happy about that."

She looked behind, saw something and then ran past us all. A few seconds later another woman with thick glasses and spiky hair stumbled over and grazed her elbows and knees. Boden went over to help her up, and without a word of thanks she just got to her feet and began staggering down the street. We heard more screaming coming from the adjacent bars and people spilling out into the street.

A man cried out in a high-pitched voice, "Zombies! Lesbian Zombies!"

We all looked at each other and began laughing. "Yeah right," said Corbier, "Zombians!"

He put his arms out in front of him, rolled backed his eyes and began walking like the Mummy, "Puuussssy!" he drooled,

"Me eat puussssy!" He didn't see a fat woman fall out into the street chewing on a forearm.

People screamed and we all stepped back. Like a school of fish huddled together for protection, the swell of onlookers ran away in one direction. Instinctively we joined them, unsure exactly where we were going. We turned a corner onto West-Bulford Street and saw four zombies sharing a meal. Two of the zombies were gorging on opposite ends of a long string of intestine, their heads drawing closer and closer to each other until we assumed it would end in a *Lady and the Tramp* kiss. It didn't, they just growled at each other and spooned out more guts.

And as we gazed in revulsion while the other two zombies feasted between the legs of one poor woman, Corbier remarked, "They're eating more pussy than cervical cancer."

A few trannies wearing high heels fell over near us as their ankles gave way to the momentum. We turned and noticed men and women running into buildings and a few more frantically hitting the buttons on their mobile phones. We ran a little further before finally stopping beside a bridge to catch our breath.

"It can't be zombies, right? They're not real, right?" asked Boden.

Before we could even muster up an answer, we heard a woman scream from below. Gordon looked over the bridge, and on the embankment a woman with bleach-blonde curls was holding her friend in fear. Hobbling toward them were three zombies.

"Whatever the fuck they are," said Gordon, "there's three about to eat those girls down there."

Gordon shouted that we were on our way. He lowered himself over the side of the bridge, landing on the embankment with a heavy thump. Corbier followed him while Boden and I watched on with bewilderment and surprise.

When Corbier was eight years old he watched the *Karate Kid* seventy-six times and became obsessed with learning Karate. He weighed close to eleven stone and had about as much grace as a heifer wearing stilettos. He lost of a lot of his puppy fat masturbating vigorously during his teen years, but it had been almost twenty years since I'd even seen him try the crane, but right then, with a moaning, flesh-eating, pallid-faced lesbian approaching him, there he was, arms raised and one leg cocked. Gordon stood behind him, his very own Mr. Miyagi whispering in his ear. I felt this was more than just a simple homage to a movie for Corbier—it was the little fat kid inside him getting revenge against all the girls who never once looked his way when he was a kid.

When we heard Gordon shout, "Now!" both Boden and I watched in awe as Corbier jumped from one foot to the next, striking the zombie in her tits and knocking her into the river. With his confidence build up, he roundhoused the other one into the river and put his fist through the face of the last. The two women cheered and ran toward him and Gordon. The pretty girl was called Pela, and her friend was Gayle, the only two straight women in the village.

For the first time since I have known him, Corbier spent his time in the company of another woman without once farting or acting chauvinistic or vulgar. He offered his coat to Pela and remained by her side the whole time. Providence shone on Gordon, too. Gayle had just been through a messy divorce as well, and upon noticing his t-shirt, spent most of the few minutes comparing notes on the appalling behaviour of her ex partner.

Boden and I just watched on, caught in this surreal world that was unfurling before us where women were running for their lives and these "zombians" were dragging their heels in an attempt to find fresh meat. And as the streets became more frantic, and the gutters brimmed with fresh blood, it was suggested that we hole up for a while someplace safe.

We jostled the crowds and realised that we didn't know any way out of this place. It wasn't safe on the streets, so we found the nearest empty club, Al's Jizzera. Inside we found limbs scattered across the dance floor, heads with Ellen Degeneres hairstyles strewn left and right. The DJ was slumped over the decks, a lanky women covered in tattoos and a gaping hole in her neck big enough to accommodate a sleeping cat.

We found a back office and secured the door with a table. There were no windows—which was good—but there was a fire exit leading into the alley. Boden made coffee using an expresso machine, but Gordon had snagged a bottle of brandy from behind the bar before we entered the office. The women drank the brandy, and so did Gordon and Corbier.

We tried the phone on the table but it was dead. Pela had a mobile with her and got through to the police. She told them that they were needed at the gay village, and that people were dying. The person on the other end told her that the police would be there soon. The clock on the wall told us it was nearing 1:30am.

Corbier was sitting on a small leather couch with Pela, his finger circling a small freckle on her knee. Gordon sat on the floor next to Gayle talking about Susie, and Boden was lost in the contents of his miniature cup. Me, I was just glad to be out of the streets.

Boden asked if there was any brandy left for his coffee, and Gordon poured him a little. "Crazy shit out there," said Boden, and no one said anything. "What do you think will happen?" asked Boden.

Gordon answered, "We'll stay here until the police arrive. As soon as they see what's happening, they'll send for back up."

Boden nodded. I noticed Corbier's hand moving toward Pela's exposed thigh. He whispered something in her ear and she smiled. I was almost jealous of the guy.

"I just don't understand how these women can be dead and walking around, eating other women," said Gayle.

Gordon put his arm around her and told her not to worry. "They're not dead," he said. "It'll be a virus of some kind, like rabies. We'll get home tonight, turn on the news and they'll tell us it was all down to an escaped monkey. A lab experiment gone wrong."

Boden jumped in, "I wish that was true, but no virus I've ever seen turns women into cannibals. No woman is safe tonight."

Gordon gestured with his eyes to shut up, and when Boden saw the look of terror on Gayle's face he apologised and agreed it was probably just a virus.

Corbier got to his feet, stretched his arms out and announced, "I need a smoke. Does anyone want to join me?" Neither Boden, Gordon nor I smoked, and from what we knew, Corbier didn't either.

"What do you mean, join me?" asked Gordon.

Corbier frowned, "Well, it's a little stuffy in here, and I wouldn't be wanting to blow smoke all over the place. I figured I'd slip out of the fire exit and have a quick fag, figuratively speaking."

Pela got to her feet and handed Corbier a lighter and pack of cigarettes from her bag, "Yeah, sounds good. I think the fresh air will do me good, too."

I looked over to Boden and Gordon who were both staring at Corbier with distrust. "I don't think that's a good idea, buddy," said Gordon. "Those things are still out."

Corbier waved his hand, "Pish. We'll be fine. In and out, promise. Look, I'll even take this envelope opener in case any shit goes down." Corbier picked the small silver knife from a shelf and pressed down on the bar-handle of the door. As soon as it was opened, Corbier dragged Pela out into the darkness.

Corbier wasn't just in and out. Five minutes passed and we could hear him and Pela giggling outside and the Velcro sound of their lips pulling away from each other. Gordon announced he was going back into the bar area to find another bottle of brandy, and instantly Gayle offered to help.

When only Boden and I were left, I looked to him and rolled my eyes. "Horny bastards," I said, and Boden smiled. A moment of silence followed where I reflected on my life, and how shit it had been. I was nearing thirty years old and had never had a serious girlfriend. I was renting some crummy flea-infested dive that wasn't worth the money, and my job had little in the way of prospects. Nothing ever exciting had happened to me, and that's what was more frustrating than anything else because I believed something *was* going to happen. I don't know what, but I always felt special, gifted, but not in the clever way. I just felt like the type of person that was aiming toward something.

Sitting in that office, a little drunk from all the shots and beer, I realised I wasn't special, and that my life was pitiful. I aspired to the mediocre, playing everything safe. I never took risks. Everything was thought out...planned. I was a pawn advancing along a monochrome chessboard, movements deliberate and logical. And here I was, in the gay village surrounded by flesh-eating lesbian zombies, holed up waiting for the cavalry to arrive and save us all. Well, at least I still didn't live with my mother, like Boden. I stared over at him, and he too looked in deep contemplation.

"Shit like this makes you think, doesn't it?" I said to Boden, but he didn't acknowledge the remark. I began to walk around the room, looking at the posters of half-naked men with masculine faces wearing lip-gloss and eye shadow, and all the Lady Gaga posters. On a small table was a paperweight shaped into a large cock. The letter underneath was addressed to a Christopher Deal congratulating him on subscribing to Hard Times, a local gay TV channel.

Boden spoke, "You remember when we were kids and we went to the docks?" I nodded. "You and Gordon went skinny dipping. It was so cold Gordon panicked and began to thrash about." Boden began looking into his cup. "He would have drowned if you hadn't been there," he said.

"You were there, too," I said. "I'm sure if I wouldn't have saved him, you would have jumped in."

Boden looked up at me, his eyes burning. "I wouldn't have," he said. A confession, and now of all times? I asked him what all this was about, and he said, "You ever see me swim?"

I cast my mind back. "Can't say I have."

Boden's voice splintered under the weight of the words lodge in his throat, "Didn't you ever wonder why I never got changed with you guys in the locker room?"

I could sense there was some deep-rooted confession brewing, so I tried to make light of it all, "I figured you had a small dick."

Boden spoke again, "How many girlfriends have I had?"

I thought for a moment before replying, "You were seeing that blonde from work for a few weeks. What was her name, Monica?"

Boden began to shake his head. "I made her up. I made Paquita up too from accounts, and when I fingered that girl in the park when I was fourteen, I just dipped my fingers in a packet of prawn cocktail crisps. I need to tell you something because I'm scared I might not get out of here tonight."

He seemed genuinely scared. I assumed he was gay. It was the only explanation to why he lied about those girls.

He took a deep breath, "If you weren't there that day at the docks, Gordon would have drowned because I didn't want to risk getting changed out of wet clothes in front of him."

I sat down and put my arm on his shoulder. "Dude, look around you; we're surrounded by gays. It's not so taboo now. People are coming out left, right, and centre. There's even TV shows especially for gay people. In fact, tonight has opened my eyes up to the gay community. They're just like us, but more stylish. I'm totally cool with it and I'm sure the guys will be, too. Maybe Corbier might take a little persuading, but give him time and he'll come around to the idea, I'm sure."

Boden turned to me, his brow caving in. "I'm not gay," he said.

"Then what's the big deal?" I asked.

"I was born with..." he tapered off, still unsure whether or not to say the words.

I told him, "Regardless of how bad it is, once it's out in the open you're bound to feel a lot better."

He smiled, reassured. "You're a good friend," he said, "which is why I'm not afraid to show you."

Boden stood up, undid his belt and pulled down his jeans and boxer shorts. As he exposed himself to me, an act which had taken great courage and made vulnerable the final few strands of dignity he had left, I couldn't help think that if Kirk Douglas was still alive and wanted to know what his face would look like after being pummelled with a mallet, then he should look no further than Boden's genitals. From the cleft of an underdeveloped vagina poked this pug-nosed phallus beneath which hung two rounded testicles that gave them a chin-like quality.

"You're a hermaphrodite?" I asked him, still transfixed on this mutant cock-and-vagina combo.

"No," he said looking down at it all. "I'm an intersex, born with the chromosomes of a man, but the external organs of a female *and* man."

I looked closer, "You telling me that's a clit hanging out of you?!"

Boden did up his pants and moved toward the fire exit. "Man, if I knew you were going to freak out."

I stood up, "Dude, I've seen some weird shit tonight; lesbian zombies, limbs and blood flying about, Corbier acting like a gentleman, Gordon happy, but you got to admit, your junk is fucked up."

Boden shook his head and looked at the floor, "I thought out of everyone, you would be okay with this."

Outside we could hear Pela moaning. "I'm sorry, man. It's just a lot to take in," I said sympathetically. "I guess it can't have been easy living with that…what did you call it?"

Boden replied quietly, "Intersex, or pseudohermaphroditism."

To be honest, it all sounded Greek to me, but this was a big moment in Boden's life. It couldn't have been easy for the kid growing up knowing he was different than everyone else. Guess when you are different, you always feel like an outsider. It was clear he needed a friend, one willing to look beyond his condition.

I replied accordingly, "Boden, all those years we've known each other and I told you to go fuck yourself. I never knew you could." As I began to walk toward him, the landscape of my face shifting with compassion, Boden looked up and smiled. I will always remember that smile because it implied the weight he had carried on his shoulders all these years had been lifted, and I remember it fondly because it was also his last.

Corbier screamed, closely followed by Pela. The fire door swung back on its hinges and in came an elderly zombie dressed a blue tabard, wild hair, and a nametag scribed J.L.Smith. Clenched in a hand the colour of grapes were two human fingers. Over her shoulder, Corbier stood in the ally, bent over holding his hand. Pela was standing next to him, her arm on his shoulder.

I looked back and before I could warn Boden to move, his mouth whispered the words, "thank you." His eyes closed, as if preparing for her teeth upon his flesh. The old woman crunched into his throat, triggering a cascade of blood. As she pulled away his larynx and began mauling at the exposed gristle, Boden's body relaxed and fell to the ground. He never once made a noise.

I looked around and grabbed the penis paperweight and cracked it over the head of the zombie. The cock broke in two so I rammed the clay trunk and testicles into her mouth. She bit down hard; the breaking of her teeth sounding like tiny ice cubes in a warm drink.

Corbier ran inside, his hand stained red. "That bitch took my fucking fingers! Boden! What the fuck!"

He looked down at the convulsing body of our friend, eyes closed, skin ashen. Stamping his heel on the zombie's head, Corbier shouted, "First my fingers...and now my friend!"

Over and over he stomped his foot on her head, interchanging it with a few well-aimed kicks. The spine snapped like burning wood, eyes popped from her skull, green puss oozed from each orifice. Pela ran in, and upon seeing the carnage of brains, cartilage and shards of porcelain skull, she fainted. Corbier grabbed her before her head hit the floor, blood from his exposed knuckle dying her hair from platinum blonde to auburn at the temples.

"We need to get the shit out of here," I said. "Corbier, did you hear me? We need to go."

Corbier was looking into Pela's eyes with a sadness he should have reserved for Boden. "I can't leave her, dude," he said.

I knew there was no point in arguing. "Fine," I said. "We'll carry her to the toilets; splash some water on her face." I grabbed her legs, and Corbier took her head and shoulders.

As we lifted her up and guided ourselves out of the office, Corbier looked at me and said, "Even though she's on the rag, she offered to blow me." I guess it was love.

The bar area of Al's Jizzera appeared quiet. I shouted out for Gordon and heard no reply. I looked over the dance floor and saw the toilet signs. "Over there", I said to Corbier. As we shuffled over the dance floor I heard the faint sound of teeth grinding and the mulching of tissue and muscle.

I indicated with my eyes that something was behind the bar. Corbier wasn't bothered and whispered to me that we should just get to the toilets. He was right; we couldn't risk one of those zombies getting a whiff of Pela's menstruating vagina.

We heard Gordon when we began to move, his voice weak and raspy. I lowered Pela's legs gently and Corbier did the same on his end. We gingerly approached the bar, the noise of chewing getting louder. I peered over and found a woman with matted hair gnawing on one of Gayle's tits. Gayle's stomach had been torn open, intestines hauled out to resemble some fucked up aqua park ride. Next to her was another zombie; teeth nibbling at what looked like a boiled egg. In her other hand was a penis, chewed up at the end. I looked over to Gordon, his crotch a swamp of purple veins and red matter. He was still alive the poor fuck.

Corbier jumped over the bar, found a bottle of brandy and smashed the top off. He poured the liquid all over the zombie and then yanked her off Gordon. He pulled out Pela's Zippo from his pocket, flicked the lid and produced a flame. "Dykes don't dig on dicks!" he said before throwing the lighter.

A propane flame the colour of UV lamps crawled over her body toward her head. Flesh bubbled and blistered and the pixie cut hair turned the flames pumpkin orange. The zombie flailed around as her eyes burnt out from their sockets. She ran into the optics, smashing bottles of tequila and vodka, their contents surging over the end of the shelf in an azure flame waterfall.

Corbier jumped back over the bar, reached for a barstool, broke off one of its legs and returned, piercing the head of the zombie eating out Gayle. The bar was swimming in pools of fire, heat bloating the varnished veneer of the bar.

I leapt over and knelt before Gordon, his eyes lost between worlds. "Least you got to fuck someone better looking than Suzie," I said.

Gordon pulled back from the death's divide and caught my eyes. With his final breath he pulled me close to his ear and said, "Don't let me leave without my cock." I understood. It's bad enough entering the afterlife without your eyes, but to walk eternity without your manhood had to be mortifying.

I leant over and prized the soggy, flaccid lump of flesh from the zombie's hand and placed it delicately on the latticework of bloodied veins and tendons. "There you go, buddy," I said. "Now you can fuck as many angels as you want."

I guess he was just holding on long enough to hear me say that because he soon closed his eyes, a wry smile pulling the corners of his mouth. I stood up and looked to Corbier.

Backlit by a blaze of feral flames the pall of his silhouette looked fiendish. He pulled the barstool from the skull of the zombie and wiped its brains on his jeans. "Let's get us some fucking revenge!" he screamed. I didn't need telling twice.

We moved Pela into the women's toilets, laid her in a cubicle and headed out into the streets. Corbier was armed with his barstool leg and I had two bottles of Jack Daniels in both hands, the bases smashed to form jagged splinters of glass.

The first zombie we found chewing on the labia of a petite girl with perky tits, Corbier rammed the tip of his weapon up her arsehole. He jammed it in as far as she could go, a foul stench of shit and blood oozing out from the sides. The second was mine, a rotund woman with piercings. I ran toward her and thrust the razor-sharp glass in her face, twisting it round until I could hear cartilage and flesh tearing. "Have a drink on me," I said before kicking her in the crotch. I left her rolling along the road, the bottle wedged firm in her face.

We ran the length of the street, slicing zombie throats and breaking bones. By the time we reached a bar called, Calebia, we were both out of breath and covered in the ooze of at least twenty walking dead.

We looked back at the carnage, the puree of gizzards and marrow, and beyond to where a raincloud of smoke scaled the walls of Al's Jizzera. "Pela," said Corbier already running toward the bar.

The fires that had cremated our friend and Gayle had knitted together to form a dense smog of potent smoke. Feral and unwavering, the blaze tore up the back walls closest to the bar and crawled like yellow vines across the ceiling. Both Corbier and I could just make out the toilet doors, and with heads held low, we ran toward them like prisoners escaping an erratic searchlight.

Inside the air was clear, save for a foul decaying aroma we had become accustomed to. I shut the exterior door to stop any smoke filtering in and heard Corbier cough and then yell Pela's name. I turned to find him pulling a skinny zombie from the twitching body of Pela, her eyes rolling back into her skull to that darkend place where mortality awaits.

2:33am. Al's Jizzera. The inferno beats its fetid breath under the toilet door, filling the room with the toxic mix of plastic, varnished wood, lube juice and alcohol. Sirens pierce the endless night sky like a hundred wailing robot babies with colic, and Corbier, my only living friend, kneels before his latent love, brushing her hair back over her ears with his remaining fingers.

A washbasin's drain burbles as a foetus-looking mishmash of matted hair, brain juice and bone that was once a zombie head makes its way into the sewage system. Shoes strike the road outside in rapid succession, a twisted melody of stricken voices cry out for aid, absolution, God and all his backbiting angels.

I hear a man call out toward me. "Are you okay?" asks the voice, and I look out of the window to see a police officer in full-body protection. "Are you injured?"

I tell Corbier the police have arrived, but he just keeps rocking Pela in his arms. "The bar is on fire," I tell the police officer.

"How many of you are trapped?" he asks, and I tell him just me and Corbier.

Another police officer joins him and after a quick confab the first officer calls out to me again, "Is there any other way out, another door perhaps or fire exit?"

I tell him there is one in a small office, but it's on the other side of the bar. "I'm PC Thomas, and this is my partner, PC Rathke. He will stay with you while I get the fire service to the front of the building. Don't worry, we'll have you out in no time."

And with that the officer runs off down the street, talking into a small radio on his lapel. I glance at PC Rathke. He appears no older than twenty-five. He keeps looking nervously from side to side as if expecting something to jump out and bite him.

I shout down, "They only go for women!" PC Rathke looks up and nods his head as if he understands, but I don't know how he does.

"I've just never seen anything like this before," he says.

"None of us have," I reply.

Corbier breaks away from Pela's death embrace, his face half-smeared with her blood. "Who you talking to?" he asks. I tell him it's a police officer and that they're going to help get us out of here. "Tell him there's no point," he says. I ask him what he means.

Corbier lowers Pela's head gently to the floor, and making sure she's comfortable, he stands up, brushing down his jeans. His eyes are waterlogged, a silver leach of snot coating his lips. "We're not leaving," he says, his voice is without inflection or emotion.

I jump off the counter and in the distance hear PC Rathke call out to me. "What do you mean, we're not leaving?" I ask Corbier.

He wipes his mouth, his hand returns stained red. The air around us is a thin web of smoke, the fumes more palpable. "Look, I know you're upset," I say, "but you're talking like a fucking loon. The fire service will be here in a matter of minutes. They'll bust that door down and pull our skinny white arses into the cold night air, and this fucking nightmare will be over."

Corbier looks over briefly to Pela and then returns to me again. "You think this shit happens every night?" he asks. "You think it's normal for the dead to rise up and begin killing, and that the people they kill rise up and start killing?"

There was something about that line that sounded familiar to me. I tell Corbier, "It isn't normal and that's why we need to leave."

"Someone left open the door to Hell," he says.

I reiterate his madness, and he grabs me by the shoulders, his face so close I can smell the pungent mix of Pela's saliva and the fusty stench of decay. "We're fucked, and there ain't nothing we can do about it."

I assume it's the virus in him, making him talk bollocks, so I humour him, agree that it's all wrong and that maybe he's right about zombies escaping from Hell.

"Don't you see?" he says, smiling, "They've not escaped... We've found our way in."

And as he says this a wiry shadow drifts across the tiles behind him, and over his shoulder she appears, eyes like Greek statues, silt oozing from her mouth and nose. Pela rips off the side of Corbier's face that is stained with her blood, revealing a row of uneven teeth framed by the new hole in his cheek. As Corbier tries to let out a scream, his tongue falls through the opening, dangling over his jaw like some swollen slug. I search for the barstool leg and, snatching it from the floor, Corbier grabs my hand. He shakes his head and mumbles something that tells me he doesn't want her slaughtered.

Feasting on half of his face, Pela is oblivious to all this. Corbier turns and places one hand on her shoulder and she looks up at him. Beyond each lifeless eye I sense Pela recognises Corbier, that she remembers something of their brief time together. A flash of trust and compassion is exchanged between her dead soul and his fading heart, because for the briefest of moments they seem connected in more than just rancid flesh. Corbier leans in and, stretching his mouth open to reveal jawbone, he kisses her on bloodied lips.

It's sickening to observe, but its gesture beautiful. And as envy rises from my gut, two bullets whizz past my ears, cracking open Corbier's skull and taking off the front of Pela's head. Watching their bodies collapse to the ground in the eternal encirclement, and sensing Hell's wrath breathing upon my nape, the world I know and hate didn't seem all that bad.

It was not as bleak as I imagined, and my future not so apocalyptic in design. I have life, a life where the grotesque has no place, and a life that could, if given the chance, be fashioned to include happiness. If Boden could relinquish his fear of social rejection, Gordon unshackle himself from an ill-starred love, and Corbier find happiness within the arms of zombie, then anything was possible in this new world. They say in the midst of life we are in death, and it seems so very true of this night, but in death I have found a reason to live.

From behind me, instructions are being pushed through a Government Issue smoke mask telling me to turn around slowly, and this I do with a great weight lifted from my shoulders. My liberator is a tall figure in tactical attire, a heavy-duty rifle scribed with the words, KORPON CORP, pointing toward me. Another figure wearing an identical outfit joins him.

I ask, "Are you here to save me?" and one of my saviours tilts his head slightly to one side and raises his gun. The last word I hear is "infected" and the sound of skull splintering into a hundred tiny pieces.

Keeping it Together
Starring DK Mok

No one aspires to be the pizza delivery guy. It's a summer job, or something neurosurgeons do after fleeing their war torn country.

When I was a kid, I wanted to be a bandit monk when I grew up. But that was a long time ago.

It's 3am on a Thursday night, my last delivery on a shift full of weeknight drunks and cackling science majors. I've got a chilli cheese monstrosity burning a hole through the vinyl beside me, and a timer that says my mark's about to go from 'Satisfied Customer' to 'Ravenous Psycho'.

It's summer in Calam City, and the heat makes everyone a little crazier. Which is a big deal in a city where serial killers are at the vanilla end of the spectrum. Thankfully, most people don't pay attention to the faceless cap that drops off their box. The pay is lousy, and the prestige is below halitosis test subject, but the anonymity suits me fine.

I ring the bell on apartment sixty eight, and the guy who answers is unexpectedly sober, sane, and looks uncannily like a friendly baguette. He's tall and skinny, with whitebread colouring, ending in a vigorous puff of crust coloured curls. Admittedly, everyone reminds me of food these days. The woman at the local bakery reminds me of a ripe tomato. I can't taste tomatoes anymore because of my condition, but the memory of their soft, aromatic flesh still makes me drool.

"Please sign here, confirming the pizza was in the box when you got it," I say.

347

I flash open the greasy box, and the baguette's gaze swirls around the chunks of marinated bok choy.

"Thanks, it looks—"

He stops, and I follow his gaze to something floating on a pool of congealed bocconcini.

It's a finger.

I glance at my right hand, still holding the lid of the box. God, I hate summer.

I scoop out the finger and press it quickly to the stump on my hand, shoving the box into the guy's arms.

"I'll get a free one sent out," I holler as I run down the stairs.

"Did you just put your finger back on?" He's following me down the stairwell.

"It's a prosthetic," I yell.

"I work with people with disabilities," says the guy. "That wasn't a prosthetic."

I'm running to my car now, jamming the key into the wonky lock. "It's a condition," I shout. "Like gangrene."

"Gangrene is where bits fall off. Not when you stick them back on."

I kick the ignition into gear, and he's chasing the car as I swerve down the road. Swearing shadows stumble out of the way, and a garbage can bounces down the sidewalk.

"Hey!" he yells. "I just want to—"

"Please don't sue us!" I call out the window, leaving him behind in the sticky predawn.

Pizza delivery is something I fell into   expecting to climb back out of. I can still pass as a college student, but at my actual age, I should be retired on a private, motorised island. I blame it on my condition, but the truth is, all my friends have faced their own challenges and done pretty awesome for themselves anyway. Stanik has her own surgery, Chandler has made partner in the city's most terrifying law firm, and Yelen's a hotshot detective in Calam police special ops.

But more than that, there are plenty of people who have it far worse than me; the illiterate woman in rural Zimbabwe with untreated hepatitis; the gay teen living in a country where they still hang people for religious reasons. Compared to them, I have it sweet.

And to be honest, I don't mind delivering pizza. I tried telemarketing once, and decided if I was going to be at the bottom of the career barrel, I'd rather be a pizza jockey than a cubicle zombie. But nights like this make me think I've got to get my act together.

I pull up outside Chandler's penthouse. I feel like having a self-pity rant, and he sleeps irregular hours anyway. I've known him for almost four hundred years, but he doesn't look a day over thirty five. His hair's fashionably scruffy and walnut brown now, but there's still a trace of outlaw underneath the Armani.

"Hey, Crumb," says Chandler, "anything new on the menu?"

I sag onto his post modern sofa. "If a contaminated pizza is delivered to a customer," I say, "does the legal liability fall on the pizza company, or on the delivery driver, if, hypothetically, the contamination was inadvertently caused by the delivery driver?"

"Did they deserve it?" says Chandler.

"How did you get through law school?"

"Ruthlessly," replies with a grin Chandler. "You worry too much, Crumb. What if this…what if that? No one's going to sue you for spitting on a pizza."

"I didn't spit on a pizza," I say defensively.

Chandler tilts his head slightly. "Oh, you mean your ear," he says.

"My ear?"

I touch the side of my head, and feel a damp patch where I should have felt a pinna.

"Oh crap."

It's almost dawn by the time I get to Stanik's surgery. She isn't a morning person, but it doesn't show. Her starling hair is pulled back into an airtight bun, and her spotless lab coat radiates toxic levels of disinfectant.

"Got into another fight?" says Stanik dryly.

"Racing someone for the last tin of peaches doesn't count as a fight," I say. "And no, this time it came off by itself."

Stanik inspects my crooked finger, and I wince as she adjusts it. Not that it hurts, but old habits die hard.

I met Stanik fifteen years ago, when she was a post grad student with a virulent case of ambition. She thought my condition would be her career-making paper, until she conceded that the science to explain it was still decades away. In her words, what I have is less like a variant of rabies, and more like what would happen if someone put a voodoo curse on someone with a variant of rabies. I just tell people I had rubella as a baby.

I try not to think about how I managed before I met Stanik. She's got an arsenal of antibacterial creams and ointments that stop my skin from oozing, and she's a pocket ace in emergencies like this.

Stanik snips off the suture thread at my knuckle, and flicks on the otoscope. "No internal damage," says Stanik, peering into my ear canal. "But the whole pinna's gone. I'll need to order the implants and prosthetic, but there's a three month backlog after that whole imploding smartphone battery debacle."

"Three months? You could grow one on a mouse in that time."

Stanik taps at her tablet screen. "You could wear a deerstalker hat," she says.

I tug at my wiry hair, trying to cover the absent ear. It's hard enough holding down a job without looking like a prison movie extra.

"You have to be more careful, Crumb," says Stanik.

"I was fine," I snap. "It was that stupid guy chasing me down the street. I think I ran over something trying to lose him."

"Something like a beer can, or like a small child?"

"I don't think it was a person. It didn't make a noise."

"Maybe it was a mime."

"Then I did the world a favour." I sigh and rub my temples. "Thanks for the checkup, Doc," I say.

Stanik doesn't look up from her tablet. "How's your eyesight lately?" she says casually.

I pause at the door. "Fine," I say, and head out into the muggy morning.

My apartment's a bolthole in the shadow of the Bruhath Bridge. Eighteen lanes of gridlock hell. In the morning, the bridge looks like a skeletal monster rising from the water, all black spines and monolithic legs, crawling with angry parasites.

The walls of my apartment sweat, and the cupboards sigh with humidity. Mould grows faster than I can scrape it off, and last week I found a forest of mushrooms growing under my bed. I keep meaning to move somewhere less fetid, but real estate's tight on a minimum wage.

I toss my keys onto the coffee table, one wobbly leg jammed with a copy of *Why Vampires Don't Get Fat*. My eyes are killing me, but I refuse to contemplate glasses. I'm a walking joke as it is.

It's too early to sleep, and I keep thinking about the baguette guy chasing me down the street. I'm not worried. I've survived mobs and wars and occult priests, but I wonder if I'm getting too old for this. I pull a tattered manila folder from under my mattress, dog-eared papers poking out. Almost everything I know about my condition is in this folder. It's disappointingly slim.

I'm pretty sure there's no way to reverse what's happened to me, but until I find the original catalyst, I'm not ruling anything out.

There's a scratching noise from the landing, then footsteps outside my door. I don't get visitors, and no one robs this neighbourhood—the only thing you'd leave with is scabies. I grab a baseball bat and wait beside the door.

Nutters don't usually hunt people like me. Vampires and werewolves get harassed all the time—Yelen's got the scars to prove it—but people like me usually wander around until they get hit by a truck or a herd of wildebeest. Then again, my condition's a bit atypical.

There's a tense silence, then a knock at the door.

"I just want to talk to you." The baguette guy.

He must have called Sugoi Pizza and gotten my address. Bastards.

"I want to return something to you," he continues. "But maybe you didn't...hear me."

Bloody damn.

I open the door and glower at the baguette guy. He's dressed in a crisp white shirt and tan slacks like a freshly baked loaf wrapped in a brown paper bag. I force my mind away from food.

"Hello," smiles the man. "Can I come in?"

"No."

"You dropped an ear in my foyer," says the man. "I'm guessing you want it back?"

I stand aside reluctantly, and he steps into the damp living room. "I'm Prentice," he says, holding out a hand.

I ignore it. He'd probably snag himself a fistful of fingers.

"Sorry about the pizza," I say. "Can I just have my ear back?"

Prentice sits on the armrest of my mangy couch.

"So, what's your story?"

My story. It was the size of a Babylonian library with the qualitative content of a fridge magnet. At the end of the day, my story could fit on a square of toilet paper.

"I'm a zombie. Deal with it."

I'd once used the line 'I'm a zombie. So sue me'. Chandler had to sort out that mess. Prentice doesn't bat an eye.

"And what does that mean for you?" he says, like I've just told him I have the hiccups.

"It means if you don't give me back my ear right now, I'm going to tear open your head and eat your brain like a crème brulee."

Prentice pauses, his hands still folded neatly on his knees. "I'm a Health and Lifestyle Optimisation Officer—" he begins.

"I don't need a social worker."

Prentice glances around the studio, and the sallow walls exhale slowly. He stands up, and hands me a ziplock bag with a familiar, fleshy crescent inside. "The next person who gets extra toppings might not be so cool with it," he says.

I maintain a dignified silence. Prentice pauses in the corridor. "You just seemed like you could use some help," he says.

It's 9am, and Stanik has back-to-back patients until lunchtime. I hate to admit it, but Prentice is right. I obviously don't belong in the food industry, and it's only a matter of time before I run into a lawsuit Chandler can't fix. What I need is a sedentary office job with lots of air conditioning and snack breaks. Maybe even something with career prospects.

I flick through the job ads but I'm kidding myself. I only shuffle a little when I walk, but I've never been able to get rid of the twitch. I'm the only driver in the Sugoi Pizza fleet who uses my own car because they couldn't get the mysterious smell out of the vans I used. People like me don't get office jobs. We don't get nice apartments. Or normal friends.

I call a few of the job ads, but inevitably hit a wall after 'Hello'. I end up playing a vintage version of The Sims for several hours before I head out to the surgery. I've only just hit the freeway when I get a call from Yelen.

"Meet me right away. Usual spot," she says.

Yelen doesn't waste time on small talk or sentimentality, but she's one of the good guys. We met twelve years ago when she was a rookie cop building a reputation for hunting down crims no one else could find. She doesn't care if you're a small time grit or king of the underworld, if you mess in her city she'll stake you to the courthouse wall.

We meet at the freeway underpass. It's a cool stretch of concrete columns, a colossal mausoleum to the motor industry. Yelen likes to meet here because there's always shady business going on. Once, we came across a guy burying half a hippo. I never got the other half of that story.

"Run over anyone lately?" says Yelen. She's got her patrol sunnies on, so all I can see is my own distended reflection. She's in a khaki tank top and jeans today, her mocha hair in a short ponytail. Honesty's the best policy with Yelen. She rarely asks a question she doesn't already know the answer to.

"Was it a mime?" I say.

"Bicycle courier," said Yelen.

I wince.

"Are they okay?" I say.

"One of Amin's couriers," continues Yelen.

I feel my stomach decomposing faster. Amin's a pillar of the community, which means he owns half the city and runs a nasty chunk of the underground. He's over my head by galaxies, and I've just landed on his hit list.

"Are they pressing charges?" I ask.

"Not yet," says Yelen. "But Amin's looking for you."

My insides are bubbling, and I wipe the slime of sweat from my forehead.

"Just a heads up," says Yelen, climbing back into her unmarked car.

I close my eyes and listen to my heart not quite beating. The ear will have to wait.

Amin's two hundred years younger than me, but he invested wisely, took calculated risks, and killed all the right people.

Which is why guys like him mulch their lawns with people like me.

I've managed to stay out of his way until now, but Amin'll be looking for his dead man walking. The only reason I'm not already a splatter -zone is because he figures I can't run. Not fast, anyway.

Usually, I'd lay low—even Amin's grip hits static in the sewers. But in my current state, I may as well throw myself into a compost bin. Can't run, can't hide. I've lived my life low key, but I always swore I wouldn't die cornered.

It's afternoon by the time I pull up outside his electrified gates. Amin's mansion is like Area 51 meets Disneyland. The chariot track's adjacent to the crocodile tanks, and the carnivorous garden encircles the Roman bath house. Tabloid choppers sometimes try to flyover, but invariably crash in flames with bats tangled in the rotors.

Security jostles me through the checkpoints, looking at me like something that fell out of the wrong side of a rhino. Amin and his pals might have great skin and teeth, but in my opinion, if you're stuck on a liquid diet with no sunshine, you may as well spend eternity in a nursing home.

Amin doesn't look happy to see me, but every day's a bad day when you're a guy like Amin. Time is money, and I'm a dime that's fallen in the bog.

Amin's hair is slick and treacle blonde these days, which looks strange against his light-coffee skin. He's the product of an Indian diplomat, an Irish boxer, and some seriously crazy times. Amin's had so much cosmetic surgery he should look like the love child of Errol Flynn and Jake Gyllenhaal, but his face keeps trying to revert to an eighteen-year-old boy who hasn't lost his puppy fat. He looks maybe twenty-four today, and mean.

"My courier was carrying an artifact worth more than the Louvre when you ran her off the road," says Amin. He throws me a parcel with a tyre mark on it. It rattles. "It's not supposed to make that noise," says Amin flatly.

"You know, they have these carbon fibre postal cases—" I begin.

"You have no capacity to compensate me," says Amin. "So do I send you to prison or let you go?"

I keep out of Amin's business, but I've been around long enough to know how it works. 'Send you to prison' means a nasty frame up that'll see you cemented in the Supermax convicted of cannibalising orphans. 'Let you go' means a visit to the woodchipper.

"How long would you last in a human prison?" says Amin with a freeze-dried smile.

Longer than you, I figure. Amin might have flourished, but I'd *survived*. And after every flourishing civilization falls, the survivors cling on. Accreted in the corners like antibiotic resistant staph.

"I have a very good lawyer," I say. "I'm here because I don't play games and I don't raise debts. If you're going to do something, do it here, do it now."

My skin is tingling, which means what's left of my nervous system is going absolutely gorgonzola.

Amin leans back slightly, his eyes going flat. "Do you know why your friends control empires, and you're delivering baked lard to obese children?" says Amin.

Pizza ain't gonna deliver itself. But I keep my mouth shut. I've dug as deep as I'm going to.

"It's because you don't play games," says Amin. "You don't raise debts. You don't gamble, so you don't win."

I don't know where he's going with this, but I don't like it.

"You've rotted through your days in the shadow of security," continues Amin. "But if you'll pardon me saying so, Crumb, you don't look so fresh."

"What do you want, Amin?"

"Perhaps the question is, what do *you* want?"

Amin twirls his fingers lazily, and a primitive votive figurine appears in his hand. It's stained ivory, a roughly hewn figure with its mouth open unnaturally wide. It has no eyes. A shock of nausea hits me, and I clench my fists to stop my hands from shaking. I haven't seen one of those in four hundred years.

"There's a curious story behind this," says Amin. "My curators say it belonged to a bokor—a voodoo sorcerer—but it was found continents away from Africa in Ugistan. Crumb, isn't that where you're from?"

My head is spinning, a sickening milkshake of hope and dread slushing through me.

"Who was the bokor?" I say.

"There's a charity ball at Solstice Feria's manor tomorrow night," says Amin. "Do something for me there and the bokor's artifacts are yours. And I'll call it even regarding my courier."

Dread hungrily swallows the hope. Solstice Feria is ancient. Some say she's a fallen angel, an immortal witch, a time traveller. The only certainty is you'll be squished from existence if you cross her.

"What exactly did you want me to do?" I say.

"Your commitment first, then we talk specifics," says Amin dismissively. "You have until dawn tomorrow to give me your answer."

My thoughts are a mess as I head west on the motorway. That's what Amin does. He gets to people.

I've been trying for centuries to track down the bokor behind my condition. Although, when I say 'trying', I guess I mean 'wishing', in between stumbling through odd jobs and napping more than I needed to. Success takes so much effort, and I guess I never had the guts to make it happen. But I'm running out of time.

The midday sun is scorching by the time I get to Calam Necropolis. All the graves here are over a century old, and no one tends to them now. It's a hazard of snakes and sunken graves. Crooked gravestones rise from random hillocks, and skinny brown rabbits flash through the grass.

I wade over to a fallen, granite crucifix, the words weathered blank. It takes me an hour to clear the grass enough to dig up a tin box wrapped in plastic. Under the shade of an over-grown fig tree, I pry open the tin, the rusted lock coming apart.

My chest pangs—or I imagine it does—as I touch each for-lorn relic. A hand inked map of Ugistan, a copper pendant shaped like a beetle, a shred of frayed and bloodied tunic. Rem-nants of a wasted life.

My finger traces a faded red circle on the rumpled map. The answers are there, I can feel it, but I've never scraped up enough for a ticket. Even if I survive the next forty eight hours, Amin's right. People like me don't get answers. People like me die won-dering.

Unless something changes.

With my right ear stuffed, I should see Stanik before I plow into a walking bus of pre-schoolers. But what I need now isn't an ear, it's a fresh pair of eyes.

It isn't hard breaking into Prentice's apartment. Laws change so often it seems pointless to keep track of the fiddly ones. 'Don't kill' is the big one. Everything else is moral decora-tion.

I only glimpsed his place last night through a haze of vola-tile pizza, but in the syrupy afternoon sun, it's like walking into a bread basket. The couch is a buttery loaf against one wall, and beside the fruitcake slab of coffee table, three rustic dinner rolls slouch in their beanbag repose. The carpet is sandwich white, skirted with walnut crust, and even the scalloped lights are remi-niscent of croissants. Either this guy really likes his carbohydrates, or my food fixation is getting worse.

Prentice is unperturbed to see me when he arrives late after-noon, toting a bag of sourdough rolls.

"Tell it to me straight," I say. "How bad is it?"

"Excuse me?" says Prentice.

"My life."

Prentice looks at me thoughtfully.

"Do you care what I think?"

"I want a human opinion," I say.

I technically stopped being human a long time ago, but I like to think I'm still human where it counts. But it's hard sometimes, remembering what that means.

"You don't have any human friends?" says Prentice.

"One, sort of."

Stanik's mostly human. Chandler says there's a taint of faerie blood, but Stanik calls it heightened cognitive processing. She's great with a suture, but when it comes to personal stuff, she can be a little clinical.

I don't have a circle of friends so much as a stunted blot of acquaintances. Chandler, Stanik, Yelen. We don't exactly have movie nights. We went to karaoke once, but Yelen's bloodcurdling rendition of Blue Moon got us kicked out at *katana*-point.

"I don't know enough about you to give you my professional opinion," says Prentice. "How about I accompany you for the next few hours, build a profile?"

I can't afford to let Amin get under my skin, and a bit of perspective is just what I need.

"Sure."

I get to Stanik's surgery just after closing time. Prentice isn't taking notes, but I get the feeling a mental filing cabinet is being accessed.

"Hell of a day," says Stanik. "I had three different patients come in with tekko-kagi injuries. What's wrong with people?"

Stanik glances at Prentice, but doesn't comment. She inspects my bagged ear, not entirely convinced I haven't accidentally given her a slice of pepperoni.

"Crumb, I hate to say it," says Stanik. "But you're not holding together so well these days."

"It's just stress," I say.

"From what?" says Stanik, then softens her tone. "Your body's showing signs of senescence. I'm not saying we need to go into palliative care mode, but you've had a good run, Crumb."

A long run, maybe. Not a good one.

Stanik fixes my ear and loads me up with a chiller full of pills and potions. She pauses just before we leave, and turns to Prentice.

"Best quality?" she says.

"Optimism," says Prentice.

Weird, I think. But that's Stanik.

I'm running late for my shift at Sugoi, and my car's feeling the bitumen tonight. If Prentice notices the smell, he doesn't say anything.

"Why pizza delivery?" he says.

"It makes people happy." Plus, Sugoi's gourmet selection includes deep fried pigs' brains, and I only pick off a few pieces.

"Does it make you happy?" says Prentice.

It does when I'm crunching deep fried brain. "It's a job."

"That sounds like a no," says Prentice.

"It doesn't matter," I say. "I can't have what makes me happy." I can see Prentice making mental notes and I have the urge to scoop out his brain with my hand and step on it.

"What would you rather be doing?" says Prentice.

Neon lights streak past, humid pink and green.

"I wanted to be a bandit monk," I say. "Sort of like a forest ranger."

"Why aren't you?"

"It's hard to conduct a feral cat census when condors are picking chunks off you," I say.

"Have you ever actually applied for a forestry position?"

"I keep having to tell people I'm recovering from necrotising fasciitis as it is. That doesn't make you popular at job interviews."

Prentice blinks at me, and it looks just like blue smarties in a finger bun. My stomach growls.

"It sounds like you're making obstacles for yourself," says Prentice.

Before I can snap a retort, or his neck, a red and blue light flares in the rear view mirror. The last thing I need is another ticket I can't pay, but outrunning the cops in this car is assisted suicide. I wind down the window and try not to scowl.

"What's the hurry?" says Yelen. She's in uniform tonight. "Who's the snack pack?"

"Not a good time, Yelen," I say. Sugoi's wage docking policy is longer than a German opera.

"Just checking youdidn't leave Amin's place in a doggie bag," says Yelen.

"I'm fine," I say. "You don't know anything about some party tomorrow night at the Feria estate do you?"

"I know you're going to be nowhere near it," says Yelen. "Every supernatural psycho's got a ticket. You wouldn't know so many people cared about ending human trafficking."

Great. I doubt Amin's plans for me involve helping with the catering.

"Not my scene," I say.

"You bet," says Yelen. "By the way, both of your tail-lights, your plate light, and your left headlight are out. And you're missing your right side mirror."

Damned courier. But by the sounds of it, that's the least of my problems.

By the time I get my first smoking payload, I've been docked half my wages, and I'm not the type who gets tips.

"I think I'm starting to see how some of these problems are perpetuating," says Prentice.

"I'm just unlucky," I say.

"According to scientific studies, luck is an attitude," says Prentice.

"According to scientific studies, there's no such thing as zombies."

Through the corrosive steam of *bhut jolokia* peppers, I can sense his smartie eyes on me.

"How long have you been this way?" he says.

"A while."

"Longer than most humans get, am I right?"

I shift on the cracked vinyl. The chilli vapours are prickling my skin.

"That's unusual for a zombie, isn't it?" he continues.

"What are your qualifications anyway?"

"Life is precious," says Prentice. "Whatever form it takes, however long it lasts. You should do something only you can do."

"Chase after screaming crowds while rotting flamboyant-ly?"

"I'm just saying you should consider doing something where your heart, your hopes and your hands are aligned," says Prentice.

His words stick in my head, and it's nearly dawn when I drop him back at his place. He stops on the curb for a moment.

"I always thought zombies had no personal volition," he says.

"The myths got it wrong," I say.

"Hmm," he says, and waves goodnight.

I've had four hundred years. Four hundred years of scraping by, and trying not to eat people. Four hundred years, and it's still not enough.

I look at my palms, dull and colourless. This time, it won't get better if I just ignore it. I sneezed the other day and about a teaspoon of veins blurted out, which is gross even by zombie standards. The truth is, I'm just not ready to go.

Amin looks unsurprised to see me, although far from happy.

"Your target tonight is a coral circlet in an oak casket locked in an electronic vault on the fifth floor," says Amin.

"You want me to steal from Solstice Feria?"

"It doesn't belong to her," says Amin.

"Sounds like it doesn't belong to you either."

Amin's expression becomes even more dour. "Don't eat anything for the next twelve hours," says Amin. He tosses me something wrapped in waxed paper. "Bathe using this one hour before returning here for final instructions."

I unwrap a bar of translucent brown soap. "Why does this smell like ham?" I say.

"Be here at seven tonight exactly," says Amin. "I'm giving you a chance to do something right for once. Don't screw it up."

Knowing the right thing to do is easy. Leave the unhealthy relationship. Go after that exciting job. Don't eat that second jam donut. It's the doing that's hard.

I spend the morning tying up loose ends. I have no doubt tonight's job is the sort Amin gives to people he doesn't plan on seeing again. If he's doing me a favour, it's the kind of favour done to old, blind dogs with stomach cancer. But I'm short on options.

I meet Chandler for lunch at the Welcome Hello. My shout. I won't need tomorrow's rent money at this rate. The Welcome's my favourite restaurant in Calam City—a place for those who don't fit in at the pretentious Goth clubs, or the howlers' road houses. Zombies don't really hang out—sometimes we mob, but it's not the same. So it's nice to have somewhere to grab a bite without feeling like the unwashed kid at school.

"This is nice," says Chandler, sliding into a padded booth. "Who died? Or got resurrected?"

"Can't I take you to lunch just because I feel like it?" I say.

"Sure," says Chandler. The waiter delivers a roasted tomato salad and a whole crumbed brain. "Is there something you want to tell me?"

"Just...thanks," I say.

I stare at the buttery, deep fried lobes on my plate. God, life goes fast. It doesn't feel like four centuries ago that I first dragged Chandler from a pit of corpses while hunting for a snack. He's the one who first gave me my nickname. 'Cruimh'—old Irish for worm. I wasn't in the best shape back then.

"I haven't seen you this depressed since the last outbreak of CJD," says Chandler.

"I'm going to Solstice Feria's charity ball tonight," I say.

"You say it like you're announcing you have undead cancer."

"I'm not going to live like this," I say. "Waiting until I fall to gooey pieces."

"Death by charity ball. Classy," says Chandler. "Look, you don't want to get messed up with Feria. There'll be so many attempted assassinations, hexes and countercurses flying around you'll be lucky not to end up a prehistoric smear in another dimension."

That's probably what Amin's counting on. Amidst the epic power struggles, no one's going to notice a disoriented zombie.

"Just one question," I say. "Is there even really a charity involved?"

Chandler shrugs.

"There's some kind of auction for the Halena Foundation. But no one's there for the feelgood speeches. Crumb, you don't have anything to prove."

Except that I was human, once.

I've forgotten what it feels like to dream about the future. To imagine a life full of friends, family, triumphs, and a graceful fade out. I've let each day blur into a streak of identical years, and stopped asking myself 'why am I here?'.

Chandler says 'human' is just a sequence of genes. Integrity, decency and heroism come from what you do, no matter who or what you are. He's a good guy, Chandler. I wish I knew exactly what he was, but I guess it doesn't matter.

I don't bother cleaning out my apartment. It'd be easier to take a torch to the place, but I've had that done to me enough times for it not to be cathartic anymore. When I get downstairs, I find someone leaning against my car.

"Why do you smell like bacon?" says Prentice.

"Why do you look like a bread stick?"

Prentice doesn't move from the driver's side door. "You're going to Feria's ball, aren't you?" he says.

"You said I should get out of my comfort zone."

"I meant getting a new job, or joining a book club," says Prentice. "No one ever finds their solution by going to the casino, or smuggling endangered lizards in their underwear, or crashing homicidal undead parties. The answer never begins with your circumstances, but with you."

"Prentice, I appreciate your advice." I gently move him aside. "But you were right. It's time I moved forward."

Amin's waiting for me in the basement of his mansion. It's all covert labs and arcane dungeons down here—where war criminals find employment after the ICC. A white-haired man in a dinner suit starts painting calligraphic runes over my skin, the symbols stinging their tendrils over my face and arms.

"This'll wash off, right?" I say.

"You will have several layers of protection against Feria's security," says Amin. "My team will provide support, but your job is to get to the vault."

A holographic blueprint zips into life beside him, a glowing red path winding up several floors.

"Memorise this route," says Amin. "Directions, distance, elevation. Inside Feria's estate, you won't be using your eyes."

The white-haired man finishes his runes, and opens a long case full of gleaming implements.

"You can control your limbs, even when detached from your body, can't you?" says Amin.

I had a hunch I wasn't sneaking in as a waiter, but this is a whole new level of 'what the f—" I swallow the part of me that's screaming all kinds of hell.

"I don't know."

I've only been separated from an entire limb a few times, in chaotic, frenzied situations. I could still sense them, perhaps move them, but only in a desperate, adrenaline soaked way. Nothing calculated. Nothing involving five blind floors of precision navigation.

"Each of your limbs, and your head and torso, will be shipped into Feria's estate via crates of salted pork," says Amin. "Once inside, my team will do their best to secure a path for you. Only one of your limbs needs to make it to the vault. The runes should do the rest."

I think I'm going to bring up crumbed brains all over his tiled floor. I force my stomach to settle. I've spent my life trying to keep it together, but maybe it's time to let go a little. Or a lot.

My gaze skims the blueprint. No worse than a midnight pizza run during Mardi Gras.

"Make the cuts clean," I say. "I need my nerve ends as intact as possible if I'm going to get this bastard done."

Disembodied. Dismembered. Dying.

Strands of consciousness stretch between my parted limbs; fungal threads of memory. Remember...remember I was whole.

I can feel the press of cold flesh, the creak of pine. Disjointed sounds and vibrations, clashing inputs from each lonely part of me.

A sudden draft, a haze of grey light. I'm staring at a concrete ceiling, the world a tepid blur. Amin's team have hidden my torso in a storage room at Feria's manor, but I'm too far away. On the other side of the estate, I feel my fingers twitch.

I lever myself across the floor, not looking at my bandaged stumps. I am whole. Not together, but still whole.

I feel the prickle of witchery shielding me from slicing eyes. No one notices the limbless torso writhing down the halls. My hold is tenuous, but I can just curl my mind around it. I urge my solo arms and legs into a military crawl, freeing them from their numb slumber.

A dark maze, fingers dragging. Carpet, concrete, marble floors. My fingernails are splitting, but I'm getting closer. I sense the hum of my destination, the ink on my skin licking the air. I feel Amin's agents falling away, one by one.

I'm a puppet in pieces. Everything aches, burning cold. I rest my torso on a quiet balcony overlooking the ballroom. Below, a swirling current of tuxedos and gowns, champagne glasses and violins. My energy seeps away into the void. I can just see...

Solstice Feria on the podium. Ageless Eurasian features framed by dark hair and opal beads. The Halena Foundation chairwoman is beside her with a digital envelope. They're about to announce the auction winner, but no one's listening. Beneath the polite chatter, lives are being gambled and lost.

I can't move anymore. I channel my thoughts into my distant fingers. A warm panel of glass, my aching fingers tap a desperate legacy. The screen is daubed with blood, but I smile.

They're watching the wrong hand.

The touchscreen blinks confirmation against my skin. A far-away voice, fading to black.

"The winner of the silent auction is...Varian Amin." Pause. "Eighty million dollars."

Stunned silence sweeps the hall. Through the charms on my skin, I feel Amin's surprise turn to rage.

I smile against the freezing tiles.

I did something right, for once.

The darkness bleeds to grey. I can't feel my body. All that's left is an echo of consciousness, chasing my final regrets. I imagine voices, drifting by like sailboats in the summer.

"Crumb's not your average zombie, is she...?" Prentice, soft and crunchy.

"Everyone knows what happens when a zombie eats your brains." Chandler, warm and bitter. "But no one talks about what happens when you eat a zombie's brains..."

"She...?"

"She's just different."

Warmth. A blanket lies over me, or maybe a shroud. I can feel my fingers and toes, but my body aches unbearably. My vision blurs into Stanik's recovery room, with Chandler and Prentice sitting by the trolley bed. Yelen is lounging over a folding chair, and Stanik's putting away rolls of gauze.

"What happened?" I mumble.

"I was representing Chandler & Calvin at the Halena fundraiser," says Chandler, "when I noticed all these zombie bits crawling around on the floor."

"Luckily, I was on security detail," says Yelena, "and managed to scoop up the pieces before you got chucked into the posole."

"I didn't get an invite," says Stanik. "Not that I wanted to hang around self-absorbed psychos. I dated a vampire once in high school. Pretentious twit."

"Thanks..." I say.

I feel a hand rest gently on my shoulder.

"Get some sleep," says Prentice. "You've had a busy night."

It's almost a week before I'm on my feet again. My lurch is worse now, but I'm lucky to be undead. I'm surprised it takes this long for Amin's white-haired henchman to find me, and I'm even more surprised when he doesn't douse me in napalm.

"You and Amin had an agreement," says the henchman.

"Here's a message for Amin," I say. "Consent under duress isn't really consent. And next time Amin wants to bully a zombie, remember that vampires aren't the only ones who bite."

The white-haired man smiles very faintly.

"I'll pass that on," he says.

"And I'm sorry about the courier," I say. "But she was on the wrong side of the road."

I'm glad I didn't raze my apartment, although a blast of kerosene would probably do it good. It's still hard getting around, but at least it gives me time to find a new job.

Prentice makes an unexpected visit, bringing macrobiotic takeout and community college pamphlets. "They have ecology courses. And this was outside your door," says Prentice, passing me a silver embossed envelope. "How are you feeling?"

"Almost human," I say. "For the record, about what Chandler said that night..."

Prentice crosses his hands on his lap patiently.

"It was the fifteenth century," I say. "It was rural Ugistan. Merchants had taken over the farms, started up cane fields. They brought in some guy to rustle up a cheap workforce. I saw what he did to them—they worked until they fell to pieces. When they rounded me up..."

The scent of blood and smoke. Blank eyes, blank eyes on every side.

"I didn't eat his brains," I say. "But I bit him."

Prentice blinks mildly.

"It was a pretty big bite," I concede. "Well, I bit a lot of people that night, but I got away without so much as a hickey." I shift uncomfortably. "I got sick after that," I say.

The rest is history.

"You should have the salad before it gets warm," says Prentice. "Are you going to open the envelope?"

I crack open the seal and slide out a sheaf of marbled paper:

Solstice Feria, the Halena Foundation, and survivors of human trafficking thank you for your contribution. We look forward to future cooperation.

"Made a new friend?" says Prentice, laying out folded napkins.

I look across at him, and today, he doesn't look so much like a baguette. "I guess I have."

So maybe the clock's on countdown, but what's left of my life is mine. Whether I'm a pizza grunt or a bandit monk, what matters is I have a choice.

And that's close enough to human.

The unthinkable has happened. The dead are walking! Humanity's fragile thread may be reaching its bitter end. Individuals and groups struggle to survive…some at any cost. Will there be anybody left? Or, is this just…
The Ugly Beginning?

DEAD:REVELATIONS

The zombies have risen, the world has spiraled into chaos. Small pockets of survivors continue to struggle each day to survive. The best and worst of humanity fight the undead and themselves as they come to grips with a new, violent reality. See the world through Steve's eyes as he tries to balance the duties of leading a band of survivors while caring for a young, Hispanic orphan girl. Ride along with a band of self-professed "zombie-geeks" who are discovering that living through the apocalypse is vastly different than watching it on television. Peek in at horrifying snapshots of men and women…good and bad. This is- Dead: Revelations

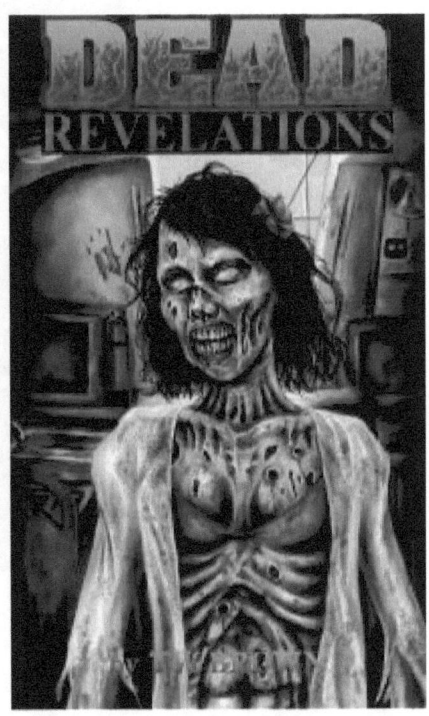

THE DEAD WALK!

Samuel Todd is a regular guy:
...Failed husband...
...Loving father...
...Dutiful worker...
...Aspiring rock star.
He had no idea if anyone would care, or take the time, to read his daily blog entries about his late night observations. But what started as an open monologue of his day-to-day life became a running journal of the first-hand account detailing the rising of the dead and the downfall and degradation of mankind...

Meredith Gainey is a survivor...and determined to retain that status as the zombie apocalypse wipes out most of humanity. Unable to accept an existence behind walls and fences, she finds herself in constant danger...and she wouldn't have it any other way.

Look for Zomblog: The Final Chapter

Anthologies from MDP

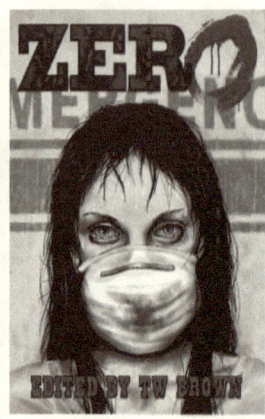

Pencil Pet Art

Get beautifully drawn original pencil
portraits of furry loved ones from your photos.
custom sizes, color or black and white
quality prints and matting available.
www.pencilpetart.com

LOOK CLOSELY
THESE ARE DRAWINGS, NOT PICTURES

To have your pet art done, Contact Denise @
dlbrown@maydecemberpublications.com

MAY DECEMBER
Publications

The growing voice in horror and speculative fiction.

Find us at www.maydecemberpublications.com

Or
Email us at contact@maydecemberpublications.com